KEYS TO THE KINGDOM

Drowned Wednesday

KEYS TO THE KINGDOM

So far . . .

#1 Mister Monday

#2 Grim Tuesday

#3 Drowned Wednesday

GARTH NIX

KEYS TO THE KINGDOM

BOOK THREE
Drowned Wednesday

SCHOLASTIC INC.

New York Toronto London Auckland Sydney
Mexico City New Delhi Hong Kong Buenos Aires

No part of this publication may be reproduced, stored in a retrieval system, or transmitted in any form or by any means, electronic, mechanical, photocopying, recording, or otherwise, without written permission of the publisher. For information regarding permission, write to Scholastic Inc., Attention: Permissions Department, 557 Broadway, New York, NY 10012.

ISBN 0-439-43656-7

12 11 10 9 8 7 6 5 4 3   6 7 8 9 10/0

Printed in the U.S.A.   40

First paperback printing, March 2006
The display type was set in Dalliance and Albertus.
The text type was set in Sabon.

Book design by Steve Scott

To Anna and Thomas, and
to all my family and friends

KEYS TO THE KINGDOM

Drowned Wednesday

Prologue

A three-masted square-rigger with iridescent green sails that shone by day or night, the *Flying Mantis* was a fast and lucky ship. She sailed the Border Sea of the House, which meant she could also sail any ocean, sea, lake, river, or other navigable stretch of liquid on any of the millions of worlds of the Secondary Realms.

On this voyage, the *Flying Mantis* was cleaving through the deep blue waters of the Border Sea, heading for Port Wednesday. Her holds were stuffed with goods bought beyond the House and illnesses salvaged from the Border Sea's grasping waters. There were valuables under her hatches: tea and wine and coffee and spices, treats for the Denizens of the House. But her strongroom held the real treasure: coughs and sniffles and ugly rashes and strange stuttering diseases, all fixed into pills, snuff, or whalebone charms.

With such rich cargo, the crew was nervous and the lookouts red-eyed and anxious. The Border Sea was no longer safe, not since the unfortunate transformation of Lady Wednesday several thousand years before and the consequent flooding of the Sea's old shore. Wednesday's Noon and Dusk had been missing ever since, along with many of Wednesday's other servants, who used to police the Border Sea.

Now the waters swarmed with unlicensed salvagers and traders, some who would happily turn to a bit of casual piracy. To make matters worse, there were full-time pirates around as well. Human ones, who had somehow gotten through the Line of Storms and into the Border Sea from some earthly ocean.

These pirates were still mortal (unlike the Denizens) but they had managed to learn some House sorcery and were foolish enough to dabble in the use of Nothing. This made them dangerous, and if they had the numbers, their human ferocity and reckless use of Nothing-fueled magic would usually defeat their more cautious Denizen foes.

The *Flying Mantis* had lookouts in the fighting tops of each of its three masts, one in the forepeak, and several on the quarterdeck. It was their task to watch for pirates, strange weather, and the worst of all things — the emergence of Drowned Wednesday, as Lady Wednesday was now known.

Most of the ships that now sailed the Border Sea had incompetent lookouts and inferior crews. After the Deluge, when the Border Sea swept over nine-tenths of

Wednesday's shore-based wharves, warehouses, counting rooms, and offices, more than a thousand of the higher rooms had been rapidly converted into ships. All these ships were crewed by former stevedores, clerks, rackers, counters, tally-hands, sweepers, and managers. Though they'd had several thousand years of practice, these Denizens were still poor sailors.

But not the crew of the *Flying Mantis*. She was one of Wednesday's original forty-nine ships, commissioned and built to the Architect's design. Her crew members were nautical Denizens, themselves made expressly to sail the Border Sea and beyond. Her Captain was none other than Heraclius Swell, 15,287th in precedence within the House.

So when the mizzen-top lookout shouted, "Something big . . . err . . . not that big . . . closing off the port bow . . . underwater!" both Captain and crew reacted as well-trained professionals of long experience.

"All hands!" roared the mate who had the watch. "Beat to quarters!"

His cry was taken up by the lookouts and the sailors on deck, followed only seconds later by the sharp rattle of a drum as the ship's boy abandoned his boot polish and the Captain's boots to take up his sticks.

Denizens burst out from belowdecks. Some leapt to the rigging to climb aloft, ready to work the sails. Some stood by the armory to receive their crossbows and cutlasses. Others raced to load and run out the guns, though the *Flying Mantis* only had eight working cannons of its usual complement of sixteen. Guns and gunpowder that worked in the House were very hard to come by, and always contained dangerous specks of Nothing. Since the toppling of Grim Tuesday fourteen months before, powder was in very short supply. Some said it was no longer being made, and some said it was being stockpiled for war by the mysterious Lord Arthur, who now ruled both the Lower House and the Far Reaches.

Captain Swell climbed onto the quarterdeck as the cannons rumbled out on the main deck, their red wooden wheels squealing in complaint. He was a very tall Denizen, even in stockinged feet, who always wore the full dress coat of an admiral from a small country on a small world in a remote corner of the Secondary Realms. It was turquoise blue, nipped in very tightly at the waist, and had enormous quantities of gold braid on the shoulders and cuffs. Consequently Captain Swell shone even more brightly than the green sails of his ship.

"What occurs, Mister Pannikin?" Swell asked his First Mate, a Denizen as tall as he was, but considerably less handsome. At some time Pannikin had lost all his hair and one ear to a Nothing-laced explosion, and his bare skull was ridged with scars. He sometimes wore a purple woollen cap, but the crew claimed that made him look even worse.

"Mysterious submersible approaching the port bow," reported Pannikin, handing his spyglass to the Captain. "About forty feet long by my reckoning, and coursing very fast. Maybe fifty knots."

"I see," said the Captain, who had clapped the telescope to his eye. "I think it must be . . . yes. Milady has sent us a messenger. Stand the men down, Mister Pannikin, and prepare a side-party to welcome our illustrious visitor. Oh, and tell Albert to bring me my boots."

Mister Pannikin roared orders as Captain Swell refocused his telescope on the shape in the water. Through the powerful lens, he could clearly see a dull golden cigar-shape surging under the water towards the ship. For a second it was unclear what propelled it so quickly. Then its huge yellow-gold wings suddenly exploded ahead and pushed back, sending the creature rocketing forward, the water behind it exploding into froth.

"She'll broach any moment," muttered one of the crewmen to his mate at the wheel behind the Captain. "Mark my words."

He was right. The creature's wings broke the surface and gathered air instead of water. With a great flexing leap and a swirl of sea, the monster catapulted itself up higher than the *Flying Mantis*'s maintop. Shedding water like rain, it circled the ship, slowly descending towards the quarter-deck.

At first it looked like a golden, winged shark, all sleek motion and a fearsome, toothy maw. But as it circled, it shrank. Its cigar-shaped body bulged and changed, and the golden sheen ebbed away before other advancing colors. It became roughly human-shaped, though still with golden wings.

Then, as its wings stopped flapping and it stepped the final foot down to the deck, it assumed the shape of a very beautiful woman, though even the ship's boy knew she was really a Denizen of high rank. She wore a riding habit of peach velvet with ruby buttons, and sharkskin riding boots complete with gilt spurs. Her straw-colored hair was restrained by a hairnet of silver wire, and she tapped her thigh nervously with a riding crop made from the elongated tail of an albino alligator.

"Captain Swell."

"Wednesday's Dawn," replied the Captain, bending his head as he pushed one stockinged foot forward. Albert, arriving a little too late, slid along the deck and hastily tried to put the proffered foot into the boot he held.

"Not now!" hissed Pannikin, dragging the lad back by the scruff of his neck.

The Captain and Wednesday's Dawn ignored the boy and the First Mate. They turned together to the rail and looked out at the ocean, continuing to talk while hardly looking at each other.

"I trust you have had a profitable voyage to date, Captain?"

"Well enough, Miss Dawn. May I inquire as to the happy chance that has led you to grace my vessel with your presence?"

"You may indeed, Captain. I am here upon the express command of our mistress, bearing an urgent dispatch, which I am pleased to deliver."

Dawn reached into her sleeve, which was tight enough to hold no possibility of storage, and pulled out a large thick envelope of buff paper, sealed with a knob of blue sealing wax half an inch thick.

Captain Swell took the envelope slowly, broke the seal with deliberation, and unfolded it to read the letter written on the inside. The crew was quiet as he read, the only sounds the slap of the sea against the hull, the creak of the timbers, the momentary flap of a sail, and the faint whistle of the wind in the rigging.

Everyone knew what the letter must be. Orders from Drowned Wednesday. That meant trouble, particularly as they had been spared direct orders from Wednesday for several thousand years. They were almost certainly no longer going home to Port Wednesday and the few days' liberty they usually received while their precious cargo was sold.

Captain Swell finished the letter, shook the envelope, and picked up the two additional documents that fell out of it like doves from a conjurer's hat.

"We are instructed to sail to a landlocked part of the Secondary Realms," the Captain said to Wednesday's Dawn, the hint of a question in his voice.

"Our mistress will ensure the Sea extends there for the time it takes for your passenger to embark," replied Dawn.

"We must cross the Line of Storms both ways," added the Captain. "With a mortal passenger."

"You must," agreed Dawn. She tapped one of the documents with her riding crop. "That is a Permission that will allow a mortal to pass the Line."

"This mortal is to be treated as a personal guest of milady?"

"He is."

"This passenger's name will be required for my manifest."

"Unnecessary," Dawn snapped. She looked the Captain directly in the eyes. "He is a confidential guest. You have a description, a location, and specific sailing instructions drawn up personally by me. I suggest you get on with it. Unless of course you wish to challenge these orders? I could arrange an audience with Lady Wednesday if you choose."

The crew members all held their breath. If the Captain chose to see Drowned Wednesday, they'd all have to go as well, and not one of them was ready for that fate.

Captain Swell hesitated for a moment. Then he slowly saluted.

"As ever, I am at Milady Wednesday's command. Good day, Miss Dawn."

"Good day to you, Captain." Dawn's wings stirred at her back, sending a sudden breeze around the quarterdeck. "Good luck."

"We'll need it," whispered the helmsman to his mate as Dawn stepped up to the rail and launched herself in a long arcing dive that ended several hundred yards away in the sea, as she transformed back into a golden winged shark.

"Mister Pannikin!" roared the Captain, though the First Mate was only a few feet away. "Stand by to make sail!"

He glanced down at the complex sailing instructions

that Dawn had given him, noting the known landmarks of the Border Sea they must sight and the auguries and incantations required to sail the ship to the required place and time in the Secondary Realms. As was the case with all of Drowned Wednesday's regular merchant marine, the Captain was himself a Sorcerer-Navigator, as were his officers.

"Mmm . . . Bethesda Hospital . . . room 206 . . . two minutes past the hour of seven in the evening. On Wednesday, of course," muttered the Captain, reading aloud to himself. "House time, as per line four, corresponds with the date and year in local reckoning in the boxed corner, and where . . . odd name for a town . . . never heard of that country . . . what will these mortals think of next . . . and the world . . ."

He flipped the parchment over.

"Hmmph. I might have known!"

The Captain looked up and across at his running, climbing, swinging, rolling, swaying, sail-unfurling, and rope-hauling crew. They all stopped as one and looked at him.

"We sail to Earth!" shouted Captain Swell.

Chapter One

"What time is it?" Arthur asked after the nurse had left, wheeling away the drip he didn't need anymore. His adopted mother was standing in the way of the clock. Emily had told him she'd only pop in for a minute and wouldn't sit down, but she'd already been there fifteen minutes. Arthur knew that meant she was worried about him, even though he was already off the oxygen and his broken leg, though sore, was quite bearable.

"Four-thirty. Five minutes since you asked me last time," Emily replied. "Why are you so concerned about the time? And what's wrong with your own watch?"

"It's going backwards," said Arthur, careful not to answer Emily's other question. He couldn't tell her the real reason he kept asking the time. She wouldn't — or couldn't — believe the real reasons.

She'd think he was mad if he told her about the House, that strange building that contained vast areas and was the epicenter of the Universe as well. Even if he could take her to the House, she wouldn't be able to see it.

Arthur knew he would be going back to the House sooner rather than later. That morning he'd found an invitation under the pillow of his hospital bed, signed Lady Wednesday. *Transportation has been arranged*, it had read. Arthur couldn't help feeling it was much more sinister than the simple word *transportation* suggested. Perhaps he was going to be taken, as a prisoner. Or transported like a mail package . . .

He'd been expecting something to happen all day. He couldn't believe it was already half past four on Wednesday afternoon and there was still no sign of weird creatures or strange events. Lady Wednesday only had dominion over her namesake day in the Secondary Realms, so whatever she planned to do to him had to happen before midnight. Seven and a half hours away . . .

Every time a nurse or a visitor came through the door, Arthur jumped, expecting it to be some dangerous servant of Wednesday's. As the hours ticked by, he'd become more and more nervous.

The suspense was worse than the pain in his broken leg. The bone was set and wrapped in one of the new ultra-tech casts, a leg sheath that looked like the armor of a space marine, extending from knee to ankle. It was super strong, super lightweight, and had what the doctor called "nanonic healing enhancers" — whatever they were.

Regardless of their name, they worked, and had already reduced the swelling. The cast was so advanced it would literally fall off his leg and turn into dust when its work was done.

His asthma was also under control, at least for the moment, though Arthur was annoyed that it had come back in the first place. He'd thought it had been almost completely cured as a side effect of wielding the First Key.

Then Dame Primus had used the Second Key to remove all the effects of the First Key upon him, reversing both his botched attempt to heal his broken leg and the Key's beneficial effect on his asthma. But Arthur had to admit it was better to have a treatable broken leg and his familiar, manageable asthma than to have a magically twisted-up, inoperable leg and no asthma.

I'm lucky to have survived at all, Arthur thought. He shivered as he remembered the descent into Grim Tuesday's Pit.

"You're trembling," said Emily. "Are you cold? Or is it the pain?"

"No, I'm fine," said Arthur hastily. "My leg's sore but it's okay, really. How's Dad?"

Emily looked at him carefully. Arthur could see her evaluating whether he was fit enough to be told the bad news. It was bound to be bad news. Arthur had defeated

Grim Tuesday, but not before the Trustee's minions had managed to interfere with the Penhaligon family finances . . . as well as causing minor economic upheaval for the world at large.

"Bob has been sorting things out all afternoon," Emily said at last. "I expect there'll be a lot more sorting to do. Right now it looks like we'll keep the house, but we'll have to rent it out and move somewhere smaller for a year or so. Bob will also have to go back on tour with the band. It's just one of those things. At least we didn't have all our money in those two banks that failed yesterday. A lot of people will be hurt by that."

"What about those signs about the shopping mall being built across the street?"

"They were gone by the time I got home last night, though Bob said he saw them too," said Emily. "It's quite strange. When I asked Mrs. Haskell in number ten about it, she said that some fast-talking real estate agent had gotten them to agree to sell their house. They signed a contract and everything. But fortunately there was a loophole and they've managed to get out of it. They didn't really want to sell. So I guess there'll be no shopping mall, even if the other neighbors who sold don't change their minds. The Haskell place is right in the middle, and of course we won't be selling either."

"And Michaeli's course? Has the university still got no money?"

"That's a bit more complicated. It seems they had a lot of money with one of the failed banks, which has been lost. But it's possible the government will step in and ensure no courses are cancelled. If Michaeli's degree is discontinued, she'll have to go somewhere else. She was accepted by three . . . no, four other places. She'll be okay."

"But she'll have to leave home."

Arthur left another sentence unsaid.

And it's my fault. I should have been quicker to deal with the Grotesques. . . .

"Well, I don't think she'll be too concerned about that. How we'll pay for it is a different matter. But you don't need to worry about all of this, Arthur. You always want to take too much on. It's not your responsibility. Just concentrate on getting better. Your father and I will make sure everything will be —"

Emily was cut off by a sudden alert from the hospital pager she always wore. It jangled a few times, then a line of text ran around the rim. Emily frowned as she read the scrolling message.

"I have to go, Arthur."

"It's okay, Mom, you go," said Arthur. He was used to

Emily having to deal with gigantic medical emergencies. She was one of the most important medical researchers in the country. The sudden attack and then abrupt cessation of the Sleepy Plague had given her a great deal of extra work.

Emily gave her son a hurried kiss on the cheek and a good luck rap of her knuckles on the foot of the bed. Then she was gone.

Arthur wondered if he'd ever be able to tell her that the Sleepy Plague had come from Mister Monday's Fetchers, and had been cured by the Nightsweeper, a magical intervention he'd brought back from the House. Though he had brought back the cure, he still felt responsible for the plague in the first place.

He looked at his watch. It was still going backwards.

A knock on the door made him sit up again. He was as ready as he could be. He had the Atlas in his pajama pocket, and he'd twisted numerous strands of dental floss together so he could hang the Captain's medallion around his neck. His dressing gown was on the chair next to the bed, along with his Immaterial Boots, which had disguised themselves as slippers. He could only tell what they really were because they felt slightly electric and tingly when he picked them up.

The knock was repeated. Arthur didn't answer. He

knew that Fetchers — the creatures who had pursued him on Monday — couldn't cross a threshold without permission. So he wasn't going to say a word — just in case.

He lay there silently, watching the door. It slowly opened a crack. Arthur reached across to the bedside table and picked up a paper packet of salt he'd kept from his lunch, ready to tear it open and throw it if a Fetcher peered around.

But it wasn't a dog-faced, bowler-hatted creature. It was Leaf, his friend from school, who had helped save him from a Scoucher the day before, and who had been injured herself.

"Arthur?"

"Leaf! Come in!"

Leaf closed the door behind her. She was wearing her normal clothes: boots, jeans, and a T-shirt with an obscure band logo. But her right arm was bound from elbow to wrist in white bandages.

"How's your arm?"

"Sore. But not too bad. The doctor couldn't figure out what made the cuts. I told him I never saw what the guy hit me with."

"I guess he wouldn't believe the true story," said Arthur, thinking about the shape-changing Scoucher and its long, razor-tendrilled arms.

"What is the true story?" asked Leaf. She sat down on the visitor's chair and looked intently at Arthur, making him uncomfortable. "I mean, all I know is that last week you were involved in some weird stuff with dog-faced guys, and it got even weirder this week, when you suddenly appeared in my living room on Monday with a kind of history girl who had . . . wings. You ran up the bedroom stairs and vanished. Then yesterday, you came racing into my yard with a monster chasing after you, which could easily have killed me, only it got . . . destroyed . . . by one of my dad's old silver medals. Then you had to run off again. Then today I hear you're in the next ward with a broken leg. What's going on?"

Arthur opened his mouth, then hesitated. It would be a great relief to tell Leaf everything. At least she could see the Denizens of the House, when no one else could. Perhaps, as she'd claimed, it was because her great-grandmother had possessed the second sight. But telling Leaf everything might also put her in danger.

"Come on, Arthur! I need to know," urged Leaf. "What if one of those Scoucher things comes back to finish me off? Or something else. Like one of those dog-faces. I've got a couple of Dad's medals for the Scouchers, but what do I do about the dog-faces?"

"Fetchers," Arthur said slowly. He held up the paper sachet. "The dog-faces are called Fetchers. Throw salt on them."

"That's a good start," said Leaf. "Fetchers. Where do they come from? What do they want?"

"They're servants," Arthur explained. He started to talk faster and faster. It was such a relief to tell somebody about what had happened. "Creatures made from Nothing. The ones you saw were in the service of Mister Monday. He is . . . was one of the seven Trustees of the House —"

"Hang on!" Leaf interrupted. "Slow down. Start at the beginning."

Arthur took a deep breath, as deep as his lungs allowed, and started at the beginning. He told Leaf about his encounter with Mister Monday and Sneezer. About Monday's Noon pursuing him through the school library with his flaming sword. He told her how he got into the House the first time, and how he met Suzy Turquoise Blue and the First Part of the Will, and the three of them together had ultimately defeated Mister Monday. How he'd brought back the Nightsweeper to cure the Sleepy Plague, and how he'd thought he would be left alone till he grew up, only to have that hope dashed by Grim Tuesday's Grotesques, whose appearance had led to his return to the

House, his descent into the Pit, and his eventual triumph over Grim Tuesday.

Leaf occasionally asked a question, but most of the time she just sat there, taking in everything Arthur had to say. Finally, he showed her the cardboard invitation from Lady Wednesday. She took it and read it several times.

"I wish I had adventures like you do," Leaf said as she traced her finger over the writing on the invitation.

"They didn't feel like adventures," said Arthur. "I was too scared most of the time to actually enjoy anything or get excited about it. Weren't you scared by the Scoucher?"

"Sure," Leaf said, with a glance at her bandaged arm. "But we survived, didn't we? That makes it an adventure. If you get killed it's a tragedy."

"I could do without any more adventures for a while." Arthur thought Leaf would agree with him if she'd had the same experiences. They sounded much more exciting and safer just as stories. "I really just want to be left alone!"

"They're not going to leave you alone, though." Leaf held up Wednesday's invitation, then flipped it over to Arthur, who put it back in his pocket. "Are they?"

"No," Arthur agreed, resignation all through his voice. "The Morrow Days aren't going to leave me alone."

"So what are you going to do to them?" said Leaf.

"What do you mean?"

"Well, since they won't leave you alone, you'd better get in first. You know, attack is the best form of defense."

"I suppose . . ." said Arthur. "You mean I shouldn't wait for whatever Wednesday is going to do, but go back into the House now?"

"Yeah, why not? Get together with your friend Suzy, and the Will, and work out some plan to deal with Wednesday before she deals with you."

"It's a good idea," admitted Arthur. "The only thing is, I don't know how to get back into the House. I can't open the Atlas because I've used up all the power I had from holding on to the Keys. And in case you haven't noticed, I do have a broken leg. Though I suppose . . ."

"What?"

"I could phone Dame Primus if I had my phone box, because it'll probably be reconnected now that Grim Tuesday's bills have been paid."

"Where's the phone box? What's it look like?"

"It's at home," said Arthur. "In my bedroom. It's just a velvet-lined wooden box about this big." He held his hands apart.

"Maybe I could go get it for you," said Leaf. "If they ever let me out of this hospital. If it isn't one thing, it's another. Quarantine this, quarantine that . . ."

"Maybe," said Arthur. "Or maybe I could . . . what's that smell?"

Leaf sniffed the air and looked around. As she looked, the pages of the calendar on the wall started to flutter.

"I don't know. I think the air-conditioning just came on. Feel the breeze."

Arthur held up his hands to feel the air. There was a definite rush of cold coming from somewhere, and a kind of salty odor, like when they stayed at the beach and the surf was big. . . .

"It smells kind of damp," said Leaf.

Arthur struggled up to a sitting position, reached over and grabbed his slippers and dressing gown, and hurriedly put them on.

"Leaf!" he cried. "Get out! That's not the air-conditioning!"

"Sure isn't," Leaf agreed. The wind was getting stronger every second. "Something weird's going on."

"Yes, it is . . . get out while you can!"

"I want to see what happens." Leaf backed up to the bed and leaned against it. "Hey! There's water coming in under the wall!"

Sure enough, a thin film of frothy water was slowly spreading across the floor, like the leading wash of a wave across the sand. It ran almost to the bed, then ebbed back.

"I can hear something," said Leaf. "Kind of like a train."

Arthur heard it too. A distant thunder that got louder and louder.

"That's not a train! Grab hold of the bed!"

Leaf grabbed the rail at the end of the bed as Arthur gripped the headboard. Both turned to look at the far wall just as it disappeared, replaced by a thundering gray-blue wave that crashed down upon them. Tons of seawater smashed everything else in the room to bits, but the bed itself was carried away by the wave.

Dazed, drenched, and desperate, Arthur and Leaf hung on.

Chapter Two

The hospital room vanished in an instant, replaced by the savage fury of a storm at sea. The bed, submerged to within an inch of the mattress-top, had become a makeshift raft. Picked up by the first great wave, the raft rode the crest for a few seconds, then fell off the back, sliding down and down into the trough behind.

Leaf cried out something, two words lost in the thunder of the waves and the howl of the wind. Arthur couldn't hear her, and he could barely see her through the spray that made it difficult to tell where the sea ended and the air began.

He felt her grip, though, as she clawed herself fully onto the bed and grabbed his foot. Both of them would have been washed off then, if Arthur hadn't managed to get his arms wedged through the bars of the headboard.

Fear lent her strength, and Leaf managed to crawl up to the headboard railings. She leaned over Arthur and screamed, "What do we do now?"

She didn't sound like she was enjoying this adventure.

"Hold on!" Arthur shouted, looking past her at the towering, office-block-high wall of water that was falling towards them. If it broke over the bed, they would be smashed down and pushed deep into the sea, never to surface.

The crest of the wave curled high above them, blotting out the dim, gray light of the sky. Arthur and Leaf stared up, not breathing, eyes fixed on the curving water.

The wave didn't break. The bed rode up the face of the wave like a fisherman's float. As it neared the top, it tipped up almost vertically and started to roll over, until Arthur and Leaf threw their weight against the curl.

They were just in time. The bed didn't roll. It leveled out as they made it to the crest of the second wave. They balanced there for a few seconds, then the bed started its downward slide once more. Down into another sickeningly deep trough in front of another giant, blue-black, white-topped cliff of moving water.

But the third wave was different.

There was a ship surfing down it. A hundred-and-sixty-foot-long, three-masted sailing ship with sails that glowed a spectral green.

"A ship!" yelled Leaf, hope in her voice. That hope rapidly fled as the bed continued to run down into the trough at alarming speed, and the ship surfed down the opposite side even faster still.

"It's going to hit us! We have to jump!"

"No!" shouted Arthur. If they left their makeshift raft he felt sure they'd drown. "Wait!"

A few seconds later, waiting seemed like a very bad decision. The ship didn't waver in its course, a great wooden missile coming at them so fast that it would run right over them and the crew probably wouldn't even notice.

Arthur shut his eyes when it got within the last twenty yards. The last thing he saw was the ship's bow plunging down into the sea, then rising up again in a great spray of froth and spray, the bowsprit like a spear rising from the water.

Arthur opened his eyes when he didn't feel the shocking impact of a ship ramming them. The ship had turned just enough at the last instant to meet the bed in the very bottom of the trough between the waves. Both had lost speed, so that the bed would be right next to the ship for a matter of seconds. It was an act of tremendous seamanship by the captain and crew, particularly in the middle of such a mighty swell.

Through the blowing spray, Arthur saw two looped ropes like lassos come down. One loop fell over Leaf. The other, clearly aimed for Arthur, fell over the left bedpost instead. He scrambled for it and started to lift it off. But before he got it clear, both ropes went taut. Leaf went up like a rocket, up towards the ship.

The other rope tipped the bed over.

Arthur lost his grip and tumbled into the sea. He went down several feet, his breath knocked out of him. Through the veil of water and spray, he saw Leaf and the bed spinning up to the ship's rail high above. The bed went up several yards, then the rope came free and it fell back down.

He kicked as best he could with one immobilized leg, and struck out with his arms, desperate to get back to the surface and the ship. But by the time his head broke free of the sea and he got a half-breath of spray-soaked air, the vessel was already at least fifty yards away, surfing diagonally up the wave ahead, moving faster than the swell. New sails unfurled and billowed out as he watched, accelerating its passage.

The bed was much closer, perhaps only ten yards away. It was his only chance now. Arthur started to swim furiously towards it. He could feel his lungs tightening, an asthma attack closing in on him. He would only be able to swim for a few minutes at most. Panicked, he threw all his energy into getting back to the bed, as it started its rise up the front of the following wave.

He just made it, grabbing a trailing blanket that had

twisted through the bars at the end of the bed. Arthur frantically pulled himself along that, hoping it wouldn't come loose.

After a struggle that used up all his remaining strength, he managed to haul himself up onto the mattress and once again wedge his arms through the bars.

He shivered there, feeling his breath getting more restricted as his asthma got worse. That meant that wherever he was, it wasn't the House. This sea was somewhere in the Secondary Realms.

Wherever it is, I'm probably going to die here, Arthur thought, his mind numbed by cold, shock, and lack of breath.

But he wasn't going to go easily. He freed his right hand and pressed it against his chest. Perhaps there was some shred of remnant power from the First Key in his hand, or even of the Second Key.

"Breathe," whispered Arthur. "Free up. Let me breathe."

At the same time, he tried to stop the panic that was coursing through his body. Over and over, inside his head, he told himself to be calm. Slow down. Take it easy.

Whether it was some remaining power in his hand or his efforts to stay calm, Arthur found that while he still couldn't breathe properly, it didn't get any worse. He started to take stock of his situation.

I'm kind of okay on the bed, he thought. *It floats. Even wet blankets will help me stay warm.*

He looked up at the wave the bed was riding up. Maybe he'd gotten a bit used to these enormous waves or just couldn't get any more terrified, but it did seem a bit smaller and less curling at the top than the first few. It still scared him, but it felt like less of a threat.

He thought about what else he might have. He was wearing hospital pajamas and a dressing gown, which weren't much good for anything. The cast on his leg looked like it might be disintegrating already, and he could feel a dull throbbing ache deep in the bone. His Immaterial Boots kept his feet warm but he couldn't think of anything else they could be used for. Other than that, he had —

The Atlas! And the Mariner's whalebone disc!

Arthur's hand flashed to his pajama pocket and then to the multiple strands of floss he'd woven into a string for the whalebone disc. The Atlas was still in his pocket. The Captain's medallion, as he'd come to think of it, was still around his neck.

But what use were they?

Arthur wedged his good leg through the bars and curled up as much as he could into a ball. Then he gingerly let go with his hands and got out the Atlas, keeping it close to his chest to make sure that it couldn't get washed away. But as he'd half-expected, it wouldn't open. He slowly put it back in his pocket.

The Captain's whalebone disc, on the other hand, might work. Tom Shelvocke was the Mariner after all, son of the Old One and the Architect (by adoption), a man who had sailed thousands of seas on many different worlds. He'd told Suzy Turquoise Blue to warn Arthur to keep it by him. Perhaps it might summon help or even communicate with the Captain.

Arthur pulled the disc out from under his pajama top and looked at the constellation of stars on one side, and then at the Viking ship on the other. They both looked like simple carvings, but Arthur thought there had to be some kind of magic contained in them. Because it seemed more likely to be of immediate help, Arthur concentrated on the ship side, and tried to will a message to the Captain.

Please help me, I'm adrift on a bed in the middle of a storm at sea, he thought over and over again, even whispering the words aloud as if the charm could hear him.

"Please help me, I'm adrift on a hospital bed in the middle of a storm at sea. Please help me, I'm adrift on a hospital bed in the middle of a storm at sea. Please help me, I'm adrift on a hospital bed in the middle of a storm at sea. . . ."

It became a chant. Just saying the words made Arthur feel a little better.

He kept up the chant for several minutes, but had to

give up as his lungs closed down and he could only just get enough breath to stay semiconscious. He lay next to the headboard, curled up as much as he could with one leg straight and the other thrust through the bars. He was completely sodden, and the sea continually sloshed over him, so he had to keep his head up to get a breath.

But the waves were definitely getting smaller and the wind less ferocious. Arthur didn't get a bucketful of spray in his eyes and mouth whenever he turned to face the wind.

If I can keep breathing, there's some hope, Arthur thought.

That thought had hardly crossed his mind when he felt an electric thrill pass through his whole body, and his stomach flip-flopped as if he'd dropped a thousand feet in an aircraft. All the water around him suddenly looked crisper, clearer, and a more vivid blue. The sky turned a charming shade of eggshell blue, and looked closer than it had before.

Best of all, Arthur's lungs were suddenly clear. He could breathe without difficulty.

He was in the House. Arthur could feel it through his whole body. Even the ache in his broken leg subsided to little more than an occasional twinge.

Hang on, he thought. *That was too easy. Wasn't it?*

This thought was interrupted by what sounded like an explosion, far too close for comfort. For a moment Arthur thought he was being shot at by a full broadside of cannons from a ship like the one that had taken Leaf. Then it came again, and Arthur recognized it as thunder.

As the bed reached the top of another wave, he saw the lightning — lightning that stretched in a line all the way across the horizon. Vicious forks of white-hot plasma that ran in near-continuous streams between sea and sky, constant thunder echoing every flash and bolt.

The bed was being taken straight towards the lightning storm. Every wave that it rode up carried it forward. There was no way to turn it, stop it, or avoid the collision.

To make matters as bad as they could possibly be, the bed was made of metal. It had to be the biggest lightning conductor for miles. And any lightning that hit would go through Arthur on its way to connect with the steel frame.

For a few seconds, Arthur's mind was paralyzed by fear. There seemed to be nothing he could do. Absolutely nothing, except get fried by a thousand bolts of lightning all coming down at once.

He fought back the fear. He tried to think. There had to be something. Perhaps he could swim away . . . but there was no way he was strong enough to swim against the direction of the swell. It would be better to die instantly by lightning than to drown.

Arthur looked at the line of lightning again. Even in only a few minutes he'd gotten much closer, so close he had to shield his eyes from the blinding bolts.

But wait, thought Arthur. *The ship that took Leaf went in this direction. It must have gone through the lightning storm. I just have to get through. Maybe Lady Wednesday's invitation will protect me. . . .*

Arthur checked his pocket. But there was only the Atlas. Where could the invitation be?

The pillows were long gone, lost overboard, but the sheets were partially tucked in. Arthur dived under the drenched linen, his hands desperately groping into every corner as he tried to find the square of cardboard that might just save him.

The bed rose up the face of a wave, but did not reach the crest. Instead, bed, wave, and boy rushed towards the blinding, deafening barrier of thunder and lightning that was the Line of Storms. The defensive inner boundary of the Border Sea, which no mortal could cross without permission.

The penalty for trying was a sudden, incendiary death.

Chapter Three

Arthur never saw the lightning or heard the water boiling where the bolts struck, the noise lost in the constant boom of thunder. He was under the sheet, a soggy piece of cardboard clutched in one trembling hand. He didn't even know if it was the invitation from Drowned Wednesday, his medical chart from the end of the bed, or a brochure about the hospital telephones.

But since he was still alive a minute after the blinding glow beyond the sheets faded, he guessed it must be the invitation in his hand.

Arthur slowly pulled his head out from under the sheet. As he blinked up at the clear blue sky, he instinctively took another deep breath. A long, clear, unrestricted breath.

As the bed moved in the mysterious current, the swell it was riding subsided to a mere ten or twelve feet, with a much longer interval between waves. The wind dropped, and there was no blowing spray. It also felt much warmer, though Arthur couldn't see a sun. He couldn't see any clouds or lightning either, which was a plus. Just a brilliant blue sky that was so even and perfect that he supposed it must be a painted ceiling, like in the other parts of the House.

Arthur took several more deep breaths, reveling in the rush of oxygen through his body. Then he took stock of his situation once more. The one thing he had learned about the House was that you couldn't take anything for granted. This warm, rolling sea might turn into something else at any moment.

Arthur tucked the Captain's disc back under his pajama top and slid Lady Wednesday's sodden and barely legible invitation next to the Atlas in his pocket. Then he braced his cast against the headboard, stood up, and looked around.

There was nothing to see, except the sea. The bed rode too low in the water. Even standing up, Arthur's view was blocked by the next wave. What he could see was much closer and immediately obvious.

The bed was sinking. Even in this calmer ocean, the mattress was now totally submerged, losing its buoyancy as it absorbed more and more water, the steel frame dragging it down.

It wasn't going to sink in the next five minutes, but it was going to sink.

Arthur sighed and sat back down, water splashing

almost up to his waist. He looked at the cast on his leg and wondered if he should take it off. It was very lightweight and it hadn't dragged him down before, but that had been a truly panic-driven swim and it would be hard to swim any real distance with it on. But if he took it off, his leg might snap apart again or hurt so much that he couldn't swim anyway.

He decided to leave the cast on and got out the Captain's disc again. This time he just held it in his hand and tried to visualize the ship with the glowing green sails coming back to pick him up.

He hoped that was a good thing to visualize. At the back of his mind was a nagging worry that Leaf hadn't been actually rescued but had gone from one trouble to another. What would the Denizens do to her? They would have been after him, not her. He hoped that since Lady Wednesday had sent him an invitation instead of an attack squad, she might be at least kind of friendly. But maybe that was just a sneaky plan to get him where she wanted. In which case, Drowned Wednesday might take out her bad feelings on Leaf. . . .

If Leaf survived that line of lightning, Arthur thought guiltily. *Surely that ship would have had some protection. . . .*

The bed gurgled under his feet and sank a bit more, reminding Arthur of his immediate problem.

"A ship!" he called out. "I need a ship! Or a boat! A better raft! Anything!"

His voice sounded alone and empty, lost amid the waves. He was answered only by the sloshing of the sea under, through, and around the mattress.

"Land would do," said Arthur. He said this directly to the Captain's disc, but once again it didn't appear to do anything. It was just a carving of a boat on a piece of whalebone.

No land came in sight. Though he still couldn't see any sun, it got warmer, and then positively hot. Even the seawater now constantly washing over Arthur didn't cool him down. It was tepid and very salty, as he found when he tasted some on the end of his finger. He was getting very thirsty, and had started to remember all kinds of terrible stories about people dying of thirst at sea. Or going crazy from thirst first and hurling themselves into the water or attacking their friends and trying to drink their blood. . . .

Arthur shook his head several times. It looked like he was already starting to go crazy, thinking of stuff like that. Particularly since he knew he couldn't die of thirst in the House. He might feel like he was, and of course he could still go crazy. . . .

Better to think of something positive to do. Like send a signal, or catch a fish. If there were any fish in this strange sea within the House. Of course, if there were fish, there might also be sharks. A shark would have no trouble pulling him off the bed. It hardly qualified as a raft anymore, it had sunk down so far.

Arthur shook his head again to try and clear away the negative thoughts.

Stop thinking about sharks! he told himself.

Just at that moment, he saw something in the water not far away. A dark, mostly submerged shape. A shadow largely under the surface.

Arthur yelped and tried to stand up against the headboard, hopping as his immobilized leg got caught under a fold of sheet. This violent action changed the balance of the bed, and one corner went down several feet, releasing a huge air bubble.

This downward progress halted for a few seconds as air bubbles continued to pop to the surface, then the bed sank like the *Titanic,* one end briefly sticking straight up before it subsided beneath the waves. Arthur let go of it just in time and pushed himself away. He thrashed out a rough backstroke for a few yards to make sure he wouldn't be sucked down, then trod water with one leg and his arms circling, as he frantically looked around for the dark shadow again.

There it was, only a few yards away! Arthur braced

himself for the shock of a shark's attack, his body rigid. His head sank under the water as he stopped moving, then broke free again as he instinctively struggled to swim again.

The dark shape didn't attack. It didn't even move. Arthur stared at it and saw that it wasn't a shark. He swam closer to confirm that it was, in fact, a dark green ball about six feet in diameter. It had an irregular surface rather like matted weeds and was floating quite deep, so that only a curve fourteen inches or so high rode above the sea.

Arthur splashed over to it. On closer inspection, it was clearly a buoy or some floating marker, totally covered in green weeds. Arthur reached out to touch it. A huge strand of green weeds came away in his hand, revealing a bright red surface beneath.

Arthur touched that. It felt slightly sticky, and some of the red stuff came away on his hand. It was like chewing gum, impossible to get off. Arthur crossly wiped his hands but that only smeared it across his fingers, and his head dipped under. His broken leg wasn't weighed down that much by the cast, but he couldn't bend his knee and he couldn't tread water well enough just with one leg to really try and clean his hands, since he had to make swimming motions as well.

Arthur started to clear the weeds away with one hand. While doing that, he noticed that the buoy didn't move far with the swell. Each time one of the bigger waves came past, it swept Arthur five or six yards away and he had to swim back. The buoy didn't move anywhere near as much.

It had to be fixed to something. Arthur duck-dived down and, sure enough, a barnacle-encrusted chain led down from the buoy, down through the sunlit water and into the dark depths.

He resumed cleaning the weeds away with new enthusiasm and so got a lot more of the sticky stuff on his hands. It was tar, or something like tar, though it didn't smell.

The buoy has to mark something, Arthur thought. *It must be used by someone, who'll come past. I might even be able to climb up on it.*

When the buoy was almost clean it rode much higher in the water. Arthur had hoped he might find some handles on it, or projections he could hold on to, because he was getting very tired. But there weren't any. The only part of the buoy that was of any interest was a small brass ring right near the top. Arthur could only just reach it.

The ring was about the size of the top joint of Arthur's little finger, far too small for him to hold on. It also felt a bit loose. Arthur gave it a pull, hoping that it might come out and he could somehow make the hole bigger to create a handhold.

It came out with a very loud popping sound, followed

immediately afterwards by a ten-foot-high shower of sparks and a loud ticking noise as if a large and noisy clock had started up deep within the ball.

Arthur started frantically backstroking away from it, his body almost reacting faster than his brain, which had rapidly processed the fact that this floating ball was some sort of floating bomb — a mine — and it was going to explode.

A few seconds later, with Arthur only ten yards away, the buoy did explode. But it was not the lethal blast Arthur feared. There was a bright flash, and a rush of air above Arthur's head, but no deadly rain of fragments.

Smoke poured out of the ball, dark black smoke that coiled up into the air in a very orderly fashion, quite unlike any smoke Arthur had seen before. It started to whip about like a snake, dancing all over the place. Eventually its "head" connected with its "tail" to form a giant smoke ring that hovered ten feet above the buoy, which was still intact, though its upper half had broken open into multiple segments like a lotus.

The smoke ring slowly closed in on itself to become an inky cloud that spun about for a minute or so, then it abruptly burst apart, turning into eight jet-black seabirds that shrieked "Thief!" above Arthur's head before they each flew off in a different direction, covering the eight points of the compass rose.

Arthur was too tired to worry about what the seabirds were doing, or who they might be alerting. All he cared about was the fact that now the top half of the buoy was open, he could pull himself up on it and have a rest.

Arthur had only just enough energy to drag himself over and into the buoy. It was full of water, but he could sit in it quite comfortably and rest. That was all he wanted to do for a while. Rest.

But after only twenty minutes, according to his still-backwards but otherwise reliable and waterproof watch, Arthur found that he had rested enough. Though there was still no visible sun, it felt like one was beating down on him. He was really hot, and he was sure he was getting sunburned and that his tongue had started to swell from lack of water. He wished he'd managed to keep a sheet from the bed to use as a sunshade. He took his dressing gown off and made that into a makeshift turban, but it didn't really help.

At that point, Arthur started to hope that whoever the birds were supposed to alert would show up. Even if they thought he was a thief. That implied there was something to steal here, which didn't seem to be the case. The buoy was just a big, empty, floating ball with the top hemisphere opened up. There was nothing inside it except Arthur.

Another baking, uncomfortable hour passed. Arthur's

broken leg began to ache again, probably because the painkillers he'd had in the hospital were wearing off. The high-tech cast didn't seem to be operational anymore and Arthur could see distinct holes in it now.

Arthur picked at one of the holes and grimaced. The cast was falling apart. He was definitely sunburned as well, the backs of his hands turning pink, as if trying to match the bright red stain on his palms. According to Arthur's watch it was nine o'clock at night, but there was no change in the light. Without being able to see any sun, he couldn't tell whether night was approaching. He wasn't even sure there would be a night. There was in the Lower House, but that didn't mean anything. There might not be any relief from the constant heat.

He wondered if he should try and swim somewhere, but dismissed the idea as quickly as it came up. He was lucky to have found this buoy. Or perhaps it wasn't luck, it was the Mariner's disc that had led him here. In any case, Arthur couldn't swim for more than half an hour at the most, and there wasn't much chance of finding land in that time. Better to sit here and hope that the smoky seabirds brought someone.

Two hours later, Arthur felt a much cooler breeze waft across the back of his neck. He opened his puffy eyes to see a shadow passing across the sky. A veil of darkness advanced in a line across the horizon. Stars, or suitable facsimiles of them, began to twinkle as the light faded before the approaching line of night.

The wind and the lapping sea grew cold. Arthur turned his turban back into a dressing gown, shivered, and hunched up into a tighter ball. Clearly he was going to be sunburned during the day and then frozen at night. Either one would kill him, so not dying of hunger and thirst was no great bonus.

As he had that thought, Arthur saw another star. A fallen star, quite close to the sea, and moving towards him. It took another moment for his heat-addled brain to recognize that it was in fact a light.

A light fixed to the bowsprit of a ship.

Chapter Four

The fallen star grew closer, and the ship became more visible, though it was still little more than a dark outline in the fading light. A rather rotund outline, for this ship looked to be very broad, wallowing its way through the waves. It had only two masts, rather than the three of the ship that had picked up Leaf, and its square-rigged sails were definitely not of the luminous variety.

Arthur didn't care. He stood up gingerly, his muscles cramping from weariness and confinement in the buoy, and waved frantically.

"Help! I'm over here! Help!"

There was no answering shout from the ship. It rolled and plunged towards him, but he could see some of the sails being furled, and there were Denizens rushing about on the deck. Somebody was shouting orders, and others were repeating or questioning them. All in all, it didn't appear very organized.

Particularly as the ship sailed right past him. Arthur couldn't believe it. He shouted himself hoarse and almost fell out of the buoy from jumping up and down. But the ship kept on its way, till Arthur could only see the glow of the single lantern that hung from its stern rail.

Arthur watched till the light disappeared into the darkness, then he sat down, totally defeated. He rested his head in his hands and fought back a sob.

I am not going to cry, he told himself. *I will work something out. I am the Master of the Lower House and the Far Reaches. I am not going to die in a buoy in some rotten sea!*

Arthur took a deep breath and lifted his head up.

There will be another ship. There must be another ship.

Arthur was clutching at this hope when he saw the light again, followed by another.

Two lights!

They were a hundred feet apart and perhaps two hundred yards away. It took Arthur only a second to understand that he was looking at the bow and stern lights of the ship. He'd lost sight of the stern light as the vessel turned, but now it was heaved-to, broadside on to him.

A few moments later, he heard the slap of oars in the water, and Denizens chanting as they rowed a small boat towards him. Arthur couldn't make out the words till they were quite close, and the light of a bull's-eye lantern flickered across the water, searching for Arthur and the buoy.

"Flotsam floats when all is sunk.
Jetsam thrown isn't just junk.
Coughs and colds and bright red sores
Waiting for us, so bend yer oars!"

The yellow beam of light swept over Arthur, then back-tracked to shine directly in his face. Arthur raised his arm to shield his eyes. The light wasn't bright enough to blind, but it made it hard to see the boat and its crew. There were at least a dozen Denizens aboard, most of them rowing.

"Back oars!" came a shout from the darkness. "Yarko was right! There *is* a Nithling on that buoy! Make ready your crossbows!"

"I'm not a Nithling!" shouted Arthur. "I'm . . . I'm a distressed sailor!"

"A what?"

"A distressed sailor," replied Arthur. He had read that somewhere. Sailors were supposed to help one another.

"What ship? And what are you doing on that treasure marker?"

"Uh, my ship was the *Steely Bed*. It sank. I swam here."

There was a muttering aboard the boat. Arthur couldn't clearly hear all the words, but he heard "claim," "ours," "stick 'im and sink 'im," and the sound of someone being knocked on the head and grunting in pain. He hoped it was the Denizen who said "stick 'im," since he was fairly sure he was the "'im" being referred to.

"Give way," shouted the Denizen in charge. The oars dipped into the sea again, and the boat moved forward. As it came alongside the buoy, Arthur got his first real look at the crew, with the Denizen holding the bull's-eye lantern opening its shutters to spread the light around.

They were not a good-looking bunch. There were eight men and five women. They might have started with the usual handsome features of Denizens, but the great majority of them had eye patches, livid scars across their faces, and an illustrated catalog of tattoos, ranging from ships to storms to skulls and snakes, up and down their forearms, on cheeks and foreheads and bared midriffs. They wore many different styles of clothing, all in bright colors, the single common feature being a wide leather belt that supported a cutlass and knife. Half of them also had red knitted caps, and the leader, a broad-shouldered male Denizen with scarlet sunbursts tattooed on his cheeks, wore a leather Napoleon hat that looked a little too small for him.

He smiled at Arthur, revealing a mouth with most of its teeth missing. Of the remaining four or five, three were capped in gold.

Pirates, Arthur figured.

But there was something strangely nonaggressive about them too. Something that reminded Arthur of people playing dress-up. Surely real pirates would just kill him without a second thought, not sit quietly looking at him. And one of them was drawing a picture of the scene with a charcoal stick in a sketchbook.

"The *Steelibed*," said the leader. "Can't say I've heard of her. When did she sink? Carrying any cargo?"

"Maybe a day ago," said Arthur cautiously. "Not much cargo. Um, cotton and stuff."

"And stuff," repeated the leader, with a wink at Arthur. "Well, with a treasure marker in front of us, we'll not bother with 'cotton and stuff' if there's anything below. The question is, are you claiming salvage?"

"Uh, I don't know," said Arthur cautiously. "Maybe. I might."

"Well, if you're not sure, then it don't matter!" declared the leader, with a laugh that was echoed by the crew. "We'll just have a look below and if there's anything left, we'll have it up. Then we'll be on our way, and you can get on with your own business."

"Hold on!" cried Arthur. "Take me with you!"

"Lizard, take a line and have a glance under the buoy," said the leader to one of the crew, a small woman who had blue scales tattooed all over her face. At least Arthur *hoped* they were tattoos and not actual scales. She undid her belt, kicked off her boots, and quickly dived over the side with a rope held between her teeth.

"Please, I need to get to land," said Arthur. "Somewhere I can make a phone call."

"Ain't no phone calls in the Border Sea," said one of the Denizens. "Exchange got flooded and they never built a new one on the high ground."

"Shut yer trap, One-Ear," instructed the leader. He turned back to Arthur. "You want to come aboard the *Moth* as a passenger, then?"

"That's your ship?" asked Arthur. "The *Moth*?"

"Aye, the *Moth*," replied a Denizen who had a shark's toothy mouth tattooed around his own. "What's wrong with that? Moths can be extremely frightening. If you get trapped in a cupboard with a whole passel of moths —"

"I didn't mean anything bad about the name," said Arthur. He thought quickly. "It's just I was surprised to be picked up by such a famous ship."

"What?" asked one of the other Denizens. "The *Moth*?"

"Yes. Such a famous ship and its crew of . . . uh . . . such renowned pirates!"

Arthur's speech was met by a sudden silence. Then the crew of the boat erupted, falling over themselves as they tried to run out the oars again. All of them shouted at once:

"Pirates! Where?! What pirates?! Back to the ship!"

"Hold hard!" roared the leader. He waded in among the crew, slapping them openhanded across the backs of their heads till they subsided onto the slats. Then he turned to Arthur.

"I ain't never heard anything so insulting. Us! Pirates! We're Salvagers, and proud of it. We don't take anything that hasn't been thrown away first or sunk and come up. Or treasures left in the open sea."

"Sorry," said Arthur. "It was just the eye patches and the clothes and the tattoos and everything . . . I was confused. But I really would like to be a passenger."

"Just because we're only Salvagers doesn't mean we can't dress nice and wear an eye patch if we want," muttered Shark-Mouth. "Or two eye patches, come to that."

"Can't wear two, you idiot," said another Denizen.

"Can so," replied the first. "Get some of that one-way leather from the Doctor —"

"Shut up!" roared the leader. He turned back to Arthur and said, "I'm not saying you can be a passenger, right?

I'm only the Second Mate of the *Moth*. Sunscorch is my name. But we'll take you back to the ship. The Captain can decide your fate."

"Thanks!" said Arthur. "My name's Arth —"

He stopped halfway through. Better to keep his name to himself, he thought.

"Arth? Well, get aboard Arth."

Two of the closer Denizens held the boat against the buoy, and another one helped Arthur across.

"Gettin' yer leg ready to cut off, are yer?" asked the helping Denizen with a grin. He slapped Arthur's cast and waved his own leg, showing off a wooden peg that started below the knee. "They grow back too quick, though, I'm telling yer."

Arthur grimaced at the sight and quickly suppressed a flash of fear that his leg might have to be cut off. And his wouldn't grow back, unlike a Denizen's.

"I've had this one chopped a dozen times," continued the peg-legged crew member. "Why, I remember —"

He stopped in midsentence and recoiled, staring at Arthur's red-stained hands.

"He's got the Red Hand!"

"Feverfew's mark!"

"We're all doomed!"

"Quiet!" roared Sunscorch. He peered down at Arthur.

"It's only red tar or something from the buoy," said Arthur. "It'll wash off."

"From the buoy," whispered Sunscorch. "This here buoy?"

"Yes."

"There wasn't any smoke, was there?"

"Yes."

"What about birds? That smoke didn't turn into cormorants, did it? Smoky black cormorants that screamed out something that might have been 'Death' or 'Dismemberment' or anything like that?"

"There were birds," admitted Arthur. "They screamed out 'Thief' and flew away. I thought they must have brought you here."

Sunscorch took off his hat and wiped his bald head with a surprisingly neatly folded white handkerchief that he took out of a pocket.

"Not us," he whispered. "Lookout saw the open buoy and the Captain thought it worth a glance. That there treasure marker must be one of Feverfew's. The birds will have flown to find him, and his ship."

"*Shiver*," intoned the crew. "The ship of bone."

As they spoke, the Denizen with the lantern shuttered it

right down to the merest glimmer, and everybody else looked out at the sea all around.

Sunscorch ran his tongue over his remaining teeth and kept wiping his head. His crew watched him intently, till he put away his handkerchief and clapped his hat back on.

"Listen up," he whispered. "Seeing as we're probably dead or headed for the slave-chain anyway, we might as well see what's below. Lizard? Where's Lizard?"

"Here," came a whisper from the water. "There's a chest all right, a big one, sitting pretty as you please atop a spire of rock, ten fathom down."

"The chain?"

"Screwed to the rock, not to the chest."

"Let's be having that chest, then," whispered Sunscorch. "Bones, you and Bottle back oars. Everyone else, hands on the line. You, too, Arth."

Arthur joined the others to grab hold of the rope. At Sunscorch's hoarsely whispered commands, they all hauled together.

"Heave away! Hold on! Heave cheerily! Hold on! Heave away! Hold! One more!"

At the last command, a dripping chest as long as Arthur was tall and as high as his waist scraped over the gunwale and was manhandled into the boat. As soon as it was settled, there was a mad dash to the oars. With Sunscorch whispering more commands and the rowers very gently dipping their oars, the boat moved ahead and then turned towards the lights of the *Moth*.

"Hope we get back to the ship in time so as we can all die together," whispered the Denizen on the oar next to Arthur. "It'd be better that way."

"What makes you so sure we're going to die?" asked Arthur. "Don't be so pessimistic."

"Feverfew never leaves any survivors," whispered another Denizen. "He slaves 'em or kills 'em. Either way they're gone for good. He's got strange powers. A Sorcerer of Nothing."

"He'll torture *you* first, though," added one of the women, with a grin that showed her teeth were filed to points. "You touched the buoy. You've got the Red Hand that shows you tried to steal from Feverfew."

"Quiet!" instructed Sunscorch. "Row quiet, and listen!"

Arthur cupped a hand to his ear and leaned over the side. But all he could hear was the harsh breathing of the Denizens and the soft, regular swoosh and tinkle of the oars dipping in and out of the water.

"What are we listening for?" Arthur asked after a while.

"Anything we don't want to hear," said Sunscorch, as he looked back over the stern. Without turning around, he added, "Shutter that lantern, Yeo."

"It is shuttered," replied Yeo. "One of the moons is rising. Feverfew will see us miles away."

"No point being quiet, then," said Sunscorch.

Arthur looked where the mate pointed. Sure enough, a slim blue-tinged moon was rising up on the horizon. It wasn't very big and it didn't look all that far away — a few tens of miles, not hundreds of thousands — but it was bright.

The blue moon rose quickly and rather jerkily, as if it was on a clockwork track that needed oiling. By its light Arthur could easily see the *Moth*, wallowing nearby. But he could also see something else, far away on the horizon. Something that glinted in the moonlight. A reflection from a telescope lens, atop a thin dark smudge that must be a mast.

Sunscorch saw it too.

"Row, you dogs!" roared the Second Mate. "Row for your miserable lives!"

Chapter Five

Their arrival aboard the *Moth* resembled a panicked evacuation more than an orderly boarding. The boat was abandoned as most of the Denizens clawed their way up the side ladder or the untidy mess of netting that hung along the *Moth*'s yellow-painted hull, all of them shouting unhelpful things like "Feverfew!" and "*Shiver!*" and "We're doomed!"

Sunscorch managed to drag several Denizens back and get them to take the line from the chest. But even he wasn't able to get the crew to do anything about retrieving the boat. As it began to drift away, he jumped to the ship's side himself, reaching back to help Arthur get hold of the netting.

"Never lost salvage nor a passenger," he muttered. "No thanks to the scum of the sea I have to sail with. Mister Concort! Mister Concort! There's a boat adrift!"

"Concort's the First Mate," he confided to Arthur as they climbed the side. "Amiable, but hen-witted. Like most of this lot he was with the *Moth* when it was a counting house. Chief Clerk. You'd think after several thousand years at sea he'd have learned . . . but I'm misspeaking meself. Up you go!"

Arthur was pushed up and over the rail. He fell onto the deck, unable to get his bad leg in place in time. Before he could get up himself, Sunscorch gripped him under each elbow and yanked him upright, shouting at the same time.

"Ichabod! Ichabod! Take our passenger to the Captain! And get him a blanket!"

A thin, nontattooed Denizen neatly dressed in a blue waistcoat and an almost white shirt stepped out of the throng of panicking sailors and bowed slightly to Arthur. He was thinner than most of the other Denizens, and moved very precisely, as if he was following some mysterious dance pattern in his head.

"Please step this way," he said, doing an about-turn that was almost a pirouette and would have looked more in keeping on a stage than on the shifting deck of a ship.

Arthur obediently followed the Denizen, who was presumably Ichabod. Behind him, Sunscorch was yelling and slapping the backs of heads.

"Port watch aloft! Prepare to make sail! Starboard watch to the guns and boarding stations!"

"Very noisy, these sailors," said Ichabod. "Mind your head."

The Denizen ducked as he stepped through a narrow

doorway. Though Arthur was considerably shorter, he had to bend his head down too. They were in a short, dark, narrow corridor with a very low ceiling.

"Aren't you a sailor?" asked Arthur.

"I'm the Captain's Steward," replied Ichabod severely. "I was his gentleman's gentleman when we were ashore."

"His what?"

"What is sometimes called a valet," replied Ichabod as he opened the door at the other end, only a few yards away. The Denizen stepped through, with Arthur at his heels.

The room beyond the door was not what Arthur expected. It was far too big to be inside the ship, for a start: a huge, whitewashed space at least eighty feet long and sixty feet wide, with a decorated plaster ceiling twenty feet above, complete with a fifty-candle chandelier of cut crystal in the middle.

There was a mahogany desk right in the middle of the room with a green-shaded gas lantern on it, and a long row of glass-topped display cases all along one wall, each illuminated by its own gently hissing gaslight. In the far corner, there was a curtained four-poster bed with a blanket box at its foot, a standing screen painted with a nautical scene, and a large oak-paneled wardrobe with mirrored doors.

It was also absolutely quiet and completely stable. All the noise of the crew and the sea had vanished as soon as the door was shut behind Arthur, as had the constant roll and sway of the deck.

"How —"

Ichabod knew what Arthur was asking before the boy even got the question out.

"This is one of the original rooms. When the Deluge came and we had to turn the counting house into a ship, this room refused to transform to something more useful, like a gun deck. Eventually Doctor Scamandros managed to connect it to the aft passageway, but it isn't really in the ship."

"Where is it, then?"

"We're not entirely sure. Probably not where it used to be, since the old counting house site is well submerged. The Captain thinks that this room must have been personally supervised by the Architect, and retained some of Her virtue. It lies within the House, that's for sure, not out in the Realms."

"You're not worried that it might get cut off from the ship?" asked Arthur as they walked over to the bed. The curtains were drawn and Arthur could hear snoring behind them. Not horrendous "I can't bear to hear it" snoring, but occasional drawn-out snorts and wheezes.

"Not at all," said Ichabod. "The ship is still mostly the counting house, albeit long-transformed and changed. This room is of the counting house, so it will always be connected somehow. If the passageway falls off, some other way will open."

"Through the wardrobe maybe," said Arthur.

Ichabod looked at him sternly, his eyebrows contracting to almost meet above his nose.

"I doubt that, young mortal. That is where I keep the Captain's clothes. It is not a thoroughfare of any kind."

"Sorry," said Arthur. "I was only . . ."

His voice trailed off as Ichabod's eyebrows did not return to a more friendly position. There was a frosty silence for a few seconds, then the Denizen twitched his nose as if something had irritated his nostrils, and bent down to open the blanket box.

"Here is a blanket," he said unnecessarily, handing it to Arthur. "I suggest you wrap yourself in it. It may stop that shivering. Unless of course it is merely an affectation."

"Oh, thanks," said Arthur. He hadn't realized he was shivering, but now that Ichabod mentioned it, he realized he was very cold, and little tremors were running up and down his arms and legs. The heavy blanket was very welcome. "I am cold. I might even have a cold."

"Really?" asked Ichabod, suddenly interested. "We

must tell Doctor Scamandros. But first I suppose I should wake the Captain."

"I'm already awake," said a voice behind the curtain. A quiet, calm voice. "We have a visitor, I see. Anything else to report, Ichabod?"

"Mister Sunscorch is of the opinion that we are being pursued by the awful pirate Feverfew, on account of stealing one of his treasure chests."

"Ah," said the voice. "Is Mister Sunscorch doing . . . um . . . things with the sails and so on? So we can, ah, flee?"

"Yes, sir," said Ichabod. "May I present the potential passenger Mister Sunscorch took aboard from Feverfew's buoy? He is a boy and, I believe I am correct in assuming, a true mortal. Not one of the Piper's children."

"Yes," said Arthur.

"First things first, Ichabod," came the reply. "Second-best boots, third-best coat, and my, ah, sword. The proper one with the, err, sharpened blade."

"The sharpened blade? Is that wise, sir?"

"Yes, yes. If, ah, Feverfew catches us . . . now, mortal boy, what is your name?"

"My name is — look ou —!" said Arthur as Ichabod walked straight into the wardrobe mirror. But the Denizen didn't hit it. He went right through, like a diver into a pool of still water, the silvered glass rippling as he passed.

"Lookow?" asked the Captain.

"Sorry, I got distracted," said Arthur. "My name is Arth."

"Lookow sounds better than Arth," said the Captain. "Pity. Names can be a terrible burden. Take mine, for example. It's Catapillow. Captain Catapillow, at your service."

"Caterpillar?" asked Arthur, not sure he'd heard it right through the bed's curtains.

"No! Cat-ah-pillow. See what I mean? Suitable name for the manager of a counting house, but hardly the stuff of nautical legend."

"Why don't you change it?"

"Officers not allowed to," came the muffled reply. "Name was issued by the Architect. Inscribed in the Register of Precedence. That's why I'm Captain. Most senior aboard, 38,598th in precedence within the House. Prefer not to be, but no choice in the matter. Mister Sunscorch is, um, the only professional sailor aboard. Boots?"

"Here they are, sir," said Ichabod, inserting boots, coat, and sword between the curtains. Arthur hadn't seen him come back through the mirrored door of the wardrobe, but there he was.

There was a muffled curse from the bed and the curtains billowed out. Then the boots thrust out under them, half on Captain Catapillow's feet. Ichabod helped him ease them on all the way, and Catapillow slid out of the bed and stood up and bowed to Arthur.

He was tall, but not as tall as Dame Primus or Monday's Noon. He was also not particularly handsome, though not exactly ugly either. He didn't have any tattoos, or at least none visible. He just looked very plain and ordinary, with a rather vacant face under a short white wig with a kind of ponytail at the back tied with a blue ribbon. His blue coat was quite faded, and he only had one gold epaulette, on his left shoulder.

"Now, young Arth," Catapillow said as he tried to buckle on his sword-belt and failed. He stood still while Ichabod fixed it up. "You want to be a passenger aboard a ship that will shortly be sunk and everyone on it put to, umm, the sword or made slaves by the pirate Feverfew?"

"No," said Arthur. "I mean I want to be a passenger, but surely we can escape? I saw that ship, the pirate one, but it was a long way away. We must have a good lead."

"A stern chase is a long chase," muttered Catapillow.

"But they'll, you know, probably catch us in the end. I suppose we should go and, er, have a look. Mister Sunscorch might have some — what-do-you-call-'em — ideas. Or Doctor Scamandros. Just when I was going to examine some new additions to my collection. I suppose it will be Feverfew's collection soon, and he won't appreciate it."

Arthur started to ask about the Captain's collection. He could tell from Catapillow's fond gaze that it was housed in the display cabinets along the wall. But before he could get the words out, Ichabod trod on his foot and coughed meaningfully.

"What's that?" asked Catapillow, looking back at the boy.

"The Captain's needed on deck!" said Ichabod in a loud, firm voice.

"Yes! Yes!" said Catapillow. "Let's see where that vile, um, vile ship of Feverfew's has got to. We can talk about your passage fee later, Arth. Follow me!"

He led the way back to the door. As soon as it opened, Arthur heard the deep roar of the sea, the groan of the ship's timbers, and the continuing shouts of the crew and Sunscorch.

He had to shut his eyes as he left the room and stepped into the corridor because the floor of the ship was rocking but the room's wasn't, creating a very sick-making feeling at the back of his eyes. But it passed as soon as he was in the ship proper again, though the ship was pitching up and down so much he had to use a hand to steady himself every few paces.

It was bright out on the main deck. The moon was high above them, its light cool and strong. Arthur could even have read by it, he thought, and he noticed that it was strong enough to cast shadows.

He hugged his blanket tighter around his shoulders as he felt the wind. It had grown colder still, and stronger. Looking up at the masts, all the sails were full. The *Moth* was heeled over quite steeply to starboard and was plunging ahead at quite a rate.

Unfortunately, when he looked over his shoulder, Arthur saw that the pirate ship was sailing even faster. It was much smaller than the *Moth*, and narrower too, with only two masts and triangular sails rather than the square ones on the merchant vessel.

"The ship looks white in the moonlight," said Arthur. "And are those sails brown?"

"They're the color of dried blood," said Ichabod. "A shade called 'vintage sanguinolent' by tailors. The hull is supposedly made from a single piece of bone, that of a legendary monster from the Secondary Realms. Feverfew himself is said to be a pirate from the Realms, once mortal, who mastered the darker depths of House Sorcery and is now half-Nithling, half —"

"That will . . . that will do, thank you, Ichabod," said Catapillow nervously. "Come with me."

He led the way up to the quarterdeck, where two Denizens wrestled with the wheel, and Sunscorch shouted orders at the Denizens aloft and on the deck, trimming sails and yards. There were two other Denizens there as well. One stood next to Sunscorch, nodding sagely at every order but saying nothing. He looked rather like Captain Catapillow, with a bland face and similar clothes, so was clearly an officer. Probably the First Mate, Arthur thought. The one who used to be the Chief Clerk in the counting house.

The other Denizen was completely different. He was crouched on the deck next to the wheel. A strange, small figure not much taller than Arthur, he was almost completely lost inside a voluminous yellow greatcoat with rolled-up cuffs. He was bald and his face and head were completely covered in small, colorful tattoos that Arthur realized after a moment were animated, moving and shifting around. Tattoos of ships and sea creatures, birds and clouds, maps and moons and stars and suns and planets.

"Mister Concort, who is First Mate," whispered Ichabod, pointing to the Denizen next to Sunscorch. "And

Doctor Scamandros, our most accomplished sorcerer and navigator. He's casting the haruspices to see where we might be able to go. No one must interrupt, take note. Dreadful things would happen."

At that moment, a gust of wind hit the *Moth* hard and she heeled over even farther. As everyone on the quarter-deck scrambled to keep their footing, Arthur stumbled against Captain Catapillow, and both of them ended up sliding across the deck and into the rail.

Arthur almost went over, into the dark sea that was surprisingly close below. He managed to save himself and, at the last second, his blanket, but at the cost of a jolt to his broken leg that sent a savage, stabbing pain up his side and into his head.

As the ship righted itself in response to Sunscorch's shouted commands, Arthur noticed that almost everybody else had ended up on the starboard rail, apart from the two helmsmen clinging to the wheel, Sunscorch next to them, and Doctor Scamandros to the side. He was still crouched where he'd been, as if he were glued to the deck. All the things he was studying were also still there, which seemed impossible. Several maps were laid out on the deck, with a pair of gilt-bronze dividers on top, a ruler, and the skull of a small animal that had been converted into a cup to hold a dozen or so pencils.

There were also lots of small pieces of colored cardboard strewn apparently at random next to the map. Doctor Scamandros was studying them and whistling through his front teeth. After a few seconds, he gathered them up into his cupped hands and threw them down again. To Arthur's surprise, they joined together as they fell, and he realized they were jigsaw pieces. When they hit the deck, nearly all of them had joined, but two or three pieces remained separate. The jigsaw was incomplete.

Doctor Scamandros stopped whistling and the wind, as if in response, eased a little. The Denizen gathered the jigsaw pieces together again and put them in a cardboard box that had a picture of a sheep on it, which he then put inside his yellow greatcoat. After this was done, he stood up. This was obviously the point at which he could be interrupted, because Catapillow and Concort rushed over to him.

"What are the signs, Doctor?" asked Catapillow. "Is there a course out of here?"

"No," said Scamandros. His voice was very high and pure, and reminded Arthur strangely of a trumpet. "There is some power interfering with both the goat and sheep auguries. I dare not try the ox in such circumstances. Without guidance, I can find no true course."

"Is it Feverfew?" asked Sunscorch. "Even so far away?"

"No," said Scamandros. He had caught sight of Arthur for the first time, and his dark eyes were staring straight at the boy. "It is much closer. Who is that?"

"Arth," said Sunscorch. "A mortal boy. We picked him up with Feverfew's treasure."

"He holds an object of great power," said Doctor Scamandros, excitement in his voice. He rummaged inside his coat and pulled out a pair of glasses with gold wire rims and thick smoked-quartz lenses, which he slipped onto his forehead, not over his eyes. "Bring him here."

Arthur stepped forward of his own accord and staggered across the deck. Sunscorch caught him and held him, loosely enough for the grip to be either a friend helping out or a guard about to secure a prisoner.

"What is in your pocket, boy?" asked Doctor Scamandros. "It is interfering with my augury and, thus, my navigation of this ship."

"It's . . . it's a book," said Arthur. "It won't be of any use to you."

"I'll be the judge of that!" Scamandros exclaimed. He reached forward to Arthur's pocket, and Sunscorch tightened his grip on the boy's arms. "What have we —"

As he touched the top of the Atlas, there was a loud report, like a pistol shot. Scamandros's hand came back so quickly Arthur didn't even see it, and then the navigator was hopping around the deck with his fingers thrust into his armpit, screeching, "Ow! Ow! Ow! Throw him overboard!"

Sunscorch hesitated, then picked up Arthur in a bear hug and tottered to the starboard rail, crashing into it with considerable force.

"Sorry, lad," he said as he lifted Arthur up and prepared to heave him into the waiting sea. "We need the Doctor."

Chapter Six

"No!" screamed Arthur. Then, as Sunscorch continued to lift him up, "I'm a friend of the Mariner! Captain Tom Shelvocke!"

Sunscorch lowered Arthur to the deck.

"Prove it," he said coldly. "If you're lying, I'll carve you a set of gills before I throw you over."

Arthur reached with a shivering hand into his pajama top and pulled out his makeshift floss-chain. For a dreadful moment he thought the disc was gone, then it slid free and hung on his chest.

"What are you waiting for, Sunscorch?" yelled Doctor Scamandros angrily. "Throw him overboard!"

Sunscorch looked closely at the disc, flipped it with his finger, and looked at the other side. Then he sighed and let go of Arthur. Just then, the ship rolled to port and back again, almost sending Arthur over the side anyway.

"Do as the Doctor says, Mister Sunscorch!" called Catapillow. "We must have a course to get away!"

"I can't, Captain!" shouted Sunscorch. "The boy has

the mark of the Mariner. If he asks for aid, as sailors we must give it."

"I *am* asking," said Arthur hastily. "I don't want to be thrown overboard. I only want to send a message to the Lower House. Or the Far Reaches."

"He has the what? The who?" asked Catapillow.

Sunscorch sighed again and helped Arthur along the sloping deck to the group gathered around the wheel. Doctor Scamandros still had his hand under his arm. He scowled at Arthur.

"No seaman will go against the Mariner," said Sunscorch. "The boy has the Mariner's medal, so you'll have to figure something else out, Doc. He ain't going over the side."

"The Mariner," said Scamandros. "A figure of reverence for the nautically inclined. One of the Old One's sons, I believe?"

"Yes," said Arthur, though the question hadn't been asked of him. "And the Architect's."

"Perhaps I was a little hasty," Scamandros continued. "I thought perhaps you had something in your pocket we wouldn't want aboard. But any friend of the Mariner . . . please do accept my apology."

"Sure," said Arthur. "No problem."

"Well, ah, welcome aboard," said the Captain. "We're

delighted to have you here. Though I fear that our voyage is, um, about to be cut short."

Everyone looked back over the stern. The *Shiver* had closed in, and was now less than a mile away.

"She'll be firing her bowchasers soon," said Sunscorch. "If they've any powder. They've the weather gauge too. We'll have to fight it out."

"Oh," said Concort. He swallowed and frowned at the same time. "That doesn't sound very good."

"Can you get us a better wind, Doctor?" asked Sunscorch. "Untie one of your knots?"

"No," replied Scamandros. "Feverfew is already working the wind, and his workings are stronger. There is no escape within the Border Sea."

"And is there, er, no plausible course out to the Realms?" Catapillow pulled his sword partly out of its scabbard as he spoke, and almost cut his nervous fingers on the exposed blade.

"There is one possibility that I may have overlooked due to extreme pain in my hand," said Scamandros. "I cannot cast the haruspices because of magical interference. But the young have natural ability, so this boy may be able to. Can you read portents of the future in the strewn intestines of animals, young sir?"

"No," said Arthur with a grimace of revulsion. "That sounds disgusting!'

"They don't use actual intestines anymore," whispered Ichabod. "Just magical jigsaw puzzles of intestines."

"Indeed, the art has grown more orderly and less troublesome for the laundry," said Scamandros, who clearly had very superior hearing. "Though personally I believe it is best to be trained the old way, before coming to the puzzles. So you are not a haruspex or seer?"

"No . . ."

"Then you shall cast the pieces and I will read them." Scamandros took a large box out from under his coat — bigger than the one he'd put away before — and handed it to Arthur. There was a picture of an ox on the box, the back half cross-sectioned to show its innards. "Quickly now. Take the box and empty the pieces into your hands."

As Arthur opened the box, something shrieked overhead. It sounded like a cross between a train whistle and a terrified parrot. Sunscorch looked up, then muttered, "They've got powder! That's a ranging shot!" and started to shout more commands to the helmsman and crew. The *Moth* lumbered and rolled to port as the wheel spun and the crew hauled on lines to trim the yards, the horizontal spars on the mast that the sails were attached to.

Arthur knelt down on the deck and put his hands in the box. Though all he could see were pieces of colored cardboard, he recoiled as he touched them.

"Ugh! They feel like raw mince or . . . or worse!"

"Ignore that!" instructed Scamandros. "Pick them up and cast them on the deck! Quickly now!"

Arthur shuddered and hesitated. Then he heard the whistling again, and a huge plume of water exploded just behind the *Moth*, showering them all with freezing water.

"Over and under," said Sunscorch grimly. "They'll have the range inside a minute."

Arthur took a deep breath and plunged his hands into the box. Picking up the pieces was like picking up handfuls of dead worms. But he got them all, raised them up, and threw them at Scamandros's feet.

As before, the jigsaw came together as it fell. But this time all the pieces joined to make a perfect rectangle. The colors ran and shimmered like spilled paint, then formed into lines and patterns. In a few seconds, a picture appeared. A picture of a rocky island, a mound of tumbled yellow stones, surrounded by a sea of curious color, more violet than blue.

Scamandros looked at the picture, muttering to himself, then he rolled up the chart at his feet and immediately unrolled it again, revealing a completely different map.

"Forlorn Island, Sea of Yazer, on the planet we call Gerain," said Scamandros. "That'll do!"

"Err, Mister Concort . . ." said Catapillow.

"Ah, Mister Sunscorch . . ." said Concort.

"Prepare to Cross the Line!" roared Sunscorch. "Idlers take a hold!"

Catapillow and Concort rushed to the rail and gripped it. Sunscorch joined the two Denizens on the wheel. Scamandros picked up the jigsaw, which didn't fall apart, and stood by them.

"Grab hold of a rope or the rail," Ichabod instructed Arthur. "When the Doctor shouts, look down and close your eyes. And whatever you do, don't let go!"

Arthur did as he was told, taking a firm grip on the portside rail. He looked back at Doctor Scamandros, who was holding the jigsaw and muttering to himself, with occasional instructions to Sunscorch.

"Port five, steady," he said. "Starboard ten and back again amidships, hold her as she goes, port five, port five, starboard ten . . ."

The *Moth* rolled and tilted first to one side and then the other, but didn't seem to change its actual direction very much for all the turning of the wheel this way and that. But Doctor Scamandros kept ordering small changes of direction.

Arthur heard a muffled bang come from behind them and looked astern, just in time to see the flash of the *Shiver*'s bowchasers, followed by that same whistling screech. This time, it didn't end in a waterspout or a pass overhead. Just as Doctor Scamandros shouted something unintelligible and threw the jigsaw in the air, Arthur heard a terrible splintering, crashing noise that momentarily blotted out all other sounds.

But he didn't look. He closed his eyes and bent down as instructed, hoping that whatever the cannonball had hit wasn't going to fall down on his head.

There was a moment of silence after the terrible sound of some major part of the ship breaking, immediately followed by a flash so bright Arthur's eyes were filled with white light, even through shut eyelids. That flash was accompanied by a crash of thunder that shook the whole ship and stirred a vibration so strong it made Arthur's limbs and stomach ache.

Arthur knew what was happening at once. His hand went to the invitation card in his pocket and he hunkered down as low as he could, still clutching his pocket.

They were about to pass through the Line of Storms again!

The thunder was so deafening that its echoes lingered in Arthur's ears and head, so even when it ceased it took him awhile before he stopped trembling and his hearing started to return. The afterimage of the lightning remained in patches, and dark spots danced around his eyes.

Arthur opened his eyes to a scene of destruction and wonder. One of the huge horizontal spars from the *Moth*'s mainmast had been struck by the cannonball and broken off. Half of it was sprawled over the deck, and half was in the water, a tangled mass of timber, ropes, and canvas.

Arthur only glanced at that. His attention was drawn ahead of the ship. There, extending upward from the sea into the sky, was a huge gilt picture frame, easily four hundred feet long and three hundred feet high. It bordered an enormous, brightly glowing version of the jigsaw picture Arthur had made, with the yellow stone island and the violet sea. But this didn't look like a picture. The sea was in motion, there were purple-tinged clouds drifting above the island, and birds or birdlike things were flying around. Arthur could still see the jigsaw piece outlines — much narrower and more wriggly pieces than in a normal jigsaw — but the lines were very faint.

"Starboard Watch! Cut away that yard! Quickly now!"

The *Moth* rolled as Sunscorch spoke, sending its sails flapping, to make a sound like sarcastic applause.

"Helm! Hold her steady!" shouted Sunscorch.

The *Moth* was trying to sail straight for the framed image, Arthur saw. He understood it was not an image. It was a doorway to another world, out in the Secondary Realms.

"Did we lose 'em?" asked Sunscorch to the Doctor.

Scamandros looked astern, lowering his smoked glasses over his eyes to stare at the now surprisingly distant Line of Storms.

"I'm not . . . no!"

Arthur looked back, too, blinking at the still-bright flashes of lightning, though they were now several miles away. At first he couldn't spot anything, then he saw the silhouette of the *Shiver*'s dark sails. She had dropped back but would soon catch up again, particularly with the *Moth* slowed by the broken spar over the side, which acted like a large and clumsy sea anchor.

"They'll try and follow us through the portal," said Sunscorch.

"Um, is there anything . . . some maneuver or other?" asked Catapillow anxiously.

"Get that spar cut away!" roared Sunscorch. Arthur winced. Clearly Sunscorch got louder the more anxious he was.

Doctor Scamandros looked ahead at the vast gilt-framed doorway to the violet-hued sea. It was several hundred yards away. He looked back at the pursuing ship, took out a pencil, and made some calculations on the cuff of his big yellow coat.

"At our current speed Feverfew will board us short of the portal," he said. "Even if they don't take down a mast or hole us below the waterline."

"He won't fire again," said Sunscorch. "Don't need to, does he? We're slow enough now. Anything more might damage the loot."

This confident assessment was immediately undermined by the report of a cannon astern, resulting in another plume of water, this time well short.

"Then again, he might sink us for sport," added Sunscorch. He looked down at the main deck where the Denizens were hacking ineffectually with axes at the fallen yard. "Cut away! Don't slap at it! Cut! Doctor, if there's anything you can do, do it. No seamanship can save us now! I'm for an ax!"

"Carry on!" Catapillow called out as Sunscorch leapt down the companionway to the waist of the ship.

Arthur looked at the rapidly gaining pirate vessel, then at the living picture in its vast gilt frame. Even without calculating anything, it was clear the *Shiver* would catch them before they could get to the transfer portal. It was too far away. . . .

Arthur suddenly had an idea.

"I don't know any sorcery or anything," Arthur said. "But that big painting is like a transfer plate you step on, isn't it?"

Scamandros nodded distractedly.

"So if we can't get to it in time, can it somehow be moved to us?"

Scamandros frowned, then cocked his head as if struck by Arthur's suggestion. Arthur noticed that all the small tattoos on the doctor's face were showing scenes of trouble. Storms at sea. Sunken ships. Exploding suns. Imploding planets.

Just as the Doctor opened his mouth to speak, the *Shiver* fired again.

"Interesting. Yes, it is theoretically possible to —"

Whatever Scamandros was going to say was lost as a cannonball struck the *Moth*'s side just behind and below the wheel, smashing the heavy timber into a spray of deadly foot-long splinters that went whistling across the quarterdeck.

Chapter Seven

The next thing Arthur knew, he was lying on the deck, right up against the rail, with his good leg hanging overboard. He could hear screaming all around him, and shouting. For a moment he thought he'd suffered a sudden asthma attack and had passed out from lack of air. But his breathing was fine, or so his mind reported before it suddenly switched back to the current situation. The splinters flying through the air —

Arthur pulled his leg in, sat up, and stared around him. He was vaguely aware that his broken leg hurt, but that was nothing new. There was blood on his dressing gown, but it was bright blue. A pain in his left hand made him lift it up. There was blood there too — red blood, but not much of it. Arthur focused on his middle finger, and pulled out a needle-shaped splinter that had sliced across a knuckle and was still hanging there.

"Will you look at that?! Ruined!" said a voice next to Arthur. The boy slowly turned to look. There was a large hole on the far side of the deck. The planking was gouged all around and there was blue blood splattered all over the place, amid shattered wood and splinters.

Ichabod was pointing at his waistcoat. A splinter as long as Arthur's forearm was sticking out of the Denizen's stomach. Blue blood was trickling out of the wound and into his waistcoat pocket.

"Doesn't it hurt?" asked Arthur. He was in shock and part of his mind was telling him to check himself over again. He knew the Denizens could recover even from a beheading, but that didn't help. It also didn't apply to him. A wound like Ichabod's would kill him for sure.

"It certainly does hurt," replied Ichabod with a grimace. "But just look at my favorite waistcoat!"

Arthur looked along his own arms and legs. They were fine. He gingerly felt his stomach and head. They seemed fine too. Only his finger had been touched.

The Denizens around the wheel had not been so lucky. Arthur could hardly bear to look at them, they were so pierced by splinters. At least the blue blood didn't look so serious as real human blood would. And they were still standing, and complaining about their bad luck.

"Seriously wounded to the Captain's quarters!" instructed Doctor Scamandros. He didn't appear to be injured, but blue fluid dripped from the sleeve of his yellow greatcoat. "You too, mortal! You could be killed up here! Get below at once. Ichabod, take charge of our valuable passenger!"

Arthur struggled to his feet and hesitantly walked to the gangway, Ichabod at his side.

"Are you going to do something, Doctor?" asked Captain Catapillow plaintively, as he stared down at the spot where his foot and one of his third-best boots used to be. "I think that cannonball was coated in Nothing."

"You'd feel a lot worse if it was, Captain," said Doctor Scamandros. "As I was saying, it is *theoretically* possible to accelerate the transfer by bringing the portal to the traveler, rather than the other way around. It is of course exceedingly difficult and dangerous."

Everyone looked at the pirate vessel astern. It fired again, a great gout of water exploding out of the sea a little ahead and to the port side of the *Moth*.

"What could happen that would be worse than eternal slavery or a slow and torturous death by Nothing-based sorceries at the hands of Feverfew?" asked Concort. He didn't sound like he really wanted to know.

"If I fail, we shall transfer not into that Secondary Realm, but into the Void of Nothing, and be immediately expunged from existence."

"My collection too?" asked Captain Catapillow.

"The ship and everything on it or connected with it,"

said Scamandros. "Including all your stamps, sir. So what are your orders?"

Arthur hesitated on the steps, waiting to hear Catapillow's commands. Surely there was some other way? Perhaps he could escape via the Infinite Stair . . . no . . . not in his current state. He probably didn't have the power anymore. . . .

"I can't have the collection fall into Feverfew's hands," said Captain Catapillow in a small voice. "All or . . . or Nothing!"

Arthur saw Scamandros open his yellow greatcoat. The inside was lined with dozens of pockets and loops for magical implements and apparatus. Scamandros selected two lengths of bronze rod with curved-back hooks set near their pointed ends. Though they were in miniature under his coat, only a few inches long, they expanded as he dragged them out, till they were at least a yard in length.

"Fire irons," said Ichabod. "Matching set. Very nice. Come along!"

Arthur started to follow Ichabod down the port-side ladder to the waist, where Sunscorch and the crew had finally succeeded in cutting away the last of the broken yard and its accompanying debris. But Arthur stopped on the companionway to look back. He saw Scamandros reaching out with a fire iron in each hand, the bronze rods continuing to extend till they became shafts of curdled sunlight that reached up into the sky, and to each side of the ship.

Only a few seconds later, the transformed fire irons reached all the way to the vast gilt-framed portal to the Secondary Realm. The hooks on the end were now easily thirty feet long. The irons wavered outside the edges of the frame, then Scamandros brought them in and seated them. As sun bronze met magical gilt, there was a horrendous metallic noise, like an angle grinder suddenly cutting into steel, magnified a hundred times.

Everyone on the ship stared up at the portal and the Doctor's two levers. Ichabod didn't protest or try to make Arthur go below. Like everyone else, he wanted to see what would happen next.

Scamandros shouted something, a word that passed through Arthur like a hot wire, causing him to cry out and clap his hands to his ears. The doctor shouted again, and Arthur, suddenly stripped of strength, fell down the ladder onto the deck, taking a surprised Ichabod with him.

Then Scamandros yanked the fire irons back towards himself. This action was magnified all along their sun-curdled length. With the squeal of ten thousand fingers on a giant blackboard, the entire vast doorway to Forlorn Island shuddered towards the *Moth*.

At first, it looked like all was going well. The portal rapidly grew closer, and the *Moth* continued to sail straight at it.

Then, when it was only yards away, the portal began to totter and shake, and the top edge started to lean forward. Behind it, in place of the normal sky, was a dark mass that glittered like some volcanic stone.

The Void of Nothing.

"Faster!" shouted Scamandros, fear in his voice. "Make the ship go *faster*!"

Denizens who had been frozen in awe sprang into action, goaded again by the now unbelievably loud voice of Sunscorch. Yards were trimmed, ropes hauled, sails hoisted where sails were hardly ever seen.

"Faster!" screamed Scamandros. The portal was falling towards them now, and instead of dragging it with the fire irons, the Doctor was trying to hold it up. Darkness rippled behind it. "We must get through before it drops!"

The portal fell farther, and the bowsprit of the *Moth* pierced its shining jigsaw-crazed surface. Then the bow passed through, and the rest of the ship followed. The light changed to a softer, golden tone, and the breeze around Arthur became instantly warm.

As the sternpost of the *Moth* passed the portal,

Scamandros fell to the deck, his fire irons clattering at his side, no longer anything more than lengths of bronze. The portal, its work done, collapsed in on itself. The threat of Nothing was gone.

But there were other troubles for the *Moth*.

"Splashdown! Brace!" roared Sunscorch. "Take hold!"

Arthur instantly shuffled back and wound his arms through the port-side ladder. He knew from the volume of Sunscorch's order that this was serious.

The *Moth* had come through the portal all right, but because of the angle of entry, they had not come through at the same level. The ship had entered this new world thirty feet above the water.

Now it was crashing down into the sea.

Before the echo of Sunscorch's shout had gone, the ship tilted precipitously forward. Arthur saw Ichabod slide past, till the Denizen managed to grab hold of a grating. Other Denizens tumbled along farther down the deck and some fell or jumped from the rigging, though as far as Arthur could tell they went into the violet sea.

Then the ship struck. Arthur's legs went up in the air but he managed to keep hold of the ladder. His good foot kicked desperately for a hold as he tried to avoid sliding down the deck to the bow, which went completely under-water. For a dreadful second it looked to Arthur like the whole ship was going to nosedive straight into the deeps. But though the forward twenty feet or so were completely covered in foaming water, the *Moth* somehow came back up with a violent rolling action that spilled more Denizens into the sea.

Arthur was covered in spray, but he kept his grip. Gradually, the *Moth*'s roll slowed. Ichabod got up, dusted himself off with a *tsk*-ing noise, and walked back to Arthur. The splinter that had been in his stomach was gone, but the waistcoat was still sodden with blue blood.

"Come down below," said Ichabod. "I've stopped bleeding but I have to help the Doctor if there's anyone really seriously wounded."

"Is it safe to stand up?" asked Arthur. He didn't want to even guess what *really seriously wounded* might mean.

Ichabod looked around.

"I trust that is the case," he replied. "We have made it clear through the Transfer Portal. The sea here is quite placid, at least at present."

Arthur climbed wearily to his feet, grimacing as pain shot through his leg. When that subsided a little, he looked around. Sunscorch was giving orders, but not very loudly. Denizens were climbing back up the rigging and the ones that hadn't fallen off were already inching their way out across the yards, getting ready to furl the sails.

It all looked surprisingly calm, until a Denizen stuck his head out of a forward hatch and shouted, "Mister Sunscorch! She's cracked a dozen strakes or more! There's four foot of water in the well!"

Arthur looked at Ichabod.

"I believe that means we are sinking," Ichabod said calmly. "Doubtless we shall hear more in a moment. Allow me to remove some flecks of wood from your coat."

Without waiting for permission, Ichabod started to remove tiny pieces of wood from Arthur's shoulders, reminding the boy how easily they could have been larger splinters that would have killed him.

He had to get out of the way as Sunscorch ran back to the quarterdeck, jumping halfway up the steps. There was a confused milling about going on around the wheel. As far as Arthur could tell, Doctor Scamandros was barely conscious, but he had all the maps. They needed the maps to work out what to do before the ship sank, which was going to happen within the next thirty minutes at the rate they were taking in water through the cracked hull.

Though Captain Catapillow and First Mate Concort were both there, once again it was Sunscorch who really took charge.

"I'm guessing you'll want us to beach her dead ahead on Counter-Crab Beach, Captain?" Sunscorch asked, quite calmly. He pointed at Forlorn Island, which was only a mile or so away. "I've been here before, more than once. Good deep sand, quite steep. Once we're aground we can warp her about and career her."

"Um, yes, very good, carry on, Mister Sunscorch," said Catapillow. "I'm just going to . . . ah . . . see to the situation belowdecks. Counter-Crab Beach, eh? Excellent. Excellent. Mister Concort, I believe we may leave the ship to Mister Sunscorch."

"Pardon?" asked Concort. The back of his coat was peppered with many holes, some of them stained with his own blue blood. "Aye, aye, sir."

They both left the quarterdeck, trooping down past Arthur and Ichabod. Neither looked at the boy and they seemed in a hurry to get back to the Captain's cabin. Catapillow was muttering something about humidity, gum Arabic, and perforated edges.

"Exciting times," said Ichabod. "We don't normally have these sorts of goings-on going on. Not for a hundred years or more, we haven't. Come on."

"Can't we stay on deck?" asked Arthur as they walked away. He was still feeling very shaky after the shock of the cannon blast and, as he had expected, was already having a little trouble breathing now they had left the House. He also had little inclination to see the "really seriously wounded" and had a strong inclination to stay out in the open air. If he went below he thought he might throw up from reaction to shock. He needed fresh air and distraction.

"I suppose we might," said Ichabod. "The Captain and Mister Concort will be checking over the collection. They won't notice anything else. And Doctor Scamandros will call if he needs me. We shall ask permission to join Mister Sunscorch on the quarterdeck."

Ichabod called up, and after a moment Sunscorch nodded and waved them both up. The original two helmsmen had gone below to have their wounds treated, accompanied by Doctor Scamandros. They had been replaced by two of the Denizens who had brought Arthur in from the buoy.

"A fine bit of sailing and no mistake," said Sunscorch as Arthur rejoined him. The Denizen seemed very cheerful. "There's not many as can say they showed the *Shiver* a clean pair of heels."

"But aren't we sinking?" asked Arthur.

"We're taking water, that's certain," said Sunscorch. "But we'll be on the beach afore she drowns. And just as well, for there's at least a week's worth of repairs to be done."

"A week!" Arthur protested. He coughed as he spoke, sudden anxiety making his chest tight. A week out in this Secondary Realm might mean a week lost in his own world. He still didn't understand how time worked between the House and the Secondary Realms, but it couldn't be good to be out here for so long. What if he lost a week at home? His parents would freak out. So would Leaf's. Plus, he didn't have any asthma medication, so he might not even survive a week. What if his broken leg got worse?

"I can't spend a week on some deserted island!"

"You'll have to, 'less you're a better swimmer than you look," replied Sunscorch. "There's precious little on this world. Lots of islands, some things you might call fish and fowl, and a bit of useful timber, that's all. A safe haven from both Feverfew's pirates and any nosy parkers from the House."

"Nosy parkers?"

"Officials. Inspectors. Quaestors. Auditors. You know."

"Officials? Why would we be hiding from them?" asked Arthur. Not that he wanted to meet any himself. Too many of them served the Trustees who were his enemies.

"We're in the Secondary Realms without a license," explained Ichabod. "It's the Original Law, and there's fierce penalties to be here without permission. Not that there's much chance of trouble, not since Lady

Wednesday's mind went adrift and she ate up half her officials and drowned —"

"Avast that!" interrupted Sunscorch. "We are still in Her Ladyship's service!"

"True! True! Mister Sunscorch, I beg your pardon."

"In any case, we have good reason to be here, which might prove sufficient excuse," said Sunscorch, after a moment. Though he spoke to Arthur, his gaze continued to roam over the masts and rigging, the ship and the crew. "As soon as we're able, we'll be back to the Border Sea and our business of salvage. Now we must shorten sail. We're riding deep and the sand is soft, but we've still too much way on."

Immediately Sunscorch raised his volume enormously, bellowing out some incomprehensible orders involving clewgarnets, buntlines, leechlines, and slablines. These were all met with sudden activity by the crew.

"Now, all we need to do is get her safely lodged before teatime," said Sunscorch cheerfully, without looking away from the rapidly closing beach. "Try as I might, I can never get them to give up their afternoon tea. Once made clerks, always clerks, no matter how much salt they taste."

The ship slowed as sails were furled, and even Arthur could tell she was lower in the water and more sluggish to answer the helm. But they were only a few hundred yards from the beach, a wide crescent of sparkling sand that looked much like an earthly beach, save that the sand was a very light blue.

"We'll make it," said Sunscorch. But as he spoke, a bell rang from somewhere deep inside the ship. The peal quickly repeated several times. In answer to it, the crew left their posts, abandoned lines, and slid down from the rigging. The Denizens who'd fallen overboard stopped treading water and started to swim for the ship, showing near-Olympic speeds without Olympic-standard grace or style. Even the helmsmen made as if to join the throng milling about a grating on the main deck of the ship, till they were physically restrained by Sunscorch.

"Oh, no you don't," he cried. "How many times do I have to tell you? If you're at the wheel you can't both go to afternoon tea. You have to take it in turns."

Arthur stared down at the main deck. The Denizens were accepting cups of tea in fine bone china cups that appeared out of the grating, even though there was no one below handing them up. Small biscuits also materialized in the air and were delicately taken and eaten in modest bites. The sight of both made Arthur aware that he was extraordinarily thirsty and hungry, despite the drink of water

Sunscorch had given him in the boat. He knew he didn't need food or water, but he felt as if he did.

"How . . . where are the cups coming from?"

"It's one of the things that didn't change when we remade the counting house," said Ichabod. "Some department in the Lower House is still supplying us with afternoon tea, wherever we are in the House or the Secondary Realms. I would venture to suppose that an order was given long ago, and it has never been rescinded. It's quite convenient, of course, and we are the envy of many other ships."

"It's a cursed nuisance," said Sunscorch. He cupped his hands around his mouth and shouted, "All hands come aft! Hold yer cups and saucers!"

The crew was slow to respond, and Sunscorch shouted again. The beach was only fifty or sixty yards distant.

"They're best aft. We might lose a mast when we strike," Sunscorch explained to Arthur. "But it'll go for'ard, like as not."

Arthur looked up at the two very tall masts and their mass of spars and rigging. They had to weigh tons, and if one or both of them came down backwards instead of forward, they'd crush everyone.

"Take a hold!" roared Sunscorch.

Chapter Eight

Arthur hardly felt the *Moth*'s initial impact with the beach. The deck shuddered a little under him, but he was sitting down with his bad leg straight out and he had a very firm grip on an iron cleat next to the rail.

More serious shudders followed, as the ship ground its way up and through the deep sand. Arthur watched the masts carefully, and though they shivered and the rigging rattled and a few ropes and blocks fell down, nothing worse occurred.

After a few more yards' progress, the *Moth* gave a final creaking groan and slid forward no more. It sat upright for a few moments, then slowly heeled over till the deck was at an angle of twenty degrees. Arthur wondered if it was going to go over completely on its side, but the deep sand around the hull held it in place.

Amazingly, not one of the crew appeared to have dropped his or her teacup. While Arthur gingerly crawled to the side and looked over at the blue sand, Ichabod went and got a cup of tea to offer to Arthur.

Arthur drank it gratefully, though it was very strong,

very sweet, and very milky. When the cup was empty, he handed it back to Ichabod, who asked, "More?"

"Yes, please," said Arthur. He was quite surprised when Ichabod simply handed the cup straight back, but the cup was full again. Strangely, this time the tea was black and, while still sweet, had been made so by something like treacle. Arthur drank it anyway.

"Just say 'more' if you want more," Ichabod explained. He handed Arthur a biscuit and added, "Similarly, as long as you have a crumb left of biscuit, just say 'more' and you'll get another one. Till afternoon tea is over, which is in about five minutes by my reckoning."

Arthur nodded and concentrated on the business of drinking and eating, with occasional, mouth-full mumblings of "more."

Precisely five minutes later by Arthur's backwards watch, his cup and half-eaten biscuit disappeared. This disappearance was followed by a stream of bellowed orders from Sunscorch, who had clearly bottled them up till afternoon tea was over. As far as Arthur could gather, the orders related to propping the ship up so it didn't fall over, getting out some anchors, and carrying lots of different things ashore.

Without imminent danger threatening, and with a full, warm stomach, Arthur found himself yawning. His watch said it was ten past ten, but he knew he must have spent more than seven hours (counting backwards) just sitting in that buoy, let alone the time on the bed in the storm.

Remembering the buoy made Arthur look at his hands. The red color still hadn't come off. It hadn't gotten any lighter either. It looked deeply engrained, almost as if it was in the skin, rather than just on it.

"The Red Hand," said Ichabod. "Doctor Scamandros might be able to clear it. Feverfew marks all his treasure caches such. The stain is supposed to last forever. Well, until Feverfew tracks the thief down and exacts his terrible punishment. What were you doing on the buoy anyway?"

"I . . . I was shipwrecked," said Arthur.

"From the *Steelibed*," interrupted Sunscorch as he slid down the deck. "Or so you say. The Captain, Mister Concort, and I will want to hear Arth's tale, Ichabod, so hold your questions till dinner. Which will be served ashore, so you can begin by getting the Captain's table on the beach. Arth, you go ashore too, and stay out of the way."

"Aye, aye," said Ichabod, without great enthusiasm.

"And look lively, you loblolly boy."

Being called a *loblolly boy* made Ichabod both cross and active. Bent over almost double to keep his balance on the tilted deck, he crawled over to the companionway and hustled below. Arthur was left alone.

He wanted to ask Sunscorch some questions, about almost everything, but particularly about the green-sailed ship that had taken up Leaf. But the Second Mate was too busy, shouting orders and stamping about the quarterdeck.

After a few minutes watching the crew, the boy climbed down from the quarterdeck and made his way through the working crowd of Denizens, equipment, and cargo that was being rigged or moved above or through the hatches in the waist of the ship. Eventually he found his way to the forecastle at the front of the vessel. There were several broad rope ladders over each side. Arthur waited for a space in the line of Denizens climbing down with their loads, then carefully lowered himself over the side and climbed down.

It was quite difficult with his leg immobilized by the cast, but he made it. There was still water around the ship, so he splashed into it, and was relieved to find it was very shallow. The blue sand seemed much the same as sand back home. Difficult to walk in, even without a leg in a cast. Arthur found himself imitating one of the Denizens with a wooden leg, not so much walking as stumping his way up the beach.

One of the things the Denizens had brought ashore already was the chest from Feverfew's trove. Arthur walked over to it. It looked ordinary enough, just a big wooden box with bronze reinforcement at each corner and bands of bronze across the lid. He wondered what was inside. What would Feverfew the Pirate value so much?

Arthur sat down and leaned back against the chest. He felt very tired, but he didn't want to go to sleep. He had to work out what to do next. Not that there seemed to be many choices. He felt that he should do something to make sure Leaf was okay, but he couldn't think of anything. And he should try to contact Dame Primus or Suzy. And he should try and get home as soon as possible, but Leaf was right, he ought to sort out Lady Wednesday first and that meant finding the Third Part of the Will, claiming the Third Key. . . .

Arthur's thoughts trailed off into a confused mishmash of different problems and unlikely solutions. His body was too tired, and it had finally gotten its message through to his brain.

The boy slid farther into the sand and his head slumped down. As the Denizens toiled to lighten the ship by removing cargo and prop her up with spare yards and topmasts, Arthur slept.

He awoke at sundown. At first, he was totally

disoriented. Not only was he lying on a blue beach, but there was an enormous vermilion sun sinking into the sea on the horizon. Its weird light mixed with the violet hues of the sea and the blue of the sand sent alarming messages to his brain.

The reason he'd woken was instantly obvious. Doctor Scamandros was sitting next to him, peering at his leg through what looked like a very short telescope. He also had a small bellows with him, a leather-lunged apparatus that looked to Arthur like the original ancestor of an air-bed pump.

"What are you doing?" Arthur asked suspiciously. He sat up and glared at Scamandros. The doctor looked quite different, though it took Arthur a second to work out why. His animated tattoos were gone, and he was wearing a woolly cap with a long tassel that hung down next to his neck.

"Your leg has been recently broken," said Doctor Scamandros. "And set."

"I know," Arthur replied. His leg was hurting again. He wondered if Scamandros had been prodding it. "That's why it's in a cast. Or was . . ."

He added the last bit because the ultra-high-tech cast had almost completely fallen apart. There were only thin strips of it remaining, and Arthur could see his pale and puffy skin in the gaps between.

"Usually, I could fix that leg for you," said Doctor Scamandros. "But my examination reveals a very high and unusual level of magical contamination that would resist any direct action to repair the bone. I could, however, equip you with a better brace and exert some small magic that would lessen the pain."

"That would be good," said Arthur hesitantly. "But what do you want in return?"

"Merely your goodwill," said Scamandros with a half-hearted chuckle. He tapped the bellows at his side and added, "Though I understand from Ichabod that you might have a cold? If so, I should like to harvest any sneeze, nose-tickle, or phlegmatic effusion that you feel coming on."

Arthur wrinkled his nose experimentally.

"No, I haven't got a cold. I just thought I might."

Scamandros was looking through his short telescope again, this time at Arthur's chest.

"There is also a disturbance in the interior arrangement of your lungs," he said. "Most interesting. Again, there is magical contamination of a high order, but I think I could probably lessen the underlying condition. Would you like me to proceed?"

"Uh, I'm not sure," said Arthur. He took a breath. He couldn't completely fill his lungs, but it wasn't too bad. "I think I'll wait. It'll be all right when I get back in the House."

"Just the leg brace, then," said Doctor Scamandros. "And amelioration of the pain."

He slid his stubby telescope into one pocket of his greatcoat and, reaching inside, took out a flat tin labeled with the picture of a bright red crab. It had a key stuck to it, which Scamandros now broke off, connected to a tab, and used to wind back the metal lid. There was a whole small crab inside, but the Denizen only broke off one of its legs. He put the leg on the sand and passed his open palm across the tin, which disappeared.

Arthur watched with both curiosity and anxiety as Scamandros picked up the tiny crab leg and held it high in his left hand. A thick carpenter's pencil appeared in his right hand, and he used this to lightly sketch several lines and asterisks on Arthur's leg. Then he clapped his hands, still holding both pencil and crab leg.

The two objects disappeared and at the same time, the remnants of Arthur's modern cast were instantly replaced by an armored section of red-and-white-speckled crab exoskeleton, jointed at the knee and ankle.

"As for the pain," Scamandros said, scribbling on a piece of paper with a pen that trailed glowing crimson ink, "take this prescription."

Arthur took the page of heavy, deckle-edged paper. It was very hard to read, but he made it out eventually:

Apply pain-lessening paper to painful area once
Dr. J. R. L. Scamandros, D.H.S. (Upper House, Failed)

"What does D.H.S. stand for? And . . . excuse me . . . why do you put 'failed' on it?" Arthur asked as he touched the paper to his leg, directly above the break, where it hurt most. The paper crumbled as he spoke, paper-dust forming a miniature tornado that appeared to go straight through his new cast and into his leg. A moment later, the dull pain there started to ebb.

"It stands for Doctor of House Sorcery," said Scamandros. "A very high degree, which I so very nearly possess. Honesty necessitates me to reveal my failure, but it was only in my final year. Seven hundred and ninety-eight years of successful examinations, only to fall at the end. Politics, you understand! But I do not wish to speak of that.

"Let us talk of you instead, Arth. You hold a magical book of great potency in your pocket, too potent for me to even touch without your leave. Your very flesh and bones reek of past magics. You are found on a buoy of the infamous pirate Feverfew, in the Border Sea of the House. Yet you are a mortal, or mostly so. Tell me, on what world in the Secondary Realms do you make your home?"

Arthur almost answered "Earth," but restrained

himself just in time. Scamandros had certainly helped him, but there was something about the look in his piercing brown eyes that made Arthur think the fewer secrets he knew the better.

"Passenger Arth! The Captain's compliments, and you are to join him for a beachside supper!"

Ichabod's call was very welcome. Arthur struggled to his feet, pleasantly surprised to find that his leg was well supported by the crab armor. Scamandros helped him find his balance.

"We shall speak more, and soon, Arth," the Doctor said. Arthur noticed that his tattoos were starting to crawl across his face again, emerging from the skin like a blush. The Denizen leaned in close as Arthur started to step away, and added, "Or should I say Arthur, Master of the Lower House and Lord of the Far Reaches?"

Chapter Nine

Arthur felt as if Doctor Scamandros was watching his back the whole time it took to stomp across the beach to an open-sided tent, where he could see Captain Catapillow, Concort, and Sunscorch sitting at a long, white cloth–covered table. Lanterns hung at the tent's corners, their soft yellow glow in stark contrast to the strange scarlet twilight.

As he walked across the beach, Arthur was thinking furiously. Was Scamandros threatening to reveal his real identity? It hadn't sounded like a threat, but he couldn't be sure. What did the sorcerer want? Who did he serve? He was trained in the Upper House . . . or so he said. He could easily be a servant of one of the Morrow Days, who would do anything to stop Arthur from liberating anymore of the Will.

"Mind the barrels," said Ichabod, leading Arthur between two pyramids of different-sized barrels. There was a huge amount of stuff on the beach, all of it very carefully stacked and ordered. Barrels and boxes and crates and bags. And there in the tent, in front of the table, was

Feverfew's chest. Arthur wondered how they'd taken it away without waking him up. Perhaps he'd already slid forward into the sand by that point.

"Bring the passenger forward, Ichabod," ordered Captain Catapillow. He had a writing book open in front of him, and a pen and inkwell, as did Concort. Sunscorch had a huge, thick, leather-bound tome the size of several bricks.

It looked more like a court bench than a dinner table. And "passenger" had sounded awfully like "prisoner."

"Stand in front of the Captain and bow," whispered Ichabod, nudging Arthur forward. The boy complied, inclining his head not just to the Captain, but also to Concort and Sunscorch. Catapillow and Concort gave the slightest nods back, and Sunscorch winked, which Arthur found encouraging.

"Now, due to, ah, the irregular nature of the last day, we have not been able to, er, keep up-to-date the log of our good ship *Moth*," said Catapillow, leaning forward to fix Arthur with his unsteady stare. "Wishing to be, ah, beforehand with such records and intending to inscribe you as a passenger has reminded me that we do not, ah, know who you are, where you are going, or what fare you should be charged. There is also the matter of this treasure."

He leaned back when he'd finished talking and folded his hands together.

"You want to know who I am?" asked Arthur. He wasn't sure whether Catapillow's speech actually needed to be answered.

"Indeed," said Concort. "That is of the essence. Who are you? Where are you from? Where are you going? How did you come to be on Feverfew's buoy? Why did you remove the telltale red pitch from the marker so that we didn't know whose treasure it was below? Do you claim the treasure yourself?"

"Well . . ." said Arthur slowly, stalling as he tried to think of some answers that wouldn't get him into trouble. Clearly, Scamandros already knew or strongly guessed who he was. Would it be any worse if the others knew as well? He needed help — to find Leaf, for a start.

It would be a big gamble. Sunscorch would support him, he thought, because he had the Mariner's disc. Ichabod seemed to like him. Catapillow and Concort were kind of stupid, even if they were technically in charge, so perhaps they didn't matter too much. Doctor Scamandros . . . Arthur really wasn't sure about that Denizen, but after he'd recovered from having his fingers burned by the Atlas he'd been nice enough. The crab armor on Arthur's leg worked really well. . . .

"Speak up!" ordered Concort. His voice suddenly squeaked, which removed all authority from it.

"My real name is Arthur Penhaligon," Arthur said slowly. "I am a mortal from Earth. But I am also Master of the Lower House and of the Far Reaches, though I have given up my Keys in trust to Dame Primus, who was once Parts One and Two of the Will of the Architect."

Catapillow's mouth curled up at one end as Arthur spoke. Then he broke out in uproarious laughter, followed a second later by Concort. Sunscorch neither smiled nor laughed, but looked down at the huge book in front of him.

"Very good, very good," Catapillow chortled. "Master of the Lower House and the Far Reaches! Arthur Penhaligon! Most amusing!"

"But I am Arthur Penhaligon!"

"Yes, yes, you've had your joke," said Catapillow. "Now you must answer our questions."

"Most specifically, do you intend to claim this treasure?" added Concort.

"No, I really *am* Arthur Penhaligon! Why don't you believe me?"

"Don't be silly," replied Catapillow. "Everyone knows Lord Arthur is a mighty fighter! Why, he defeated Mister Monday in personal combat and wrestled Grim Tuesday to the ground and broke both his hands. Besides, I've seen a picture of Lord Arthur. Huge, broad-shouldered chap, carries a bag full of magical apparatus he invented himself."

"Not to mention he always travels with his giant half-bear, half-frog assistant," said Concort. "And an assassin girl who used to be the Piper's bodyguard."

"What?" asked Arthur. "You mean the Will and Suzy Blue?"

"It's all here, you know," said Concort, pulling out a tiny book from his sleeve. It expanded into a large hard-cover, bound in red, with the title embossed in enormous gilt letters on both the spine and front cover, *The Epic Adventures of Lord Arthur, Hero of the House.*

"Look, the frontispiece is a portrait of Lord Arthur."

Concort held the book open to show a color plate that had been stuck in next to the title page. It showed a very tall, handsome man who looked and dressed rather like Monday's Noon. He was posing next to an open carpetbag that was glowing with rainbow-colored light. A bizarre, hunched-over monster that had the legs of a frog and the upper body and front paws of a bear crouched next to him, and in the background an Amazon woman in silver armor was cutting the head off a misshapen semihuman creature that was clearly supposed to be a Nithling.

"So, who are you?" asked Concort again, snapping the book shut. "And let's be clear this time, what about the treasure?"

"What about the treasure?" asked Arthur as he tried

to gather his thoughts. It hadn't even occurred to him that they might doubt his identity. But it was clear that both Concort and Catapillow's main concern was the treasure. "I don't even know what the treasure is. Do I have a claim to it?"

Catapillow and Concort looked at Sunscorch.

"It looks as if that's so," said the Second Mate, tapping the book in front of him. "Doctor Scamandros had a reading of the laws for me, and it looks to be that young Arth here is entitled to ninety percent of the value of this treasure."

"Ninety percent!" exclaimed Catapillow and Concort. Catapillow added, "Doctor Scamandros! How can this be so?"

Arthur hadn't seen the Doctor, but the Denizen stepped into the light from beside the table, so he must have followed Arthur and then stood in the shadows.

"According to *The Blue Book of Admiralty*, a fixed buoy treasure marker is itself considered a vessel. This young mortal here was in command of the vessel by virtue of being on it. Mister Sunscorch took him off at his request, but Arth did not relinquish command of the buoy, which marked the treasure, and which was not taken in tow. By taking the chest and not the buoy as well, the vessel is still considered to be afloat and the treasure it marked notionally still of it, though no longer marked by it. The matter is further complicated as the treasure was the property of a pirate outlawed by direct writ of Lady Wednesday. So it is considered immediately forfeit and property of the House authorities, with a reward equal to an amount of ninety percent of the value of the treasure being paid to the finder. We are not the finder, Arth is, as demonstrated by the unfortunate fact that he is marked with the Red Hand. We are in the position of having salvaged the finder, and must come to some arrangement with him. But should Arth wish to be returned to that buoy with the chest, we must do so."

"I'm not sure I followed that," said Arthur. "You're saying the treasure has to be given to Wednesday because it belongs to a pirate? And I'm entitled to a reward equal to ninety percent of its value because I found it first?"

"Yes," said Scamandros. "However, we do not have to help you. We can simply return you and the chest to the treasure marker. There is also the matter of the original owner of the treasure. So there is room to negotiate, I think."

"Sure." Arthur tried to smile as he spoke. It sounded crazy to him, but no crazier than some of the court reports on the news back home. Murderers who weren't murderers because of weird technicalities. Companies that didn't have to pay debts because of odd loopholes. "What do you suggest?"

"We should first find out what's in the chest," said Doctor Scamandros. "Do we have your permission to open it?"

"Yes!" exclaimed Arthur. He was surprised they hadn't opened it already. He would have if they'd been asleep all afternoon.

"I have taken the precaution of examining the chest with various magical instruments," Scamandros continued. "And I have neutralized a number of nasty little traps. So it should be quite safe to open. Just flip back those two catches and turn the key."

"There wasn't a key there before," said Arthur.

"Yes, I had to fashion one to fit," said Scamandros. "Go ahead, open it."

"Why do you want me to open it?" asked Arthur. Scamandros knew who he really was, and there was still something slightly shifty about the sorcerer. He wouldn't quite meet Arthur's gaze. "What if there's a trap you missed?"

"I am merely following correct procedure. It is your —"

"Stand back, lad," interrupted Sunscorch, who had left the table. "Best to let a Denizen bear the brunt of any trickery. You mortals are too fragile."

"Thanks," muttered Arthur. He felt a bit bad now, as if he'd been a coward, but Sunscorch seemed to think it was perfectly sensible of him to refuse. He smiled and nodded at the boy as he walked past and knelt before the chest.

Sunscorch lifted the two clasps at the same time. They snapped back with a loud click, immediately followed by a strange popping noise that made Arthur jump, till he realized that it was actually the sound of the entire crew of the *Moth* drawing in breaths of anticipation. They were all gathered around in a half circle up the beach, beyond the lantern light. The last of the vermilion twilight had faded, so the Denizens were just dark outlines, but Arthur could sense their concentration on Sunscorch and the chest.

The Second Mate turned the key. It played musical notes as it turned several times in the lock.

Ting-ting-ting-ting-ting . . .

Each note seemed like it would be the last. Finally the key stopped, and instead of a jangled note, there was a soft *snick* as the lock released. Sunscorch leaned forward and lifted the lid.

"Ahhhh!" came from a hundred throats.

"Is that all?" asked Arthur, looking over Sunscorch's shoulder. The contents of the chest looked very disappointing to him. It was full of little off-white blocks carved with letters. They looked like cheap mah-jongg pieces.

Sunscorch didn't answer. He seemed quite stunned. Looking around, Arthur saw that nearly everybody else was as well. They were all staring with their mouths open.

Except for Doctor Scamandros. He bent down and picked up one of the small blocks and tilted it so the character carved into its surface caught the light.

"A deep, racking cough," pronounced Scamandros. "Fixed in auriphant ivory from Senhein. Good for twenty years or more, as House time flows."

He put it back again and took out another piece.

"A roseola rash around the neck, head, and ears," said Scamandros. "Fixed in wood-fired clay. Good for at least a decade in the House."

Arthur knew that human diseases were valued by the Denizens of the House. They would get the symptoms, but not feel the effects. So these little blocks of ivory and clay were how the diseases were actually used by the Denizens, and would presumably be in demand. But what were they worth?

"This is a great treasure," said Doctor Scamandros. "A very great treasure. There must be twenty thousand coughs, rashes, swellings, and other diseases here, all of the highest virulence and fixed by first-class sorcery. I would guess its value to be in excess of a million simoleons of gold."

His words were met by a vast cheer from the crew, who began to sing and dance around and throw their caps in the air.

"And ninety percent of it is mine?" asked Arthur. He could barely make himself heard above the uproar.

"Notionally," replied Scamandros. "As I said, if you want both yourself and the treasure to remain salvaged, you must come to an agreement with Captain Catapillow."

"Feverfew will never bear this loss," muttered Sunscorch, who was still staring at the open chest. He pointed at a small bronze plaque set on the underside of the chest's lid. As his finger touched it, the letters engraved there burst into red fire, and a booming voice roared across the beach:

"THIEVES! THIEVES! THIEVES! This be the treasure of Captain Elishar Feverfew! The Red Hand marks you! Feverfew's vengeance shall be swift and slow: swift in the taking, slow in the making. Regret and repentance shall prove no —"

Whatever else the voice was going to shout stopped as Doctor Scamandros tapped the plaque with an ebony paper knife that materialized in his hand. Silence fell over the beach, the only sound the lapping of the waves on the shore. The Denizens' songs and cheer were gone, replaced by a mood of dread.

"I'm the only one with the Red Hand," said Arthur. "Aren't I?"

"Yes," said Doctor Scamandros. "Though Feverfew would kill or enslave anyone sailing with you, or giving you aid."

"You're a sorcerer — can't you get rid of it?"

"No. It is beyond my power. Feverfew is an expert in magics I do not wish to know."

Arthur looked down at the treasure, then at his red hands.

"So you're all at risk from Feverfew while I'm around?"

"Indeed. Though, in truth, Feverfew kills or enslaves everyone he encounters anyway. But the Red Hand marks you for a particularly long and unpleasant ending, and we would probably share in it."

"Can you send messages to other parts of the House? And can you find out what's happening to someone if they're in the House? I mean, by sorcery."

"Yes, on both counts."

"In that case," said Arthur, turning back to Captain Catapillow, "I am prepared to offer you, and the crew of the *Moth*, all of my share of the reward in return for some help. I want to get a message to Dame Primus. . . ."

Captain Catapillow nodded his agreement.

"I need to find out what's happened to my friend Leaf, who I think is aboard a ship with glowing green sails. . . ."

Once again Catapillow nodded, this time with a smile.

Arthur paused, thinking about what he might need.

"And I might . . . I might want passage as quickly as possible to wherever I can meet Drowned Wednesday."

"What!" shrieked Catapillow. "Are you totally mad?"

Chapter Ten

"Take you to Drowned Wednesday!" repeated Catapillow. "Do you think us fools?"

"Uh, no," said Arthur. "I only said I *might* want to go and see her. I'm not sure where I should go next. But I have been invited to have lunch with Lady Wednesday —"

"You mean to *be* lunch!" scoffed Concort. He paled and added, "Excuse me! I didn't mean to say that!"

"I'm sure we can work something out with regard to the treasure," said Catapillow. "Doctor Scamandros will help you find your friend, send messages, and so forth. We will even carry you to Port Wednesday. But I'm sure you will be as grateful as we will be to not encounter our most esteemed but sadly submerged ultimate mistress."

"Why?" Arthur asked, wondering why Catapillow and the others seemed unreasonably terrified at the idea. But they were in her service, or at least they operated in her demesne of the House. Presumably she gave them orders or sent them instructions from time to time. But perhaps she was slothful, like Mister Monday, and the administration of the Border Sea was all fouled up like it had been in the Lower House.

"By the way," Arthur continued, "do you have any orders about Lord Arthur? I mean, if you happened to pick him up, what would you do with him?"

"Pick up Lord Arthur? Well, naturally, we should do whatever he wanted us to do," replied Catapillow. "He's lord of two domains within the House!"

"We wouldn't want to cross that half-frog thing," said Concort. "Or the killer girl either."

"So you haven't been instructed by Lady Wednesday or her officers to do anything to Arthur if he does show up?"

Sunscorch snorted. Catapillow and Concort looked at each other. Eventually Concort muttered, "Very busy these days, Drowned Wednesday, what with eating . . . with various things . . . unfortunately Noon and Dusk went missing some years ago, the confusion arising out of the flooding. . . ."

"What Mister Concort means," cut in Doctor Scamandros, "is that the *Moth* has been largely forgotten these six or seven thousand years. I don't believe we have had any instructions in that time. We simply cruise the Border Sea, take our salvage from it, and sell it and replenish our stores at Port Wednesday or, if we are pressed, at less salubrious anchorages both in the Border Sea and out in the Secondary Realms. Now tell me, have you really been invited to luncheon with Lady Wednesday?"

"Yes," said Arthur. He reached into his pocket and drew out the soggy invitation. Doctor Scamandros took it, raised his eyebrows at the almost complete absence of readable type upon it, and set it on the table. He took an oval-shaped felt blotter out of his coat and rolled it across the card several times. With each pass, the card dried and the ink returned to its former density and blackness. Catapillow and Concort craned over the table to look, and even Sunscorch tilted his head to get a proper view.

Arthur watched the two officers' faces change as they read the invitation, going from curiosity through puzzlement to shock. Sunscorch, though he moved his lips to read, did not seem unduly affected.

LADY WEDNESDAY

TRUSTEE OF THE ARCHITECT AND

DUCHESS OF THE BORDER SEA

HAS GREAT PLEASURE IN INVITING

ARTHUR PENHALIGON

TO A PARTICULAR LUNCHEON

OF SEVENTEEN REMOVES

"I don't understand," said Catapillow. "Then you must be —"

"But you can't be," said Concort. "You're just a boy!"

"He is," said Scamandros. "Who else might have *A Compleat Atlas of the House* in his top pocket and the mark of the Mariner's favor on a string around his neck? Not to mention this very curious invitation."

"Why is it curious?" asked Arthur. For the first time since the wave picked him up he had time to ask some questions instead of just trying to stay alive, or recover from the effort of staying alive. "Why is everyone scared of her? Why do you call her Drowned Wednesday? And what was the Deluge and all that?"

Catapillow and Concort still looked stunned. Sunscorch looked at Scamandros.

"Best if the Doctor explains all that to you," said Sunscorch after a moment. "The Captain and Mister Concort have duties to attend to, as do I."

"I trust you'll join us for supper, Lord Arthur?" murmured Captain Catapillow, without meeting Arthur's eye. "Without any, ah, hard feelings as to our regrettable lack of, er —"

"Sure," said Arthur. "I understand. It's just that the

book makes me seem more like a big hero. Who wrote it anyway?"

Concort opened the book again and showed Arthur the title page. Catapillow looked embarrassed and walked off, muttering something to Doctor Scamandros as he went past.

"It is, um, written by someone called Japeth, 'Official Biographer, Chronicler, Annalist, and Recorder of Lord Arthur,'" said the First Mate. "Published by the Dayroom Press of the Lower House."

"I see," said Arthur with a frown. Japeth was his friend, the Thesaurus he'd met in the Pit. He had asked Dame Primus to give him a job, but he hadn't expected it would be writing something that was basically propaganda. He wondered what the point of it was. Why make him out to be such a big hero?

"If you would care to walk with me, I shall attempt to answer your questions about Lady Wednesday and the Deluge," said Doctor Scamandros. He lifted his hand and a candle appeared there, lighting up as he blew softly on the wick. "We shall wade in the shallows, so that the sea shall cloak our conversation. There are some matters it is best not to excite the crew with."

Arthur hesitated. While he thought about whether it would be smart to go off with the Doctor alone, he looked at Sunscorch and tapped the Mariner's medallion. The Second Mate gave a slight nod.

"All right," said Arthur. "Lead on."

He followed the Denizen out of the bright pool of lantern-light, down the beach, and past a line of very neatly organized piles of spare clothing. Each pile was individually labeled.

Scamandros saw him looking at the tidy arrangement and guessed what he was thinking.

"The crew was originally the staff of a counting house," he said. "A warehouse where goods were sorted and valued. They were made for that purpose and, being Denizens of a low order, they change and learn very slowly. Hence they are not very good sailors, but excel at the movement and ordering of cargo. Here we are. I shall just take off my shoes and roll up my breeches."

Doctor Scamandros thrust the candle in the sand and sat to remove his shoes. Arthur sat down too, and took off his Immaterial Boots.

"We must be careful," Scamandros said as he took up the candle again and waded into the froth. "The beach shelves very steeply. We shall stay near the tidemark."

They started walking along, Doctor Scamandros on the lower slope, nearer the sea, so he was almost the same height as Arthur. He was very short for a Denizen, Arthur thought. Shorter even than the miserable Coal-Collaters in the deep cellars of the Lower House.

"Where shall we begin?" asked Scamandros.

"What's the story with Wednesday?" asked Arthur. "Why is everyone afraid of even going near her?"

"I can answer more easily than most, because I am a volunteer on the *Moth* and not in fact in her service," said Scamandros. "I also have made something of a study of both the Border Sea and its ruler. I am sure you are familiar with the Will of the Architect, the breaking of it by the Trustees, and so forth?"

"Yes," said Arthur. "You could say that."

"Around that time, Lady Wednesday began to be afflicted by an enormous hunger, something no Denizen usually has to any degree. We merely eat for amusement. She ate and ate and ate, and would normally have grown larger and larger. However, by using the power of the Third Key, she was able to keep this growth in abeyance. This continued for some two thousand years, even though by that time she was eating tons and tons of food every day.

"I am not sure exactly what happened then. Either the power of the Key failed, or she misdirected it. In any case, she was transformed into a shape and size appropriate to the amount of food she was eating. She became a Leviathan."

"A what?"

"A Behemoth."

"Um, I don't —"

"A monstrous white whale. A stupendous whale! One-hundred twenty-six miles from tail to head, and thirty-two miles in width, with a mouth when open that is two miles high and ten miles wide."

Arthur stopped walking to think about this. A whale 126 miles long! Doctor Scamandros kept walking and talking so he had to scurry to catch up and missed a few words.

". . . transformation and immersion in the Border Sea displaced a vast quantity of water. Fortunately the transformation took place over a week or more, allowing time to prepare the docks and foreshore buildings, most of which were turned into ships like the *Moth*. A new port was partly prepared on the ridge of Wednesday's Lookout, now Port Wednesday.

"But the greatest destruction to actual Denizens was not wrought by the Deluge, but by Lady Wednesday herself. In the shape of a Leviathan she was hungrier than ever, and in her early years, she ate not only the usual plankton, krill, and other small creatures by the ton, but also many of her own servants, including her Noon and Dusk. No one has dared approach her for millennia, save her surviving Dawn, who it is believed she communicates with by moving the pupils of her massive eye in some code, so Dawn need not get too close.

"That is why it is strange that you should be invited to lunch with her. How can you have lunch with a Leviathan? Particularly one that eats everything that comes anywhere near her?"

"Why is she called Drowned Wednesday?" asked Arthur. "I mean, she's obviously not drowned."

"I believe that when she first began to transform she flung herself into the Border Sea and was presumed drowned," said Scamandros. "A nasty fate for a Denizen, since some consciousness would remain until the fishes completely nibbled you away. I also suspect that the term 'Whale Wednesday' is shied away from by her still-loyal Denizens."

Arthur nodded and hopped forward to completely catch up. They were quite a long way along the beach now, the lights of the camp a hundred yards or more behind. Arthur glanced at Doctor Scamandros's face. Most of it lay in shadow, only the lower part of his visage illuminated by the candle. His tattoos were moving and shifting, but it was too dark for Arthur to make out what they were showing, save for one of a ship that was cruising across the Denizen's cheek with all sails set.

"Perhaps we should turn around," said Arthur nervously.

Scamandros halted and looked at Arthur.

"We have come far enough to try a little sorcery that may find an answer to your questions," he said, walking up the beach to set his candle down. Arthur followed, the blue sand sticking to his wet feet.

"What was it you wanted first?" asked Doctor Scamandros. "A message to Dame Primus or news of your friend?"

"I want to see what's happened to Leaf," said Arthur. Even though she hadn't listened when he'd told her to get out of the hospital room, he still felt responsible . . . and guilty. He hoped she was all right.

"Your friend was picked up by another ship?"

"Yes," said Arthur. "A bit like the *Moth*, but thinner and longer, with three masts. It had sails that glowed green. I think it was meant to pick me up, like it said in the invitation. 'Transport has been arranged.' Only they got Leaf instead."

"The ship sounds like the *Flying Mantis*. One of the ships of Wednesday's original merchant marine. Which would make sense. Now, do you have anything that belongs to your friend? A lock of hair, perhaps?"

"No!" said Arthur. "I mean, she's just a friend. Like a fairly new friend too."

"Mmm, that makes it more difficult, even though knowing the ship will narrow things down," mused Scamandros. "Did you shake hands with her? Or have anything she may have touched, like a cup or bottle?"

Arthur shook his head. He tried to think back to the hospital room. Leaf had sat on the bed. . . .

"She did read Wednesday's invitation. Will that do?"

"That will do," said Doctor Scamandros with satisfaction. "May I have the invitation, please?"

Arthur handed it over. Scamandros took out a tortoise-shell-inlaid penknife and cut a small, curling sliver off the surface of the card, which he deposited in a tiny tin pillbox. Reaching once more into his greatcoat, he removed a cardboard chessboard — or something divided into colored squares like a chessboard — which he unfolded. On this board he laid down with some exactitude a small round shaving mirror and a conch shell the size of Arthur's fist. He then placed the tin pillbox down as well, arranging it so mirror, shell, and pillbox formed a triangle against the red-and-black-checkered background.

"A trigon on my work-square," he said, taking out a quill pen and a small bronze bottle labeled ACTIVATED INK.

BEWARE! "Arthur, please place your hand flat above the trigon, not quite touching."

He indicated the three objects. Arthur complied, holding his hand level just above the mirror, conch, and pillbox.

"Now I shall have to write on your hand. It may sting," said Doctor Scamandros, in the tone doctors and dentists use when something is going to hurt. He set the bronze bottle down, carefully unscrewed the lid, and dipped his feathery pen.

"This is going to help me find out what happened to Leaf?" asked Arthur. He had a strong urge to pull back his hand and run down the beach, back to the camp.

Sunscorch did nod okay, thought Arthur. *So Scamandros must be mostly trustworthy. . . .*

"Yes, yes," said Scamandros. "Hold still."

Arthur held still. Scamandros poised the pen above the back of the boy's hand. A tiny drop of ink fell from the pen and splashed on Arthur's skin like molten metal, sending up a small plume of Nothing-laced smoke.

"Aahhhhh!" screamed Arthur as intense pain shot through him.

Chapter Eleven

Doctor Scamandros didn't pause. With incredible speed, he wrote a word on Arthur's hand even as the boy snatched it away, the ink leaving a trail of fire across his skin.

"It will only hurt for a moment," Scamandros promised, as Arthur rushed to the sea and thrust his hand in. "If I'd warned you, you wouldn't have kept still."

Arthur couldn't speak. The pain occupied his entire mind — but only for a few more seconds. Before Doctor Scamandros had finished speaking, the pain ebbed and was gone, as if it had been washed out with the last wave.

Arthur walked the few yards back up the beach. Scamandros had already packed away the board and the pillbox, leaving only the shell and the mirror. He held these out to Arthur, who didn't notice, as he was holding the back of his hand to the candlelight. As far as the boy could tell, there weren't any scars or ink stains. He couldn't see any writing either.

"What did you write?" asked Arthur.

"My signature," said Doctor Scamandros. "Most

House Sorcery is done with prepared apparatus that will only work for the authorized sorcerer."

"Was there Nothing in that ink?"

"Yes. A very small, refined amount. Not made by me, I hasten to add. I do not work directly with raw Nothing. Though it is true most House Sorcery depends upon apparatus or consumables originally created from or with Nothing."

"Right," said Arthur. He took the mirror and the shell suspiciously. "What do these do, then?"

"I have, I hope, attuned the mirror to show the current situation of your friend Leaf," said Scamandros. "And the conch so you may listen as well. It should work for some days, before the spell degrades and begins to show other persons or places. I should not use it once that occurs, as it may well show you to those who look for such open passages into the mind."

"How do I make it work?"

"Merely hold the shell to your ear and gaze into the mirror. It will work best somewhere quiet, with a little but not too much light shining into the mirror. Here, with the candle, would be ideal. It is generally best to have someone watching over you, as you will not be aware of what is happening around your corporeal form."

"Thanks," said Arthur. "I think I'll try this a bit later. Closer to the camp."

"As you wish. Now, as to messages, I'm afraid that neither telephone nor telegraph will work for us. Though we are not in the Border Sea, we are of it, and any connection would thus normally go through there and the exchange has been long flooded. However, I can send a message by slower means. Have you paper, pen, and ink?"

"No."

"Here you are, then." Scamandros handed Arthur a cracked leather case tied closed with a blue ribbon. "Write a letter while I prepare the messenger."

Arthur opened the case. It was like a pop-up book, with an inkwell, a pile of paper, and several pens rising up as he opened it. Arthur selected a pen, dipped it in the ink, which he noticed was turquoise blue, and wrote.

Dame Primus
Monday's Dayroom or Tuesday's Pyramid
    Dear Dame Primus,
      Lady Wednesday invited me to luncheon and sent a ship for me, but due to an accident I am now in another Secondary Realm with a different, wrecked ship, called the Moth. *A House Sorcerer called Dr. Skamandross is sending this letter for me. I think I might try*

to find the Third Part of the Will, since I'm here. If you can send help or advice that would be good. Also my friend Leaf got picked up by accident and I think is on a ship called the Flying Mantis. *If you can help her get back home that would also be good.*

Yours sincerely,

Arthur Penhaligon

P.S. Say hi to Suzy for me, and Sneezer and everyone.

Arthur looked at what he had written. He hadn't even been sure he was going to try to find Part Three of the Will until he'd written it. But the idea must have been growing in his head ever since Leaf had said that he should do something first instead of waiting for the Trustees to do something to him.

The only problem was where to start.

"Finished?" asked Doctor Scamandros. "Fold it over and write the addressee on the front. Then press your thumb on the fold and it will seal."

Arthur did as he was instructed. When his thumb pressed down, a spray of rainbow light ran around the edges of the paper, and when he lifted his hand, there was a thick round seal that showed his own head in profile with a laurel wreath around his temples.

"Now, don't tell Captain Catapillow or Concort," said Doctor Scamandros. "Having a shortage of prepared stamps, I have taken something suitable from their collection."

He showed Arthur a large, colorful stamp that pictured a bird with a dark body, a white rump, and a forked tail. It was labeled in small type *Leach's Stormy Petrel* and there was a large number 2 and an unfamiliar currency sign.

"From your Earth," said Scamandros. "A nocturnal seabird. I shall just dab a drop of activated ink on its eye and utter a little incantation. You might wish to stand behind me, Arthur. Some of the Architect's words are inimical to mortals."

Arthur quickly moved behind Scamandros and put his fingers in his ears. He remembered the effect of the words the sorcerer had used on the ship.

Scamandros bent over the folded letter, opened his bronze ink bottle, and, using a tiny eyedropper, sucked up some ink. He then carefully dropped just a speck of the liquid on the eye of the bird in the stamp, at the same time muttering something that Arthur couldn't hear, though it made his elbows and knees twinge and ache.

The bird twitched and flapped its wings. It poked its head up and out of the stamp and, fluttering its wings furiously, worked its whole body out. As it left the stamp, it grew larger and the letter grew smaller. It continued to grow until it was about two feet long and its wings spanned six feet. The letter was tiny by then, a rectangle only an inch long. The bird, a bright twinkle in its eye, picked the letter up in its beak and swallowed it before waddling down the beach, slowly beating its wings till it was able to take off, immediately becoming graceful and swift.

"Well, I shall just clear up here," said Doctor Scamandros. "I have to spread some of this magic-tainted sand around and so forth. If you want to try the mirror and shell, I suggest you ask Mister Sunscorch to watch over you, and sit between the Captain's tent and the sea."

"Thanks," said Arthur. Doctor Scamandros was being very helpful.

Maybe I'm too suspicious, thought Arthur. *He must have some reason of his own for helping me. . . . I wonder what it is. . . . I wonder if he can read my thoughts —*

"How long will it take the letter to get to Dame Primus?" Arthur asked quickly, just in case Doctor Scamandros *could* read his mind and was offended that Arthur still didn't trust him.

"It's difficult to say. Barring accident or interception, a day or two in our time here. What that would be in the House, I cannot say without considerable calculation.

Time does not run true between the House and the Realms."

Arthur nodded. It looked like he was stuck here for a week anyway, till the *Moth* could be repaired. Since there was nothing he could do about that, he might as well use the time to work out what to do. And to do that, he needed to find out what had happened to Leaf.

"I'll go back now," said Arthur. "I will ask Sunscorch to watch over me. Thanks for your help, Doctor."

Scamandros bowed.

Arthur turned away and started to walk back along the beach. It was dark without the candle, but he could see the lights of the camp, which weren't that far. Even so, he started to walk quite fast.

He was halfway there when something made him turn around and look back. He could see the glow of the candle, and a partial silhouette that might have been Doctor Scamandros. But there was something else there as well. Another shape, a dark cutout against the candlelight. Arthur only saw it for a moment, then it was gone. But in that instant, he thought he recognized what it was.

Another stormy petrel. Doctor Scamandros was sending a message to someone else.

I knew it, thought Arthur fiercely. *He's probably trying to sell me out to Wednesday or one of the other Trustees.*

They might send Superior Saturday's Dusk if that's who it was who attacked me in Grim Tuesday's Pit. If he comes back with his sword I'll be helpless without a Key, though maybe the crew of the Moth *would defend me because of the Captain's disc. I still don't understand why Saturday would want Nothing to destroy the House. There is definitely something going on with the Morrow Days and Nothing. But what? Why is everything so difficult —*

Arthur's thoughts submerged into his subconscious as he was hailed by a sentry near the camp.

"Halt! Who there goes? I mean, who goes there? Recognize me and advance!"

"Um, I think your name is One-Ear, isn't it?" said Arthur. The Denizen was only partially illuminated by the lanterns on Catapillow's tent, a dozen yards away. "It's Arthur, I'm just coming back from a walk. Doctor Scamandros will be along in a while."

"Advance, friend!" called out One-Ear. He lowered his crossbow and waved Arthur in. As the boy passed, the Denizen muttered, "Actually my real name is Gowkin, but One-Ear sounds so much better. I was a Third-Class Box Shifter before the Deluge. Now I'm a forecastle hand —"

"One-Ear! Watch your front!"

Arthur recognized that shout. Sunscorch came stomping down the beach. Arthur could just make out another sentry behind him, scanning the darkness, his crossbow ready.

"Aye, aye, sir!" called One-Ear. "Just admitting a friend."

Sunscorch gave a slight bow as he met Arthur, which the boy returned.

"The Doc done what's needful?" asked Sunscorch.

"I think so," said Arthur. He held up the mirror and shell. "He's given me something I can use to see what's happened to my friend Leaf. Only I need someone to keep watch while I'm using it. I was hoping you wouldn't mind . . ."

"Watch over you? Aye, I can do that. I have to finish going round the sentries first, since we don't want Feverfew and his lot arriving unannounced."

"I thought we left them behind!" said Arthur as he fell into step with the Second Mate.

"Maybe, maybe not," said Sunscorch. "Feverfew's an uncommon clever sorcerer. Doctor Scamandros would outdo him in book learning, but that pirate must have dozens of filthy tricks the Doc don't know about. Watch your front!"

The next sentry scrambled to her feet and picked up her crossbow. Sunscorch gave a disgruntled snort and kept on.

"Doctor Scamandros told me he was a volunteer,"

Arthur said. He needed to know more about Scamandros. "What did he mean? Why would he volunteer?"

"Before the big flood there were only Navigator-Sorcerers on the regular ships," explained Sunscorch. "So when all the extra ships were being built, they advertised for volunteers with enough sorcerous training to come aboard. Some of the regular sailors were transferred to the new ships too."

"Like you," guessed Arthur.

"Yes, sir, like me," said Sunscorch heavily. "Fourth Mate of the *Spiral Waterspout,* I was, and you never saw a better ship and a finer crew."

"But why would Doctor Scamandros volunteer to be a navigator if he was a top-class sorcerer trained in the Upper House?"

Sunscorch shrugged.

"He probably lost something. That's why most folk from other parts of the House come to the Border Sea."

"I don't understand."

"Anything that's ever been lost anywhere turns up in the Border Sea sooner or later," said Sunscorch. "Finding it again can be more than a mite difficult, though. And it has to be lost by accident — not on purpose, or stolen."

They were almost down to the sea again. A Denizen stood in the wash, looking out to the water, a crossbow at her side. There were a few very red, very bright stars in one patch of the sky, but it was mostly cloudy, and there was no moon of any kind. Possibly no moon circled this world.

"Halt!"

"It's Sunscorch and the passenger," said Sunscorch. "All quiet?"

"Nothing save the waves," said the Denizen. Arthur recognized her voice. It was the one with scales all over her face. Lizard.

"Mind your eye," said Sunscorch. "If they come, like as not it'll be straight from the sea."

"Aye, aye!"

Sunscorch turned back and started walking up the well-trodden patch of sand between two of the larger piles of boxes.

"That's my rounds done. Where do you want to look into that mirror of yours?"

"Somewhere quiet, with a bit of light," said Arthur. He pointed to a patch of sand where there were no resting Denizens, not too far from the lanterns on the tent. "Over there would do, I guess."

Sunscorch followed Arthur over, and stood behind him as Arthur sat down cross-legged on the sand. The boy looked in the shell, holding it up to the light, and shook it a few times to make sure there was nothing inside. Then he gingerly put the shell to his ear, raised the mirror, and tilted it so it caught some of the lantern light.

All Arthur could hear at first was the soft roar of the sea inside the shell, and all he could see in the mirror was his own reflection. He tried thinking about Leaf, but for some reason he couldn't remember exactly what she looked like. He could remember her voice, though, and he concentrated on that, recalling what she had said when she'd come into his hospital room.

The roar in the shell cut off, to be replaced by the rattle of iron and the creak of wood. The mirror clouded as if Arthur had breathed on it, then cleared to show not his reflection, but another dark scene, lit by a different light.

Arthur stared at the mirror. He could see Leaf, inside a very cramped, dimly lit room.

She was a prisoner.

Chapter Twelve

Leaf was sitting slumped in a narrow space, with an inch or so of water around her legs. A heavy chain joined the manacles on her wrists to the manacles on her ankles, then ran to a dark iron ring set into the wooden wall. From the way the water gently sloshed from side to side, she was clearly aboard a ship. The only light came from a swinging, smoke-grimed lantern that hung from a hook in the planked ceiling, barely a foot above Leaf's head.

Something moved in the darkness in the corner of the vision. Arthur shifted his head to try to see it, but that didn't work. The mirror was like a TV set or a stage. Anything that happened to either side or behind it was invisible.

The movement came again. Leaf raised her head and looked around. Seeing nothing, her head slumped forward. It looked like she was totally despondent, till Arthur noticed that she was doing something to the manacle on her left ankle. Trying to pick it, he guessed, catching a glimpse of a nail file or something similar.

Arthur was concentrating so hard on what Leaf was

doing to the manacle that it took a moment for him to realize he'd seen movement again. This time, the movement ended within the mirror's frame and Arthur had a clear look at what it was.

A rat. But not just any old rat.

This was a four-foot-tall brown-haired rat that stood upright on its hind legs. It was also wearing clothes. It had on an old but well-kept swallow-tailed coat of dark blue with gold facings over a cream shirt and silver waistcoat, with white breeches that were rolled up to be out of the sloshing water. Its feet were bare and its pink, hairless tail flicked around behind.

The rat lifted its broad-brimmed but low-crowned hat of oiled leather and said in a voice that squeaked when it took in a breath, "Excuse me, miss. Are you by any chance a mortal from Earth?"

Leaf started and scuttled back, her chains rattling.

"I beg your pardon," said the rat. "I didn't mean to startle you. I would not intrude, save that I have a commission regarding a mortal from Earth."

Leaf shook her head and blinked a few times.

"Sorry," she said. "I just kind of . . . wasn't expecting . . . a . . . a visitor."

"Allow me to introduce myself," said the rat. "I am

Commodore Monckton, officer in charge of the Raised Rats of the Border Sea."

"Raised Rats?" asked Leaf weakly. "Border Sea?"

Commodore Monckton's whiskers twitched before he answered.

"The Raised Rats, young lady, are those rats that formerly served the Piper, and were brought by him to the House. The Border Sea is a demesne of the House, notionally ruled over by Lady Wednesday, self-styled Duchess of the Border Sea and Trustee of the Architect."

"Oh, I see," said Leaf sarcastically.

"I beg your pardon?"

Leaf shook her head again. "Never mind. Yes, I suppose I am a mortal from Earth. A pretty dumb mortal."

"Yet you speak."

"I mean *dumb* like *stupid*," said Leaf. "Anyway, what do you want with a mortal from Earth? Can you help me get out of here?"

Monckton took a paper out of his coat pocket and held it out to Leaf. It was Post-it note size when he handed it over, but as Leaf picked it up it grew to full letter size.

The paper showed an engraved portrait of a boy. It was quite a good likeness of Arthur. Underneath it were a few lines of type:

REWARD

Information as to the whereabouts of one

Arthur Penhaligon,

a mortal boy from Earth.

Send particulars by telegram or message to

Monday's Tierce, Suzy Turquoise Blue

"Arthur!" said Leaf. "And Suzy was the girl . . . the one with the wings."

"Ah," said Monckton. "You know Arthur? Do you know where he is?"

"I might," said Leaf. Arthur could tell she was thinking from the way her eyes had narrowed a bit. "I guess you want the reward?"

"Naturally," said Monckton. "Though in this case we have already been paid a small retainer. We are known to be expert searchers and finders."

"I'll tell you what I know if you help me escape," said Leaf, holding up her manacled wrists. "And help me get in touch with Suzy Blue."

"Hmmm," mused the Rat. "We can't help you escape, as that would be counter to several agreements we have with various authorities within the House. However, I would be honored to act as your counsel in the forthcoming court of inquiry into your criminal activities."

"Criminal what? What! The only thing I've done is let them drag me onto this ship! They took one look at me, asked my name, and then threw me down here in chains!"

"I believe that you will be charged with being a stow-away," said Monckton, adding emphasis with a flick of his tail. "The penalty is likely to be one or two hundred lashes, which I suspect you would not survive. Or, to be quite frank, being mortal, you would *definitely* not survive."

"Lashes? You mean like whipping?"

"Indeed. With the cat-o'-nine-tails. Perhaps you've heard of it?"

"I don't want to hear about it! Or feel it either! This is crazy. There must be something I can do."

"It depends upon the court," said Monckton. "I suspect there is a logical flaw in the charge, which if correctly argued would result in you being spared punishment."

"What is it?"

Monckton inclined his head a little to the side and looked at Leaf with one bright eye.

"We are mercantile rats, miss," he said. "That is to say, you tell me what you know about Arthur, and I shall act as your counsel at the court."

"How do I know that you'll do anything for me once I tell you about Arthur?" asked Leaf.

"I give you my word as a Raised Rat and former mortal

inhabitant of Earth," said Monckton, placing one claw over his neatly waistcoated heart. "In the name of the Piper, who brought us here."

Leaf looked at the Rat carefully. He met her gaze and didn't blink.

"Okay," said Leaf. "I suppose I don't have much choice. You sound convincing, at least. Better than the guy who sold my dad his last car. I was visiting Arthur in his hospital room, back on our . . . back on Earth. Arthur had an invitation from Lady Wednesday, to have lunch, and he was telling me about the House and everything. Then a giant wave came through the hospital room and swept us out to sea, on Arthur's bed. We were getting washed up and down these really big waves when a ship with bright green sails picked me up with a rope, but they missed Arthur. I guess he's still floating on his hospital bed some-where. If it hasn't sunk or been picked up by someone else. That good enough for you?"

"It is an excellent lead, thank you," said Monckton. "It also explains why the Captain and crew of this vessel have been so tediously closemouthed and have chosen to raft up here at the Triangle. Were it not for some of the reg-ular rats, I would not even have known there was a mortal aboard. I suppose the *Mantis* was meant to pick up Arthur for Lady Wednesday, and having failed in their mission,

Captain Swell is biding his time trying to work out what to do next. Besides get rid of you, the unfortunate evidence of having picked up the wrong mortal."

"Raft up? The Triangle? Where are we?"

"We are aboard the *Flying Mantis* on the orlop deck," said Monckton. "A ship of Wednesday's regular merchant marine. The *Mantis* is rafted up, which is to say moored to another ship, which is moored to another ship, and so on, all of them ultimately joined to a giant triangular mooring-post that is all that remains above sea level of the old Port Wednesday lighthouse. Hence, the Triangle. Which is, of course, in the Border Sea of the House."

"Which is the center of the universe," said Leaf. "At least that's what Arthur said. My parents'd freak if they knew it was like this."

"I beg your pardon?"

"They think there's some big tree at the center of the universe, with little branches going off everywhere. And animals living in harmony and being nice to each other and everything."

"It sounds rather pleasant," said Monckton. "If only it were so. Now, I must be getting back to my ship. I shall stop off on the way and inform Captain Swell that I shall be your counsel. I imagine the court will sit anytime within the next few days."

"The next few days!" exclaimed Leaf. "They haven't given me anything to eat or drink. I could starve or die of thirst!"

"Not in the House," said Monckton. "You may get hungry and thirsty, but you won't die from it."

"So you're just going to leave me here chained up? That's it? To wait for the court or whatever?"

"Yes," said Monckton. "You have it exactly. A pleasure doing business with you. Good-bye."

"Wait!" shrieked Leaf. But the Rat was gone. Arthur caught a flash of his tail as he left the mirror's field of view.

"Wait! You can't just leave me! What if the ship sinks —"

Leaf's shout was suddenly cut off and the mirror flickered between Leaf's situation and Arthur's face in the lantern light, before settling on the latter. Arthur felt a wave of nausea at the sudden change of perception, but that was banished in an instant as Sunscorch clapped him on the shoulder and whispered, "Arthur! Get ready, lad. There's something coming in from the sea!"

Arthur blinked, stood up, and hurriedly put the mirror and shell in the pockets of his dressing gown. That reminded him briefly that he really needed to change into something more sensible, the thought only lasting for a second before it was gone.

Ichabod continued to ask questions, handing Arthur an item of clothing or equipment every few seconds. Finally he fell silent, and Arthur quickly got undressed and put on his new clothes. Surprisingly, everything fit him perfectly. Arthur hadn't deliberately chosen any particular combination, but when he was mostly dressed he found that he had on pretty much the same uniform as Catapillow. A blue coat over a white shirt and blue waistcoat with white breeches.

As Arthur had half-expected, as soon as he changed clothes his Immaterial Boots transformed from hospital slippers into knee-high boots, the left one wider in the leg to accommodate his crab-armor cast. Arthur thought for a moment, then slipped the Atlas and Wednesday's invitation down inside his right boot and the shell and mirror down the left boot. Immaterial Boots were proof against water, as they were to almost everything, and they would keep these articles safe and dry.

"I don't know what to do with this collar," Arthur said a few minutes later. The collar was separate from the shirt and he couldn't figure it out.

"Allow me," said Ichabod. He quickly stepped in and fastened Arthur's collar. Before the boy could protest, Ichabod had wrapped a red cloth around his neck and tied it as a necktie as well. "Arms up, sir, for the belt."

A broad leather belt seemed to be the last thing to put on, but when it was buckled up and Arthur tried to take a step out, Ichabod held up his hand and gave a slight bow. "Your sword, sir. One mustn't venture into a prospective battle without one's sword."

"I suppose, er, one mustn't," repeated Arthur.

I'm even starting to sound like Catapillow, he thought. *I hope I don't turn into someone like him. I'd rather be like Sunscorch. Someone who gets things done.*

Ichabod picked up a scabbarded sword from the floor and fastened it to Arthur's belt on his left hip. At the same time, Arthur tied the knife he'd been given by Sunscorch onto the other hip.

"This is a naval pattern sword, reduced in length and weight by the armorer specifically for your lordship," said Ichabod. He stood up and saw Sunscorch's knife, his mouth twisting a little in distaste. "If I may say, milord, the knife does little for the ensemble. Perhaps if you allow me —"

"I want to keep the knife," Arthur said quickly. "And I have to go and join Mister Sunscorch now. Thanks for your help, Ichabod. I don't know how you got the clothes my size so quickly."

"Oh, I cut them down from the Captain's and Mister Concort's best while you were off with Doctor

Scamandros," said Ichabod proudly. "Then a few minor tweaks were all that was required, as I have a very good eye, even if I say so myself. 'Always anticipate!' That's the motto of the true gentleman's gentleman!"

"Um, thanks," muttered Arthur. He hoped Catapillow and Concort wouldn't mind their best clothes getting cut down. "Thanks again."

"And should your lordship be wounded in the forth-coming action, be assured that I have applied my motto to my other profession," said Ichabod.

"What?"

"Surgeon's Mate," said Ichabod. "Or as the *extremely vulgar* call it, Loblolly Boy. I assist Doctor Scamandros. We have never had to operate upon a mortal, but I have all my equipment ready. Knives, saws, drills — all newly sharpened!"

"Great!" said Arthur, faking a cheerfulness he didn't feel. "Well done! Keep up the good work!"

He hurried away before Ichabod had a chance to show him any newly sharpened surgeon's tools. He was halfway through the camp to where the two cannons were pointing out to sea when he heard the sudden clang and clatter of the ship's bell, and Sunscorch's bellow.

"Stand to your guns! Make ready your crossbows! Cutlasses and boarding pikes to the tidemark!"

Chapter Thirteen

Arthur broke into a limping, partly rolling run, joining a dangerous crowd of cutlass- and pike-wielding Denizens heading towards the sea. Two of the *Moth*'s cannons had been taken off the ship and emplaced there, facing the waves.

Near the guns, the crowd split to either side of the emplacement, while Arthur stopped next to Sunscorch and one of the cannons. The weapon didn't look too sturdy or safe to Arthur. The black iron of the long barrel was pitted and rough and its wooden carriage was splintered and cracked, with uneven wooden wheels. Both cannons were stationed on a kind of wickerwork carpet laid over the sand, and that didn't look very solid either.

"Stand away from the gun," warned Sunscorch. "She'll buck when she fires. Break your other leg or your back if you're behind."

Arthur hastily walked over to Sunscorch's right, putting the large Denizen between him and the guns.

"Can you see them yet?" Arthur asked as he peered into the darkness. Apart from the lanterns farther up the beach and the glow from the gunner's slow matches — smoldering lengths of what looked like big fat shoelaces — there was no other light. Or was there? Arthur shaded his face with his hands and squinted to get a proper look straight ahead.

"There is a faint glow in the distance, isn't there?"

"Sure enough," said Sunscorch. "But it's too low in the water to be a ship. And it's moving too fast to be a raft or a longboat or suchlike. I can't fathom it, myself. Unless it's those Rats. . . ."

"Rats?" asked Arthur. "Raised Rats?"

"Aye," said Sunscorch. "They have some uncommon vessels. But I dunno —"

He broke off as the glow in the sea suddenly shot up in the air, eclipsing a red star low on the horizon with its sudden brightness. Then it arced down again, reentering the sea and diminishing.

Sunscorch muttered something, and Arthur heard the gunners nearby whispering nervously.

"What is it?"

"It's a Denizen with marine wings and a veritable glimlight of sorcery about him," said Sunscorch quietly. "Most likely Feverfew has come by himself to reclaim his treasure."

"By himself? But surely we're . . . we've got these

cannons . . . and there's a hundred of us and Doctor Scamandros. . . ."

"We've little powder for the cannons," said Sunscorch. "And Feverfew is a master of dark sorceries the Doc wouldn't touch. He'll turn the sea and the sand against us, like as not, same as he made the rigging of the *Oceanus* choke the life out of its crew. But we've a better chance ashore with our lot than in a sea fight, so you never know. If you get a go at him, Arthur, try to take off his head with a single blow, and get a handful of sand or grit on the neck-stump. Or lay the flat of your blade there, if there's nought better to hand."

Arthur swallowed and looked back at the rapidly approaching light in the water. Then he drew his sword, resting the blade on his shoulder like the Denizens with their cutlasses.

I will cut off his head, Arthur told himself. *I have defeated Mister Monday and Grim Tuesday. I've been wounded before. I know I can take it. I'm not going to be killed by a pirate. . . . I hope my leg doesn't give way suddenly. . . . This crab armor is good and the joints work well but what if it locks up or it just gets weak as I'm fighting Feverfew and . . .*

"Stop it!" Arthur whispered to himself. "Whatever happens, I will make the best of it. I will win."

"Wait for it to leave the water!" roared Sunscorch as the light grew even closer. "Point-blank!"

The glow streamed towards them, growing brighter and brighter, like the headlights of an oncoming car. Arthur felt transfixed by the light, unable to move as it got closer and closer. He could make out a dark shape inside the light, inside the wave. An inhuman figure, like a shark, with huge wings propelling it along. It broke the surface and began to surf in on a wave. The gunners grunted and cursed as they shoved and levered at the cannons with handspikes, trying to point them just where the thing was going to come out of the water.

Sunscorch took a breath and opened his mouth, the word "Fire!" already forming there, when suddenly Doctor Scamandros came capering about in front of the cannons, shouting.

"Hold! Hold hard! Don't! Don't fire!"

At his last word, one of the cannons went off with a tremendously loud bang, a spray of sparks and an eruption of thick white smoke that completely enveloped Arthur. Coughing and choking, he stumbled away, only to find his feet suddenly wet.

He was in the wash of the surf, and the thing from the sea was standing over him, its light shining through gunsmoke and darkness. It had not been hit.

It wasn't a "thing" anymore, though it still had huge wings of metallic yellow-gold feathers. It was a very beautiful, very tall woman, with bright yellow hair tied back in a wire net. She was wearing a green velvet dress with a darker green, fur-trimmed jacket that hung loose on her left shoulder, the arms swinging behind. She held a short, white, scaly whip in her right hand.

She looked down at Arthur, and at the unscathed Doctor Scamandros, who had come up next to him, and at Captain Catapillow, who Arthur hadn't even seen around, but was now bowing and scraping and mumbling.

"Doctor Scamandros?"

Her voice was cold and clear. It made Arthur's ears hurt slightly, as if they were being touched by an icy breeze.

"Yes, ma'am. I am Scamandros."

"I received your message. Introduce me to Lord Arthur. I am in a hurry."

Scamandros bowed to her, indicated Arthur with his right hand, and bowed again to both of them.

"Lord Arthur, may I present Lady Wednesday's Dawn?"

Arthur bowed. He had already half-guessed the identity of their surprise guest. She had the hauteur that all the chief servants of the Trustees possessed. A kind of look that said, *I am superior and you had better admit it.*

"Greetings, Lord Arthur," said Wednesday's Dawn. "Please accept Lady Wednesday's apologies for the sad miscarriage of our transport arrangements. Unfortunately I have not yet been apprised of the exact nature of the incident that led you here, but I trust that you are now ready to accompany me to the promised luncheon?"

Arthur looked up at Dawn's beautiful but cold face.

She would cut my throat if ordered to, Arthur thought. *But what choice do I have?*

"I'm not sure," he said aloud. He still had his sword on his shoulder, and Sunscorch's advice about dealing with Feverfew would probably apply equally well to Wednesday's Dawn. He tensed, ready to strike, as he slowly said, "I've heard some scary talk about how Lady Wednesday is kind of . . . well, you know . . . a giant whale that eats everything. And I don't want to get eaten."

"It is a temporary indisposition," said Dawn. She looked at Scamandros and Catapillow. "Which those of lesser orders would do well not to gossip about. However, you may be assured that Lady Wednesday intends to resume her traditional human form for this luncheon. That is in indication of the importance given to your visit, Lord Arthur. It is currently a regrettable strain for milady to take human shape. She has not chosen to do so for many centuries."

"What does she want from me?" asked Arthur. There seemed no point beating around the bush. "She's in with the Morrow Days. She's a Trustee who didn't do what she was supposed to. I'm the Will's Rightful Heir."

"These are not matters to discuss in public," sniffed Dawn. "Is it enough to say that my mistress recognizes a need for negotiation, not battle?"

"Maybe," said Arthur.

"Excellent. Then I take it, Lord Arthur, that you are ready to come with me?"

"Where exactly?"

"Back to the House," said Dawn. "To the Border Sea. I have many duties, so we must not waste any time. Do you need to breathe?"

"What?"

"Do you need to breathe? You are a mortal of sorts, are you not? If I am to carry you back, we shall spend large amounts of time underwater. If you have not already been ensorcelled to need less air, then I shall have to take care of that before we depart."

"I'm not and I don't think I want to be," said Arthur. "I have asthma and I don't want my lungs messed up any more with magic or anything. And I don't want to turn into a Denizen."

"It is a very straightforward spell," said Dawn. She

gave a small flick of her riding crop, as if to illustrate how small a matter it was. "It merely allows you to survive on far fewer breaths. Perhaps, Doctor Scamandros, you can allay Lord Arthur's concerns. You are a university-trained sorcerer, I note, though I do not recall your name and station in the Index of Navigator-Sorcerers in the employ of Lady Wednesday."

"Ah, dear lady, I was a volunteer after the Deluge," said Scamandros. He made some nervous shuffling motions and almost tripped over his own feet. "So the paperwork may be a little, that is, not quite in order. But, as to the breathing spell, it is one of suspension, I take it? Perhaps the formulation known as 'A Thousand and One Breaths'?"

"It is a peg, purchased at Port Wednesday," said Dawn, removing a small cloth bag from her sleeve and proffering it to Scamandros. "I am unaware of its provenance. I believe it is worn on the nose."

Scamandros took the bag, opened its drawstring, and emptied a small wooden clothespeg onto his palm. He held it up to Dawn's light and looked at the tiny writing on it with his unaided eyes and through his smoked-quartz glasses.

"It is a straightforward spell," he said to Arthur. "One breath will serve for a thousand, till it wears off. There will be a little magical residue, but far less than that already within your flesh and bone."

Arthur took the clothespeg dubiously and opened and shut it, feeling the strength of the spring.

"How will I know when it wears off?"

"It will fall off your nose," said Doctor Scamandros. "You may take it off, of course, and reapply it — though in that case I should be careful not to be too far away from a source of air. It will work less and less well with each reapplication."

"Can't the *Moth* take me to meet Lady Wednesday?" asked Arthur. "I don't think I want to use this spell. Or be carried underwater. No offense, it's just I don't like the idea."

"Time is of the essence," said Dawn. "Lady Wednesday cannot hold her human shape long, and the luncheon is scheduled to begin at noon, House time, on the day I left. We must hurry. No ship can carry you there in time, and unless I am mistaken, this '*Moth*' needs considerable work. I also have numerous important tasks that need my attention. The Border Sea must be constantly tended, lest it spread into the Realms, or conjoin with Nothing."

"Do you swear that I will be returned somewhere safe after meeting Lady Wednesday?" asked Arthur. "Swear by the Architect, and the Will, and Lady Wednesday."

Wednesday's Dawn scowled and her riding crop whistled back and forth through the air. But finally she said, "Yes. I shall do everything in my power to ensure you are returned to a place of safety after your luncheon with Lady Wednesday. I swear this by the Architect who made me, by the Will, and by my mistress, Lady Wednesday."

"Okay," said Arthur. "I guess I'd better go."

He looked at Doctor Scamandros, who shuffled again and bent his head close to Arthur.

"Captain Catapillow thought it best to inform Miss Dawn," muttered the sorcerer softly so only Arthur could hear. "Not wanting the *Moth* to be entangled in things beyond us, and afraid of what the Red Hand you bear might bring. I have to follow orders, you know. But I made sure your letter went first. Only Miss Dawn was already looking for you."

Arthur shook his head, but when Doctor Scamandros offered his hand, the boy sheathed his sword and took it. He still wasn't sure if the Denizen was lying, but Doctor Scamandros *had* fixed his leg up. Hopefully Arthur's letter really *was* going to Dame Primus.

"A pleasure to have you aboard the *Moth*," said Captain Catapillow, who was practically hunched over with his constant bowing to both Arthur and Wednesday's Dawn. "Farewell."

Arthur nodded but didn't offer to shake hands. He looked around instead. There was Sunscorch up by the cannons, surrounded by what looked like the whole crew, gathered in close to stare at the luminous Dawn.

"I won't be long," Arthur said. He raced up the beach to the Second Mate. This time, he did offer his hand, which was taken in a firm grip and shaken so soundly that his shoulder ached.

"Thanks, Sunscorch," said Arthur. "For picking me up from the buoy and everything."

"Fare thee well," said Sunscorch. "Mention Second Mate Sunscorch of the *Moth* to the Mariner, if you ever walk a deck with him again."

"I will," Arthur promised. He saw Ichabod standing primly amid a gaggle of tattooed, unkempt salvagers and waved.

"Thanks for the clothes, Ichabod!"

Ichabod bowed deeply. Arthur waved again and ran back to the sea.

"Take a deep breath and peg your nose," said Doctor Scamandros. He leaned close again and Arthur felt him drop something in the pocket of his coat. "And if I may be of service, do not hesitate to send word. I should like to serve the Rightful Heir."

Arthur felt in his pocket as he stepped back. The object

was round, heavy, and metallic. Before he could investigate further, Dawn spread her wings and gestured for Arthur to approach.

"I shall have to take you under my arm," she said with a fleeting look of distaste. "We shall achieve the best speed if you remain still and don't squirm. Please also ensure your sword stays at your side."

Arthur nodded and stood next to Dawn. Before she picked him up under the arms like a parcel, he took a deep breath, as deep as he was able, and put the peg on his nose. It hurt, but not enough for Arthur to need to take it off.

Dawn spread her wings and, with one mighty flap, launched into the air. As she rose, she began to change. She grew larger and longer, skin and clothing transforming into rough sharkskin with a golden sheen. Her arm changed too, becoming a thick tentacle, its many suckers sticking on to Arthur with nasty pops of displaced air.

Arthur shut his eyes. He didn't want to see the tentacle.

He kept them closed as they dived into the sea, the cold shock of the water smashing into his chest. For a moment he was scared that the peg spell had failed and he would drown. But he felt no need to draw breath, and as long as he kept his eyes closed, he could almost kid himself that he was just in the bath, or mucking around in a swimming pool.

Almost. The water was rushing past too quickly, and the tentacle felt too strange. Arthur suddenly thought of something he should have asked.

How long is it going to take to get back to the House? How long will I be underwater? How long will my thousand breaths last?

Chapter Fourteen

It was a terrible journey, one that seemed to Arthur to last for days, though he knew it was merely hours. At intervals, Dawn would erupt from the water for a long gliding flight, at the same time calling out to Arthur, "Breathe!"

He would take a breath, then down they would plunge, back into water of varying temperature, though always more cold than warm. The light changed too, often quite radically, from total darkness to daylight of different hues. Arthur realized that Dawn was taking them through several different Secondary Realms. How, he didn't know, since there were no obvious portals and they didn't go through the Front Door. He supposed it was something to do with the nature of the Border Sea and of Wednesday's Dawn. Perhaps she could go wherever there was a sea of some kind.

Arthur survived the experience by going into a state where he was neither awake nor asleep. He kept his eyes closed most of the time, and his mind retreated into semi-consciousness, so he had almost no coherent thoughts or memory of any particular time within the journey. It all felt like one ghastly, overtired waking nightmare.

Finally, Dawn leapt up from the sea. Arthur heard the crack and boom of thunder and saw lightning bolts scrawl jagged paths across the entire horizon. He screwed his eyes shut and tucked his chin in tight, holding like that as the thunder got louder and louder and the white light broke through his eyelids. All of it was just too much to bear and then . . . it was gone.

They were through the Line of Storms and in the House, spiraling up and up as Dawn climbed higher into the sky, till they were many thousands of feet up. Arthur started to get worried about hitting the ceiling, then realized it was much higher here than the parts of the House he'd been in before.

Fortunately it wasn't cold. In fact, it seemed to be warmer, which was strange, until Arthur figured out that while there was no sun, the ceiling, no matter how distant, must provide heat as well as light. And he couldn't tell whether the air pressure was decreasing, because he wasn't breathing. The peg was still securely on his nose and his last breath had been only twenty minutes before.

"Nearly there," said Dawn, her voice strange and horrible from her shark-toothed maw. "Look to the left."

Arthur looked down. All he could see for miles and

miles was the sea, a blue expanse flecked here and there with white. Then as his eyes blurred from the rush of the wind, he saw something long and white, reaching up to the horizon. A mountain chain. No, a mountainous island. It was long and narrow, and the snow-covered central ridge looked like it rose higher than Arthur and Dawn were flying.

"We're going to an island?" he shouted, his words almost smothered by the constant flapping of Dawn's wings.

Dawn laughed, a scornful laugh that made Arthur shudder. There was something intrinsically wrong with a laugh coming from a winged shark.

But there was reason for her scorn, Arthur saw as he looked again. What he'd thought was an island was moving. He could see the vast white wash behind it, which he'd mistaken for surf breaking on a very long reef. And the size and shape of the island changed, as it rose and fell in the water.

It wasn't an island. It was a gigantic white whale. A Leviathan. One hundred and twenty-six miles long. A Behemoth. Thirty-two miles wide. A mouth ten miles wide and two miles high —

Dawn stopped flapping her wings and began to glide slowly down.

Down towards Drowned Wednesday.

"Hey!" Arthur shouted. "You said Wednesday was going to be in human form!"

"She will be. She eats tons of fish and krill until the last moment, to satisfy her hunger. You see the ship in front of her?"

Arthur peered down. He could see a tiny brown fleck at least a hundred miles ahead of the vast white whale. It was like a speck of dust on the floor, with a commercial cleaner's mop heading straight for it.

"Yes!"

"Milady has already begun to reduce, and will be fully in human form by the time she reaches it."

"What happens when she needs to change back?" asked Arthur.

Wednesday's Dawn did not answer, instead diving more sharply, her wingtips lifting and angling to control their descent.

"I said, 'What happens when she needs to change back?'" Arthur repeated, knowing it was important.

"We flee," said Dawn.

"What about the people . . . the Denizens on the ship?"

"There are none," said Dawn. "The ship was readied at my orders and the crew taken off. It is not an important vessel."

"Right," muttered Arthur. More loudly he said, "Don't forget your promise."

"I will not forget," said Dawn. "In any case, you are probably milady's only hope."

"What?"

This time Dawn did not answer at all. As they glided steadily down, Arthur watched the approach of the Leviathan. Maybe she was getting smaller, but she still looked like a mountainous island, with enormously high cliffs of chalk at the front. Something too big to be mobile.

Then she raised her tail. Even though they were still twenty miles away or more, Arthur flinched in Dawn's tentacular grasp. The tail rose up at least a mile and came crashing down with a rumbling explosion that Arthur could feel through the air as much as hear. He could see the wave it generated too, and was surprised that by the time the wave got to the ship it was just a slightly higher crest in the swell.

"She's changing," said Dawn confidently. "Already only half her normal size."

Arthur found that hard to believe, but he supposed Dawn would know. They were circling above the ship now, still a long way up, but disturbingly no higher than Wednesday's mighty white brow. It loomed closer and closer, and Arthur started to use his hand as a measure, holding five fingers out at arm's length and counting the number of fingers from sea level to the top of the whale's head. It wasn't very scientific but Arthur was somewhat relieved to see that by this crude measure, the whale was reducing in size.

Not that it looked any smaller.

"Shouldn't we fly up a bit?" he asked, repeating the question in a shout when Dawn did not answer.

"No," Dawn roared. "That would show disrespect. I trust milady!"

Arthur took another measure from sea level using his fingers. The whale was definitely getting smaller, but she was still what he could only think of as humongous.

"I don't think it would be disrespectful to not go any lower," shouted Arthur. "I mean, I'm the visitor. Shouldn't we let her get on the ship first?"

Dawn didn't answer. But she also didn't fly any lower.

Arthur kept looking at Drowned Wednesday. Because of her enormous size, he hadn't really taken in how fast she was approaching. The distance between them was rapidly disappearing, and she still loomed higher than they were flying. He felt like an ant watching a freight train approaching, and he was stuck to the railway line.

At least she's got her mouth shut, thought Arthur. She was close enough for him to see one of her huge eyes now, a thing the size of a racetrack. There were oily tears the size of buses rolling across the face of the eye, each one leaving a rainbow trace behind.

The pupil in the eye suddenly moved up and down a few times, then left and right. It looked like a weird code.

Instantly Dawn's wings pumped the air and she veered away from the onrushing whale, circling to gain height. Arthur, taken by surprise, rotated in Dawn's grip and found himself staring at her sharkskin belly. He urgently pushed and pulled himself around, desperate to see what was happening.

It took him a minute or more, a very long minute, with the expectation that when he next looked he would see the giant mouth open and them going straight into it, no matter how hard Dawn tried to fly away.

But he didn't. He saw the top of Drowned Wednesday's head, only a hundred feet or so below. A huge expanse of white whale blubber and, a few seconds later, a blowhole that looked like a billionaire's sauna.

Which was not that big, Arthur thought. The Leviathan had shrunk considerably. She was now no more than a mile long and he could actually see the shrinking taking place. It was like watching a balloon slowly losing its air, while it still kept its basic shape.

"A minor miscalculation," said Dawn as they began to glide around and down again. There was something in her tone that suggested to Arthur that she'd done it on purpose to scare him, perhaps on Wednesday's orders.

Whether it was intentional or not, Dawn made no mistake with the landing on the ship. She circled a few times, watching the approaching white whale get smaller and smaller. Then, when Drowned Wednesday was no more than fifty feet long, Dawn swooped down onto the poop deck, dropped Arthur, and transformed herself back into human shape.

"Go down to the main deck," said Dawn. "Milady will meet you there."

Arthur unpegged his nose and slowly climbed down the companionway to the quarterdeck and then to the waist of the ship. Tables had been laid end to end on both the port and starboard sides, from the forecastle back to the mainmast. They were covered in fine white tablecloths and loaded with many different kinds of food on fancy silver platters and trays and china plates and bowls.

This, Arthur guessed, was the luncheon of seventeen removes, though all seventeen courses were already laid out and, as far as he could see, there were no places set, or chairs.

The slap of water on deck made him look to the side

ladder. A pulpy-fingered, dripping hand gripped the top rung, followed by another.

Drowned Wednesday was coming aboard.

She did not look good. Her skin was pallid and strangely lumpy, and her arms and legs were of different sizes, the left much puffier than the right. She was wearing a one-piece garment that looked like a huge flour sack with holes cut for her head and arms. Her hair hung limp and wet like a bunch of brown seaweed on her head, obscuring much of her face. Arthur could see that once she must have been beautiful, as were all the superior Denizens, but the fine bones of her face were lost in fat.

She had a rope tied around her waist in place of a belt, and thrust through the rope was a long silver fork — perhaps a short trident. Arthur's eye was drawn to it at once, and he knew without being told that this was the Third Key. Right in front of him! He could run forward and snatch it out —

"Greetings, Lord Arthur," muttered Lady Wednesday as she staggered past him to the table and picked up a huge, meaty bone. She immediately began to gnaw at it, tearing off huge chunks of meat, which she swallowed down with barely a chew. "Wouldn't believe how tired . . . I am of krill and . . . microscopic shrimps!"

Arthur tried to keep the look of disgust off his face as

she threw the bone away and picked up an enormous cake and forced it into her face.

"Repulsive, aren't I?" mumbled Wednesday. "Not my choice, you understand. Can't stop eating."

"Why?" asked Arthur. "I don't understand. What's wrong with you? What do you want with me?"

"Cursed," came the indistinct reply, as Wednesday moved to a huge silver tureen of soup and started to drink it down. "Or something similar. Never should have gone in with the other Trustees. Started getting hungry back then, almost as soon as I took my part of the Will. But held it in check with the Key. Pass me that turkey."

Arthur looked at the table. It took him a moment to locate a huge roast bird that had to be the turkey, though it was twice the size of any he'd ever seen. He lifted it up with some effort and handed it to Wednesday, who grabbed it one-handed and managed to get her jaws around two-thirds of the huge bird in one go.

Arthur had thought of snatching the Key as he handed over the turkey, but he couldn't bring himself to get close enough. Lady Wednesday's hunger was really frightening and it took all Arthur's courage just to stay and listen to her — from a distance.

"As I was saying . . . this good . . . started getting hungry but held it in check for a couple of thousand years without too much trouble . . . sauce for this duck, ah . . . ate a huge amount but didn't matter . . . then I realized wasn't just my appetite getting out of hand . . . cucumber sandwiches excellent, only four dozen, pity . . . the Border Sea was spreading without my direction . . . extending into the Secondary Realms, which was bad enough, but also into Nothing . . ."

She paused to eat a huge, towering jelly-cake, shoving handfuls of it into her maw in quick time. Then, between mouthfuls of bread torn from a loaf the size of Arthur himself, she continued.

"I could stop the Sea spreading when I noticed it, using the Key . . . ugh, fish, you can have that . . . but I didn't like what was going on. Eventually I concluded that the problem went back to our actions with the Will. So I decided —"

She stopped suddenly and flung herself on a platter of small chocolate desserts, smearing chocolate all over her pasty face. Then, through bubbles of chocolate, she continued what she was saying.

"I decided that I would free Part Three of the Will and relinquish the Key. That I was not equipped to deal with whatever was wrong with the Border Sea and with myself."

Wednesday stopped eating for a few seconds. Her face screwed up with a look of pain.

"Unfortunately I also decided to share my plan first

with my friend, the so-called Superior Saturday, who I thought might do the same. Two of us would have a better chance against the others. Or so I thought."

She took a deep breath and staggered down the table to a barbecue plate that was sizzling away without any visible source of heat. It was crowded with thick, succulent sausages, which Drowned Wednesday picked up by the half dozen and crammed into a mouth that Arthur noticed was already bigger and wider than it had been moments before. Drowned Wednesday herself had also grown a foot or two in every direction while she was speaking.

"Saturday betrayed me! The other Trustees, save that somnolent fool Monday, called me to a meeting. I was ambushed, five Keys against my one. They stripped me of my power and I was cast down into the Border Sea, my shape lost, my appetite unsuppressed!"

She punctuated her last remark by eating an entire watermelon, rind and all, washing it down with a huge flagon of ale that spilled down her front.

"Ahh! Since then, I have not been fully able to wield the Key. All the power I have is directed at growing no larger, else I eat up everything in the Border Sea and beyond!"

"What about the Will?" asked Arthur. "Why didn't you just release it like you were going to?"

"Stolen!" roared Wednesday as she slavered over a side of suckling pig. "They reached into my mind and stole out the secret of its location, then Saturday or one of the others sent that pirate Feverfew to take it. But you will get it back, Lord Arthur! You will get the Will, and I shall give you the Key, and all will yet be well. Oh, how I long not to . . . eat! Eat! Eat!"

She threw herself on the table, sliding along with her mouth gaping open like some sort of awful giant vacuum cleaner, scooping up food, plates and all. As she ate her way along the table, her torso grew larger and larger, and her arms and legs shrank back into her body.

"Where did Feverfew take the Will?" Arthur shouted. He started to back even farther away from the feeding frenzy, darting glances at Dawn, who did not look at all ready to fly away.

"Aaaarrch homp homp ugh," Wednesday gurgled and spat, bits of mangled silver falling from her jaws. "Don't know! The pirates have a secret harbor. I know it is in my very own Border Sea, I feel it in my gut! But I cannot find it. You must! Now run! Run!"

She focused on the last few yards of piled-high food on the table and swallowed the lot down in one sweep of her now enormous mouth. Then she turned towards Arthur and slid onto the deck, a huge blubbery cylinder that was not yet whale but no longer human, her now vestigial arms and legs writhing and her vast mouth chomping, the ridges of bone that had once been teeth making a hideous clattering sound.

Arthur wasn't on the deck anymore. He was halfway up the main mast, almost jumping from ratline to ratline. He climbed so quickly that he made it to the cross-trees and was working himself onto the small platform there when Dawn caught up with him and plucked him away and into the air.

Below them, Wednesday continued to grow and grow, threshing and rolling in her hunger, biting at the timbers of the ship until her own rapidly increasing weight broke the vessel's back and sent it to the bottom.

Dawn did not waste any time letting Arthur have a look at Wednesday's transformation. She started flying directly away, her wings beating rapidly and full, gaining height as well as speed. It took Arthur a moment to understand that even now they might not get away, that Dawn was pushing herself to the limit in order to escape Wednesday's remarkable growth and even more remarkable hunger.

Neither of them spoke for some time, till it was clear

that their flight had taken them out of Drowned Wednesday's ravening path.

"Where do you wish to go?" asked Dawn finally. "I will do as promised, and take you to a place of safety, if you so desire."

Chapter Fifteen

Arthur didn't reply immediately. He felt himself at an important crossroads, and his choice here would decide not only his own fate but the fate of many others as well.

"If safety is your prime concern," Dawn continued, "then I must take you to Port Wednesday. It is the only place in the Border Sea where there are elevators to take you elsewhere within the House, and thence wherever you wish to go."

Arthur was silent, thinking this through. It would be so easy to go to Port Wednesday, take an elevator to the Lower House, and then go home through the Front Door or Seven Dials. That would be the safe course to follow. But deep inside he felt that there were no safe courses for him anymore. Not in the long run.

"How far are we from the Triangle?" he asked.

"A half-day's journey, by way of an ocean in the Secondary Realms," replied Wednesday. "Or a week or more if we stay within the House. Port Wednesday is even closer, only a few hours away, again by way of a suitable sea on another world in the Secondary Realms. There's nothing for you at the Triangle."

"My friend Leaf is there, and some Raised Rats. Have you asked them to try and find the pirates' secret harbor?" asked Arthur.

"No," said Dawn. "We do not deal with Rats. Milady Wednesday wished to ban them from the Border Sea, but they possess a patent of authority from the Architect herself, allowing them to roam where they will within the House. What can you possibly want with the Raised Rats?"

"They're expert finders and searchers," said Arthur, thinking back to the vision he'd seen of Leaf and the Commodore. "Or they say they are."

"They are braggarts and not to be trusted," Dawn scoffed. "They sell their services and the secrets of others. They have never answered to any authority within the House, save the Architect's, and since her disappearance I doubt they have grown more obedient to anyone, not even Lord Sunday."

"He's ultimately in charge of everything, right?"

"After a fashion," replied Dawn. "Superior Saturday has the day-to-day management of affairs, as it were. Lord

Sunday's mind dwells upon higher things, not for any lesser beings to know."

"They're both traitors to the Architect," Arthur stated boldly. "Saturday and Sunday, and all the other Morrow Days."

"Where do you wish to go?" asked Dawn, her tone even frostier than usual.

"The Triangle," Arthur answered firmly.

"The Triangle," Dawn confirmed. "I cannot approve of this desire to deal with the Rats, but does this mean you will go in search of the Will? To aid milady?"

"Yep," said Arthur. Somehow *yep* seemed the most positive thing he could say. Stronger than *yeah* and more heroic than *yes*. He hoped he could live up to it.

He pushed on. "I'm going to rescue Leaf and get the Raised Rats to help find the pirates' secret harbor. Then I guess I'll work out some way to release the Will and set everything straight. Including Lady Wednesday."

Dawn was silent for a while, save for the sound of her constant wingbeat. In a small voice that sounded strange and half-strangled, she finally said, "Thank you."

Then she folded her wings and dove towards the sea, with Arthur just managing to take a breath and put his nosepeg back on before they plunged through a slow rolling wave.

The journey to the Triangle was much quicker than Arthur had thought it would be. Even the Line of Storms didn't bother him this time. He just shut his eyes and put his fingers in his ears. He figured that if the lightning hadn't fried him the first few times it wasn't going to now.

Shortly after crossing the Line, the sea suddenly changed color and temperature, and they were swimming through lukewarm, orange-tinted seas full of tiny floating flowers. Sometime later the orange sea transformed to a body of freezing, black water, full of small, regularly shaped chunks of faintly luminous ice. It was as if millions of radioactive ice cubes had been dumped into the sea. Fortunately Arthur did not feel the full effect of the cold, for the golden radiance of Wednesday's Dawn surrounded him and kept him warm. In any case, they were not in this chill sea for long, leaving it abruptly for the blue waters of the Border Sea and, very soon after, another crossing of the Line of Storms.

Somewhere just past the Line, the clothespeg suddenly fell off Arthur's nose. Without meaning to, he breathed in a large amount of water and panicked. He had no idea how deep they were swimming, or how long it would take to get to the surface. He just wanted air immediately and instinctively threshed around in the grip of Dawn's tentacle, fighting against her as he tried to push up to where he imagined the surface was.

Dawn didn't release her hold, but she quickly slanted upward. Her huge wings gave one enormous beat that sent her bursting out of the sea and into the air. Arthur tried to take a breath but had too much water already in his lungs, so he broke into a coughing fit that ended in him throwing up what seemed like gallons of water. Even more came out of his nose and ears.

Finally he managed a few racking breaths, interspersed with bouts of coughing, till he hung exhausted in Dawn's grasp, unable to stop thinking about what might have happened if the peg spell had failed when he was underwater in that black, freezing sea.

"We are nearly there," said Dawn. "Though it will take longer now that I cannot go by water."

Arthur nodded, unable to speak. Her flying speed seemed quite fast enough.

Eventually the water stopped coming out of Arthur's nose, and he could breathe normally again.

"The Triangle lies dead ahead," Dawn informed him. "Though it is unusually empty. There were reportedly thirty or forty ships there a few days ago. Now, I only count eight. . . ."

Arthur looked down. At first all he saw was the sea, with the white tops of the waves relentlessly moving in the same direction. Then he shifted his gaze and saw eight ships of different sizes floating next to one another, in the lee of what at first sight appeared to be a sheer rock that thrust out of the sea. On closer inspection, Arthur realized the protrusion was actually the top of a pyramid, its stones heavily weathered by wind and ocean. It rose several hundred feet above the sea, and was perhaps half a mile long on each side. If it had once ended in a point, that was gone, leaving a flat platform about the size of a basketball court, which was almost completely occupied by a huge iron ring. There was a single six-foot-thick rope tied to the ring, swinging down the lee side of the pyramid into the sea. The ships were either tied up to this rope, or rafted up to a vessel that was.

"Can you see the *Flying Mantis*?" asked Arthur. "Or the Rats? What kind of ship do they have?"

"The *Mantis* is not there," said Dawn. "As for the Rats, one of their putrid, smoky steamers is tied up on the eastern side of the raft, next to the four-masted ship *Undine*."

"A steamship? The Rats have steamships? Why doesn't everyone else?"

"They are forbidden by Drowned Wednesday," said Dawn. "With good reason, for they are foul and unclean. But the Rats have their exemptions. Besides, only the steam vessels made by Grim Tuesday work in the Border

Sea, and they are fueled with Accelerated Coal, made from Nothing. As with everything from Grim Tuesday, the price of this coal is exorbitant."

"That'd be right," said Arthur. "Where is the Rats' ship again? I can't see it."

"Next to the big four-master on the eastern side, as I said."

Arthur looked again. This time, he saw the Rats' vessel. It was only a third the size of the four-masted barque next to it, and his eye had been momentarily confused because the Rats' ship could sail as well as steam, having two masts and square-rigged sails as well as a large central funnel that was not currently smoking.

"We will land on the *Undine*," said Dawn, "and see what is happening. It is unusual for so few ships to be here. Everything looks strangely quiet."

She began to spiral down. Arthur closed his eyes as their rapid descent made him feel dizzy. He didn't open them again until he suddenly felt a solid deck under his feet and Dawn let him go.

She had already transformed back into human form. This time, she was wearing a kind of naval uniform, with a very dark blue coat that was almost black, hung with medals and supporting two very large silver epaulettes. Arthur wondered how she managed to instantly change clothes.

There was no one on board to greet them. Dawn looked around, a frown wrinkling her forehead. There was no one to be seen on any of the other ships either. The only sounds were the groan of the wooden hulls, the high-pitched squeaking of the mooring ropes, and the wash of the sea.

Dawn opened her hand and gripped the air, and a flaming harpoon appeared in her fist. Arthur flinched, but though it was obviously magical, it was not like the Mariner's harpoon. It didn't make him feel odd when he looked at it, so he hoped it wouldn't have the horrible side effects the Captain's harpoon did when it was used.

"The guard boat is missing," said Dawn. "This is what comes of having all one's faithful Nisser . . ."

She restrained herself, but Arthur knew she had been going to say *eaten.*

"I suppose the crews are hiding inside the Triangle," Dawn continued. "Fearful of a pirate attack, no doubt. Which reminds me — put these on."

She pulled a pair of white leather gloves out of her sleeve and handed them to Arthur.

"No need to cause panic at the sight of the Red Hand," she said.

Arthur put on the gloves as Dawn stalked across the poop deck and looked over the port side, across to the pyramid. As she walked away, Arthur heard a shout to starboard.

"Ahoy the *Undine*!"

Arthur went to the rail and looked down. The shout had sounded high-pitched, so he wasn't that surprised to see a four-foot-tall Rat wearing a blue cap, blue breeches, and a loose white shirt hailing him from the forecastle of the steamship. A ship, Arthur noticed, that despite Dawn's disdain looked very spick-and-span. It also had a name, painted in white on the bow. *Rattus Navis IV*.

"Ahoy to you too," Arthur called out. "Where is everyone?"

"A score or more ships sailed within the last few hours, and of those that are left, most of the crews are quivering inside the Triangle," replied the Rat. "It started with the sea level dropping four fathoms for half an hour yesterday. Then the *Shiver* was sighted to the south this morning. What with the rumor of someone afflicted with the Red Hand and all, a dreadful fright got among the Denizens. The braver ones decided to chance it on the high seas, preferring not to be sitting here. Those less brave thought to barricade themselves inside the pyramid and leave the pickings to Feverfew."

"But he has not come," interrupted Dawn, looming up

at Arthur's side. "Or he has become uncommonly gentle with his prey. Has *Shiver* been seen again today, Rat?"

The Rat doffed his cap before replying.

"No, ma'am."

"Is your captain aboard?"

"Captain and crew, ma'am, awaiting custom."

"Who are you?"

"Gunner's Mate First Watkingle, ma'am."

"And your captain?"

"That would be Longtayle, ma'am. Do you wish to come aboard?"

"No. I have other pressing matters to attend to, but my companion here has business with your captain. This is Lord Arthur, Master of the Lower House and the Far Reaches. For some reason he believes you Rats might be useful. He is an honored guest of Lady Wednesday and is to be treated with all courtesy."

Watkingle bowed low, but didn't answer.

"Farewell, Lord Arthur," said Dawn, offering her hand. "I hope you succeed."

Arthur wasn't sure what to do, but he took it and gave a kind of half bow and a little shake.

"I'll do my best."

Dawn nodded, withdrew her hand, and took a standing

jump over the rail and onto the deck of the next ship, without even flapping her wings.

"Just come down the *Undine*'s ladder amidships, sir," called up Watkingle. "Then jump down, if you don't object."

As Arthur walked along to the waist of the ship, Watkingle called out something and more Rats came on the steamship's deck, arranging themselves in a line opposite the *Undine*'s ladder. When Arthur climbed down and jumped across to the deck of the *Rattus Navis IV*, one of them played several piercing notes on a silver whistle. All the Rats immediately stood to attention.

Watkingle saluted Arthur, then said, "Welcome aboard, sir. Please follow me. Mind your head."

Though the deck was wooden, as soon as Arthur followed Watkingle through a door between the two quarterdeck companionways, his feet rang on iron. Arthur stopped to look around, and felt the rivets in the iron wall. He had to bend his head a lot lower than he had in the *Moth*, as the ship was built to Raised-Rat scale.

"She's an iron ship, sir," said Watkingle. "Timbered up to ease the sensibilities of Wednesday and her officials. Built by Grim Tuesday himself, four thousand years ago, and still as sound a vessel as anyone would wish."

He knocked on a door at the end of the passage.

"Lord Arthur, Master of the Lower House and the Far Reaches, sir!"

The door was opened immediately by another seaman Rat, dressed like Watkingle but rather more neatly. Beyond him, there was a large stern cabin with dinner-plate-sized portholes on three sides, a map table loaded with charts and augury puzzle boxes with pictures of animals on them, several upholstered chairs, and a couple of riveted iron chests. Two Rats stood over the table, both in blue coats with gold epaulettes. Arthur recognized one of them as Commodore Monckton. The other was a black Rat, not brown, taller and younger-looking, his whiskers shorter and not as white.

The black rat said, "Thank you, Watkingle, that will be all. Lord Arthur, welcome aboard the *Rattus Navis IV*! I am Captain Longtayle, and may I introduce Commodore Monckton."

Both Rats inclined their heads and snapped their tails like whips, the crack echoing through the cabin. Arthur jumped in surprise, then bowed.

Longtayle pulled out a chair from the table and offered it to Arthur. When he sat, so did the two officers. The Rat who had opened the door immediately put a glass in front of Arthur and poured what looked like red wine from a silver jug.

Arthur looked at it and wished it wasn't wine.

"Cranberry juice," said Longtayle, correctly judging Arthur's expression. "An antiscorbutic for our rare ventures into the Secondary Realms. While we are Raised, we are not Denizens. Like the Piper's children, some diseases may still get hold of us out in the Realms. Scurvy is one of them."

Arthur nodded over the rim of the glass. The juice tasted very good indeed.

"Before we go on to discuss your particular business, Lord Arthur," said Commodore Monckton, "I believe I should tell you that we have been employed by Monday's Tierce, Miss Suzy Blue, to find you and accordingly I have just a few minutes ago sent a message to the effect that you have been found. We have also claimed a reward."

"That's okay," said Arthur. "I knew you were working for Suzy. What I want to know right now is what's happened to my friend Leaf."

The two Rats exchanged a surprised look.

"We are expert searchers and finders of information as all else," said Monckton. "But clearly your sources are as good. It was only five days ago that I entered into an agreement with Miss Leaf."

"Five days," Arthur repeated, mystified. Yet again the

weird time shifts between the House and the Secondary Realms were confusing him.

"Yes, five days," Monckton confirmed.

"That was for her court thing, right?" said Arthur impatiently. "What happened?"

"The court was held this morning, before Captain Swell chose to sail away. Miss Leaf was charged with being a stowaway —"

"I know! What happened to her?"

"With the potential punishment being a death sentence for a mortal, I was acutely aware of the stakes. However —"

"*What happened*? Is she . . . ?"

Chapter Sixteen

"No, no, she's not dead," replied Monckton. "But she has been pressed."

"Pressed!" Arthur exclaimed. "What do you mean? Like crushed?"

He couldn't believe it. Whipping was bad enough, but to be pressed flat —

"No, no! Pressed, as in forcibly enlisted," said Monckton. "I was able to prove that she did not go aboard the *Flying Mantis* of her own free will, so she was not a stowaway. But she was not a passenger either, nor a distressed sailor. Ultimately the only thing she could be was one of the crew. So she was pressed into service as a ship's boy."

"Ship's girl," said Arthur.

"Ship's *boy*," said Monckton. "They're always called ship's boys, even when they're girls. There are plenty of both aboard the ships of the Border Sea. Though apart from your friend Leaf, they're all the Piper's children, of course, and therefore our brethren. We help one another, where we may."

"But what will happen to her?"

"It's a hard life, but the *Mantis* is a well-found ship and a fair one," said Longtayle. "Your friend might work her way up, become an officer, even captain her own ship in time. Mortals learn much faster than Denizens, so there's no knowing where she'll end up."

"But she won't want to be a ship's boy! She has to get home! She has a family and friends!"

"She signed the ship's articles," Longtayle reported. "There's no breaking them."

"Except by executive order from Drowned Wednesday," corrected Monckton.

"So I could release her once I get the Will to make me Master of the Border Sea," said Arthur. "Or Duke, or whatever it is."

Both Rats nodded in agreement. They didn't seem surprised that Arthur was planning to assume control over the Border Sea.

"I suppose Leaf will be safe enough on board the *Mantis*," Arthur said in a hopeful tone. She was probably better off than he was, being out of the trouble he was heading into, but still he wished he'd gotten to the Triangle earlier and could have helped Leaf get off the ship and go home.

I'll have to check, he thought. *With the mirror and the shell . . .*

"She'll be safer than most at sea, for the *Mantis* is a good ship, but there's always storm and wrack," said Monckton.

"And pirates," added Longtayle. "The *Shiver* has been sighted too often in recent times for my liking, not to mention some of Feverfew's lesser brethren, such as Captain Blooddreg of the *Nightdream*."

"That's why I'm here," said Arthur. "Kind of. I need to find Feverfew's secret harbor, and I need to go in there and get something. I must ask for your help."

"We are mercantile Rats," said Monckton. "That is to say, we do not do anything without payment of some kind."

"Do you actually know where Feverfew's harbor is?" Arthur asked. "Or can you find out fairly quickly? I mean, there's no point talking about payment if you can't do anything."

"We think we know where it is," said Longtayle. "That is to say we have deduced its location from some evidence, but we have not actually been there ourselves. As for getting you there . . . if we're right then that's an even more difficult proposition."

"Okay," said Arthur, ready to bargain. "What payment do you want for the location, to start with?"

"We deal in information," said Monckton. "So if we answer your questions, we'd like you to answer an equivalent number of ours."

Arthur had been expecting to pay a ransom in gold or treasure. This seemed too easy. . . .

"Is that all?" he asked.

"That may be more than it seems," Longtayle advised.

Arthur shrugged. "I don't have anything to hide. At least I don't think I do."

"Then you shall ask three questions of us," said Monckton. "And we shall ask three of you."

"There's no trick to this, is there?" Arthur asked suspiciously. "I mean, what I just asked doesn't count as a question, does it? Because I'm not agreeing to that."

"Only significant questions count," said Monckton. "So, you want to know what we know about Feverfew's secret harbor?"

"Yes," said Arthur. "That's my first question. Where is it?"

In response, Longtayle unrolled a very large map that took up most of the table. It was labeled the border sea and was nearly all blue water, with occasional small flecks of land, each neatly marked in tiny cursive script.

Arthur looked over the map eagerly, taking in place names like Port Wednesday, the Triangle, Mount Last, and Swirleen Deep. At first glance, he couldn't see anything labeled Feverfew's Secret Harbor, so he went back to the top left corner to start a systematic search up and down, only to be interrupted as Longtayle carefully placed a small ivory carving of a white whale on the map and tapped it twice.

"It's there," he said. "We believe Feverfew's secret harbor must actually be inside Drowned Wednesday."

"Inside her!"

"More exactly, we believe the secret harbor is a miniature worldlet that is anchored inside Drowned Wednesday's stomach. It can be accessed in only two ways. One is via a unique augury puzzle that Feverfew possesses, made for him by Grim Tuesday, like the worldlet itself. The other is directly from Wednesday's stomach."

"But it can't be inside her," said Arthur. "She returned to her normal human form. How could a whole secret harbor still be in her stomach?"

"I am not a metamathic sorcerer," said Longtayle, "but I believe the explanation is something like this: The secret harbor is contained within a bubble of the Secondary Realm that has been brought into the House. The size of that bubble may change from minuscule to gigantic without affecting the world it contains. When Lady Wednesday used the Third Key to return to her former shape, the bubble shrank with her. When she grew again, it grew. But the world inside the bubble did not change."

"And you can get into it from Wednesday's stomach?"

"We believe so," said Longtayle. "Or out of it. We think Feverfew had the worldlet sorcerously placed inside Wednesday for two reasons. It would be the ideal hiding place, but also would provide unparalleled opportunities for recovering salvage. You are aware that anything lost always turns up eventually in the Border Sea?"

Arthur nodded. He'd been told that by Sunscorch.

"A great part of what is lost lies in the very deeps and is unrecoverable, unless it floats up before it sinks to one of the places where the Sea now impinges upon Nothing and is dissolved. But there is still considerable salvage in shallower water, and it, along with everything else in Wednesday's path, ends up in her stomach, at least for a time. Feverfew uses his slaves to harvest the salvage Wednesday has swallowed, adding greatly to the plunder he takes from the ships of the Border Sea."

"How do you know about this?" asked Arthur.

"One of the advantages granted us by the Piper is the ability to return to our former shape and size for a time," explained Monckton. "It is unpleasant and potentially dangerous, should we forget that we are Raised, but we are able to masquerade as normal rats. One of our number managed to infiltrate the *Shiver* in this fashion, and observe the transition to the secret harbor. While there, she also saw slaves being sent out somewhere, the survivors returning with salvage. Later, we deduced the location of that harbor and the nature of the slaves' activities. Captain Longtayle, show Lord Arthur the map and the sketches."

Longtayle took a leather case from under the table, opened it, and took out several rolled-up pages. He laid these out on the table.

The first one was a map, drawn in pencil and entitled in large uneven letters FEVERFEW'S ISLAND. It showed a body of land shaped like a skull. Under the title there was a note that read: *The isle is roughly 4,500 double paces long and 3,200 double paces wide.*

The left eye socket of the skull had LAKE LEFT written on it. The right eye socket was broken and open to the sea. This was labeled HARBOR and there were some smaller notations indicating a jetty, a shipyard, eight warehouses, a dozen large buildings marked as slave quarters, and a star-shaped construction called Feverfew's Fort.

The nose cavity was labeled as HOT MUD CRATER a note underneath that said *Nothing?*

Down by the skull's jawbone, there were lots of squiggly lines described as TEETH MOUNTAINS and *Followers of the Carp. Escaped Slaves.*

There was sea around the island, but it only extended for about 850 double paces according to the indicated scale, till it met a line marked *Extent of Bubble* that circled the map. Not far from the harbor mouth, near this line, there was a narrow peninsula that thrust out into the sea, with a dot on the end of it and the inscription: *Exit to salvage grounds.*

The second page Longtayle unrolled showed several rough charcoal sketches. One drawing showed the harbor with half a dozen ships present, one of them easily recognizable as the *Shiver.* The other ships looked derelict, and were all piled up against one another in one corner of the harbor, while the pirate schooner was tied up to the jetty.

The second drawing showed a line of slaves wearing bizarre-looking diving helmets, each of them hobbled with a long chain and equipped with a sack and net.

The third drawing was incomplete, a partial scene captured over the shoulder of a pirate who was kneeling on the deck of a ship. He had the lid of a box next to him, the lid illustrated with something that looked like a cross between a squid and a man.

The fourth and final drawing showed a line of small mountains or large hills, which were covered in thick jungle. The caption under the drawing read *Followers of the Carp must be escaped slaves. Potential here.*

"How did your spy get back out with these?" asked Arthur.

Longtayle shook his head.

"She didn't. The map and the drawings came by simultaneous bottle."

"By what?"

"Simultaneous bottles are a form of communication we developed ourselves, with some assistance from certain parties. Essentially, they are pairs of magical bottles. Anything put in one simultaneously appears in the other bottle as well. But they do not work outside the Border Sea, and are very expensive to construct, so only our most important agents are equipped with them. Our various vessels also use simultaneous bottles to keep in touch. We have over a hundred simultaneous bottles aboard."

"So these two papers were the last thing to come through from your agent with Feverfew?"

"Not quite," said Monckton grimly. "The last thing to come through before the bottle shattered was a severed tail. So you see, one gallant Rat has already given up her life for this information."

"This drawing, is it of Feverfew himself?" Arthur asked, indicating the sketch of the pirate kneeling on the deck. "And what's on the lid of that puzzle box?"

"We believe it's Feverfew," said Longtayle. "He was once a mortal man, though greatly changed by sorcery and his long existence in the House, and this drawing shows a man of mortal dimensions. The augury puzzle he is using is not one that is listed anywhere we can find. The creature it portrays is a Gore-Draken, a rare form of Nithling that is very occasionally created when certain lost items within the Border Sea come in contact with Nothing. This suggests the augury puzzle was created from the intestines of a Gore-Draken specifically for Feverfew, which could only have been done by a very superior Sorcerer or one of the Morrow Days. Since Feverfew's private bubble was made by Grim Tuesday, it's likely the Grim made the augury puzzle to go with it. Who paid for it to be made is another question, which we do not know the answer to."

"Probably Superior Saturday," said Arthur. "That's who Drowned Wednesday went to in the first place, to get his help to return the Keys to the Will."

"*Her* help," said Monckton. "Superior Saturday is female. Or she was, last we heard. Now, I think you will agree, we have answered your first question. So we shall ask one in return. Why do you want to go to Feverfew's secret harbor?"

Arthur thought for a moment. There seemed to be nothing to be gained from trying to not answer the question, or fudging the answer. He liked the Rats. They seemed very straightforward, and he knew he would need more of their help.

"I believe the Third Part of the Will is there. Drowned Wednesday doesn't have it anymore, and she says Feverfew took it, with help from the Morrow Days. I want to get to the Will and release it. Then I can get the Third Key from Drowned Wednesday, fix her up, get Leaf back, and . . ."

The two Rats leaned forward as Arthur hesitated.

"Then . . . I'm not sure. I guess I'll need to go back home for a little while, to make sure everything's okay. But if I manage to get the Third Key, I suppose I'll have to work out what to do about Sir Thursday and just . . . get on with it."

"That is a generous answer, Arthur. Please, your next question."

"It's not exactly a question," said Arthur. "I need to get to that secret harbor. If there are only two ways in, and one of them is Feverfew's augury puzzle, it looks like I'll have to get in through Wednesday's stomach. Which means I have to survive getting swallowed up. The only way I can think of doing that would be to be in a submarine or something like it. I've heard you have lots of strange ships, so my question is this:

"Do you have a submarine or know where one is, and can I borrow it?"

Chapter Seventeen

"A valuable question, Lord Arthur," said Monckton. He hesitated, his whiskers shivering, then went on. "We do indeed have a submersible boat, a craft we keep secret. But I am afraid it is laid up underneath our dock at Port Wednesday, for lack of an essential component, which we have been waiting on for some time."

"What kind of component?" asked Arthur. "And who's making you wait? Uh, only answer if that doesn't count as another question."

"That can be accounted as part of your second question, Arthur," replied Monckton. "The submersible boat was made for us in the Far Reaches, by Grim Tuesday's minions. The component it lacks is, in fact, a canister of Accelerated Coal, which must be replaced every century or so. However, since the fall of Grim Tuesday, very few of our orders are coming through from the Far Reaches."

"Yeah, well, I'm sure Dame Primus is doing her best to sort everything out," said Arthur defensively. "Grim Tuesday was using way too much Nothing —"

"That was not a criticism, merely an observation," said Monckton. "We are aware that changes were necessary in the Far Reaches, and we have been advised that we will get a new fuel canister within the next thirty or forty years."

"Thirty or forty years! That's hopeless," said Arthur. He thought for a moment, then said, "How about I get you a new fuel canister? Will you then let me use the submersible to get into Drowned Wednesday's stomach?"

"Will you allow me to confer with Lieutenant Longtayle for a moment?" Monckton asked. "The submersible is very valuable, and it would not be easy for even it to survive a passage into the Leviathan's interior — and out again."

"Sure, go ahead."

Monckton and Longtayle retreated to the other side of the cabin to whisper, while Arthur studied the drawings and the map again. His head was full of rapid thoughts darting around and linking together to lead him into new ideas.

Okay, if I can get into Wednesday's stomach and then into Feverfew's private worldlet, I still need to find the Will and release it and get back out again. Presuming the place will be full of pirates, it would be dumb to go in there by myself. . . . This is kind of like working out how to rob a bank or something. . . . I need to get a team together to help me. . . .

There're the Rats, of course, to run the submarine. . . . I wonder if the Rats can fight. . . . I probably need some Denizens who can fight the pirates, though we should try and sneak in, but just in case. . . . I wonder if Dawn would come along. . . . Then there is the sorcery angle, so if I could get Doctor Scamandros to help out . . . and Sunscorch, he'd be a good fighter, though the rest of the Moth's crew wouldn't be up to much —

Monckton and Longtayle came back to the table and sat down. Arthur looked at them expectantly.

"We have agreed," said Monckton. "You may have the use of the submersible *Rattus Balaena* and its crew if you can secure a new power canister for it. We will do our best to deliver you into the belly of the whale."

"Great!" exclaimed Arthur. "And they'll take me out again too, right? With the Will."

"Yes, if at all possible, the *Balaena* will stand by to take you off the worldlet again and return out to the Border Sea. But the crew will not be able to help you against Feverfew in the worldlet itself. That is too great a risk."

"What about taking on extra passengers, as well as me? I'll need to get some help."

"There is limited space aboard the *Balaena*. It was

built for us Rats, but there is room for you and perhaps another six normal-sized Denizens, if no one minds being a little cramped. There might be some bumped heads too."

"Great! I'd better write a message to Dame Primus to get that power canister delivered. Do you have someone in Port Wednesday with one of your bottles, so I can send it to them to pass on?"

"Certainly," said Longtayle. He opened a drawer and offered Arthur a thick sheet of paper, a quill, a bottle of ink, and a small pot of sand. "We shall consider our next question while you write."

Arthur dipped the quill in the bottle and wrote quickly. The smooth black ink ran a little too freely, causing blots and blotches along the way.

Dear Dame Primus,

I don't know if you got my other letter. Anyway, I'm in the Border Sea and I talked with Lady Wednesday and she explained how she got turned into a whale by the other Trustees and how she wants to release the Will and give the Key to me. But the Will got stolen by a pirate called Feverfew who works for the Morrow Days. I've done a deal with the Raised Rats and they've told me that Feverfew's secret harbor is inside her and they'll let me use their submarine to go there so I can try to get the Will and fix everything up. Only the Rats need a power canister from the Far Reaches for the submarine, so can you please hurry that up so they get it straight away. I mean, really straight away, not next year or whatever. Immediately. Right now.

Also can you send Suzy to help me out? And if you can get in touch with the Mariner, can you ask him to come and help me out too?

Regards,

Arthur

P.S. Send a reply via the Rats at Port Wednesday and their simultaneous bottles, so I get it quicker.

P.P.S. Can you check what's happening back on my world? I want to know what the Border Sea did to the hospital. Thanks.

Arthur finished by spreading some sand over the paper to dry up the ink, as he'd seen done in the offices of the Lower House. He lifted the page to pour the sand back into the pot, then folded the paper, wrote Dame Primus's name on it, and sealed it with his thumb. As before, his thumbprint shone and rippled like a rainbow and became a proper seal, showing Arthur's laurel-wreathed profile.

"If the power canister is delivered quickly, how long will it take before we can get going in the submarine?" asked Arthur.

"Well, the *Balaena* is at Port Wednesday, so we will

have to get there first," said Longtayle. "Under full steam, that will be five days. The *Balaena* can be readied in that time, so we would be able to depart in her immediately."

"Five days!" exclaimed Arthur. "I guess there's no choice . . . I hope I still get back home just after I left, like I've done before. I suppose I might need the time to get in touch with the helpers I need. . . ."

"Our simultaneous bottles are at your service," said Longtayle. "I presume we can send the bill for their use to Dame Primus?"

"Yes," said Arthur. "But no jacking up the price or anything — we'll only pay the regular fee."

"That is understood. Are you ready for our second question?"

Arthur nodded.

"What has the Will told you about the disappearance of the Architect?"

Arthur was surprised by the question, but tried not to show it. He wondered if he was supposed to be repeating what the Will told him. But a deal was a deal — and in this case, he didn't think giving out the information would hurt. "I think it just said she went away," he told the Rats, "leaving the Will behind."

"Are you sure of the exact words?"

"Pretty sure. Yeah, it was back when the Will was a

frog in Suzy's throat. It said something like 'The Great Architect went away' or 'The Architect then went away.'"

"It never said that She was killed or slain by her own servants, the Morrow Days?"

Arthur dropped the cup he'd just picked up, the cranberry juice spreading like spilt blood towards the papers, till the liquid was hastily blotted up with a cloth by the Steward.

"What?! No! The Will said something about choosing to go away or it was her own choice. It never said anything about her getting killed. . . . Do you think the Morrow Days killed her? The Architect of everything? How would they do that?"

"Some authorities claim She is dead, or returned to Nothing, which is the same thing," said Monckton. "We wanted to know what the Will had said to you, because the Will probably knows, and it would not lie to the Rightful Heir."

"I don't know about that," said Arthur. "I reckon it would lie if it suited it. And the First Part of the Will used to say it didn't know enough because it was only one-seventh of the whole Will. Though I have to say since it became Dame Primus it acts like it knows everything."

"You really think the Will might lie to you?"

Arthur thought for a moment. He couldn't think of any

time when the Will had told him an outright lie, but he still had the feeling that it would if it thought it might help its cause. It would certainly lie by omission, choosing not to tell him things if he didn't ask for them.

"Yes, I think it would, but only if it thought it needed to. You know, to make me do something the Rightful Heir should do."

"That is interesting. We had hoped to learn definitively what has happened to the Architect, but clearly that is not yet possible. Thank you, Arthur. Do you have your third question?"

"I might save it for the time being, if that's all right." Arthur didn't want to waste his last question and he needed to think things through.

"You may do so," said Monckton. "Of course that means we will also still have a question for you."

"That's fine," Arthur agreed. He sat quietly for a moment, going over a rough plan in his head. "I want to send some other messages as well," he finally said. "Do you have a bottle on board the *Moth*? The salvage ship I was on."

"I don't think so," replied Longtayle. He pulled out a small book from his pocket and started to flick through it. "I'll check the list."

"Is there any other way to get a message to them?"

"There are numerous ways," said Monckton. "But most rely on sorcery, and we do not practice House sorcery, save for navigation. If Wednesday's Dawn is still here, she might send a message for you. She has many powers within the Border Sea."

"I'd like to talk to her," said Arthur. "But she told me she had urgent business to attend to."

"We don't have a bottle or anyone on the *Moth*, but I'll send someone to check if Wednesday's Dawn is still over at the Triangle," said Longtayle. He opened the door and spoke quickly to the Rat who stood at attention there.

"Sorcery . . ." said Arthur. He suddenly remembered Scamandros had put something in his pocket. Arthur had meant to transfer it to his boot so it would be safe, but he'd forgotten. Was it still there? He reached into the deep pocket and for a moment thought it was gone. Then his fingers closed on something cool and metallic in the corner.

He realized then that Longtayle and Monckton were looking at him curiously, so he hastily pulled his hand out. The Rats were probably trustworthy, but they didn't need to know everything, particularly if they were going to be trading information with him. Arthur needed to keep some secrets in reserve.

"Would you care to be shown to your cabin?" asked Longtayle. "It will take an hour or so to build up steam, then we will be on our way. Earlier, if the wind shifts and we can sail. The breeze is against us for Port Wednesday at the moment, but it may change."

"Thanks," said Arthur. He thought he could take a look at whatever Scamandros gave him in the cabin, and maybe use the shell and mirror to check out how Leaf was doing.

"You shall have my cabin, which is opposite," said Longtayle as he opened the door and indicated another one across the passage. There was already a replacement sailor Rat on sentry outside, who stood aside and saluted. The Rats ran a much more disciplined ship than the *Moth*, Arthur noted.

Arthur bowed to the sentry, crossed the passage, and went into his cabin. It was smaller than the room he'd been in, no more than fifteen feet long and twelve feet wide, with a folded-up bunk on one bulkhead and a folded-down desk and chair on the wall.

Arthur sat down and pulled his boots off as part of the process of retrieving the Atlas, Wednesday's invitation, the shell, and the mirror. He put all these things into his inside coat pockets, then took out the metal object Scamandros had given him.

It was egg-shaped and made of gold, and there was a small curved catch on the side. Arthur flicked this up and the egg opened. One side was a watch, with an ivory face and ornate numbers picked out in tiny emeralds. The two hands were made from some kind of faintly glowing blue metal. The other side had a miniature portrait of Doctor Scamandros. It was very lifelike. As Arthur looked at the painting, the tattoos on his face began to move, and the pale blue sky behind him changed to show a background of dark smoke and dimly lit figures that were either fighting or dancing. At the same time, the Doctor's head turned away, as if he was looking behind him.

Arthur gasped, and Doctor Scamandros looked back. His wild eyes met Arthur's.

"Arthur!" shrieked the tiny figure, barely audible over the sudden din of screams, shouts, explosions, and clashing metal that came through as well. "Help! Give me your hand!"

Without even thinking about it, Arthur touched the miniature with his finger. It was instantly seized and drawn in somewhere, along with Arthur's other fingers and then his whole hand. He felt someone — or something — grip it fiercely. Panicked, Arthur pulled back as hard as he could.

It was like trying to pick up a very heavy weight — Arthur felt his elbow and shoulder joints stretch and almost crack. He leaned back and put his feet against the wall, pulling with all his strength. Then suddenly he was lying on his back and Doctor Scamandros was sprawled next to him on the floor.

"Shut the watch!" squealed Scamandros. "Shut the watch!"

Arthur leapt up. Just as he reached for the watch, he heard a strange zinging sound, and a long, oily flame shot out of the open watch and struck the iron ceiling, the flames burning off the paint and sending billows of choking smoke everywhere.

Arthur, thankful he was still wearing gloves, swiped at the watch, shutting it with one blow. The oily flame disappeared as the watch shut, but there was still lots of smoke. Arthur, coughing and rubbing his eyes, opened the door and the porthole to let it out, then turned to Scamandros, who was still lying on the floor.

"Are you all right? Where did you come from — and how?"

"Just recovering my strength," gasped Doctor Scamandros. "You called at an opportune time, Lord Arthur. Thank the Architect I had the foresight to give you my transfer watch!"

"Is that what it is?"

"Yes, one of my graduation projects." Scamandros tried to get up, but got tangled in the tails of his yellow greatcoat, till Arthur gave him a hand. "I had thought I might need to merely talk with you again, but the transfer was most fortunate."

"Why? What's happened to the *Moth* and everyone?"

"The *Moth* has been taken," said Scamandros, his eyes downcast. "By the pirate Feverfew."

"What —"

Arthur was interrupted by shouts of "Fire!" from outside, followed a few seconds later by several seaman Rats bursting in with buckets and a hose, fortunately not yet fully up to pressure so it only dribbled water.

"Where's the fire?" shouted the first Rat into the room.

"It's out," said Arthur. "Don't worry about it."

"Who's this?" asked the Rat suspiciously, looking at the bedraggled, yellow-overcoated, surprisingly short Denizen who had so mysteriously appeared. Doctor Scamandros bowed, but this didn't help. The Rat looked around, made sure there really was no fire, then nodded to Arthur and backed out.

"Stay here, please, sir, while I fetch the officer of the watch," the Rat said as she shut the door.

Arthur wasn't sure what would happen next.

Chapter Eighteen

No more than a minute later, there was a knock at the door. Arthur opened it and found Lieutenant Longtayle standing there, now wearing a sword. Behind him were half a dozen Rats wearing steel cuirasses and helmets, and carrying short crossbows or cut-down boarding pikes.

"You have a visitor, Lord Arthur?" asked Longtayle politely, but his eyes were cold and did not stray from Doctor Scamandros, who was sitting in the chair mopping his forehead with a yellow silk handkerchief.

"It's Doctor Scamandros, from the *Moth*," Arthur explained. "He came through a transfer watch."

"Are you sure it *is* Doctor Scamandros?" asked Longtayle. "It could be a Nithling masquerading as him. Transfers can be intercepted or redirected."

Arthur looked at Scamandros more carefully than he had before. The Doctor certainly looked the same. . . .

"I *am* Doctor Scamandros!" the Denizen protested weakly.

"Prove it," said Longtayle.

"You Rats! Never prepared to take anyone's word for anything," Scamandros complained. "Well, if you must insist upon proof, here are some documents for you."

He reached inside his greatcoat and pulled out a thin leather document case tied together with pink legal ribbon. He undid this and pulled out a parchment, which he handed over to Lieutenant Longtayle, who carefully looked it over. Arthur couldn't see what was on it clearly, but he caught a glimpse of a kind of three-dimensional portrait of Doctor Scamandros that moved and turned, with flowing type scrolling underneath the picture.

"This is merely a student accreditation from the Sorcery Scholar Assistant Registrar of the Upper House," said Longtayle. "If it's a true document, what are you doing here in the Border Sea?"

"Up until very recently I have been the Navigator-Sorcerer of the ship *Moth*," said Doctor Scamandros. "A post I have held for several thousand years, giving complete satisfaction, I may add. I have a letter here to that effect from Captain Catapillow."

He handed over a folded sheet of paper. Longtayle read this one too.

"What brought you to the Border Sea in the first place?"

Angry storms rolled across Scamandros's cheeks and his fingers twitched.

"That's none of your affair, young Rat!"

"You've come aboard without permission," said Longtayle grimly. "If you don't answer my questions we shall have to —"

"He's my guest!" interrupted Arthur. "I kind of . . . I guess I brought him aboard."

Scamandros waved his hand weakly. The storms on his cheeks dispersed and the ships tattooed there rode gently at anchor. A sun shone on his forehead, turning green as it slowly sank towards his right ear.

"Never mind, Lord Arthur. It's well known that these Rats never rest without prying out everyone's secrets. I came to the Border Sea to find my final exam papers, which were supposedly lost before they could be marked. I thought that if I could find them and have them properly assessed, I could gain my degree and once more be admitted into the halls of learning in the Upper House. A foolish hope, I now acknowledge. I suspect my papers were never truly lost, and so will not reappear in the Sea."

"That confirms your identity," said Longtayle. He bowed and added, "We like to be sure who we have aboard, Doctor. As it happens, your 'secret' was already known to us. If Lord Arthur wishes to confirm you as his guest, we are happy to welcome you aboard the *Rattus Navis IV.*"

"I do confirm him as a guest," said Arthur. "I was hoping to enlist Doctor Scamandros for my . . . my expedition anyway."

"Expedition?" Scamandros asked. "Well, if I could have a cup of tea and a biscuit first, I daresay I could manage a small expedition. . . ."

"We have to get to Port Wednesday before we really get started," said Arthur. "So you'll have a few days to recover —"

"Excellent!" Doctor Scamandros beamed. He cast his eyes about the cabin. "Perhaps I might lie down on that bunk over there? I feel a little weak."

"Uh, I guess you can," said Arthur. "But I want to know what happened with the *Moth*! Was . . . was anybody killed? Is Sunscorch all right?"

"They'll all be slaves now," said Doctor Scamandros gloomily as he climbed into the bunk. He looked down at his stomach, then pulled his greatcoat closed. "Those that survived. Sunscorch? I don't know. Everything was confused. There was smoke everywhere, and Feverfew cast a spell that made the planks bite at our ankles. The Captain and Mister Concort retreated to the main cabin, while Sunscorch led the defense. The *Shiver* fired a broadside of grapeshot as she closed, raking the deck, then suddenly there were pirates everywhere, all around. I ran to the forepeak, thinking to jump, when I heard the chime of my transfer watch. . . ."

"But how did Feverfew know where you were? Was the *Moth* still on the beach?"

"On the beach? No, no, we were only there for two weeks, though of course that was a week too long for Sunscorch. After the ship was fixed up we started back for the Border Sea. That was when Feverfew got us. The *Shiver* was waiting, right where we came through the Line of Storms. I don't know how Feverfew knew where we'd cross. Though one naturally loathes and detests him as a pirate, one must admire his sorcery."

"You were on the beach for two weeks? But it's only been hours for me since I left."

"Time runs true in the House and —"

"— meanders elsewhere, yeah, I know," interrupted Arthur. He was thinking about getting back home before he was missed. "But that's a big time difference."

"I've known bigger," said Scamandros. "Why, one time we left the House for a year and came back only fifteen minutes after we left. The tea was still warm in the pot I left on the corner table of Aunt Sally's Café in Port Wednesday. Quite disturbing, I have to say. Now tell me, what is this expedition you plan, Lord Arthur?"

"It's a very difficult one," said Arthur carefully. "And

getting more difficult. You see, I'm going to sneak into Feverfew's secret harbor and steal something from him. Only now I guess I'd better try to rescue the survivors from the *Moth* as well."

"That would not be wise, Lord Arthur," said Longtayle. "We consider you would have some small chance of infiltration for the purpose of finding and retrieving the object you seek. That chance would be greatly reduced if you try to free slaves as well."

"I guess I'll have to see for myself," said Arthur stubbornly. "What do you think, Doctor Scamandros — will you help me?"

"Naturally I am at your service, Lord Arthur," said Scamandros. "May I ask where the fabled secret harbor of Captain Feverfew actually is?"

"Inside Drowned Wednesday."

Scamandros's head fell back as Arthur spoke, hitting the pillow with a loud thud.

"Doctor Scamandros?"

Longtayle went to the bed and looked down on the Doctor, peeling back one eyelid.

"Fainted," he pronounced. Then his whiskers twitched and he peered more closely at the Denizen's midsection. Reaching inside the Doctor's coat, his paw came out covered in blue blood.

"Fetch Mister Yongtin!" he barked to one of the sailor Rats.

"Is he all right?" asked Arthur.

"Peppered with grapeshot," answered Longtayle. "Strange that his coat isn't . . . I wouldn't have thought he'd have fainted, though, just from these wounds. He's a Denizen. . . ."

He bent down still closer and sniffed, his whiskers all aquiver. Then he recoiled and wiped his snout with a clean white handkerchief.

"He's poisoned with Nothing," Longtayle pronounced. "Feverfew must have doctored the grapeshot. I don't know how he'd make it stick together —"

He stopped talking as a tall, piebald Rat wearing a long apron over his frock coat rushed in. This new arrival went immediately to Doctor Scamandros, pushing Longtayle out of the way. He sniffed at the Denizen, opened up his Gladstone bag, and began to pull out a number of instruments, including a large pair of pincers, which he laid on the table.

"Got to get the Nothing-laced lead out of him," said the Rat. "Clear the room so I can work, Longtayle."

"Mister Yongtin," whispered Longtayle as he ushered Arthur out and across the passageway into the great cabin where he'd met with Commodore Monckton, though the commodore wasn't there now. "An excellent surgeon, but no conversationalist."

"Is . . . do you think Doctor Scamandros will die?" Arthur asked.

"Probably not," said Longtayle. "It's very hard to kill a Denizen. It depends on whether Yongtin can get the Nothing out before it dissolves too much of him. But he'll be weak for quite a while, so I doubt you can count on him for the expedition."

"I hope he'll be okay," said Arthur. He felt a bit bad because he knew he wanted Doctor Scamandros to recover as much for the expedition as for his own sake.

"I'll show you to another cabin," said Longtayle. "It might be an idea to rest, if you can. We found long ago that though sleep is not absolutely essential within the House, we mortals and semi-mortals are happier if we do rest our tired minds and bodies."

"I could do with a rest," admitted Arthur. "Only there's one thing I have to do first, but I need someone to watch over me. Maybe, if it's okay, you could do that."

As they went into the new cabin, Arthur quickly explained to Longtayle the watching spell Scamandros had made for him so he could check that Leaf was all right. He showed the Rat the mirror and the shell.

"I can't watch myself," said Longtayle. "I am the captain

of this ship, after all. But I shall assign someone trustworthy. They will be with you in a few minutes."

He sounded a bit offended.

"Oops," muttered Arthur to himself as the Rat left. Obviously you didn't ask the captain of a ship to do something so basic as stand around watching a passenger stare into a little mirror.

As promised, a few minutes later there was a knock on the door. Arthur opened it and let in a familiar-looking rat.

"Gunner's Mate First Watkingle," Arthur said as the Rat saluted and opened his mouth to talk.

"Bless me! You remembered, sir."

"Thank you for coming so quickly," said Arthur. "Did the captain explain what I want you to do?"

"Stand sentry-like while you whip up some magic," replied Watkingle, tapping the cutlass at his side. "And if your eyes turn yellow and you start acting strange or yabbering peculiar, then I'm to give you a tap on the head with the pommel of this 'ere cutlass."

"Uh, that's not exactly . . ." Arthur started to say. Then he shrugged and nodded.

I guess if my eyes do turn yellow and I start yabbering peculiar it probably would be best to hit me on the head, he thought.

Sunlight — or the light from the ceiling of the Border

Sea — streamed in through the porthole. Arthur sat down, got out the mirror, angled it to the light, and raised the shell to his ear.

Once again, Arthur tried to think of Leaf. A few images rose up in his mind. When he'd first seen her, refusing to run, with her brother, Ed. Then in her house, with the Scoucher cutting its way through the front door.

These images briefly crossed the surface of the mirror, then it went dark. Arthur heard the hiss inside the shell change. He caught the sound of footsteps, followed by a match striking. Light flared in the mirror and the darkness ebbed.

Arthur saw a pale hand transfer the match to a lantern. Then, as the wick caught and flared, another view of a small space aboard a ship. Not the same prison area Leaf had been in before, though the ceiling was only four feet high. This was a long, narrow room.

Leaf was there. She looked quite different. She had a blue bandanna tied around her hair and was wearing a blue-striped shirt and black breeches, with the tops of her high sea-boots folded down over her knees. Even in the flickering light, Arthur could see her skin was much darker than it had been, burned brown by some otherworldly sun.

There was a boy with her, dressed in the same style. He was the one who had lit the lantern, which now hung by a hook in the ceiling.

"I don't see why we have to fight, Albert," said Leaf. "It seems kind of dumb to me. I mean, it's not as if we don't get along okay."

"Tradition," replied Albert glumly. "I don't want to fight either, but the Captain told me we have to. 'Ship's boys always fight,' he said, 'and Miss Leaf has been aboard a month without a drubbing. See to it, or you can both have twenty of the best over the twelve-pounder.'"

"What?"

"Twenty strokes of Pannikin's cane over one of the cannons," explained Albert. He was rolling up his sleeves. "Which would hurt a lot more than anything you could do."

"You're just trying to make me angry," said Leaf. She didn't bother to roll up her sleeves, instead leaning back against a curved internal strut. "Which won't work. I've studied psychology. I know what you're trying to do."

"You don't know much else," said Albert, though there wasn't much heat in his words. "I get tired trying to teach you everyday stuff you should already know."

"What, like the difference between the mizzen gaff and the mizzen topsail yard?" snorted Leaf. "As if I'd ever need to know that back home."

"I keep telling you, you won't be going home," said

Albert. "That just doesn't happen. You might as well face up to the fact that you're one of the Piper's children now, or good as."

"Arthur will find me," said Leaf. "He's the Master of the Lower House and everything. I'll be going home, sooner or later."

"Sure, and Pannikin will give us extra plum pudding for good work," Albert scoffed, then suddenly darted forward and punched Leaf fair in the face.

"Ow! What the —"

Albert darted in again, but this time when he threw a punch, Leaf ducked aside and trapped his arm with an obviously well-practiced move using her left hand and right arm. She followed this up with a swinging movement of her body that propelled Albert into the side of the ship.

He hit hard and Leaf let go. But instead of falling down or giving up, Albert turned around and punched her again, this time in the stomach. Leaf fell back, gasping, the wind knocked out of her.

"That'll probably do it," said Albert, wiping his bloodied nose with the back of his hand. "S' long as the Captain sees blood he'll be satisfied, and if you can walk around all hunched up like that for a hour or two —"

"I might have to, you idiot," complained Leaf. "If you just needed a bloody nose why didn't you say so?"

"I thought it'd be better if *you* had the bloody nose," said Albert. "Didn't know you could fight, did I? What was that wrestling trick?"

"Judo." Leaf straightened up and took a breath. "And that's not all I know either, so you watch it."

"We can be friends again now," said Albert, holding out his hand. "For about another three months or so, I reckon, before the Captain decides we should be fighting. Or if we get any more ship's boys aboard. Or we get washed between the ears and have to start all over again."

"Washed between the ears? That doesn't sound good," replied Leaf as they shook hands.

"It isn't. It's strange, now I think about it. I mean, the Border Sea is all messed up, what with Wednesday turning into a great big fish and all, but the washing between the ears is still regular. Someone always turns up to do it, every couple of decades. Never thought about that before. Can't see why anyone would bother. We're just the Piper's brats, after all."

"I'll have to ask Arthur," said Leaf. "I want to know why the Piper brought you all here in the first place too. And the Raised Rats."

Albert shrugged.

"Never thought about it all myself. Too much to do. Speaking of which, we'd better get back topside before my nose stops."

He lifted down the lantern and blew it out. Arthur listened as it was replaced, and to the soft footfalls as the two children walked away. He was about to stop watching, when a narrow beam of light entered the frame, and he saw the silhouettes of Leaf and Albert against it. They were opening a hatch and climbing out, but as they did so, there was a lot of shouting from up above. It took Arthur a few seconds to separate out some specific words from the general tumult.

"Beat to quarters!"

"It's the *Shiver*!"

As Arthur heard the words, a strange red wash crossed the mirror, like a crimson oil spreading on water. The dark image of the inside of the *Flying Mantis* was replaced with something lit by a very bright, green-hued sun, so glaring that Arthur had to squint.

"You may wear gloves," said a voice from somewhere within the bright light. "But I can still see the mark of MY RED HAND!"

Chapter Nineteen

Arthur tried to look away, but an unseen force gripped his head, keeping him staring at the mirror.

"You will come to me," ordered the voice in the light. It was little more than a whisper, but it echoed in Arthur's mind. "Reach through the mirror with your red-splashed hand."

Arthur's fingers twitched. He felt them slide across the surface of the mirror without his control, his whole hand preparing to plunge through the silvered glass. At the same time, through squinting eyes, he saw a face emerge from the light. A shriveled face that looked like an ancient bog corpse that had been burnt.

"You have stolen from Feverfew — now you must make reparations," whispered the face, which Arthur knew with dread was Feverfew's own, sorcery-ravaged and twisted by Nothing. "Reach through the mirror!"

"NO!" Arthur screamed. He couldn't shut his eyes, but he managed to turn his head, dislodging the shell. Still, Feverfew's voice remained, whispering inside his skull.

"Reparations . . . reach through the mirror . . . reach through the mirror —"

There was a sharp pain in Arthur's head, and the voice vanished. Arthur blinked several times and just managed to raise his hands in time to stop Watkingle from hitting him for the second time with the pommel of his cutlass.

"No! Don't! I'm all right!"

Watkingle lowered his cutlass.

"Wasn't sure I hit hard enough," he said. "Thought I'd start with a little tap, like on a table for ordering a drink."

"Thanks," muttered Arthur, feeling the sore spot on the top of his head. He felt a small wash of nausea pass over him and gulped. Seasickness, he figured.

"You were screaming softly," said Watkingle. "Fair gave me the shudders."

"Me too," replied Arthur. He sat up and looked around, ignoring a momentary attack of dizziness. The mirror was lying on the floor, a huge crack running across it. The shell was crushed under his foot.

A fixed gaslight burned in the corner of the cabin, and there was no longer any sunshine coming through the porthole. The ship was vibrating with a low, regular hum, and he could hear a distant sound like someone hitting a punching bag, not in time with the slight roll and pitch of the ship.

"How long was I looking in the mirror?"

"From four bells in the afternoon watch to six bells of the first," reported Watkingle. "Nine hours, more or less."

"It seemed like minutes. I guess they were a long way out in the Secondary Realms. I wonder where . . ."

Arthur's head throbbed and his throat was sore, probably from the soft screaming Watkingle had described. He shivered again as he thought of Feverfew's horribly burned face and his whispering voice.

Don't think about Feverfew, he told himself. *Think about what must be done.*

"The *Flying Mantis* was about to be attacked by the *Shiver*," Arthur said aloud, still thinking to himself.

"The *Mantis*?" said Watkingle. "That'd be a rare fight. She's a regular ship. Pirates don't normally go for the regulars. They might win, but they'd get mighty cut up."

"Feverfew's already taken the *Moth*," said Arthur. "And now he's gone for the *Mantis*. I wonder if . . ."

He knows I have something to do with those two ships, Arthur thought, the shivers coming back. *With his sorcery, he's seen the connections. I'm marked by his Red Hand and he's looking for me. I'll never get away, I'll never . . .*

"Stop!" said Arthur, stamping his good foot. His own mind was getting out of control.

"Stop what, sir?" asked Watkingle.

"Never mind." Arthur forced the little voice of fear in his head to shut up. He was going to strike first, and once he had the Will released and the Third Key, he could sort out Feverfew without any problems. Probably. Almost for sure . . .

"Is Lieutenant Longtayle awake?" he asked.

"*Captain* Longtayle," corrected Watkingle. "Not his watch, but I could wake him if it's urgent."

"No, I guess there's no point waking him," said Arthur. He massaged his temple with his fingers as he often saw his mother doing. Perhaps that would make his headache go away. "What's wrong with calling him lieutenant, anyway? The Commodore called him that."

"He's a lieutenant in the service," explained Watkingle. "But he's the captain of this 'ere ship, so he's always called Captain on board, except by higher-ranking Rats discussing matters not to do with the ship. Understand?"

Arthur shook his head. He couldn't concentrate on weird details like this.

"I'll just call him Captain all the time to be on the safe side. I suppose I should try to get some sleep."

"I would if I were you, sir," agreed Watkingle. "Always sleep when you can, that's my rule. Now, as the Captain has ordered me to keep a sentry on you for your own protection, I might just lie down on this 'ere floor if you've no objection?"

"Be my guest," said Arthur. He lay down on the bunk. There was no chance of going to sleep, he thought. He had too many ideas floating around in his head, and too many nervous fears knotting up his stomach. All kinds of worries: about Leaf, Scamandros, Sunscorch, and the crew of the *Moth*, about insanely driving a submarine into the mouth of a monstrous whale . . .

Arthur woke with a start. There was sunshine streaming through the porthole again. Watkingle was propped against the door with his tail across his lap, apparently asleep. But as Arthur sat up, the Rat opened one eye and his tail flicked over.

"What time is it?" Arthur asked.

"Just past four bells of the forenoon watch," Watkingle replied. He got up, straightened out his shirt, and brushed some cheese fragments and crumbs off his breeches.

"Which is what in normal hours?"

"Ten o'clock in the morning."

Arthur rubbed his eyes. He still felt incredibly sleepy. "So I slept for about eleven hours, right?"

"No," said Watkingle. "You've been asleep for the last four days."

"Four days! I — I can't have," stammered Arthur. "That's impossible."

"The Captain had Mister Yongtin in to look at you when you didn't wake up the first morning," said Watkingle. The Rat shuffled a bit and his tail flicked nervously. "He said that a combination of a sorcerous insult and a . . . um . . . blow to the head had laid you low and you ought to come good in a few days. After a few days, he said he wanted to open up your head and take a look —"

Arthur hastily felt his head. There were no bandages and he couldn't feel any scars or stitches.

"He was going to do it this evening if you didn't come around," said Watkingle. "So as you'd be right for when we arrive in Port Wednesday."

Arthur stopped feeling his head.

"Are we nearly there?"

"Approaching the harbor bar as we speak," said Watkingle. He scratched his nose and added, "If you're fit, the Captain and the Commodore would like to have a word."

Five minutes later, Arthur was in the great cabin sipping on cranberry juice. He felt surprisingly good. His broken leg didn't hurt at all and moved more freely, the crab cast adapting to his increased mobility. He also felt fresh and quite optimistic, no longer so weighted with fear for Leaf and the others.

I will do what I can do, he thought. *There's no point worrying about anything till I've tried my best.*

"We regret the blow to your head, Lord Arthur," said Longtayle. "Watkingle was following orders, but perhaps his idea of a little tap —"

"It's fine," said Arthur. "If he hadn't hit me, Feverfew would have totally taken me over."

"Feverfew? You saw him?"

"I saw Leaf first. The *Mantis* must have gone out into the Secondary Realms, because she'd been aboard more than a month. I guess she's fit in pretty well, from the look of things. But right at the end they were getting attacked by the *Shiver*. That's when I saw Feverfew. He was . . . pretty ugly."

"The *Mantis* was definitely being attacked by the *Shiver*?" asked Monckton. He looked at Longtayle, his tail rising up in an agitated question mark. "Feverfew grows very bold. We have no separate confirmation of this."

"Watkingle said the *Mantis* might be able to hold off the *Shiver*," said Arthur.

"It's impossible to say," said Monckton. He was obviously troubled. "If Feverfew was determined, he would probably win out. From talking to Doctor Scamandros, you were very fortunate to get away from him the first time."

"Is he all right?" asked Arthur. "Doctor Scamandros? I forgot to ask. . . ."

"He recovers well," replied Longtayle. "He will be joining us shortly. So you say that the *Mantis* was being attacked by the *Shiver* four days ago, by House time? Do you know where?"

"I think it was in the Secondary Realms, but I'm not sure."

"If Feverfew is out cruising for victims, then he and his pirates will not be in his harbor," said Monckton. "Greatly increasing your chances, Arthur. But four days ago by House time . . . he could be anywhere."

"It doesn't matter where Feverfew is," said Arthur, hoping he sounded braver than he felt. "I have to get into that secret harbor. Even more now, if Feverfew has taken Leaf and the crews of the *Moth* and the *Flying Mantis* to be slaves."

I hope that's what happened, Arthur thought. *Better than being killed. Though maybe the* Mantis *defeated Feverfew . . .*

"There is some good news," said Longtayle. "The Accelerated Coal has arrived and the *Balaena* is fully operational. I have just had a message via bottle from her, confirming that the submersible will rendezvous with us offshore in about ten minutes."

"We're not going into Port Wednesday?" asked Arthur.

"No," confirmed Longtayle. "Commodore Monckton and I decided that it would be best to keep your presence secret, and your transfer to the submersible even more so. Feverfew certainly has informers in the port and they are bound to have sorcerous means of communicating with him."

"That makes sense. Did any messages for me come through while I was sleeping? Dame Primus must have gotten my letter if you've got your fuel canister already."

Longtayle shook his head. "No messages have come through by bottle. However, there is a representative from Dame Primus aboard the *Balaena*. She has probably brought messages for you."

"She?" asked Arthur eagerly. "Is her name Suzy Turquoise Blue?"

Longtayle took a paper scroll from the pocket of his coat, unrolled it, and scanned the text.

"No name," he said. "Just 'a representative from Dame Primus.'"

"I hope it is Suzy," said Arthur. "No one else has come

aboard the sub as well, have they? Like a tall, grizzle-bearded old guy with a harpoon?"

"I presume you refer to the Mariner," said Longtayle stiffly. "If he chose to grace any of our vessels with his presence it would be reported instantly. We hold him in only slightly less esteem than his brother, our noble creator, the Piper."

"So he's not aboard, then," said Arthur. Instinctively, he touched the Mariner's medallion on his throat, to make sure it was still there. Not that it had done anything anyway. At least as far as he could tell. He'd always known it was unlikely the Mariner would show up to help him, but he had hoped. Now that small hope had all but disappeared.

"Where is Doctor Scamandros?" he asked. It was looking more and more likely that he'd have to sneak into Feverfew's secret worldlet by himself, without the team he'd been imagining would be there to help him.

"He should be here by now," said Longtayle. He strode over and opened the door to look in the passageway, startling the sentry. "Ah — here he comes."

Doctor Scamandros entered a few seconds later. He looked the same as he always had, but was walking with the aid of an ebony walking stick that had a carved parrot head for a handle.

"Lord Arthur!" he exclaimed, using his stick to balance in order to offer a low bow. "I am most pleased to see you recovered. I cannot thank you enough for my timely rescue, as it is clear that without the friendly and most expert attentions of Mister Yongtin — worth every silver real, I may add — I would have expired quite rapidly from Nothing poison."

"I'm glad you're okay," said Arthur. "I mean, that you're all right. You are basically all right now, aren't you?"

"Indeed, 'basically all right' describes my condition quite well."

Arthur looked dubiously at the little Denizen. Scamandros hadn't fully straightened up after his bow, and the tattoos on his face showed derelict hulks barely afloat amid the wreckage of battle, with sunken masts poking up through matted rafts of debris populated by desolate castaways.

"I was hoping you might be able to help me get into Feverfew's secret harbor," said Arthur. "But you don't look well enough —"

"Poppycock!" snorted the Doctor, wincing as he put his shoulders back and stood to attention. A tattooed wind blew across his face, and the hulks sprouted jury-rigged masts and sails. "Why, an hour or two of rest aboard these kind Rats' submersible and I'll be right as a trivet."

"You'll be at least a day aboard the *Balaena* unless Drowned Wednesday changes her course dramatically," said Longtayle. At the same time, Arthur asked, "What's a trivet?"

"There you are, at least a day's more rest and I shall once more be fighting fit. As to trivets, they are three-legged stands that are notionally most sound but in practice tend to fall over, so perhaps I erred in my metaphor. Right as rain is what I meant."

"What — oh, never mind. I'll be happy with whatever help you can give me. Particularly if you can disguise me. With sorcery, I mean. To fool the pirates."

"Sorcerous disguises? A snap!" declared the Doctor. "Though to be entirely accurate, while I could weave a most excellent disguise over you, it would not stand up to Feverfew's burning gaze. Ordinary pirates, yes. Feverfew himself, no."

"I don't plan to let Feverfew get a look at me," muttered Arthur. He glanced over at Monckton and Longtayle, who were taking delivery of another scroll from a messenger, clearly the latest arrival from a simultaneous bottle.

"One of our ships is shadowing Drowned Wednesday," said Monckton, indicating the ivory whale on the chart. "She is maintaining her usual course for this time of year, following fish patterns, and the *Balaena* should be able to intercept her without trouble. But we need to get you on board immediately. Drowned Wednesday moves far more swiftly than any ship, so the submersible will have to get in position directly in front of her and then steam full ahead in order to navigate the great intake of water through the straining bones of the great creature's mouth."

"Straining bones?" asked Arthur. No one had mentioned anything about straining bones. "What . . . what are they?"

"Drowned Wednesday in her Leviathan form is not just an overgrown Earth whale," said Monckton. "But she has some similarities with the larger types. As far as we have been able to ascertain, she does not have teeth as such, nor the typical baleen structure of some whales. But her upper and lower jaws hold vast vertical sheets of perforated bone, which form a lattice that strains the water that rushes into her mouth. The holes aren't big enough to admit any ship larger than a brig, but the submersible should fit easily. Provided it can aim at one of the holes, of course. It is possible that the rush of water may be too fast for the submersible to have any steerageway, and it will smash into the bone. Or end up between the upper and lower plate and be ground to pieces."

"But you think your submersible has a good chance of getting through?" Arthur hadn't thought getting swallowed by Drowned Wednesday was going to be easy, but he hadn't considered the possibility of smashing into some weird whale-teeth or getting crunched up. "What comes after the straining plates? Do we just keep on going with the flow into her stomach? And is that completely full of water or does it ebb and flow like a tide?"

"We don't know," said Monckton. "One of the reasons we have agreed to supply the *Balaena* to your expedition, Arthur, is that it will provide us with new information. The *Balaena* will send us reports via simultaneous bottle for as long as it — that is to say, we will be very interested to see what else is inside Drowned Wednesday in addition to Feverfew's private worldlet."

"We'd best be getting aboard," said Longtayle. One of his ears twitched, and Arthur realized the Rat was listening to the sound of the ship's engines, which had just grown softer. "We've heaved to. The submersible must be about to rendezvous."

"Submersible *Rattus Balaena* alongside!" reported a Rat a second later.

"Are you coming with us, Captain?" Arthur asked Lieutenant Longtayle.

"I am assuming command of the submersible," said Longtayle. "Due to the nature of the expedition, all the crew are volunteers. Are you ready to go, Lord Arthur? And you, Doctor Scamandros?"

"I'm ready," said Arthur.

"Yes, I believe I am," replied Scamandros.

"Good luck!" said Commodore Monckton. He stood and saluted as they left, as did the Steward and sentry Rats.

"And to you too," muttered Doctor Scamandros as he followed Arthur out the door.

Chapter Twenty

The submersible's conning tower was the only part of the *Balaena* visible above the surface. The sub had tied up on the starboard side of the ship, and Port Wednesday lay to port, so Arthur only had a brief glimpse of that harbor, made even less visible by the fading light from the distant ceiling as the Border Sea's strange night came on.

He saw a dark granite mountain that had been terraced into a dozen or more levels, with hundreds of houses and buildings sprawled along each terrace. Beams of light shot up and down from the higher terraces, marking the paths of elevators to other parts of the House.

Arthur couldn't see the harbor mouth, but he could see a telltale forest of masts in the middle of the lower terraces, so the harbor clearly cut deeply into the mountain, and the terraces wound around it.

"Mind your step, sir!" called a Rat.

Arthur gratefully accepted a helpful paw to jump from the ship to the conning tower. The Rat's paw felt just like a human hand, at least through Arthur's glove.

Arthur's boots rang like a bell on the ladder as he quickly climbed down into the hull. The access tube was quite narrow and would have been difficult for a fully grown man, but it posed no problem for Arthur.

The inside of the submarine was not what he expected. Though it was a gray, dark metal above, inside it was paneled with a cherry-colored timber, and there was a richly patterned carpet on the floor. Arthur peered at the design in the relatively dim light from what appeared to be electric lamps set into the bulkhead. It took him a moment to work out that the flowing lines contained text and that the whole carpet was some sort of epic poem. Or a mission statement. He'd heard of some weird companies doing that in their headquarters. But he didn't have time to puzzle it out.

There was a door forward and a door aft, the forward one open. It was wood-paneled too, but Arthur could see the metal beneath, as it was easily six inches thick.

A crew Rat beckoned Arthur ahead. He was a brindled Rat, a kind of brown-and-black mixture, wearing a blue woolen turtleneck sweater with *Rattus Balaena* embroidered around the neck in gold. He also had on a leather helmet, like the ones pilots wore in really old, open biplanes, but without the goggles.

"Welcome aboard, sir. If you would just come forr'd to the bridge. There's not much room elsewhere."

Arthur ducked as he stepped through the bulkhead door. The Rat led him along a very narrow corridor that had doors and hatches of varying shapes and sizes along both sides, till they came to another bulkhead door.

This opened to a chamber about twenty feet long and fifteen feet wide. It was also carpeted, but you could see where the carpet had been cut so the furniture could be bolted to the metal deck beneath.

The front of this chamber was dominated by a bank of glass-covered dials and instruments, numerous wheels and levers, and a crystal globe about two feet in diameter atop a central plinth. Two tall-backed leather chairs were positioned on either side of the globe, facing the controls.

The rear two-thirds of the bridge, as this room clearly was, could have been transplanted from an expensive hotel or café, though one with limited space. There were six elegant, narrow chairs, bolted to the deck in groups of three, each with a little table between them.

Longtayle and another submariner Rat were down at the controls, intent on going through a checklist. The only other person — or sentient being — there was an exquisitely dressed girl sitting demurely in one of the forward chairs, with her back to Arthur. She was wearing a pearly-white dress with puffed-up sleeves and numerous ruffles and flounces, topped with a very broad-brimmed white hat that had a spray of peacock feathers that almost touched the ceiling. She was drinking very slowly and precisely from a gold-rimmed teacup.

Arthur's heart sank. She was too small to be a Denizen, but Dame Primus had obviously sent someone else, one of the Piper's children more to her liking. Not the ragamuffin Suzy Blue.

Still, she would have messages, which could be important. With a sigh that he didn't even try to suppress, Arthur slid between the chairs to approach the girl.

She turned her head very elegantly as Arthur sighed. Though the huge hat shadowed her face, Arthur recognized the sharp, dark-eyed face underneath. He tripped over his own feet and hit the shin of his good leg on the chair next to her.

"Lord Arthur, I presume?"

Arthur recovered his balance and frowned. She looked like Suzy Blue, but her voice didn't sound quite right. She certainly didn't dress like Suzy Blue.

"Suzy?"

"My name is Suzanna," said the girl.

"Suzy Turquoise Blue," said Arthur, with more conviction. It was Suzy, just all cleaned up and nicely dressed, and putting on a different voice.

"Suzanna Monday's Tierce," corrected the girl. "That is my name and station."

"What's happened to you?" burst out Arthur. "I can't believe you're acting like . . . like . . ."

"A properly brought-up young mortal," said Suzy. "That is the standard Dame Primus has set for me and that I try to attain. Please, do sit down, Lord Arthur. Would you like a cup of this rather strong, but quite refreshing, tea?"

Arthur sat down with a thump. He'd really been looking forward to seeing Suzy again, and having her help. This beautifully dressed, ramrod-straight girl might look like Suzy, but she might as well be an imposter. He couldn't see her being much help. She probably wouldn't want to leave the submarine.

"Do you have any messages from Dame Primus?" he asked abruptly.

"Tea?" responded Suzanna.

"Just the messages, if you have any."

"La! You are in a fearful rush!" protested Suzy. She put her teacup down with agonizing slowness and took a small silk handbag out of her lap. It was a delicate shade of pink. Arthur almost couldn't bear to look at it. Suzy Turquoise Blue was a brave adventurer, not someone who carried around a tiny pink handbag and said "La!"

Suzy reached into the bag and withdrew a tiny square of

paper that grew as it came out, to become a larger envelope of stiff, heavy paper, sealed with a huge red wax seal that showed the stern profile of Dame Primus. Without a laurel wreath, Arthur noticed.

"With the compliments of Dame Primus," said Suzy, passing it over with a very fake-looking smile.

Arthur snatched the letter. As he bent it to break the seal, he saw Doctor Scamandros out of the corner of his eye. The little sorcerer was being assisted to one of the chairs by the same Rat who'd shown Arthur in.

Up the front, Longtayle and the helmsrat sat down in the control chairs. Longtayle raised a pipe to his mouth and spoke into it. His amplified words crackled out of a speaker hidden somewhere above Arthur's head, and could be heard echoing up from the corridor behind as well.

"All hands to diving stations! Sections report when secure!"

Arthur opened the envelope. Like most letters in the House, there was no separate sheet of paper. The writing was all on the inside of the envelope. Arthur unfolded it completely and paused to listen as other Rats' voices crackled and echoed through the loudspeaker system.

"Engine room ready."

"Auxiliaries ready."

"Air circulation ready!"

"Tower secure!"

"Foresnout ready."

Longtayle spoke to the helmsrat. Arthur started to read his letter.

To Arthur, Rightful Heir to the Keys to the Kingdom and Master of the Lower House, the Middle House, the Upper House, the Far Reaches, the Great Maze, the Incomparable Gardens, the Border Sea, and those Infinite Territories beyond the House commonly called the Secondary Realms

Greetings from your faithful servant, Dame Primus, Amalgam of Parts One and Two (comprising Paragraphs Three to Thirteen) of the Will of Our Supreme Creator, Ultimate Architect of All and Steward of the Lower House and the Far Reaches in trust for the Rightful Heir

This missive is conveyed to you by the hand of our good and faithful Miss Suzanna Monday's Tierce. We trust it finds you well.

Get on with it, thought Arthur.

We are delighted to hear that you have once again chosen to prosecute the campaign against the vile and treacherous Morrow Days. We are not pleased that you have chosen to make alliance with Drowned Wednesday, as we fear that she clouds her true purpose. Do not trust her!

We are currently besieged by papers, as the Morrow Days seek to render us immobile and ineffective under a deluge of administrative tasks — a clever tactic made easier for them by Monday's many millennia of sloth.

However, we are pleased to report that progress is being made to return the Lower House to efficient operation. Rehabilitation of the Far Reaches has begun, with the Pit already 0.00002% filled in.

We have not been able to locate the Mariner as you requested, but as is no doubt evident, Accelerated Coal has been provided to the Raised Rats.

On the matter of these Rats, you must be wary in your dealings with them. It is possible they are still following some obscure and eccentric plan of the Piper's, which may be in opposition to our own aims. Do not answer their questions! Their curiosity knows no bounds and they always seek knowledge forbidden to them. Unlike the Piper's children, no effective means has been found to wash between their ears, so they have gathered far too many secrets.

Arthur stopped reading and looked surreptitiously at Suzy.

That's what happened to her, he thought. He felt both sorrow and anger rising up inside him. *She got washed between the ears and Dame Primus let it happen! Or made it happen. Dame Primus never liked Suzy!*

Suzanna noticed his look. She gave him that fake smile

and said, "Dame Primus requested that you read her letter most carefully."

It's not her fault, thought Arthur as he bit back a sharp retort. The sadness overcame the anger he felt. He couldn't look at Suzy, so he went back to reading the letter.

One thing may be said for the Raised Rats. They do keep their agreements. One must merely be careful what one agrees with them.

We await further news from you, Lord Arthur, and trust that we shall soon be united, by your hand, with the Third Part of our supreme Mistress's Will.

Until then, we remain your obedient and respectful servant.

May the Will be done.

"That's a fat lot of help," Arthur said to himself. He started to fold the letter, but it folded itself instead, ending up no larger than a postage stamp. Suzy held out her hand for it, so Arthur gave it to her, and she replaced it in her pink handbag.

Up in front, Longtayle was issuing more commands. "Extend top-eye!"

The helmsrat flicked switches and, in answer, the crystal globe began to shimmer. After a moment or two, it showed a picture of the sea outside the submarine. The bottom half was just blue water, but the top half showed a view of the *Rattus Navis IV* steaming away.

"Rotate top-eye."

Arthur caught another glimpse of Port Wednesday as the scene shifted through 360 degrees, ending up back where it started, with the *Rattus Navis* still heading directly away.

"Extend snout-eye."

The snout-eye view was all blue water.

"Tail-eye."

The view in the globe changed again. It was still mostly water, but one corner of the great dark mountain of Port Wednesday was visible.

Longtayle swiveled in his chair to face the rear.

"We're ready to go, Lord Arthur. At your convenience."

Arthur looked around. There was Suzanna, calmly sipping her tea. No longer the devil-may-care, ready-for-anything friend. There was Doctor Scamandros, looking unwell, his tattoos barely visible, hardly moving. The Mariner hadn't come.

And then there's me, thought Arthur. *With a bruise on my head, one leg in a crabshell, and no real idea what I'm going to do even if we do get into Drowned Wednesday's stomach and I can sneak into Feverfew's secret little world.*

Longtayle twitched one ear.

Arthur took a deep breath and said, "Let's go!"

Chapter Twenty-one

The helmsrat moved his levers and the distant hum became a louder vibration, rattling Suzanna's teapot till she laid a firm hand on it.

"Full ahead both engines," commanded Longtayle. "Helm steady as she goes. Dive to twenty fathoms."

The view in the crystal globe became full of bubbles and blue water that slowly changed color from a light azure to a deep blue-black. The submersible angled down and Suzanna's tray slid along the table, till it was arrested by the raised lip, a feature Arthur hadn't noticed before. The incline was gentle, and didn't last long before the submarine leveled off.

"Twenty fathoms," reported the helmsrat. "Cruising speed achieved. Eighteen knots."

"Very good," confirmed Longtayle.

"Phew!" said Suzanna loudly, startling everyone. She ripped off her large white hat and threw it on the floor. "Fair thought I'd never see a ceiling again with that on!"

"Suzy!" exclaimed Arthur. He started to get up and

was surprised to find a restraining belt had automatically slid around his waist when the submarine dived. It had a buckle, but it took him a few seconds to work out how to release the old-fashioned bronze hook and clasp.

Suzy, in that short time, had torn the puffy sleeves off her dress and was reaching into her pink handbag to pull out a much larger, much scruffier leather suitcase with a broken strap. She undid her belt, put the case on the floor, and rummaged around in it.

"What were you doing?" asked Arthur. He felt quite cross that she'd been pretending, though he was also relieved. "What was with all that Suzanna stuff?"

Suzy pulled out her favorite squashed top hat and stuck it on her head with a pat to the crown that made it even more dented.

"Promised, didn't I? Old Primey wouldn't let me go excepting I swear to be all ladylike and proper on the Border Sea. So I swore, but we ain't on the Border Sea anymore, are we? We're under it."

"I'm glad to see you," said Arthur. "The real you, I mean."

"Good to see you too, Arthur," declared Suzy. She spat in her hand and held it out for him to shake. "Be even better once I get out of these ridiculous duds. I reckon you couldn't even run in this, let alone climb a wall."

Arthur took her hand with some hesitation.

"I didn't really spit," whispered Suzy as they shook. "Just did it to stir up the Rats. They're awful particular for folk who started out as vermin. Not that I hold that against them. They're good mates to all the Piper's children, long as it don't cost them any hard cash or real secrets."

"Dame Primus didn't say much in her letter," said Arthur as they sat back down. He tried not to flinch as his seat belt crept back around and refastened itself. "How is everything? How long has it been since I left you in the Far Reaches?"

"Over a twelve-month," said Suzy. She carelessly poured some more tea, letting it slop over the top of the cup. "And a busy time its been. I reckon the Morrow Days have fair got the wind up about you, Arthur. And Dame Primus. You should see the stuff they're sending down to try and keep her busy. One of the forms was eighty-two feet high when all the pages were stacked up! Mind you, that old Primus doesn't really read like normal folk. She just sits there absorbing it. Like dropping a biscuit in tea. Oops!"

"So they're just sending lots of paperwork? That doesn't sound so bad."

"Well, there's also been assassins, sabotage, and tons

more Nithlings boiling up out of the floor, and no help to deal with them," said Suzy, fishing for her biscuit with a spoon. "It's been much more exciting than it used to be. Not that Dame Primus lets me anywhere near anything if she can help it. Lessons, lessons, and more lessons, that's her idea of what's good for me. Surprised she let me come along here, though I s'pose since you asked directly she couldn't say no. Thanks."

"You do know what I want to do?"

Suzy nodded airily.

"Course I do. We sit here in comfort scoffing tea and biscuits till we get swallowed up by old Wednesday whale. Then we have to get into some crazed pirate's private world, which is stuck in her ladyship's guts, grab the next bit of the Will, and then the usual, only you reckon Wednesday's just going to hand over the Key."

"I guess that covers the main points. . . ."

"And you've got your own sorcerer along this time," said Suzy approvingly. She waved at Doctor Scamandros. "How-do. I'm Suzy Blue. Used to be an Ink-Filler."

"Pleased to meet you, young lady," said Doctor Scamandros. He leaned forward in his chair and came up against his seat belt. He looked puzzled, then subsided back again, obviously considering the three foot distance too far to travel. "I am indeed a sorcerer, though sadly not in full bloom. Doctor Scamandros is my name. I shall be assisting Lord Arthur and yourself, I believe, by constructing sorcerous disguises to ease your entry into Feverfew's hideaway."

"Disguises! What kind?" asked Suzy. "I wouldn't mind a pirate rig myself, with some tattoos like yours."

"Actually," Arthur said, "I was wondering about disguising ourselves as rats. Ordinary rats, if that's possible. I mean as an illusion, not as some kind of shape-change. I don't want to get turned into a rat. Not that it wouldn't be great to be a rat, if I had to be one —"

Arthur stopped before he got himself into any further embarrassment, since he was sure Longtayle and the helmsrat were listening to every word.

"You want anyone looking at you to see a rat," said Doctor Scamandros.

"Yes."

"It can be done," said Scamandros. "But I don't have anything prepared, so I shall have to start from scratch. It will take time. The first things we will need are noses and tails."

"Noses and tails?"

"Yes. Rat noses and tails."

Arthur winced as Longtayle's right ear rotated and quivered in attention.

"Uh, I don't think —"

"No, no. Not *real* noses and tails. We'll have to make some, and I shall imbue them with sorcerous intent as we go. Now let me see. We shall need a quantity of nice thin paper, a simple glue, some cardboard. Activated ink."

As he spoke, the Doctor pulled all these things out of his coat pockets, along with a pair of scissors, several quills, a quill-sharpening knife, and an enameled snuff box.

"Are you familiar with the craft of layering paper and glue that when dry is quite solid and three-dimensional?"

"You mean papier-mâché," said Arthur. He'd made masks for the end-of-year play at his old school. "I've done some."

"We shall make rat noses for you and Suzy out of glue and paper. I shall write on each layer of paper with Activated Ink, impressing it with a spell of illusion and misdirection. This spell will build in strength with each layer, which when complete will create a fully fledged illusion that will cloak your body and present the appearance of a rat to anyone who looks at you. I estimate that to produce two such rat noses will take at least five hours."

"I think it's going to be at least twelve hours before we even get to Drowned Wednesday," said Arthur. "So we've got plenty of time."

"We shall need it," said Scamandros. "For the rat

noses will merely fool the eyes of the pirates — excepting Feverfew, as I previously mentioned. To present them with the sounds and smells of a rat, we shall need to work on another spell, which will be housed in tails. Tails that must be woven expressly for the purpose on looms created for that spell and that spell alone."

"Looms? Ain't they great big wooden things with lots of threads in a frame?" said Suzy. "Could be tricky to get one in here, even if you've got it tucked away in those pockets."

"Looms are not always large," said Scamandros. He reached into his coat and came out with two cotton reels, no more than three inches high and two inches in diameter. They each had four nails hammered into the top of them.

"Allow me to introduce you to the wonders of the Arkruchill circle loom," said Doctor Scamandros.

"That's what you use for French knitting," said Arthur. "I know how to do that. Or I did know, once."

"French knitting?" asked Scamandros. "I learned it as Arkruchillor circle-weaving. But doubtless, as with most good ideas, it came from your Earth and was transplanted to Arkruchillor by travelers from the House. You will need small hooks and the yarn."

He handed over two small silver hook-ended needles and two balls of brown, fuzzy wool, then quickly explained how to run the wool through the cotton reel, arrange it around the nails, and start weaving or knitting, with the occasional use of the hook. After a few false starts, Arthur and Suzy quickly began to produce lengths of knitted wool.

Once they had the knack, Scamandros took the reels back.

"I have to write the spell on them first, so you'll need to start again," he explained. "In any case, we should do the noses first. They will take the most time, and will also need to dry."

The next eight hours were taken up entirely in craft activity, interspersed with occasional breaks for tea or to look at something interesting in the crystal globe. Once they passed through a large sargasso of salvage, and all kinds of things bumped past the submarine. Long-lost possessions, treasured by their owners. Many of them were children's toys, dimly seen stuffed animals and wooden figures, floating in the darkness of the sea.

Finally, the work was done. The rat noses looked like papier-mâché cones with paper whiskers. The rat tails looked like three-foot-long braids of brown wool. But if you looked closely, you could see the words of Scamandros's spell moving about in the paper, or on the wool. Tiny letters marching around, joining up into words.

Arthur couldn't read them, but when he looked at them his mind was filled with images of rats. Normal rats, the kind he used to see occasionally slipping out of the gutter near the central railway station in his old home city.

"Try them on," urged Scamandros. "But please remember, you must have both nose and tail on for the complete illusion, and if you only wear one of the two, there might be some imbalance in the spell."

"Like what?" asked Suzy.

"Suffice to say that if you put a nose on, put the tail on quickly thereafter," said Scamandros. "And vice versa."

Arthur picked up a rat nose and stuck it over his own, tying the cord at the back of his head. It felt ridiculous, a feeling made even worse when he fastened the rat tail to the back of his trousers.

"Marvelous!" said the Doctor. "Say something."

"I feel stupid," grumbled Arthur. As far as he could tell he looked just the same and his voice sounded normal. But Scamandros clapped his hands and Suzy laughed.

"I'll try mine!" she said.

Arthur slipped off his rat nose and undid the tail as Suzy put hers on. As she tied the cord at the back, she disappeared. Arthur blinked, and it took him a moment to think of looking down. There was a rat near his feet, looking up at him and waving a pink paw.

"It works!" exclaimed Arthur.

Suzy reappeared, the rat nose hanging around her neck like a strange necklace.

"I could have done with one of these years ago," she said. "How long will it last?"

"A few days," said Scamandros. "The Nothing in the Activated Ink will eventually eat through the paper and the wool. But it is a reliable, well-made charm, even if I say so myself. It might even last a little longer."

Arthur looked at Suzy. Her eyes were dreamy, indicating some thought about an additional use for the rat disguise, beyond sneaking into Feverfew's worldlet.

"Pilchards," said the helmsrat. "Or sardines."

Everyone looked at the crystal globe. It was suddenly full of flickering silver shapes, so many that Arthur had to stare and focus to work out that the *Balaena* had struck a huge shoal of fish.

"We must be approaching Drowned Wednesday," said Longtayle ten minutes later, when there was no sign of any lessening of fish. "She concentrates the fish in her path, using her powers."

He picked up the speaking tube.

"All hands! Secure for ramming stations! Close all watertight doors! Stand by all pumps! Everyone strapped in back there?" Longtayle called out.

"Yes," said Arthur.

"Indeed," said Scamandros.

"Reckon so," said Suzy.

Longtayle did not leave his chair, but he leaned around to talk to the others.

"Drowned Wednesday usually cruises near the surface, and according to our observations her mouth extends from four hundred fathoms above sea level to an estimated six hundred and fifty fathoms underneath. We have calculated that if we go in at about thirty fathoms below sea level, we should have a very good chance of finding a hole in the upper straining plates and should have no risk of being caught between her jaws. The plates are mostly holes, in fact, but we will have very little time to see one and steer for it, if we are not in the grip of too strong a current."

"We're getting a current now," reported the helmsrat. "Speed in the water has increased to twenty-six knots."

Longtayle turned back to concentrate on the controls.

"What do we do if we don't go through a hole?" asked Suzy.

"I think we get smashed to bits," said Arthur. "But like Longtayle said, it's mostly holes. And the current must aim for the holes, or get directed through them. We'll be all right."

"What happens if we don't get smashed completely to

bits, but just a bit smashed to bits?" asked Suzy after a while. "I mean, so we're still alive but drowning?"

"Suzy, please don't ask me these questions right now," said Arthur with as much restraint as he could manage.

The silver fish in the globe were rushing past at a faster and faster rate, and he could feel the *Balaena* rocking up and down and from side to side, as it was swept up by the inrush of water into Drowned Wednesday.

Suddenly, all the silver fish disappeared and the globe went dark.

"We're in her shadow!"

"Emergency power!" snapped Longtayle. "Snout-eye lights to maximum!"

Light glimmered in the crystal globe and grew brighter. The silver fish were no longer streaming past. They were going backwards, along with masses of seaweed and other objects that had to be salvage. Like the submersible, they were all being sucked into Drowned Wednesday's maw.

Something hit the *Balaena*, the sound echoing through the hull, a deep, long *bong*! It was followed by a whole series of impacts that together made a noise like hail on a tin roof. The submersible rocked and rolled, the helmsrat and Longtayle both working the levers furiously to keep it stable.

Arthur saw the glint of something white up ahead.

"The straining plate!"

Longtayle saw it too. He and the helmsrat redoubled their efforts, the submersible rolling over to thirty degrees and into a steep incline, then leveling off just as quickly. Arthur saw the solid white ahead of them replaced by a dark hole. The submersible headed straight for it, surrounded by silver fish and hundreds of pieces of flotsam and jetsam of many varying sizes.

"We're in!" called Longtayle as he flicked between the views in the crystal ball. All of them showed distant white walls. "We're going through the straining plate!"

He spoke too soon. With a resounding crash, the *Balaena* hit an obstruction big enough to really slow her down. Everyone was thrown forward, tight against their seat belts, then hurled back again as the submersible screamed to a full stop.

The water and all the smaller debris kept rushing past, not quite so quickly, but the submersible didn't move at all, even though the engine vibrations began to shake the hull.

"We're stuck," whispered Arthur.

Stuck deep underwater, in a tunnel of bone.

Chapter Twenty-two

"Stop both!" shouted Longtayle.

The engine vibrations ceased, but the sound of debris hitting the hull continued and Arthur could see a constant stream of small objects flowing past in the crystal globe.

"There's an obstruction in the tunnel," said Longtayle over his shoulder. He raised the voice-pipe again and snapped, "Damage report!"

Rat voices answered, crackling and echoing overhead. All confirmed that there was no significant damage.

"What are we up against, Foresnout?" asked Longtayle.

"The ramming spike has gone through a timber wall," reported the petty officer in charge of the submersible's front section. "Looks like the side of a big merchant vessel, wedged across the tunnel. Very solid."

"Retract the ramspike."

There was no answer for about twenty seconds. Arthur watched the view in the crystal globe. It was hard to make out what lay ahead because of the great cloud of debris flowing past, but there was a shadowy view of algae-covered timber.

"We can't retract it, Captain. Even low gear won't budge it, with everyone on the windlass."

"We'll back out, then," said Longtayle. "Helm, what's the speed of the current?"

"Nineteen knots."

"Nineteen?"

"It's varying between eighteen and twenty knots."

Longtayle's tail whipped out from behind his chair and slapped the floor in agitation.

"What's the problem?" Arthur asked nervously. He decided that he didn't really like being in a submarine. It was all so enclosed, and if anything went wrong, there was just nowhere to go. . . .

"There's a wreck wedged in this particular hole through the plate, and we've run straight into it," explained Longtayle. "Our ramming spike is stuck in it. Normally we could reverse and pull it out that way. But our maximum backing speed is eighteen knots, and the current is stronger than that."

"So we really are stuck?"

"Temporarily," said Longtayle. "Fortunately we have

time to deal with the situation. A number of options present themselves —"

"We're deeping, sir," interrupted the helmsrat.

"What?" asked Longtayle. "Within the tunnel?"

"No, sir. It must be the Leviathan herself. She's diving."

"But she hardly ever dives! How deep?"

"Forty-five fathoms. Forty-eight. Fifty-three . . ."

"Emergency diving stations!" snapped Longtayle into the voice-pipe. "Brace all watertight doors!"

A chorus of "aye, ayes" came over the speakers. Longtayle leaned over to watch the depth meter with the helmsrat, who kept calling out the depth anyway.

"She's leveling off," reported the helmsrat. "Level at sixty-seven fathoms."

"How deep can we go?" asked Arthur.

"Deeper than this," said Longtayle. "The danger is that a very small movement for Drowned Wednesday might take us down too far. We counted on her just cruising along the surface like she normally does."

"I bet she saw something to eat," said Arthur. "But we're okay for now, aren't we?"

"We have to get out of this hole in the plate," said Longtayle. "Once we have freedom to move within her, we'll be fine. But we're too deep to send divers out now, to chop away the obstruction. Perhaps, Doctor Scamandros, you might have some sorcerous solution?"

Scamandros cleared his throat.

"Hmmph, can't say anything springs to mind, sadly. Most of my practical knowledge is for wind and wave, on top of the sea, not underneath it."

"We'll try to shake ourselves out then —"

"She's diving again, Captain."

"Depth?"

"Seventy-two fathoms and getting deeper. Eighty-two fathoms. Eighty-seven fathoms. Ninety fathoms. Ninety-five fathoms."

The helmrat's impassive voice was suddenly drowned by a horrible, metallic booming that sounded like someone hitting an enormous bell. It was so loud it completely drowned out all other noise. Then it slowly eased into a host of different booms and squeals, none of them as loud, but all of them very frightening.

"We can go deeper," said Longtayle. He sounded confident, but Arthur saw that the Rat's tail had gone completely white.

"One hundred fathoms. One hundred and two fathoms."

"Send a bottle message," ordered Longtayle suddenly into the voice-pipe. "Test depth reached. DW still diving."

"Aye, aye," came the disembodied response.

"Doctor Scamandros!" Arthur turned to the sorcerer. "What about communicating with Drowned Wednesday? Is there anything you can do to . . . to, I don't know . . . cast a light in the sky so she'll look up at it?"

Scamandros was mopping his forehead with his yellow silk handkerchief. He put this away and started hunting through the numerous inside pockets of his coat. In fact, he seemed to have more pockets than it was possible to have inside a coat.

"No, no, that won't do . . . won't work from down here . . . never quite mastered that one . . . perhaps, no, used that up . . . have to be able to see the target . . ."

"How about you bung an illusion of a big hunk of roast beef on top," suggested Suzy. "I reckon she'd go for that."

"I can *make* the illusion," said Scamandros peevishly. "But I can't get it outside!"

"One hundred and six fathoms," reported the helmsrat. He turned to look at the Captain and said, without a tremor in his voice, "Estimated crush depth is one hundred and ten fathoms."

Arthur didn't need to ask what the *crush depth* was. It was obvious from the horrible booming and screeching sounds coming from all around them. He jumped as a new sound started, and turned to see water spraying up from the floor.

"One hundred and eight fathoms."

"Can Drowned Wednesday hear underwater?" asked Suzy.

"Crush depth exceeded," reported the helmsrat. "One hundred and eleven fathoms . . . and getting deeper."

As if in answer to his voice, all the lights suddenly went out. Arthur stared into the darkness, expecting any moment to hear the hull completely buckle . . . followed immediately by the cold shock of tons of water and almost instantaneous death. At least it would be quick. . . .

Everyone else seemed to be expecting the same thing. They were totally silent for about ten seconds, then Longtayle spoke.

"Switch to circuit B!"

The helmsrat moved. Through the constant booming and whistling, Arthur heard a switch click and the Rat swear under his breath. Then there was a glimmering of light in the filaments as the bulbs heated up, gradually brightening to cast a strange red glow over the submariners.

"Depth!"

Once again the passengers held their breath. Surely they couldn't still be going down, or they would already be crushed.

"One hundred . . . one hundred and thirteen fathoms! And steady!"

"What did you say, Suzy?" asked Arthur.

"I said, 'Can Drowned Wednesday hear underwater?'"

"I bet she can," said Arthur quickly. "Whales have sonar! They sing to one another! If we can make a really high-pitched loud noise, then she'll . . . she'll know there's someone stuck in her jaw. . . . That's probably not going to help, is it?"

"Why not?" asked Suzy.

"Well, she might just dive even deeper to get rid of whatever's making the annoying noise."

"One hundred and fourteen fathoms!" reported the helmsrat. "She's diving again!"

"It's not going to make things worse, is it?"

"Do whatever you can," ordered Longtayle. "The crush depth is an estimate, but —"

His voice was cut off as several jets of water burst out of the walls at the same time, accompanied by a terrible, deep groan from the hull.

"Doctor!" yelled Arthur. "Can you make a really long, really high-pitched squeal?"

Scamandros was already unscrewing the parrot head of his walking stick. He nodded as he reached inside the head and made some adjustments.

"Block your ears!"

Arthur just had time to put his fingers in his ears as the parrot head suddenly shone with a bright light and its beak opened, emitting an incredibly piercing shriek that went on for several seconds, completely cutting through the groans and bellows of the distressed submarine. Scamandros worked the parrot head like it was a puppet, pulling on little levers, and its shriek began to go up and down to a regular rhythm.

The helmsrat was trying to shout something but Arthur couldn't hear him. The parrot shriek was so loud and so high-pitched that it actually hurt. He could feel it making his cheekbones ache.

Water touched Arthur's feet. He yelped and pulled his legs up. There was at least a foot of water in the compartment and it looked like it was rising. So it hadn't worked, and they were all going to be crushed and drowned —

The screech stopped. Hesitantly, Arthur pulled one finger out of his ear, just enough to hear a confused babble of voices that included the helmsrat shrieking, all calm gone.

"One hundred fathoms and rising! She's going up! She's going up!"

Whether it was in response to the parrot shriek or not, Drowned Wednesday rose up far faster than she'd sunk. Not that either motion had been very significant for her,

Arthur thought. A bit like him bobbing his head down an inch.

"Ten fathoms and shallowing! Six fathoms! Sea level! We're out of the water. We're right out of the water."

Everyone stared at the crystal globe. All the water was running out of the hole they were in, to reveal the obstruction as a barnacle-encrusted wall of copper-sheathed timber.

"She must be lifting her head up," said Longtayle. "That'll make things easier."

He lifted the voice-pipe.

"Cox'n, prepare a diving party for outside work. Four rats with axes. Damage control, get all pumps going."

"Aye, aye!"

Arthur was watching the crystal globe carefully, so he was the first to notice the water streaming back from inside the whale. At the same time the submersible shook and tilted down at the stern, the water still in the bridge sloshing around everyone's ankles.

"We're in the sea again. Nine fathoms!" called the helmsrat. "But the current has reversed. It's coming out of her now, at six knots."

"Belay that diving party!" called Longtayle. "Full back both engines!"

The vibration of the engines had just begun when there

was suddenly a much bigger and more dramatic vibration, a shock wave that shook the whole submersible with a sound like a china cabinet falling over. Arthur held his hands against his ears as he felt his stomach flip-flop and the blood rush to his head.

"What was that?"

"Jaw clash," said Longtayle. "Guess she really didn't like that parrot noise. It might help us get free."

"Or shake us to bits," said Suzy cheerfully.

The shock wave came three more times, each more violently than the last. Arthur was very glad to be sitting down and belted in, as even so he was thrown about in his chair. The teapot and cups were long since smashed to pieces and they combined with various other bits and pieces to fly dangerously around the bridge. Arthur was cut slightly across the cheek before he covered his face with his arms.

"We're backing free!"

Arthur stared at the crystal globe. The wooden wall was receding as the submersible backed out. All the bits of flotsam were still flowing back out of Drowned Wednesday, rather more slowly than they'd streamed in, so it seemed she had stopped moving and lowered her mouth.

"Tail-eye!"

The view changed to show the open sea behind them.

"If she'll just stay still long enough for us to back right out and go through another hole . . ." muttered Longtayle. "All we need is a minute. One minute . . ."

No one spoke as they all watched the tail-eye view. It slowly changed, the debris floating more freely and the white walls of bone being left behind.

"Snout-eye."

The globe flashed and there was the immense wall of white bone ahead of them, riddled with holes.

"Do you want to pick a hole, Lord Arthur?" asked Longtayle as they continued to back through the sea.

"No! Just aim for one!"

"Port thirty and take her up," ordered Longtayle.

The submarine rattled and groaned as the engines returned to forward thrust. Ever so slowly the *Balaena* began to move towards a new hole. Then there was a strange rush of speed, and both white walls and dark hole rushed towards the submersible.

"She's moving forward again!"

"Steady helm, straight at that hole!"

"Let's hope this one's not bunged up," said Suzy.

"The currents would clean them out," said Arthur distractedly. He was trying to watch the crystal globe. They were lined up okay for the new tunnel, but it would only take a slight shift for them to miss it. "It must have been a big ship to get stuck. We were just unlucky to hit that one."

"But very fortunate to come back out again," said Doctor Scamandros nervously.

"Here we go!" cried Suzy. "Straight as an arrow!"

Chapter Twenty-three

There was no obstruction in the new tunnel. The *Balaena* passed through it at a steady pace, helped along by the steadily increasing current. Drowned Wednesday was on the move again and seawater, food, and debris were once more rushing into her gullet.

The tunnel through the plate was only a hundred yards long. As they emerged from the far end, Arthur found that he had been holding his breath. He let it out, but didn't gain any real feeling of relief. There were bound to be so many troubles and obstacles ahead. And even if they did manage to get the Will, they'd still have to come back out.

Which is going to be difficult, Arthur thought. *I guess we can go faster forward, but if the current is too strong, the* Balaena *won't be able to get out unless Drowned Wednesday stops for long enough. . . .*

Once through the straining plate, the *Balaena* followed the current into the broad lake that was the inside of Drowned Wednesday's mouth. They crossed that in twenty minutes, the engines straining to maintain steerage way as the current grew swifter, the food-laden waters gathering to pass into Drowned Wednesday's throat.

But this was almost routine work for the submersible, like navigating a tidal estuary. The throat was very wide, and though there was a lot of material being carried along, there was nothing that posed a threat to the *Balaena*. Much of it was fish and sea creatures of all kinds, mixed in with salvage.

Arthur had even started to relax a little as the pumps cleared the bridge of water and both Longtayle and the helmsrat resumed their usual calm dialogue of orders and information.

Then, about two miles down the throat, without any warning, the *Balaena* was suddenly picked up and flipped over in a complete somersault. Arthur nearly slid out of his straps, and once again was struck by flying debris, including the lid of the teapot, which gave the ring of pure silver as it hit him on the head.

At the same time, a strange electric tingle passed through Arthur's body and the ends of his fingers burst into smoky green flames that disappeared a moment later, just as he cried out and started shaking his hands.

The whole thing happened so quickly that no one had time to react. It was like being on an unfamiliar fairground ride that had suddenly whipped around and no one was sure whether it was going to do it again.

"We've passed through a sorcerous membrane of some kind," wheezed Doctor Scamandros. His greatcoat had ridden up around his throat and got tangled, and he was having difficulty pulling it back into place.

"Pressure gauges have all reset," reported the helmsrat. "According to this, we're only five fathoms down, and there's air above us. No current to speak of either. Still water, or near enough."

Longtayle scratched his ear.

"Guess we went through some kind of valve. Take us up to top-eye depth."

"Aye, aye, sir."

A few minutes later, the top-eye view in the globe revealed the surface of a sea within Drowned Wednesday, or a large lake. It was illuminated by a pinkish glow from the stomach roof high above, a glow Doctor Scamandros suggested was from the reaction of specks of Nothing with particles of the House, both of them eaten by Wednesday and caked onto her stomach lining.

"Very dangerous," the sorcerer added, staring into the globe with fascination and dread. "Too much Nothing. If enough of it managed to unfix from the House particles and it became concentrated . . ."

"Can we look for anything like a . . . well, anything big enough to be Feverfew's worldlet?" asked Arthur.

"Rotate top-eye."

The view in the crystal globe slowly moved around. At first it revealed only more monotonous, greenlit sea. Then there was a sudden flare of color, bright enough to make Arthur blink.

There, a few miles away, was a shining dome rising out of the sea. A dome easily a thousand yards high and five or six miles in diameter, its rainbow sides shimmering with all the colors of the spectrum, like a giant soap bubble in the sun.

"Immaterial Walls," commented Doctor Scamandros. "Very fine work, particularly on such a scale."

"That's it," said Arthur. "It has to be. Now we need to find the entrance."

"Keep us at top-eye depth," instructed Longtayle. "We'll do a circumnavigation, see if anything is visible. Snout-eye view."

"Probably be guards somewhere," said Suzy. "Or traps or the like. I mean, it is a pirate's secret worldlet, ain't it? If it were mine, I'd have guards and traps all over the place."

"Let's hope not," said Arthur. "I mean, it *is* inside a giant whale, to start with, and Feverfew comes and goes by sorcery. It's not as if they'd be expecting anyone to come in except the salvage slaves they sent out."

"Speaking of salvage slaves, I think that might be one there," said Longtayle. He pointed at a dim shape in the globe. "Not moving, though . . ."

Arthur leaned forward to get a better look. There was a human-shaped figure standing still on the stomach floor. As the submersible edged closer and its lights shone through the murky water, the figure became clearer. It was humanoid, rather than human. About seven feet tall, it had a human face with a beard and long hair, but its muscular bare arms glittered with green scales, and there was webbing between its fingers.

"A Nisser," said Longtayle. "But petrified or frozen."

"What's a Nisser?" asked Arthur. The creature had been stilled in the act of reaching out for something, his webbed fingers ready to grab. He looked angry, his mouth open, showing many small sharp teeth.

"Drowned Wednesday's guards," said Longtayle. "Like the Commissionaires in the Lower House, or the Winged Servants of the Night in the Middle House. She ate them up."

"This one made it through," said Suzy. "Do you reckon we can wake him up, Doc?"

Scamandros put his quartz-lensed glasses on his forehead and peered at the globe. Then he shook his head.

"He is tightly wound with a very sophisticated binding. I could unpick it, but not easily, and not underwater."

"Feverfew, I guess," said Arthur. "Hey! There's another one, closer in."

"Port ten and slow ahead," instructed Longtayle.

The submersible gently turned and progressed closer to the rainbow-hued dome. Its light spread through the water now, dimming the white beams from the submersible's front. In this ripple of colors, there was a dark silhouette. Another Nisser, this time frozen in the instant she had raised a trident for a killing thrust.

"And another two," said Suzy. "Over there, right near the dome."

She pointed at two tiny dark specks on the very edge of the snout-eye view. But when the *Balaena* drew closer, the two figures were not Nisser. They were Denizens, or rather the skeletons of long-drowned Denizens, dressed in rags and manacled at the ankles, a long, algae-covered chain stretching between them. Both clutched long rakes, the metal heads blooming with rusty flakes and curls.

Arthur was both horrified and fascinated to see that the Denizen's bones were, as far as he could tell in the rainbow light, a dull golden color.

"Interesting," said Scamandros. "Denizens don't usually

decompose. I suppose this water must have stomach acids in it, like a mortal creature. Or it may be the result of Nothing contamination. I presume this pair must be enslaved flotsam rakers."

Longtayle's tail twitched. Arthur saw him look around the bridge, as if he might see signs of the corrosive sea already affecting the submersible.

"That brings up an important matter," said Longtayle. "We must presume that the waters of this stomach are dangerous to the *Balaena*, so we cannot linger. I'm afraid we can only give you twelve hours, Lord Arthur. After that, we must attempt to leave the Leviathan."

"Is that twelve hours from when we find the way in?" asked Suzy.

"Twelve hours from now," said Longtayle.

Arthur nodded. He was still staring into the globe. There was something about the rainbow-hued wall just beyond the two skeletons. If he looked from the corner of his eye, he could see something that might be an arched doorway. But when he looked straight on, all he could see were swirls of color, shifting and changing like oil in a puddle on the road.

"Can anyone else see a door?" he asked. "An archway, about eight feet high, just behind the left-hand skeleton?"

"Nope," said Suzy.

"No," said Longtayle.

Doctor Scamandros put his glasses on his forehead and looked closely where Arthur was pointing.

"Mmmm, an archway . . . yes . . . yes, there is a two-way membrane through the Immaterial Wall. Very cleverly concealed. How did you spot it, Arthur?"

"I was just looking," replied the boy. "But I can only see it out of the corner of my eye."

"A useful talent," said Doctor Scamandros. "Particularly for you, Lord Arthur. I should make a habit of looking out of the corner of your eye. You never know what might be there, unseen."

"If there is a doorway there," said Longtayle, "we'd best drop you off, Lord Arthur, and find somewhere to hide the *Balaena*."

"How will you know when to come and get us?" asked Arthur.

Longtayle reached into his pocket and pulled out a small wooden box. Opening it, he showed Arthur a tiny green bottle packed in cotton wool.

"This is a one-shot bottle," he said. "Paired to one here. It can send only a single word, which is already in it. All you have to do is pull out the cork and the message will go. As soon as we get it, we'll come in for the rendezvous.

Also, if anything happens to us and we can't pick you up, the bottle will crumble to dust."

"Thanks," said Arthur. He turned his head to look sideways at the globe. The arched door was still there, about fifteen feet away. "Doctor Scamandros, this membrane thing in the Immaterial Wall — does that mean there'll be air on the other side of the door?"

"Probably. But not certainly."

"Have you got one of those clothespeg charms? You know, the 'thousand and one breaths' thing?"

"I fear not, Arthur. Has the one Wednesday's Dawn provided already failed?"

Arthur nodded and looked at the globe again.

"It's not far," said Suzy, correctly guessing that Arthur was worried about the distance underwater from the submersible to the door. "Bound to be air on the other side, even if we have to go up for it."

"Providing the water doesn't dissolve us or burn us," said Arthur. He knew he was procrastinating, but he couldn't help it. "And what if there's a trap, like you were talking about before?"

"Nah, you're right," said Suzy. "Why bother, if you're inside a whale?"

"I hope you're right," said Arthur. "Or I'm right. Okay, I guess we'd better get going."

He picked up his rat nose and rat tail and started to put them on.

"Are these things waterproof, by the way?"

"Hmm?" asked Doctor Scamandros, who was looking at the dome wall again.

"Are they waterproof?"

"Of course! I am a marine sorcerer, remember. Every charm and spell I have made since I signed on to the *Moth* has been highly resolute in the face of dissolution by the universal solvent!"

"So they're not exactly waterproof," said Suzy, while Arthur was still trying to work out what Scamandros had said. "How long will they stand up to a good soaking?"

A ship tattoo that was sailing across Scamandros's face suddenly hit a rock and sank, though it did manage to launch its boats, which rowed away towards his chin.

"It is very unusual to demand complete waterproofing," sniffed Scamandros. "I would expect these charms to withstand an immersion of four or five hours in normal seawater. Less in this noxious brew. It is the paper, of course, that is most at risk, though woollen yarn, once sodden, is also —"

"Thank you, Doctor," interrupted Arthur. "If we're going, let's go."

Better to get this part over with, he thought. *At least I'll be out of this metal coffin. . . .*

"There is an escape chamber towards the stern," said Longtayle. "You'll have to go out one at a time."

"I'll go first!" said Suzy.

"No, you won't," said Arthur. "I'll go first this time. It's my responsibility."

Suzy shrugged and tipped her hat, allowing Arthur to go ahead of her to the rear bulkhead door.

The submersible was longer than Arthur had thought. Having only seen from the conning tower to the bridge, he was surprised by how much corridor they had to go along, and how many doors they went through. But they encountered only one other Rat, waiting for them at a door marked Dorsal Escape Aft. Arthur was surprised to see it was Gunner's Mate First Watkingle.

"Did you volunteer?"

Watkingle grinned, which looked rather fearsome on a four-foot-tall rat.

"Always volunteer, that's my motto, sir," he said. "None of this 'don't get into trouble' namby-pamby stuff. Why, when I think of the things I might 'ave missed —"

"Thank you, Watkingle," said Longtayle quellingly. "Show Lord Arthur and Miss Suzy to the escape chamber."

"Aye, aye," said Watkingle. He turned his head slightly so Longtayle couldn't see and winked at Arthur before undogging the door and opening it. The chamber beyond was like a very small shower stall with a hatch in the ceiling instead of a showerhead. On the side of the hatch were two handles. One was painted yellow and one painted red. A brass plaque on the hatch said in inch-high letters PULL YELLOW. WAIT FOR IMMERSION TO THE RED LINE. PULL RED.

"The procedure for emergency evacuation from the craft is simple and straightforward," lectured Watkingle in a singsong voice. "First, you will enter the chamber and close the door behind you. It will automatically latch and cannot be reopened from inside. Second, grasp the yellow handle with one paw and pull. This will open a valve and water will enter the chamber. Third, when the water level reaches the red line painted around the wall of the chamber, take a normal breath. Do not take many breaths or take a deep breath. Then, grasp the red handle with one paw and pull. This will open the exit hatch. Fourth, kick off from the floor and swim out. Understood?"

Arthur looked into the chamber. The red line was about four inches from the top. He would have to crouch a bit and keep his head back to have his face out of the water for that last breath. The hatch was big enough for him to fit through without a problem.

"Okay," he said. "Get in. Pull yellow handle. Wait till the water reaches the red line. Take a breath. Pull red handle. Swim out."

"That's it, sir," said Watkingle.

"I'll swim to the door and go through," Arthur told Suzy. "I'll meet you on the other side."

"This looks like fun," said Suzy. She rubbed her hands together and added, "Sure I can't go first?"

"No," said Arthur. "As in 'no, you can't go first.' I guess we'd better put on our disguises now."

He tied on the rat nose and fixed the tail. When he looked around, Suzy was near his feet, already a rat. Arthur presumed he appeared to be a rat as well.

"I'm ready," he said.

Suzy squeaked something back at him.

"What?" asked Arthur. Then the realization hit him: They looked and sounded like rats to each other as well as to everyone else.

Arthur lifted off his rat mask and unhitched his tail.

"We won't be able to talk to each other when we're wearing these," he said. "So once we're inside, follow me."

Suzy squeaked, then was herself again, holding her rat nose.

"Whatever you say," she said.

Before Arthur could make sure she really meant it, she'd turned back into a rat.

"I mean it," said Arthur. "Follow . . . as in, stay behind me."

He slipped the rat nose back on and refastened his tail, then stepped into the escape chamber. The door shut behind him and he heard a heavy bolt or latch sliding across.

Arthur rubbed his suddenly sweaty hands against his breeches, checked that the Atlas and Wednesday's invitation were secure in his Immaterial Boot, and reached up to pull the yellow handle.

Water flowed in with shocking speed. It didn't sting or dissolve his clothes, but it did smell very strongly of ozone. Arthur barely had time to register this and take a breath before the water hit the red line. It was up around his eyes before he even pulled the red handle. Instantly, the hatch above flicked open.

Arthur clumsily kicked the floor, favoring his bad leg, so that he didn't get clear of the escape chamber in one go. He had to push against the wall till he rose up in a froth of bubbles from the small pocket of air that had been left, mixed with the atmosphere trapped under his clothes.

Orientating himself from the line of the submersible's hull, Arthur struck out for where the door was supposed to be. The rainbow light from the dome was much brighter when seen directly, so for a moment Arthur couldn't see the archway even from the corner of his eye. Panic started to rise in him, until he calmed himself with the simple thought that even if he didn't find the door, all he had to do was rise to the surface. Though if he did that, it might be hard to dive back down again.

Then he saw the archway, a little bit to the left of where he thought it was. Arthur already felt as if he needed a breath, but he was used to that feeling. He kicked harder, feeling the strangeness of his crab-armored leg, and scooped harder with his arm stroke.

The archway drew nearer. Looking down, Arthur saw that the layer of fine debris and muck below him contained many bones, broken skulls, and pieces of rusted chain. Evidence of the scores, possibly even hundreds, of slave salvagers who had either failed to return to Feverfew's worldlet . . .

. . . Or who had been thrown out, to die in the belly of the Leviathan.

Chapter Twenty-four

Arthur reached the doorway. As he touched it, the rainbow colors drifted away, to be replaced by a featureless gray. Even more disturbingly, his hand went through it as if there was nothing there.

The boy didn't stop. He kicked again, and went through the gray archway, to land sprawling on a wet stone floor.

"What was that?" asked a voice.

Arthur rolled over and sat up, ready to move. He saw that he was in a large, timber-walled room — more of a shed or barn really, since the far end was completely open and there was bright sunshine streaming in.

There were four Denizens sitting on a wild variety of chairs of different styles and eras, around a highly polished table that even to Arthur looked like a priceless antique. The Denizens were all dressed in flamboyant and ill-matching finery, mixing up everything from twentieth-century Earth military tunics to glittering, lumpy, alien-looking helmets. Every inch of their visible skin was tattooed, and they all had at least three knives in their belts, as well as short, pistol-grip crossbows on the floor next to their chairs.

"What was what?" another Denizen asked.

Arthur moved very slowly towards the wall. There was no cover at all, nothing in the room save the table and chairs, but there was a narrow band of shadow along the edge where the floor met the wall.

One of the Denizens stood up.

"I thought I heard something near the water gate."

Arthur crouched in the shadow.

It'll take a while to pump out the escape chamber ready for Suzy to come through, he thought. *But maybe she'll swim faster than I did. If she comes through now, the Denizen will see her for sure, even as a rat. . . .*

"Sit down! It's your turn!"

The Denizen slowly sat down and turned his attention to whatever was on the table. Some sort of game, Arthur saw, being played on a board with glittering pieces made from gold and gems. Not chess, because he didn't recognize the pieces, and all four Denizens were playing. They each had piles of paper in front of them too, which changed hands frequently. Not bank notes, but badly torn-up scraps and pieces with scrawled writing on them.

Arthur crawled along the wall, thinking furiously. If Suzy came out now, and they heard her, he'd try to distract them.

"What was that?"

The same Denizen stood up again. Arthur looked around and saw a rat scuttle across the floor, out of the archway.

"A rat!"

All of the Denizens erupted out of their chairs, sending them flying. As they bent down to grab their crossbows, Arthur ran straight at them. Not daring to hesitate, he jumped on the table, kicked the board over, and jumped again to the far side, almost stumbling as a sharp pain shot through his bad leg, despite the crab armor's support.

"Another rat!"

"It's mine!"

"Ware crossbow!"

A crossbow bolt zinged to the left of Arthur, sending chips of stone flying. He zigzagged and another bolt whisked past his ear. Then he was outside, in the bright sunshine, standing on sandy ground strewn with rocks. There was a stand of palm trees nearby, the first of a whole line that stretched along the narrow peninsula back to the island proper.

Arthur hurled himself towards the closest palm, continuing to zig and zag, but there were no more crossbow bolts. Once he got behind the trunk, he risked a glance back.

The four Denizens were standing by the entrance to the

shed, reloading their crossbows. They didn't look like they were going to pursue Arthur.

There was no sign of Suzy. Arthur scanned the ground, his breath coming in ragged gasps as he grew more afraid that she had been hit by a crossbow bolt. After a few breaths that didn't get properly into his lungs, Arthur tried to calm down.

This is a bubble from the Secondary Worlds, he told himself. *The bubble is inside the House but the bubble contains a fragment of a Secondary Realm. Maybe even of Earth. It looks like it. So I'll get asthma here. Have to be careful. Don't push too hard. . . .*

A sudden squeak near his foot made Arthur jump. He looked down. A rat was looking up at him, making gestures with her paws.

"Suzy!" Arthur exclaimed, before he remembered she would only hear a squeak.

Suzy squeaked some more, insistently. Arthur correctly translated this as "Get a move on!"

He turned and, jogging rather than running, moved to the next palm, and then the next. As he jogged, he looked ahead, trying to match up the geography with the map he'd seen.

There was the harbor off to the right. Arthur could see

the hulks of at least a dozen vessels all piled up on the far side. Total wrecks, or near enough. But closer, floating at anchor, were the *Shiver* and the *Moth*. And worst of all there was the *Flying Mantis*, its sails furled, their green radiance dimmed.

"So Feverfew has captured Leaf," Arthur muttered to himself.

If she isn't already dead.

He stopped, sheltered by a clump of palms, to get his breath back and look around more easily.

There were half a dozen low stone buildings clustered around the quay, clearly warehouses. Up the slight hill from there was Feverfew's fort, a building of earth and stone ramparts shaped like a star within a star, with cannons visible on many levels. Across from that, and under its guns, were three ramshackle wooden buildings, little more than long sheds, with holes for windows.

Slave quarters, Arthur thought.

There were few signs of life. The occasional glint from the helmet of a sentry in the fort, and a bit of movement aboard the *Shiver*. But the slave quarters were still. The breeze was blowing towards Arthur, but he couldn't hear anything, save the plaintive cry of some kind of seabird. He looked for that, remembering the black cormorants that had flow from the buoy to warn Feverfew, but no birds were visible.

Arthur looked away, up to the hills, where the Raised Rat spy had noted *Followers of the Carp. Escaped Slaves.* on her map.

The hills were a lot higher than he'd expected, perhaps more than a thousand feet, and were also covered in what looked like dense jungle or rain forest. It would not be easy to climb them or to find anyone there, particularly if they were trying to stay hidden.

Suzy squeaked something at him and jumped up and down on the spot, an action Arthur took to mean "get on with it."

He got on with it, walking quickly to the next clump of palms. His breathing was all right, but he knew he couldn't take any risks. He had no medication here. No inhaler, and no paramedics with beta-agonists and oxygen or emergency rooms nearby.

Suzy squeaked again and did a somersault, showing her impatience.

"I can't go any faster," said Arthur, even though he knew she'd hear only the squeak. He shrugged his shoulders up and down as well.

It did seem to pacify Suzy for the moment. She stopped being agitated and walked along with Arthur peaceably enough. They still went from clump to clump of palms, to be on the safe side, and every fifty yards or so Arthur stopped to listen and look around. The peninsula they were on was about a mile from the harbor, so he figured they should be reasonably safe.

After a while, they left the peninsula and started out across the mainland, where the palms and sandy ground gave way to thick dark earth with lots of rocky outcrops, and stunted, windblown trees with gray-green leaves. These spread low to the ground and made the going more difficult, particularly as Arthur occasionally found himself thinking he was much smaller than he was, and hit his head on a branch. This was disturbing, as it suggested Doctor Scamandros's rat disguises were having some effect on their wearers as well as observers. But Arthur couldn't worry about it. He concentrated on heading toward the hills, watching out for pirates or cormorants or other things that might serve Feverfew, and keeping his breathing steady.

The stunted, spreading gray-green trees didn't last long. As the ground continued to rise, the bare earth and stones were replaced by leaf litter, small ferns, larger ferns, and big pale-trunked trees that rose straight up for forty or fifty feet before spreading out to make a thick canopy that greatly reduced the light and heat from the sun.

The air felt much more moist too, and there were little rivulets of water to jump across every ten yards or so, usually into soft ground that was not quite mud — or if it was, it had a sufficient layer of leaves, bracken, and forest debris to make it more solid.

There were occasional small noises in this verdant undergrowth, but nothing too alarming, and Arthur hadn't seen any footprints or other signs that the pirates ever left their harborside dwelling. He was also starting to think of himself more and more as a rat, so when they had clambered up to a clearing that he thought marked the first stage of their hill ascent, he stopped and took off his rat mask and tail.

Suzy didn't take hers off. She sniffed around his feet and then sat in a begging posture, squeaking. Finally Arthur leaned down, gripped the rat by the nose and tail, both of which felt totally authentic, and pulled.

Finding himself suddenly pinching Suzy's real nose and tugging on a loose piece of cloth from her ripped-up dress, Arthur let go.

"Cor, what I wouldn't give for a piece of cheese," Suzy said as she massaged her nose. "I reckon the Doctor made those charms too strong. I was only following you that last bit cause you were another rat and I thought you might know where some food was."

"At least they worked properly to begin with," said Arthur. He peered up at the sky and then back down the slope. He could just see the topmast of the *Mantis* and a patch of blue that was the outer harbor. The harbor buildings were out of sight, obscured by a ridge lower down. But in the valley below, he could see a huge circular patch of dark brown edged in bright yellow. He realized this must be the nose cavity of the skull he'd seen drawn on the map. A lake of mud that the mapmaker had also annotated with the word *Nothing* and a question mark.

After watching the lake for a few seconds, Arthur saw that the mud must be hot, for huge bubbles appeared and the surface was in constant, low movement as the mud roiled and turned over.

"Bet that fair stinks," said Suzy, looking down at the lake. "Lucky the wind's the other way. Where to now?"

"I think we're about halfway up the first hill," said Arthur. "But I really don't know for sure. I wonder where these Followers of the Carp hang out? I mean, where would you go if you'd escaped from the pirates? Besides away from the harbor, which we've done."

"Up," said Suzy. "They're Denizens, right? They always want to go up. Up is good, inside the House. The higher the better. That's why the superior ones, like the Noons and such, make themselves tall. Got a thing about it. Bit silly really, just makes it harder to get clothes to fit."

"Up," said Arthur. "That makes sense. Unfortunately. I hope I'll be okay to keep climbing."

"What's wrong?" asked Suzy. She hadn't spent any time with Arthur in the Secondary Realms when he didn't have a Key.

"I have a . . . I guess you'd call it a breathing sickness," said Arthur. "Sometimes it comes on if I do too much exercise. Because this worldlet is part of the Secondary Realms, I might get affected by it."

"Like black lung, is it?" asked Suzy, clearly interested. "Or the greenspit cough?"

"Maybe," said Arthur. "Don't worry about it, though. I feel fine for now. Slow and steady, that's how we'll go."

"Without the rat disguises?"

Arthur nodded. "We should be okay up here. But we'd better hang on to them just in case we need to use them to get back out."

After a brief rest, they continued on. The rain forest drew in again as they left the clearing, and there were no obvious paths. Arthur simply went where the undergrowth had a gap in it or was less sparse, but he always aimed uphill.

After another half hour or so of thrashing their way upslope, Arthur paused for another rest. He wanted to wait till they hit a clearing, but there had been no sign of one and he had to take a break.

"Not much to see, is there?" said Suzy. "Smells a bit too."

Arthur sniffed at the rich odor of the forest.

"It's only all the leaves and stuff turning into mulch," he said. "I wonder whether the Followers of the Carp have built houses up here, or found caves or something. You wouldn't last long just camping out."

"Could be worse," said Suzy. "Down in the Pit or in the Lower House Coal Cellar."

"Or collecting salvage for Feverfew," said Arthur. He was thinking of all the golden bones strewn outside the dome. "They must not last long doing that."

"Who speaks of Feverfew?!" boomed a voice out of the undergrowth — a deep, powerful voice, trained to rise above the fiercest gale.

Chapter Twenty-five

"Who speaks of Feverfew?"

Arthur and Suzy leapt to their feet and drew their weapons. But there was no sign of the person who'd spoken. The rain forest around them was quiet and still.

"No one ever looks up," continued the voice. "Interesting, isn't it?"

Arthur looked up, his sword at the ready. There was a Denizen high up in the nearest tree, hanging on with the aid of hooked spurs in his boots and what looked like clawed gloves, though Arthur wasn't entirely sure if they were gloves or actually the Denizen's hands. He was wearing a shirt and breeches of light tan splattered with patches of green mold, effective camouflage for the rain forest, particularly since the mold looked like it had spread across the Denizen's skin as well.

"Now for the traditional questions," said the Denizen. "And the traditional warning. Answer correctly, or you will die where you stand. Or, to tell a truth, die a bit later, because our arrows, while tipped with Nothing-contaminated mud, are not very effective."

Arthur looked around as the Denizen spoke. There were rustlings in the undergrowth around them, and he spotted several other green-mold-and-tan-wearing Denizens moving up on them. These ones had short bows. Not crossbows, but the simple stave and bowstring kind.

"We're friends," called out Arthur. "We're looking for the Followers of the Carp."

"Can you just wait for the questions?" asked the Denizen up the tree. "Let's do this properly, please."

"Sure," said Arthur.

Suzy yawned and sat back down.

"Denizens," she muttered to herself.

"Are you now or have you ever been a pirate?" asked the Denizen.

"No," said Arthur.

"Do you serve the pirate Feverfew in any capacity?"

"No," said Arthur.

"Do you believe in the Carp?"

"Uh, I'm not sure what you mean. I want to meet it —"

"Is that a 'no'?" asked the Denizen.

Arthur took a sideways glance at the bow-wielding Denizens, who were nocking arrows and drawing bowstrings back.

"We do believe in the Carp, don't we, Suzy?"

"Sure," said Suzy. "I'll believe whatever you want."

"You must have faith in the Carp," said the Denizen. This statement was echoed in a whisper all around.

Arthur nodded vigorously several times, indicating that he had tons of faith in the Carp.

"Now, also for the record, state your names."

Arthur thought for a moment.

If the Carp is who I think it is, I can't go wrong. But if it isn't, then . . .

"This 'ere's Lord Arthur, Master of the Lower House, Lord of the Far Reaches, Hero of the House, Eater of the Biscuit, and Rightful Heir of the whole lot," said Suzy, standing up again. "And I'm Suzanna Monday's Tierce, so you'd better act a bit more respectful, if you don't mind."

"Really?" asked the Denizen in the tree. "I mean, I have faith and all, but are you really the Rightful Heir?"

"Yes," said Arthur. "I am. Can you take us to the Carp?"

"And you're going to rescue us all from Feverfew's dominion?"

"What?"

"Rescue us, like the Carp says you will."

"Uh, I have to talk to the Carp first."

"How many of you are there?" asked Suzy. She was staring out between two of the trees, where more and more green-tinged Denizens were becoming visible as they moved out of cover.

"Seven hundred and seventy-nine, at last count," said the Denizen as he slid down the tree trunk, his boot-spikes shredding bark. He landed and bowed in one smooth motion.

"Allow me to present myself. I am Jebenezer, First Follower of the Carp, and formerly Second Mate of the *Naiad*, may her wooden bones rot in peace."

Before Arthur could answer, a female Denizen pushed forward and bowed, declaring, "I am the Second Follower of the Carp, and my name is Pennina!"

"I am the Third Follower," shouted someone else, farther back. "My name is Garam. I have faith in the Carp!"

A cacophony of voices followed, with Denizens shouting out their names, their numerical ranking as Followers, and various protestations of faith in the Carp, belief that the Rightful Heir would come, and other stuff that Arthur couldn't hear properly over the din.

As they shouted, the Denizens moved closer and closer. More and more of them appeared out of the undergrowth, till there was a great crowd advancing on Arthur.

"Uh, I think I'd like to see the Carp right now," said Arthur as he retreated back against a tree trunk. Many of the Denizens had forgotten to put away their Nothing-poisoned arrows, and there were lots of muddy, sharp arrowheads sticking out ahead of them, straight at Arthur.

"The Rightful Heir says everyone take three steps back!" shouted Suzy, but even her sharp voice was lost in the tumult.

"I'm the Ninety-Ninth Follower —"

"Hundred and Sixth —"

"I believe —"

"Faith in the —"

"The Carp! The Carp!"

"Three steps back!" roared Jebenezer, at a volume to match Sunscorch's best shout.

The Denizens halted, then — after some scuffling — stepped back. Arthur took a breath, found he couldn't get a full lungful, and concentrated on staying calm.

"Lord Arthur wants to see the Carp," said Suzy.

"I'm in a bit of a hurry," Arthur added, a slight wheeze underlying his words. He looked at his watch. They'd been out of the submersible for two hours. Ten hours to go before the *Balaena* departed, and now he had nearly eight hundred Denizens thinking he was going to do something for them as well.

"Of course, sir! Follow me!" said Jebenezer. He pushed two Denizens aside and gestured at the others to move to make Arthur a path through the crowd. "It's just natural high spirits, sir, most of us having been trapped on this island for so long, and in fear of recapture. Feverfew always sinks captured slaves."

"Sinks?" asked Suzy.

"In the Hot Lake," Jebenezer continued. "If the mud doesn't drown you, or the heat burn you up, the patches of Nothing do the business. Nothing's quick, of course, or should be. But Feverfew don't let that happen. He's got a yardarm rigged up so he can lower you in a bit at a time, like a leg or whatever. A hand usually. He likes to start with the hands —"

"I get the idea!" interrupted Arthur. He felt very tense. Every minute wasted could mean disaster, and he had so many problems and so many decisions to make. And then there was the asthma, lurking. . . .

"Where is the Carp?" asked Suzy. "Is it far from here?"

"Why, the Carp is under our feet, ma'am," said Jebenezer. "When the Carp first freed the slaves, that's the first twenty, which is me and Pennina and Garam and Obelin and Herush and Peppertoe and Thin Edric and —"

"Maybe save the names for later," said Arthur. "Just tell me the basic story."

"Well, when the Carp freed us from our shackles in the dead of night, we picked him up and carried him into these hills. He said if we had faith, and looked around, we'd find a place to shelter, a fortress safe from Feverfew. And sure enough, we soon found a mighty cave, and it has served us ever since as our home. And the Carp said that we must have faith that the Rightful Heir would one day come and bring us all back to the House, and blow me down if it isn't happening, and me still here without being dissolved into Nothing or my bones bleaching out in the Stomach! Here we are."

The Denizen stopped before what appeared to be a cliff face, a vertical section of pale yellow rock, liberally covered with the same green mold or lichen that grew on his clothes and skin.

"Just step through, sir. It looks solid, but if you believe it to be a door, as the Carp says, then it'll be a door."

"That Carp sounds like a right pain in the midsection," grumbled Suzy in a low voice to Arthur. "And a faker as well. I bet it just made the cavern entrance look like this and carried on with all that belief hocus-pocus."

"We won't get that mold growing on us, will we?" Arthur asked Jebenezer.

"Oh, no, sir!" the Denizen replied. "That's the Carp's special moss, that is, not mold. It takes cultivation to get that growing right, that does."

Arthur shut his eyes and stepped forward, holding his

hands in front of his face, just in case he did run straight into a mossy cliff.

After four or five paces, when he didn't suddenly impact with rock, Arthur opened his eyes. He found himself in soft darkness, lit here and there by soft green lights. Some of the lights moved, including one close, bright clump of green lights above Arthur's head.

"The moss is luminous!" he said.

"Aye, it shines in the darkness, to illuminate our path," said Jebenezer. "As does the Carp."

"It doesn't shine very well," said Suzy. "And I can't see a path."

Arthur looked around, but he couldn't see anything more than a few feet away. But judging from the echo of Suzy's voice, and the patches of both moving and static green light, he knew he had to be standing inside a huge cavern, somewhere near the top. It looked like it extended downward for a few hundred feet and back for at least as far.

"The path to the Carp is a little difficult," admitted Jebenezer. "Even with the gift of our light. I'd better go first, and you might care to hold the back of my belt, sir. Miss Suzy, please hold Lord Arthur's coattails."

Suzy muttered something that Arthur felt he was probably glad not to hear. He reached out and hooked two fingers through the back of Jebenezer's belt. With one leg not as nimble as it should be — though the crab armor did a great job — he didn't want to take any risks in the dark. He felt Suzy grab hold of his coattails a moment later.

As a makeshift train it was a slow shuffle down. Most of the time Arthur couldn't see how narrow the path was, or how far he could fall, but every now and then they encountered a large patch of the glowing moss in exactly the right place to illuminate the danger.

Despite these momentary flashes of light and terror, they reached the cavern floor without incident. For the first time, Arthur looked back and was unnerved to see a long line of moving green light zigzagging back up behind them. It looked as if all eight hundred–odd Followers of the Carp were coming down the path. All very quiet now, in contrast to their shouting outside.

"We approach the Carp," whispered Jebenezer. He pointed ahead, indicating a straight way lit by regularly spaced clumps of luminous moss. At the far end, perhaps two hundred feet away, there was a soft, golden light that occasionally twinkled with a red glint, as if there was a distant fire caught by a mirror.

"The Carp's road is flat; there is no danger," said Jebenezer. "You should go ahead here, Lord Arthur, and we will follow."

Arthur let go of Jebenezer's belt and started walking slowly towards the gold-red light. He was having last-minute doubts with each step. Surely, the Carp had to be Part Three of the Will? But what if it wasn't? What if it was some other powerful entity, something like the Old One in the Coal Cellar? Something strange, strong, and dangerous that was expecting some other kind of Rightful Heir, somebody else entirely.

As he drew closer, Arthur saw that the greenlit road ended and there was a band of darkness. Beyond that was a kind of sunken arena or theater, a deep bowl with terraced sides where the Denizens could sit. The gold-red light came from inside the bowl, but it was deep enough that he could not quite see its source.

Arthur crossed the darkness and stepped down onto the first terrace. He paused there for a moment, looking down. The light came from a huge glass bowl about twenty feet in diameter, with a bronze lid that appeared to be riveted to the glass in some way. The bowl was full of sparkling clean water, and in the water was the biggest goldfish Arthur had ever seen. It was ten feet long and six feet high, with huge goggly eyes and long mustache-like tendrils hanging down from its mouth.

Arthur stepped down to the next terrace and the next. There were forty in all before he reached the lowest and stood in front of the glass bowl. The goldfish watched him approach, just bobbing up and down. It didn't look very intelligent.

Arthur cleared his throat, not without some difficulty, and spoke.

"Greetings! I am Arthur, chosen by Part One of the Will to be the Rightful Heir to the House!"

"I knew you were coming," said the Carp, its words mysteriously echoing all around the arena. Its voice was of a strange pitch, and could have come from either a deep-voiced woman or a high-voiced man. "It is as I have told my Followers. Hold true to your faith that the Rightful Heir will come. The pirate Feverfew will be cast down, and we shall return to the House!"

"You are Part Three of the Will, aren't you?" asked Arthur. It was hard to see through the curved glass, but he could see that the fish was actually composed of tiny shining letters, moving in lines. Its skin was like the detailed etching on a banknote. From a distance it looked like solid color, but up really close you could see what it was made of.

"Indeed I am," replied the Carp. It did a circuit around the bowl and returned to face Arthur. "What was your name again?"

Chapter Twenty-six

"**A**rthur!"

The Carp blew out a huge stream of bubbles, and a strange chuckling, gargling sound filled the air. It took Arthur a moment to realize the goldfish was laughing.

"Only joking, Lord Arthur! I am not a goldfish, though I have that shape. While it is true I depend upon newly escaped slaves for news of the House and Realms beyond this island prison, I have heard of your heroic exploits!"

"You haven't read that book about me, have you?" asked Arthur. "Because it isn't true —"

"I have read no book," said the Carp. "I have merely heard stories. Now tell me of the ships waiting to enter this worldlet, and the legions amassed to assault the vile Feverfew's fort!"

"Uh, there's just me and Suzy," said Arthur. "We had to sneak in through Wednesday's stomach. In the Raised Rats' submersible."

"Only the two of you?" asked the Carp. It did four rapid circles of its bowl, then calmed down and approached Arthur again. "And you dealt with the Raised

Rats? You are very confident, Lord Arthur. But I expect that my Followers can defeat the pirates after you have slain Feverfew himself."

"I wasn't planning to run into Feverfew," said Arthur. "I just planned to sneak in here, find you — the Will — and sneak out again. The submersible is waiting to take us back out of Drowned Wednesday. Then Wednesday can release you and give me the Key. Once I have that, I can take on Feverfew. I have to rescue my friends in the slave huts — if they're still alive — as well as your Followers, but I can't do it straightaway."

"I have faith," muttered the Carp. "But there are limits. Why did you not bring the First and Second Keys with you? I cannot feel their presence."

"Because I want to stay human," said Arthur angrily. "I don't want to turn into a Denizen. This is all your stupid fault anyway. I mean, the Will's fault. I never wanted to get involved, but now I have to sort it all out and I wish I didn't have to but I do! So how about helping me instead of complaining?"

The Carp started doing circles again and did not respond, but Arthur heard a strange whooshing sound. He looked around and saw that the Followers of the Carp had begun to file into the amphitheater and sit down on the terraces in numerical order. Suzy and Jebenezer were right behind him.

The strange whooshing sound came from the assembled Denizens all drawing in highly indignant breaths at the same time. But before they could say anything or start throwing things, which some of them looked like they wanted to do, the Carp stopped circling and came right up to the glass near Arthur.

"You are the Rightful Heir, proclaimed by the two parts of the Will that precede me. There is no doubt about that. So I must help you to help myself. It is a pity that things were not arranged otherwise, but I believe it will all turn out for the best. How do you intend to take me to this submersible?"

Good question, thought Arthur.

"Uh, I was hoping you'd be in a more . . . mobile . . . shape. Can you get out of that bowl?"

"My current shape has been fixed by the Third Key, as part of my imprisonment," said the Carp. "If you had the other Keys you could free me, but that is water under the bridge. The bowl is a later addition of Feverfew's. As the Rightful Heir, I suspect you could banish the bowl, but then I should only be able to flop around on the ground."

Arthur scratched his head with both hands and resisted the urge to pull his hair out or start smacking his forehead.

"How did the slaves carry you up here, then?" asked Suzy. "You and that bowl would be a mighty heavy load even for twenty Denizens."

"Both my person and my bowl were smaller then," said the Carp. "As my following has grown, so I have grown, reflecting the worship of my Followers."

"So you can shrink yourself and the bowl?" asked Arthur.

"I could," admitted the Carp. "But it would not befit my station to appear less than I am."

"Shrink," commanded Arthur. "I haven't got time to argue about it. Get as small and light as you can."

"That is no way to speak to the Carp!" protested someone back up a terrace or two.

"Arthur is the Rightful Heir," said the Carp. "It is my duty to obey his orders, however given. I shall dwindle to a transportable size."

"First time I've seen a part of the Will with a sensible attitude," muttered Suzy.

"We still have to get back to the water gate," said Arthur. He took the small case and checked the green bottle inside. It was intact, he was pleased to see. So the *Balaena* had not encountered trouble. Or not yet. "There's those four pirates to get past too."

"May I have my Followers sing as I shrink?" asked the Carp.

"Sure, whatever. They can dance too, if they like," said Arthur. "But please hurry."

"Song of Faith Number Eighty-One," instructed the Carp. "I shall diminish myself and my bowl as the song progresses, and at the end shall be positively minute."

"How long is the song?" asked Suzy.

"A mere hundred verses and the chorus repeated as often," said the Carp. "I shall set the key."

"No," said Arthur. He was feeling really agitated and tense, as if every second lost was vital. "You've got two minutes. Please just shrink. We'll also need some help to fight the gate guards, so maybe, Jebenezer, you can pick a dozen —"

The boy stopped in midsentence as he thought that through. The Denizens who came to fight the guards at the water gate would never be able to get back to the hills. They'd have to go with Arthur to the *Balaena*.

"No, say just four of your very best archers to come with . . . to help us get past the gate."

Arthur turned to look at all the luminous green Denizens sitting on the terraces, and raised his voice.

"And I do promise that if I make it back out and get the Third Key, I will return! I will make sure you are all brought out to the House, even if I have to use the Improbable Stair to get here."

This speech did not evoke wild cheering, but the Denizens appeared slightly happier. Arthur sighed and twisted around to look at the Carp, and was taken aback. There was no longer any huge fishbowl with a giant carp in it. There was only Suzy and Jebenezer.

"What?"

Jebenezer held up something that looked like a jam jar full of water, with a two-inch goldfish whizzing around and around in it.

"Small enough?" asked the Carp. Its voice was still as loud, and omnidirectional.

"Thank you," said Arthur. It was a heartfelt expression of gratitude. "Jebenezer, can you carry the Will . . . I mean the Carp . . . and lead us out of here? And can you get those four archers?"

"I can," said Jebenezer. "But . . . but what is to happen to us when you leave with the Carp? It is only the Carp's powers that make this cavern safe from Feverfew. Once the pirate knows the Carp is gone, he will attack, and his sorcery will invade our home."

Why is nothing straightforward? thought Arthur. *It's bad enough that I can't go and rescue Leaf and the crews from the* Moth *and the* Mantis. *Now I have to worry about all these Denizens as well. I bet heroes who had only to beat up on dragons or monsters never had to worry about whole populations and their friends, not to mention what might happen to their family back home. . . .*

"I'll be back as soon as I can," said Arthur. "Perhaps you should split up and hide all over the hills."

"You must have faith," intoned the Carp.

"We must have faith," echoed back the Followers.

"I reckon splitting up and hiding might come in handy as well," said Suzy. "I mean, faith is fine and everything, but you got to be practical."

The Carp stopped circling and peered at Suzy for a moment.

"If you have faith, all will be well," said the Carp. "But to sharpen your faith, my Followers, I shall test it. When I have left, so must you disperse among the hills, in groups of no more than three, and meditate quietly. No singing, and no loud praising of me. If you are true to your faith, Lord Arthur will return and save you. If not, doubtless Feverfew will capture you and end your doubting existences in the Hot Lake."

"The Carp is wise, long swim the Carp!" chanted the Denizens as Arthur, Suzy, and Jebenezer started to climb back up through the terraces. As they passed through the crowd, Jebenezer held the jar up above his head, and the Carp's radiance lit up the faces of his Followers, while Jebenezer singled out the archers who were to accompany them to the water gate.

Ascending the path to the cavern exit was considerably

easier with the Carp's light, though Arthur was slightly shocked to see some parts of the path that he'd blithely walked along were not only narrow but the rock was crumbling on the edges as well. This time he traversed these sections with his back against the rock wall, trying not to think about how easily he could have put a foot wrong and fallen to his death.

It was a relief to get back outside. The sun was still shining, though it was a little lower in the sky. Coming out of the darkness, Arthur thought that the sunlight was tinged a little pink, like a grapefruit skin, and so the island was probably not a piece of his Earth, pinched off to become Feverfew's worldlet, but was from one of the myriad other worlds in the Secondary Realms.

"So, do we head straight back the way we came?" asked Suzy. "Cos if we are, I hope you know the way we came. I need streets and buildings, personally. Can't find my own elbow in these woods."

"The quickest path down from here goes round the shores of the Hot Lake," said Jebenezer. "Then we can strike nor'-nor'-east to the peninsula and follow that to the water gate. Only the pirates'll probably see us coming, either from the water gate, the fort, or the *Shiver*. We'll have to run the length of the peninsula, burst through the guards, and go into the Stomach."

"Is it a lack of faith to be thinking that we're all going to be slain or captured and sunk into the Hot Lake?" asked one of the four chosen archers.

"Yes," snapped the Carp. Its voice was more restrained now that it was out in the open. "Believe in Lord Arthur. Believe in your Carp. We shall prevail."

"Provided we get a move on," muttered Suzy.

I can't run the length of the peninsula, thought Arthur as panic began to make his stomach feel tight and his breathing shallower. *I just can't run that far without having an asthma attack. . . .*

"Shall we take the quick path, Lord Arthur?" asked Jebenezer.

I can't run that far. . . . I can't run that far. . . . Arthur's thoughts were in a loop of fear and doubt. He felt like he was drowning in them, unable to think about anything else. Then all of a sudden, he felt, rather than heard, the Carp speak, inside his head. He couldn't describe it or see it, but he experienced the Carp's words as if he heard them and read them at the same time.

Have faith in yourself, Arthur. Take it one step at a time. Let us get to the peninsula. Then we shall take the next step. Perhaps we will not need to run. Perhaps you will run better than you think. One step at a time.

You can read my mind! Arthur thought back.

Not normally, replied Part Three of the Will silently, for Arthur alone. *But your fear was so great that it opened the doorways of your mind. They are closing now, and I will not*

"Arthur! The quick path or not?" asked Suzy.

"Sorry," said Arthur. He shook his head and found it clear of the paralyzing fear he'd felt a moment before. "Yeah, let's take the quick path."

"Florenza and Padraic, take scout," ordered Jebenezer. The two Denizens he'd named looked at each other nervously, then slowly advanced into the forest, bows ready.

Chapter Twenty-seven

The quick way down the hill would have been a very slow way if it had been up to Arthur or Suzy to find it, Arthur thought as they were led through seemingly impassable tangles of undergrowth, under arching tree roots, and between rocks. But within forty minutes they were back down to the flat area, skirting the Hot Lake, keeping just within the border of the forest before it died back and was replaced by bare, sulphurous yellow earth.

"It does stink," said Suzy as she tied a torn-off flounce from her dress over her face.

Arthur took a deep breath and was surprised to find that it went all the way to the bottom of his lungs. The air did smell horrible, like rotten eggs, but he could actually breathe it more easily than the cool, wet air of the hills.

Across the Hot Lake, Arthur could see Feverfew's yardarm. The pirate had simply transferred a mast and its yards from a captured ship, and set it right on the lake's edge, with a block and tackle to swing prisoners out and dip them. There was a viewing platform nearby.

"I reckon we've done it," said Suzy a little later, as they

passed the eastern shore of the lake. "Plenty of time to spare too."

"Let's not talk about it till we're actually out of here and out of Drowned Wednesday's stomach," said Arthur. "Or, better still, getting served tea by Sneezer back in Monday's Dayroom."

"If you believe, all will be well," intoned the Carp.

Its words were punctuated for the worse by the thud of two things hitting the ground just ahead of Jebenezer. For a moment Arthur thought they were coconuts or large round fruit. Then he saw that they were decapitated heads.

The green-mottled heads of Florenza and Padraic.

"Feverfew!" croaked Florenza's head.

"Sorry!" whispered Padraic's.

"Don't forget to —"

"Stick our heads back on if —"

"You win."

"Give me to Arthur!" snapped the Carp. Jebenezer just managed to thrust the jam jar into Arthur's hands before a whirl of yellow dust swept around his feet and he froze like a statue. Another gust of yellow particles wound around Suzy as she drew her knife, and she froze too, as did the two archers who were bringing up the rear.

"I can oppose Feverfew's powers to some degree," said the Carp hurriedly. "But it is up to you, Arthur!"

Arthur stuffed the jam jar in his pocket and drew his sword. The dust-laden breeze kept whipping around him, but it had no effect, other than to make it hard to see.

There was no other sign of Feverfew.

Arthur turned in a circle, his eyes darting from side to side. Everyone else was frozen around him. He could see no movement. The lakeshore, only twenty paces away, was bare and empty. The sick-looking trees and undergrowth would hide someone, but only if they stayed still.

Where was Feverfew?

No one ever looks up. . . .

Arthur jumped back and looked up, just as a shadow fell across him and a blade whistled through the air. The boy raised his own sword to block, felt a shock all along his arm, and sprang away, his back up against the rough, vine-covered trunk of a large tree.

Feverfew closed his wings and dropped to the ground, the sound of both wings and footfall clouded by the whine of the yellow wind.

He looked just like Arthur imagined a pirate captain would. Tall and dashing, his long black hair flowing, his black beard braided with jewels and smoking match-cord. He was handsome, as handsome as a superior Denizen, and his clothes were bright scarlet, rimmed with gold lace and had golden death's heads as buttons. He carried a cutlass with a blade of black iron that smoked as much as the matches in his beard.

He looked nothing like the horrid visitation Arthur had seen in the mirror. Until Arthur looked at him out of the corner of his eye.

Seen that way, Feverfew was a horrid, barely human thing. His skin was the red of severe sunburn, and shrunken against his bones. His eyes were like olive pits, black in red sockets.

He was not dressed in fine clothes, but covered in hundreds of pieces of paper. Papers of all different sizes and colors, all of them written on in a flowing, glowing script, all of them reeking of Nothing and sorcery.

"You bear the Red Hand," said Feverfew. Arthur heard the pirate's voice twice, the two voices just a little out of sync with each other. One was deep, melodious, and commanding. The other was high-pitched, whiny, and horribly penetrating. "You have stolen from me."

Arthur licked his lips and took a stronger grip on his sword. He only had one chance, he knew. A clean cut to the neck . . .

"Yet that is not all you are," continued Feverfew. "Not just a thief. But also the chosen instrument of the Architect's Will. I know who you are, Arthur."

Feverfew took a step forward. Arthur tensed, ready to step forward and swing.

"I know who you are. I know all about you. Don't I, young Leaf?"

Feverfew smiled, his cracked, too-thin lips curling back from yellow teeth.

Arthur didn't take his eyes off Feverfew, but in the corner of his vision, he saw a line of pirates slowly walk into view. Right at the front, wearing the same clothes he'd seen her in on the *Mantis*, but now with a black cap, was Leaf.

"Yes, Captain," said Leaf.

"So I know you haven't got the first two Keys with you," said Feverfew. "Of course, if you had, I'd hardly be given the time to speak, would I? And I suppose that old fish is around somewhere, talking too much about how everything is going to work out. For it, of course."

Just one step closer, thought Arthur.

"I expect you'd like to chop off my head," said Feverfew. "Now, as I'm a sporting gentleman, I thought I'd give you that chance. I have a proposition for you, Arthur. A wager, between two folk who once were mortals, as equals. What do you say?"

Arthur kept his sword up and ready. He would not blink or look away.

"What proposition?" he asked.

"Why, an exchange of blows," said Feverfew. "One each, and you can go first. If you slay me, then you and yours go free. If I slay you, then I inherit all that is yours. I become the Rightful Heir to the House!"

"I don't know if it would work like that," said Arthur. "Even if I did agree."

There has to be a catch, he thought. *Like in the story with the knight and the green giant. I know Feverfew can reattach his head, even more than most Denizens. But Sunscorch said that if I can get grit on his neck-stump, or lay the flat of my blade there . . .*

"That's my concern," said Feverfew. "There's that old fish to witness. Set it out of your pocket, so it can see the goings-on. Now, I shall give you one minute by my watch to decide. A friendly wager or a free-for-all against me and my pirate crew."

He smiled and took a jewel-encrusted watch the size of an orange out of his pocket. At the same time, he casually stepped back, so there was no chance Arthur could reach him before his own pirates came forward.

Arthur flicked his gaze to Leaf, just for a second. She looked normal enough, but she wasn't looking at him. She was staring at Feverfew.

"I get the first blow?" asked Arthur. "There'll be no interference from your crew?"

"They shall stand as trees on a windless day," replied Feverfew.

"Can you be cut by steel?" asked Arthur.

"Steel or silver, iron or bronze, all blades sunder my flesh. It is an honest wager, as I said, between two mortals, as transformed by time, the House, sorcery, and Nothing."

Arthur turned his head sideways a little and looked at Feverfew out of the corner of his eye again. The scrawny, inhuman thing clad in tattered papers would be much easier to strike than someone human-looking. His neck seemed thinner too.

"I want to talk to the Carp first," he said. "Give me another minute."

"One more minute," said Feverfew coldly. "Since it is you who asks."

Arthur kept his position against the tree, and his sword in his right hand. With his left, he pulled out the jam jar and raised it close to his head.

I'm plenty afraid now, he thought. *Can you hear me, Carp?*

I can, responded the Carp silently. *You must have faith, Arthur —*

Stop! Just tell me, as far as you know, can Feverfew be killed by having his head cut off if I lay the blade flat on his neck-stump?

Perhaps, the Carp replied. *That would work even with most superior Denizens. But Feverfew is devious.*

Perhaps!! What kind of answer . . . never mind. Is there anything you can do to free Suzy and Jebenezer and the others? Or my friend Leaf? She must be under a spell. There's no way she'd be with the pirates otherwise —

I have kept you free of Feverfew's spell. Perhaps I could free one more. . . .

There was that word again. Arthur couldn't stand it.

Perhaps! he repeated in his mind. *You're the one who needs to have some faith —*

Indeed, Arthur. I have never claimed otherwise —

"Time!" interrupted Feverfew. "Or close enough. What is your decision, Arthur?"

"I accept," said Arthur. As he spoke, he felt suddenly sick, but he willed the nausea away.

"Excellent," said Feverfew. "I shall kneel here then, and you may strike when you will. Please do ensure the fish has a good view of the proceedings."

Arthur nodded. He started to set the jar down near his feet, but changed his mind and put it down right up against Suzy's right foot. At the same time, he scooped up a handful of earth.

"I haven't got all day," said Feverfew. He had already removed his wings, and put them aside as he knelt down.

His illusory self was winding back his long black hair to bare his neck. In reality, he had almost no hair and was just going through the motions.

Arthur stepped close to him, his mind racing.

Strike fast, throw the earth on the stump, lay the flat of the blade there, to be sure.

"Oh, hurry up!"

Arthur raised his sword. It felt much heavier than it had before. He lifted it as high as he could, then brought it down with all the strength of his shoulder and the weight of his upper body.

I must keep looking, Arthur thought. *Don't be distracted. Throw the earth and lay the flat of the blade.*

It felt surprisingly like hitting a home run in baseball. There was a sudden shock through his arm, then the sword was free again.

Arthur had kept his eye on the target. He threw the earth and laid the blade firmly against the neck-stump, which was dry and bloodless. Feverfew's head rolled on the dirt for only a moment, then with frightening speed, it hurtled into the air. At the same time, his body jerked back and stood up. Arthur had to jump too, to keep the flat of the blade on the neck.

The head dropped like a hawk, landing true where Arthur's blade lay on the neck-stump. But neither earth nor blade inconvenienced it at all. Arthur watched in horror as the flesh spread up from the body's part of the neck, and down from the head's share, meeting in the middle.

Feverfew reached up and pulled Arthur's sword free of his almost totally healed neck. The point of the blade came out with a pop as the boy staggered back.

"My turn, I think," said Feverfew with a smile that was as horrible in both his true and illusory forms.

Arthur had failed.

Chapter Twenty-eight

"Just kneel down where you are," said Feverfew. He ran his thumb down the black blade of his cutlass, and flicked away a single drop of blood that was so tainted with Nothing it sizzled as it hit the earth. "I'm hoping you haven't the trick of reattachment. Many centuries it took me to learn the way of it. And twice as many to do it with complications. Young Leaf tells me you've had no such time. Kneel, I said!"

Arthur found himself kneeling, his body moving independently of his mind, which was furiously trying to think of some way out of his predicament.

We agreed to exchange blows . . . exchange blows . . . I went first. . . .

"You won't feel a thing," said Feverfew. "Which is a pity. I shall enjoy sinking your companions in the Hot Lake."

I only agreed to exchange blows . . . I didn't say I wouldn't dodge or duck. . . . I didn't even say I'd be still. . . .

Arthur tried to move, but found his muscles would not obey him. The yellow wind was winding round his wrists and ankles, holding him in place. He turned his head, and saw Feverfew raising the black cutlass.

Carp! Carp! Help me move! Help me!

Have faith in yourself.

Blinding anger filled Arthur. He couldn't believe the Carp couldn't do anything except carry on about faith!

Fury coursed through his blood and muscle, and the yellow wind flinched before it. Arthur sprang back, just as the black cutlass swept down — into the dirt.

"What!" roared Feverfew. He twisted around, his cutlass sweeping at Arthur's knees.

Arthur sprang over the black blade, cutting back with his own two-handed stroke, his sword once again severing the pirate's neck. This time, as the pirate's head bounced on the ground, Arthur tried to kick Feverfew in the chest, only to find his foot suddenly wrapped in paper and deflected towards a tree.

Arthur hit the tree and staggered back, badly off balance made worse because his crab armor was trying to keep his leg straight.

The boy teetered backwards as Feverfew's head shrieked into the air and then plummeted once again towards the stump of his neck.

It never got there. Suzy suddenly leapt across and smashed Feverfew's head to the ground with a broken branch. As it started to rise again, Leaf darted out of the ranks of pirates and, in true soccer striker–style, kicked the head as hard as she could out towards the bubbling, Nothing-laden waters of the Hot Lake.

Everyone, including the pirates, watched as Feverfew's head splashed down. Ripples spread around its impact point, but still everyone kept watching to see if it would rise again.

Arthur was staring too, when he was suddenly gripped from behind by two paper-shrouded, slithery hands that began to tighten around his neck. He just managed to get three of his fingers under those grasping hands, but he couldn't get them off, or stop them from slowly strangling him to death.

To make things even worse, Feverfew's head rose back out of the boiling mud. All the flesh, illusory and real, had been stripped from it, and it was now just a yellow-tinged skull, its teeth chattering, a sorcerous tongue of blue smoke flickering as Feverfew shouted his last words before tumbling back down into the muddy depths, to be totally destroyed by Nothing.

"Let Nothing remain!"

The hands around Arthur's neck suddenly fell away. The boy staggered forward, his crab-armored leg failing to bend at the knee, and was caught by Jebenezer, who twirled him into a sudden and unwelcome dance.

"You did it! You slew Feverfew! And I saw it happen!"

"Stop! The pirates!"

Jebenezer paused in midtwirl, sending Arthur cannoning into Suzy and Leaf, who were shaking hands. They caught Arthur and turned him so that he could see Feverfew's pirates running into the trees, throwing away their weapons as they ran.

"You don't have to worry about the pirates," said Leaf. "They're a gutless bunch. Feverfew could make them brave, but without him, they're hopeless."

"I just about had heart failure when I saw you with them," said Arthur. "What were you doing?"

"How about 'thanks for the great kick'?" said Leaf crossly. "I was staying alive, what do you think? Feverfew said he only enslaved Denizens. Or Piper's children at a pinch, because they're as hardy as Denizens and a sight cleverer. First off he was going to throw me over the side, till I told him he could get a ransom for me."

"From who?"

"From you, of course," said Leaf. "When he heard that, he got all interested."

"And you told him whatever he wanted to know!"

"Duh! I didn't have any choice! He could read my mind for starters."

"Sorry! Sorry!" said Arthur. "Let's start again. Thank

you for that wonderful kick. Thank you, Suzy, for an equally fantastic smash with the stick."

"That's better," said Leaf. "You can make the thanks official by getting me out of here and back home where I now fully realize I belong!"

"Good idea," said Suzy. She pointed up at the sky. "If we can get out."

Arthur looked up. The sun was wobbling in the sky and there were strange, streaky black clouds spreading out from it.

"Uh-oh. They're cracks!"

"This worldlet is collapsing," said the Carp, once more being carried by Jebenezer. "But we must believe in a way out, for then we shall find one."

"The augury puzzle," snapped Arthur. He turned around to look for Feverfew's body. "It must be on Feverfew somewhere. We grab that, find someone who can use it among the slaves, take a ship —"

He stopped talking. Where Feverfew's body had been there was just a big dark stain on the ground and long, thin, useless strips of curling paper.

The ground rumbled under Arthur's feet. Branches dropped from the trees and the Hot Lake bubbled more ominously. Mud began to spread beyond its shores, oozing oilily across the yellow earth.

"How long have we got?" Arthur asked the Carp. "And can you do anything to stop it or slow it down?"

"I have no power over such structures as this. I estimate the worldlet will last between six and twelve hours. Perhaps a little less, perhaps a little more. It depends on the nature of the eventual demise. Slow dissolution by intruding Nothing, or cataclysmic rupture into the Void."

"How were you going to get out, Arthur?" asked Leaf.

"By submersible," said Arthur. "One run by the Raised Rats. But it can only fit half a dozen Denizens, and —"

As he spoke, he got out the box and opened it to check the bottle. But the bottle was gone, in its place a pile of green glass dust and a tiny fragment of cork.

"— they're not going to be picking anyone up anyway. They've already left. Or been destroyed."

"So we're stuck here, which means we're dead," said Leaf.

"How about the Improbable Stair?" asked Suzy. "We did it before, Arthur. It ain't so bad. You lead the way and we all troop along behind."

"I can't get onto the Stair without a Key," said Arthur. "But maybe the Will can —"

"Not in this form," said the Carp.

"At least we destroyed Feverfew," said Suzy philosophically. "Even if it's one of those whatchamacallit victories where you win and croak before you get all the loot and everything."

"A pyrrhic victory," said Leaf. "Great. There has to be some other way out of here. We need to try and think outside the square. Or laterally. Or with different hats. Beyond the normal . . . only I guess that *is* normal here. . . ."

"There might be a way out," said Arthur slowly. "We have to get everyone to the harbor. Onto the *Moth*."

"But it's an old tub," protested Leaf. "If you think you can get a ship out, we should take the *Mantis*!"

Arthur shook his head.

"We can't get a ship out. The Rats were sure Feverfew's Gore-Draken augury puzzle was the only way to find a gate in or out, and I bet that's true. But there might be a way out using the *Moth*, because part of the *Moth*'s insides are actually somewhere else, inside the House."

"What?" asked Leaf and Suzy at the same time.

"I'll explain when we get there," said Arthur. "Jebenezer, you'd better send someone back to the cavern and order the Followers to the harbor before they start spreading out everywhere. Oh, and did anyone stick those two Denizen's heads back . . . oh, good . . . will they be all right?"

"They will survive," said the Carp. "But they will suffer

for many months, and they will not be able to drink for a year."

"Good," said Arthur absently. "Let's go! Carp, I presume you can free the slaves held down at the town?"

"Now that Feverfew is gone, I can loose their shackles even from here," said the Carp. It swelled up like a blowfish, flared as bright as the sun for a instant, then flashed around its jar in its usual shape at immense speed for several seconds. "There, it is done!"

By the time they reached the town, it was a shambles. The suddenly freed slaves had turned on any pirates still left. The most recent slaves, the crews of the *Moth* and the *Flying Mantis*, had re-formed under their officers and mates and were busy restocking their ships with supplies and the choicest pieces of salvage from the vast selection in Feverfew's warehouses. The slaves who had been there longer mainly sat around, waiting to be told what to do by somebody.

When Arthur arrived he first had a brief but very welcome reunion with Sunscorch, who was overseeing the resupply of the *Moth*. But long explanations had to wait, so after a little back-slapping that left his shoulders sore, Arthur had the Carp use its ability to make its voice heard everywhere around the harbor, to tell the former slaves that the worldlet was doomed and that if they wanted to live and return to the House, they must gather aboard the *Moth*, bringing only one small item of salvage each.

Naturally this caused a panic, only quelled by the Carp using its voice more forcefully, and Jebenezer, Sunscorch, Pannikin, and various others using their voices and belaying pins to bring order to the mass of Denizens that was trying to get on any of the four small boats that could take them from the harbor wall to the *Moth*.

Leaf also had an important role to play, convincing Captain Swell that he must abandon the *Flying Mantis,* and that even such a practiced Navigator-Sorcerer as he would not be able to find a way to sail it out. As he had already tried every augury puzzle he could find, the logic of it was clear, but it was still very hard for him to leave a ship he had commanded for nigh on ten thousand years.

Captain Catapillow presented a different problem, for he did not want to let anyone into his quarters, for fear that they would destroy his stamp collection. But when Arthur lost his temper and spoke sharply to him, he caved in and withdrew to his bed, Ichabod calmly drawing the curtains after him.

Arthur had been worried about how many Denizens would fit in the strange chamber within the *Moth*, particularly since he had promised the Followers of the Carp that he would try to save them, and as they would be last to arrive, they would be the most likely to be left behind. But the chamber was even larger than he remembered, and Ichabod moved the display cases around to create even more space, while telling him that his coat needed to be cleaned, his boots washed, and that the creation of vastly more space within a room was merely a matter of correctly arranging the furniture.

At last, five hours after they'd begun, the room was entirely packed with at least three thousand Denizens, Arthur, Suzy, and Leaf. There was no room to move at all for most of the Denizens, with everyone pressed together like standing sardines.

As far as anyone could tell, no one had been left behind.

Outside, the cracks in the sky almost stretched from the sun to the ground, and the Carp now predicted a catastrophic implosion, with the worldlet suddenly collapsing and being sucked into the Void of Nothing.

"Then, if this worldlet has been properly constructed, the breach in the Void will seal over and cause no more trouble," the Carp pronounced. "Or if shoddily made, it will spread Nothing everywhere around it and cause many more problems to the locality."

"You mean Wednesday's stomach," said Arthur.

"Yes," said the Carp. "Now, as to the matter of our

survival — I do not think this room would survive such a catastrophe, as it is linked to the ship that will be sucked into the maelstrom of Nothing."

"I know we have to get out of here too," said Arthur. "But as this room is actually somewhere else within the House, all we have to do is find a way from inside here to outside there. As I asked you to look into several hours ago."

"Indeed," said the Carp. "Unfortunately while I have found out where this room actually is, I can't find a way to get out. And even if I could, I'm not sure how much use it would be."

"Great," said Leaf. "Excellent work, Arthur."

Chapter Twenty-nine

"Why won't it help to get out of the room?" Arthur asked the Carp. "We have to!"

"This room is still where it was," said the Carp. "In the old Port Wednesday. Underwater. I don't know how far. Besides, I can find no way from here to the outside of the room."

"Because there isn't one, or because of something else?" asked Arthur.

"There may be an exit," said the Carp. "But this room is strangely twisted and I simply have not had time to work out its exact place within the fabric of the House. I doubt anybody could, save the Architect herself."

"The Atlas!" cried Arthur. He reached down into his boot and pulled out the green book. "Can you use the *Compleat Atlas of the House*?"

"No," said the Carp.

As it spoke, there was a commotion near the door out to the *Moth*. Arthur jumped up onto Catapillow's blanket box to see over the heads of the Denizens. Sunscorch, who had been handling the last few stragglers, was just inside the door.

"A piece of the sky's fallen in!" he roared over the hubbub. "And the sea is starting to turn like water going down a plughole!"

"There has to be a way out!" said Arthur. He held the Atlas and focused all his attention on it.

"Arthur —" said the Carp.

"Not now!" hissed Arthur. His knuckles were stark and white against the green book, he was gripping it so hard. "I'm concentrating!"

"Arthur —"

Arthur ignored the Carp and concentrated on his question.

Where is the way out of this room back into the House?

The Atlas stubbornly failed to open. Without a Key, it just would not respond.

"Arthur!" roared the Carp, so loud that Arthur's ears rang. "I cannot use the Atlas, but I can help you use it! Place your right hand against the glass of my jar!"

Jebenezer held up the jar and Arthur slapped his palm against the glass. The Carp came right up against it, puckered up, and kissed the side of the jar against Arthur's fingers three times. Each time it did, it shone more brightly, some of the light traveling through to bathe Arthur's fingers.

"Ask your question!"

Arthur took his hand away and gripped the Atlas again, repeating his question, willing the book to open with a determination that shut out everything else around him.

Nothing happened for three seconds, just long enough for the Carp to start to say, "We must have —"

Then the Atlas exploded open. Arthur fell off the blanket box, but was so hemmed in by Jebenezer, Suzy, Leaf, and other Denizens that his feet didn't even touch the floor.

Arthur didn't notice. He was watching the perfect, though rapid, penmanship of the invisible writer in the Atlas. Words spread across the page, Arthur shrieking them aloud as he read.

"*The chief clerk's office of the Blue Moon Company's Second Counting House has been twisted seven turns sideways and inclined twelve degrees to the impossible, due to incompetent renovation. There are three means of egress from within the office. One is to the ship* Moth, *through the former front door. The second opens on the Void of Nothing, and has been sealed under the floor ten paces to the left of the front door. The third opens in the ship tele-*

graph turret of the Blue Moon Company in old Port Wednesday, and is located through the mirrored back of the former records safe, now in use as a wardrobe —"

"No!" yelped Ichabod, but his voice was drowned out by the surge of Denizens towards the wardrobe.

"Hold!" roared the Carp. "Followers, link arms!"

"Moths, stand still!" roared Sunscorch.

"Mantises, hold yer ground!" shouted Pannikin.

"*And may be activated by peeling off the wallpaper backing*," finished Arthur. He slapped the Atlas shut, jumped down, and wormed his way between the Denizens to the wardrobe. It was a huge oak-paneled affair, easily ten feet high and fifteen feet wide.

"Ichabod!" called Arthur. "Is there any trick to going in?"

"No, sir," said Ichabod stiffly. He had managed to appear at Arthur's elbow, unruffled and calm once more. "Simply walk through. But if I may remove the Captain's clothes before they are trampled —"

He was interrupted by a very loud cracking sound, and the floor shivered under Arthur's feet. He didn't wait to hear any more from Ichabod, but strode straight at the mirror.

The inside of the wardrobe was bigger than the outside. There were racks of clothes against the side walls, and shelves of boots, shoes, and accessories. The rear wall was wallpapered with a simple blue flower pattern, and had a chaise lounge against it, next to a small table with an open book of fashion plates on it.

Arthur hurried over, shoved the table and book aside, and pulled the chaise lounge away from the wall. Then he reached up and pulled a loose corner of wallpaper. It came away easily, revealing a mirrored surface underneath. Arthur ripped some more, and then Suzy and Leaf and Jebenezer and even Ichabod were there pulling at the paper as well.

"What if it's really deep on the other side?" asked Leaf. "Will we get the bends going up? Can you get the bends in the House?"

"I don't know!" snapped Arthur. "We haven't got a choice, have we? Go through as soon as the paper's off."

"What about you?" asked Suzy.

"I've got to make sure everyone gets out," said Arthur. "You guys go or you'll get trampled."

As the paper was almost all off, he took the Carp's jar from Jebenezer and stepped back out of the wardrobe, hitting a solid wall of waiting Denizens, who were barely kept in check by the combined efforts of the Mates, some of the Carp's Followers, and the more dependable crew.

Arthur managed to squeeze through back to the blanket box. He stepped up on that, ignoring the fact that it was vibrating, along with the floor, like a badly tuned car.

"Okay, Carp, maximum volume," said Arthur. "Repeat what I say."

"I shall do so," replied the Carp.

"Quiet down!"

"*Quiet down!*"

"Don't push and wait your turn!"

"*Don't push and wait your turn!*"

"Everyone will get out!"

"*Everyone will get out!*"

"Listen carefully but don't move till I tell you to."

"*Listen carefully but don't move till I tell you to.*"

"There are two walls of mirrors to go through."

"*There are two walls of mirrors to go through.*"

"Walk slowly and carefully through the wardrobe mirrors and keep going through the next set of mirrors. You will come out underwater. Swim up and try to help anyone who needs it."

"*Walk slowly and carefully through the wardrobe mirrors and keep going through the next set of mirrors. You will come out underwater. Swim up and try to help anyone who needs it.*"

"Everyone at the back stay still. If you're in front of the wardrobe, start walking slowly forward!"

"*Everyone at the back stay still. If you're in front of the wardrobe, start walking slowly forward!*"

"As space opens in front of you, walk slowly forward! Steady! Everyone will get through!"

"As space opens in front of you, walk slowly forward! Steady! Everyone will get through!"

Arthur kept giving instructions as the Denizens shuffled forward into the mirrored doors of the wardrobe. Every now and then one would panic and Arthur would stop breathing as it looked like the fear would spread, only for everything to come back under control as calmer Denizens wrestled the panicked one back into line.

But it's all taking too long, Arthur thought as he was forced to step down from the blanket box, which was shaking itself to pieces. The floor under his feet was starting to glow a nasty, dull red — if it wasn't for his Immaterial Boots, Arthur was sure he would feel the heat.

"Let's move a bit faster!" he called out, the Carp repeating his words. Perhaps half the Denizens had gone through, so there was more room and less likelihood of a terrible crush.

Five minutes later, the walls started to weep black, tarlike tears the size of Arthur's head, and the floor was twisting and tilting by as much as six inches up and down.

"Come on, faster now!" called Arthur. "Jogging on the spot and then forward when space opens up!"

He demonstrated jogging as best he could with his

crab-armored leg on a moving surface. Perhaps two hundred Denizens remained, but the room was clearly under enormous stress, and that meant that the *Moth* and the worldlet outside must be close to final destruction.

"Can you tell what's happening outside?" whispered Arthur to the Carp as he moved to the back, smiling and waving on jogging Denizens. "I mean the *Moth* side, Feverfew's worldlet."

"It's still there because we're still here," said the Carp. "Hold on a moment. I'll check."

It whizzed around its jar several times, then stopped.

"The underlying structure is holding, though the cosmetic features, like the hills and so forth have all gone. Remarkable, really. Grim Tuesday lacked true flair, but his work was always very solid."

"How long have we got?"

"Minutes, not hours," said the Carp. "I can't say closer than that."

"Right," said Arthur grimly. There was some sort of holdup near the rear ranks of Denizens. He threaded his way over to it, to find Sunscorch, Pannikin, and Captain Swell trying to pry Captain Catapillow from a display cabinet. Arthur was only mildly surprised not to see Concort, who must have already fled through the wardrobe.

"I can't go without at least the heart of my collection,"

sobbed Catapillow. "Just one cabinet. You can help me carry it! If it can't go, I won't go!"

"Lord Arthur, please tell the Captain he has to leave the stamps behind," asked Sunscorch.

"You do have to leave them," said Arthur. "Look around! This place isn't going to last much longer. We have to hurry everyone through, and you need to set an example."

"No," said Catapillow mulishly. He hugged the cabinet. "If my collection is to be destroyed, then I'll go with it."

"I guess let him stay, then," said Arthur. He glanced over the remaining Denizens. There were perhaps fifty left, all gathered near the wardrobe, which was becoming harder to get into as the floor bucked up and down. "Everyone else, let's get through the mirrors!"

The boy turned and joined the back of the relatively orderly queue that was steadily streaming into the wardrobe. He was glad to be able to grab hold of Denizens around him, because he would have fallen over otherwise, the floor was so unstable.

"The ceiling's slanting down, isn't it?" Arthur asked as they got down to the last twenty Denizens. "From that corner. Really quickly!"

In the far left corner, the distance from the floor to the

ceiling had been cut in half, and the ceiling was still steadily moving down, like some kind of industrial stamper. It hit some of the display stands, which resisted the downward pressure for a moment, then buckled in a spray of glass and metal.

"Catapillow! This is it! Come now or you'll die!" shouted Arthur as he edged closer to the wardrobe. There were only a dozen Denizens in front of him now — and Suzy and Leaf! Arthur's head snapped around, Catapillow forgotten for a second.

"I told you to go through! We might not make it now!"

The floor broke in half as he spoke, a crevasse opening up in the middle of the room. Yellow mud boiled up out of it, preceded by clouds of stinking gas. Catapillow was on the wrong side, still clutching his display case.

Arthur held his breath and grabbed Leaf and Suzy, or they grabbed him and the three of them jumped through the wardrobe mirrors, only just making it as the crevasse split the floor even further, toppling the wardrobe over.

Inside, the wardrobe was a tangled mess of trampled clothes and broken furniture. But even worse, it had toppled forward, so that the mirrored back wall was now the ceiling, twelve feet above the three children and impossibly out of reach.

"Stand on my shoulders —" Arthur started to say, but

he hadn't seen Sunscorch, who had wedged himself in a corner. Without wasting a word, the Second Mate picked up Leaf and threw her straight up and through the mirror gate. As he turned to pick up Suzy, she jumped, got one foot on his shoulder, and leapt up without assistance.

Arthur stumbled, his crab-armored leg caught in discarded coats.

"Go!" he shouted to Sunscorch as he desperately tried to untangle himself and only made it worse. "Go!"

Chapter Thirty

Sunscorch went, but he grabbed Arthur under one burly arm, jumped on the exposed springs of the wrecked chaise lounge, and used their bounce to propel himself, Arthur, and the tangle of coats up through the gate.

It happened so quickly that Arthur barely had time to get a breath, and he didn't have time to make sure the Carp's jar was securely in his pocket. He saw it hurtle past, and then he was through the mirror and completely surrounded by water.

Arthur kicked the coats free, but Sunscorch didn't let him go. He struck out in a direction that Arthur hoped was the surface, because he couldn't see anything except dark blue and tons of bubbles.

We could be hundreds of feet down, he thought. *I've gotten through so much and then to drown at the end. . . . I'll never make it . . . the Denizens will, but I won't . . . and Leaf won't. . . . It's all my fault, I should have made her leave the hospital, how am I ever going to explain to her parents. . . . I have to take a breath, I have to take a —*

The dark blue water suddenly became lighter, interrupting

Arthur's panicky thoughts. He saw Denizens all around, some doing powerful strokes and kicks, some barely dog-paddling, a few just floating.

Then, before he could begin to think that the light must mean the surface was close, he was suddenly there. His head broke through, light and air welcoming him, and he gasped and laughed and water ran out of his nose all at the same time.

Denizens bobbed everywhere, as far as he could see, gently lifted by the small swell. Arthur's gaze moved across each survivor superfast, looking for the faces he most wanted to see — and there they were. Suzy, about ten yards away. Leaf somewhat closer. And there was a jam jar moving mysteriously across the water, into Arthur's hand.

"You can let me go now, Sunscorch," said Arthur. "Thanks."

"I might have lost the ship, but I still ain't lost a passenger," said Sunscorch. He released Arthur, who promptly sank and had to be hauled up again till he got his treading-water action going properly.

"I have summoned Drowned Wednesday," said the Carp. "She is on her way and will be here shortly."

"You what? She'll eat us! I thought we'd get on some dry land first!"

"I am sure she won't eat us," said the Carp. "Have faith, Arthur. . . ."

Arthur wasn't listening. He craned his head out of the water to look around, hoping to see some sign of solid ground, or a ship, or something. But all he could see were thousands of floating Denizen snacks looking tempting for one crazily hungry Leviathan.

"How did you communicate with her?"

"I am the Will. She is the Trustee. Now that I am back in the House, I am able to speak into her mind, much as I did into yours, Arthur."

"Well, tell her to transform into her human shape," said Arthur. "And tell her to order her Dawn to get here with as many ships as she can. Can you do that?"

"I can speak the message into her mind," said the Carp. "Whether it will totally penetrate is unclear. It is done."

"Can you speak with your mind to anyone else?" asked Arthur. "The Raised Rats, for example?"

The Carp shook its mustachelike growths back and forth.

"No. I am connected to you as the Rightful Heir, and to Wednesday as the Trustee."

"Land ho!"

The cry came from some Denizens to Arthur's right. He paddled himself around, but even before he looked, he was pretty sure what he would see.

It wasn't land, though it looked like it.

It was Drowned Wednesday, bearing down on them. Still vast and almost certainly still hungry.

"We made it!"

That was Suzy, splashing over backstroke.

"Stop saying that!" said Arthur. "We haven't made it. We're probably going to get eaten. Wednesday won't be able to help herself if she sees all these Denizens floating about. It'll be like three thousand pretzels waiting to get munched."

"Is that her?" asked Leaf, whose swimming style was very economical and practiced. She leaned back and floated easily, making circular motions with her hands. "Wow! Talk about huge!"

"If anyone has any bright ideas, now is the time to spit them out," said Arthur, spitting out some seawater himself as his mouth was splashed midsentence.

"Pity the Captain's not here," said Suzy. "It'd be real interesting to see what his harpoon could do to a whale that big."

"No way!" said Leaf. "I'm not letting anyone harpoon any whale. I'm a member of Greenpeace —"

"She doesn't mean it, Leaf," said Arthur. "And the Mariner wouldn't do it anyway. I think. I wish he was here. In a ship."

"The Mariner?" asked the Carp. "That would be the Architect's adopted son? The middle one?"

"Yes," said Arthur and Suzy together.

"I might be able to talk to his mind," mused the Carp. "Seeing as he is of the Architect's kin. I suppose I could talk to the Piper for that matter too, or Lord Sunday."

"Lord Sunday!" exclaimed Arthur. "What? Is he —"

"The eldest child of the Architect and the Old One. Their first experiment together, when the Architect inhabited a mortal woman —"

"Okay, we don't need a history lesson now!" interrupted Arthur. Drowned Wednesday was looming larger and larger, and the glad cries of "land ho" among the Denizens had been replaced by cries of fear. "See if you can communicate with the Mariner! Maybe he can get here with a ship and pick us up before Wednesday —"

"It's not as simple as that," said the Carp. "I haven't seen him for millennia, and it's not as if I'm charged with making him do anything. I'll have to try and recall what he looked like to begin with. Besides, I'm sure that Wednesday won't eat us up —"

"Why not use the Mariner's charm you wear?" Sunscorch asked Arthur. "Or is it worn out?"

"The Mariner's charm?" Arthur asked. He pulled it

out, sank below the surface yet again, and came spluttering back out. "You mean it can actually do something?"

"So legend has it," replied Sunscorch. "Doctor Scamandros would know, but he is gone now, like our late Captain Catapillow."

"I hope Scamandros is still alive," said Arthur. "The *Balaena* probably just had to leave for some reason . . . oh! You don't know. The Doctor survived the battle with Feverfew. He escaped to me, and . . . I'll tell you later. How exactly does legend say this disc worked?"

"You speak into it, and the Mariner hears you," said Sunscorch.

"I've already done that!" protested Arthur. "Heaps of times when I first got swept up! Carp, you have to contact the Mariner!"

"Did he have gray hair or was it more white?" asked the Carp.

"I reckon that whale *is* shrinking," said Suzy.

Everyone swam around to look.

"I don't know," said Arthur. "She looks just as big to me."

"Keep watching," said Suzy. "She's getting smaller."

"Aye, she's shrinking," confirmed Sunscorch. "But will she shrink enough?"

"Okay," said Arthur. "Even if she is shrinking, we

don't want to tempt her with lots of Denizens to eat up. So I'm going to take the Carp and swim towards her, and everyone else can swim off at a right angle. Okay?"

"No way," said Leaf. "I'm sticking with you, Arthur. You're my ticket home."

"I want to see what happens," said Suzy. "Besides, if she's normal size we might be able to help fight her, if we have to."

"Sunscorch, can you at least start organizing all the Denizens to swim away?" pleaded Arthur. "I really do think Wednesday might not be able to resist temptation."

"Aye, aye, sir," said Sunscorch. He touched a knuckle to his head in salute and dived under.

"That's what you two are supposed to do," said Arthur. "Say 'aye, aye' and swim away."

"Yeah, as if we would," said Leaf. "You don't have to do everything by yourself, Arthur."

Arthur didn't answer. He just started swimming towards the approaching Leviathan. But secretly he was glad not to be alone. And Wednesday was getting smaller, so perhaps it would all be straightforward after all.

"Does this mean I don't need to try to reach the mind of the Mariner?" asked the Carp. "Have you regained your faith in me?"

Arthur spat out some water and said, "Yes. You could say that."

He paused to tread water for a while and rest, and looked behind. The Denizens were very slowly beginning to swim away in the other direction. But that wasn't all that caught Arthur's eye.

"Is that a ship on the horizon?"

"A three-masted brigantine, under full sail," said Leaf, shading her eyes with one hand. "See, I didn't waste my time on the *Mantis*. Albert . . . Albert was a good teacher too."

"The ship's boy," said Arthur, suddenly horror-struck. "I haven't seen him! We couldn't have left him behind, could we?"

"No," said Leaf in a very small voice. Her eyes grew red, though Arthur could see no tears on her sea-washed face. "He . . . Albert got . . . Albert got killed when Feverfew attacked the ship. I've been trying not to think about . . . that's why I want to go home . . . I . . . I don't want any more adventures."

Arthur was silent. He didn't know what to do or say.

"He lived a long time," said Suzy. "I reckon he would have had a lot of good times, even if he couldn't remember a tenth of 'em, cos of the washing between the ears. And like all of us Piper's children, he would've died long ago if he'd been back on the old Earth. Remember what he taught you and he'll always be with you. That's what we say, when one of us goes."

"Drowned Wednesday is almost upon us," boomed the Carp suddenly. "The time has come to release me from my bowl! Lord Arthur, please unscrew the cap."

Arthur wiped his eyes, kicked hard with his legs, and picked up the jar.

"Feverfew is dead, and his bindings with him," said the Carp. "I have grown used to the bowl, but no more shall I be imprisoned in any way!"

Arthur unscrewed the lid as he sank, getting it off just as Leaf and Suzy helped him back up. They could kick much more efficiently than he could, and he appreciated their help, even if every now and then one of their kicks connected with him rather than a vacant patch of seawater.

The Carp swam free. A tiny goldfish that turned to face the onrushing whale.

"Wednesday!" roared the Carp. "I, Part Three of the Will of Our Supreme Creator, the Ultimate Architect of All, do summon thee to fulfill thy duty as Trustee of the said Will!"

Drowned Wednesday slowed, and shrank faster, though she still came forward. When she was thirty feet away, she was the size of a misshapen dolphin. It leapt into the air — and when it came down, it was a woman who stood upon the sea as if it were land.

She was not the misshapen, lumpy thing Arthur had seen before. She was beautiful, impeccably dressed in a gown of shimmering mother-of-pearl, the trident of the Third Key glowing in her hand. Only the uncontrollable trembling of that hand and the blue blood flowing down from her bitten lip indicated the difficulty she had keeping such a presentable shape.

"I, Wednesday, Trustee of the Ultimate Architect of All, do acknowledge the Third Part of the Will, and ask into whose hands shall I place that which was entrusted to me?"

Arthur knew what came next. Without prompting from the Carp, and held up by Leaf and Suzy, he spoke quickly but clearly.

"I, Arthur, anointed Heir to the Kingdom, claim this Key and with it Mastery of the Border Sea. I claim it by blood and bone and contest, out of truth, in testament, and against all trouble."

The trident flew from Wednesday's hand to Arthur's. As his fingers closed around it, he felt himself rise out of the sea, Suzy and Leaf letting go.

At the same time, Drowned Wednesday cried out in pain, and doubled over, sinking into the water. She clutched her stomach and rolled, her arms and legs ballooning.

"Be as you were," commanded Arthur, pointing the Third Key at her. "When you were never hungry, when the Architect was still here."

The puffiness retreated, but Wednesday remained hunched over, still sinking.

"Float!" commanded Arthur. He felt the trident hum in his grasp, and the sea around Wednesday momentarily shone a deep, rich blue. Wednesday bobbed to the surface, clawing at her stomach.

"Too late, Lord Arthur," croaked the Denizen. "I am poisoned within. Nothing eats at my flesh and bone, and soon I shall be no more. But I thank you, for I did not wish to end as I was, a vast thing, near mindless in hunger. Rule my Border Sea well, Lord Arthur!"

Something small and jewel-like sparkled in her mouth as she spoke. It trembled on her lip long enough for Arthur to see what it was, and in the instant that it fell, he directed the power of the Third Key upon it.

"*Balaena*," he said, naming it so his directions would not go astray. "Float over there, and stay small until you do."

He waved the trident, and the tiny metal cigar-shape that was the *Balaena* floated through the air and over to a clear patch of sea. Arthur dipped his trident and it slowly fell. As it hit the sea, there was a huge eruption of water, from which the full-sized submersible emerged, looking battered but intact.

Arthur looked back at Drowned Wednesday, but all that was left was a horrid, oily slick of Nothing that was moving against the wind towards Leaf and Suzy.

Arthur pointed the trident at it, relishing the feel of power flowing through it and into him.

"Return to the Void!" he ordered. The sea flashed gold in answer, and all that had been Drowned Wednesday vanished.

Chapter Thirty-one

Arthur hardly moved for at least a minute after he'd banished the Nothing. He felt stunned. It had happened so quickly, and now one of the seven Trustees of the Architect was not only defeated, but dead.

And the Third Key to the Kingdom was in Arthur's hand.

"How about helping us all walk on water?" asked Suzy finally, when Arthur continued to just stand there staring at the trident in his hand.

"Sorry," he mumbled. He waved the trident and visualized Suzy and Leaf rising out of the waves. This happened, but they shot up about twenty feet, then splashed down again up to their waists, before getting a proper footing.

"What happens now?" asked Leaf.

"We must commandeer that ship and get swiftly to Port Wednesday," said the Carp, who had suddenly grown up to a similar size it had been when they first met. "There will be a tremendous amount of work to see to. Ha-ha. Pardon me. There will be a great deal of work. A new Noon and Dusk will need to be appointed. I shall have to

meet with Dame Primus, with a view to . . . ahem . . . con-
solidating my paragraphs into the greater whole. I believe
the Border Sea has spread where it should not, so the
bounds will need to be reestablished. Judging from
Feverfew's loot, considerable unauthorized and dangerous
trading has been going on between the House and the
Secondary Realms and this must be regulated. . . ."

The Carp continued, but Arthur wasn't listening.
There was a whole lot of stuff popping to the surface just
near the bow of the *Balaena*. Salvage, floating up from the
depths. One item had caught his attention. Something
small and round, in a particular shade of yellow. He
walked over to it, ignoring the Carp's indignant call.

The object was a fluffy yellow elephant. A sleeping elephant, curled into a ball. Its head and trunk were bare, the
yellow fluff worn down to the cloth underneath.

Arthur picked it up. It was his elephant. The one toy
his birth parents had been able to give him before they
died. He'd had it for years and years, but had lost it on his
fifth birthday when he took it to a picnic that had been
suddenly abandoned due to rain. Bob and Emily had
hunted for it the next day, and his older brothers and sisters had as well, several times, but Elephant had never
been found.

Arthur slowly put Elephant in his pocket and turned

back to where the others were waiting. As he did so, the hatch in the conning tower of the *Balaena* sprang open behind him. A Rat, his head swathed in bloodied bandages, climbed out, then reached back in and helped Doctor Scamandros emerge.

"Lord Arthur! You did it! You defeated Drowned Wednesday!" the Doctor called.

"She helped me," said Arthur. "I'm glad you're okay. What happened?"

"Uh, the full story may have to wait," said Scamandros hurriedly. He climbed down onto the hull as more Rats came out of the conning tower and deployed an inflatable raft. "I fear this vessel is held together merely by my own poor sorcery, and that is rather coming adrift as well. In fact, if you wouldn't mind, Lord Arthur?"

Arthur pointed the Key at the submersible.

"Don't sink!"

His hand trembled as he gave that directive, and Arthur was surprised to find that it took an effort to hold the trident up. It began to shake in his hand and grow unpleasantly warm.

"Nothing contamination," gasped Scamandros as he was helped into the raft. "As soon as everyone's out you'd best let it go."

Arthur nodded. He had to grab the Key with his other

hand — it took all his strength to hold it level. It felt like the Key was some kind of lever, propping up a very heavy weight.

There was no movement at the conning tower. The Key began to slip down, then when Arthur thought he couldn't hold it up any longer, Longtayle popped out. The Rat jumped from the conning tower straight into the sea, as the raft pushed off. As it did so, Scamandros fell back in a faint. Large parts of the *Balaena* crumpled or fell off as he did.

"Go," said Arthur. "Return to the Void."

The submersible collapsed in on itself, becoming a small, dark star for just a second. Then it too was gone.

Arthur put his left hand in his pocket and felt the soft synthetic fur of Elephant, weighing it up against the heft of the Key in his right hand. He could feel the power of the Key still, flowing gently through his arm. Changing him, making him into a Denizen. Making it impossible for him to be human.

If he kept using it.

"Ho, Arthur!"

The hail was not from the Carp. It was as loud or louder, but far deeper in tone. Arthur jumped and looked around.

The three-masted brigantine was heaving-to only a hundred yards away, and its Captain was calling from the quarterdeck, without the aid of a speaking trumpet. He was tall and craggy, and cradled a harpoon that glittered and shone with unearthly light.

"I came as fast as the winds could carry me across a dozen worlds," shouted the Mariner. "Yet it seems you do not need my help at all, for now you walk where others must swim or stand upon a wooden deck!"

Arthur shook his head. All that fearful time pleading for help, hoping the Mariner's disc would do something, and *now* he came!

"I'm not walking on water for long," shouted Arthur. He put the Third Key through his belt. As it left his hand, he started to sink into the sea once again, as did Suzy and Leaf.

"So," called Arthur, just before he got a mouthful of seawater, "we do need someone to take us — and three thousand Denizens — to Port Wednesday, as soon as it can be done."

"We'll take you," answered the Mariner. "As for your three thousand Denizens, there are five vessels manned by fine Rats following not far behind. They'll take on passengers, for a fee."

"Wednesday's Noon will arrange payment," Arthur answered, the brigantine drifting closer, so he didn't have to shout so loud.

"There is no Wednesday's Noon," objected the Carp.

"He used to be called Sunscorch," said Arthur. "We'll fix up the formalities when we get ashore, provided he wants the job. There'll be a new Dusk too, if he wants the job when he regains consciousness. A Denizen called Doctor Scamandros."

"This is most irregular," said the Carp. "I believe you're supposed to consult me about such matters."

"Believe away," said Arthur. He put his head down and swam a few strokes to the net the brigantine's crew had flung over the side. "I'll see you in Port Wednesday, if you're quick."

"What? What?" asked the Carp. "What are you going to do?"

"I'm going to go home," said Arthur. "Just to make sure everything's all right. Then I'm going to come back and take on Sir Thursday. And I'm keeping the Third Key for now. I just won't use it too much."

"But you're needed here!" protested the Carp. It was goggling at him as only a goggle-eyed fish could do. "The Key is needed here! Without it the balance between the Border Sea, the Realms, and Nothing may go all awry!"

Arthur had started climbing the net, with Suzy and Leaf close behind. He stopped and hung there, looking back down at the Carp.

"I need it!" he shouted. "I'm tired of being powerless when the Morrow Days come and attack my family and my world, or drag me back here straight into trouble. Like I said, I'm only going to zip home and make sure everything's okay, then I'll come back. I don't want to, but I know I have to."

He started climbing again, but as he reached the deck he stopped and looked down at the Carp once more.

"So just leave me alone!"

"It won't," said Leaf. "Just like the Morrow Days."

"I know!" snapped Arthur. "I know —"

"Please excuse me," interrupted Suzy in a very prim and proper voice. "I must immediately find something suitable to change into. Miss Leaf, I daresay I could find a dress for you too."

"A dress!?" asked Leaf. "Why would I want to wear *a dress*?"

"She promised Dame Primus to behave properly on the Border Sea," said Arthur hastily. "So that's another good reason for all of us to get out of here."

"Indeed, I am most eager to return to more civilized regions," said Suzy. She nodded slightly to Arthur and Leaf, then hurried across the deck, pausing only to offer a curtsey to the Mariner, who tipped his cap and chuckled before striding over to offer his hand to Arthur, who shook it firmly.

"Where away, Lord Arthur?" asked the Mariner. "I've a mind to take a cruise around the Border Sea, for it's long since I sailed these waters, but I'll land you wherever you please."

"Like back on Earth?" asked Leaf.

The Mariner bent his piercing blue gaze on her.

"A ship's boy should generally include 'sir' in their questions," he said. "Yes, I could sail this ship to Earth, for wherever the Border Sea's waters have lapped a shore, so they may touch again. But I do not think it would be wise. The Border Sea has already spread too far, and that fish was right. The shores and bounds of this Sea need to be fixed once more by the Third Key."

"I said I'll be back with the Key," protested Arthur. "But for now, can you take us to Port Wednesday so we can get an elevator to the Lower House?"

"Aye," said the Mariner. "Port Wednesday it is."

"Where do we go from the Lower House?" asked Leaf.

"Through the Front Door," said Arthur wearily. He bent his left leg and looked down at the crab armor. The Third Key could remove that, but he thought he'd leave it on till the last moment. It was going to be hard to explain what had happened to the original cast. "Straight back to the hospital, I hope, a few seconds after we left."

"So it'll still be Wednesday?"

"Yep."

"Longest Wednesday I've ever had," said Leaf. "I'll be happy to get home."

"Me too," said Arthur.

Chapter Thirty-two

"**A**rthur, are you sure you're okay?" asked Emily. She was hovering over his bed again.

The boy looked at her, but did not speak or meet her gaze.

Emily turned away to check the readouts on the diagnostic equipment next to the bed.

"Come on, son," said Bob from the other side. "Just tell us you're okay. I know it must have been a terrible shock to have that water main exploding like that, but you're all checked out now. No injuries."

The boy rolled over and buried his face in the pillow. Emily and Bob exchanged glances over his back.

"We're just going outside for a little while," said Emily. She gestured at the door. "But we'll be close."

"There's no water main here, either," added Bob. "I've checked. Nothing can go wrong."

Arthur's parents tiptoed out and closed the door. In the corridor, they both took deep breaths.

"He's never been like this before," said Emily. "Never,

even when he's been barely conscious with a whole team working to re-establish his breathing."

"It was a weird accident though," said Bob. "Must have been a huge shock. That sudden over-pressure in the firefighting riser. No one's been able to explain it to me."

"Budget cuts," said Emily wearily. "The hospital hasn't been properly maintained for years. I just don't understand why Arthur won't talk. He just . . . I don't know . . . he just doesn't seem himself."

Inside the room, the Skinless Boy grinned and let the illusory flesh that covered half his body slide away to reveal the red ochre bones of the skeleton beneath.

→ NEXT →

Sir Thursday

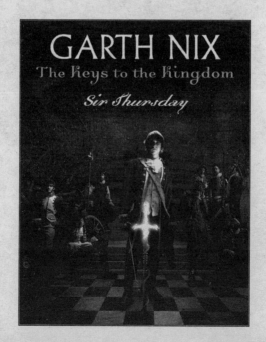

GARTH NIX

The Keys to the Kingdom

Sir Thursday

On the fourth day there was war....

GARTH NIX
The Keys to the Kingdom
Sir Thursday

In the fourth book of Garth Nix'
masterful The Keys to the Kingdom
Arthur is drafted by Sir Thursday and force
to join the Glorious Army of the Architec
Can Arthur survive basic training, avoid th
Front, and still free Part Four of the Wil

■ SCHOLASTIC

Scholastic Pres

*For my good friend Henry Kyatha—we walked the
same route for years. Now you've simply gone ahead again
and I'll meet you on the other side.*

Join the *Walking Home* journey . . .

This book is the fictional story of Muchoki and Jata, a brother and sister, and their long, incredible journey across Kenya. But everything in this story—the characters, the backdrop, even their walk itself—is based on real life.

At www.ericwalterswalkinghome.com you will find an amazing digital companion to this novel, which will fully immerse you in Muchoki and Jata's world. Pictures, video and audio clips, maps, mini-articles, and notes from the author are told side-by-side with the story found in this book!

When you see an icon in the margin of any of the pages that follow, that means you'll find material at www.ericwalterswalkinghome.com relating to a character or event or passage of text that's being described. These are the following symbols you'll see and here is what they mean:

= audio

= video

= image

= map

= author note

= mini-article

And the website has tons of other additional material, too: Find out how a manuscript becomes a finished book; how a book's cover design gets created; learn about what kind of connections you or your class can make with young people in Kenya; and discover more about the sights and sounds and traditions of this part of Africa. We're glad you've joined our journey!

Chapter One

My father led the way through the dark, my mother behind him, my sister in her arms, and I was just behind them. I kept looking over my shoulder, terrified that I'd see what I could hear in the distance, that they were closing in on us. We were surrounded by people—some relatives, some neighbors, some strangers—all of us bound together in our efforts to flee. Their looks of fear and confusion mirrored the expression that I knew was on my face. Others joined in while some scattered away, melting into the darkness, all looking for a way out, an escape. At least the night offered cover, but wouldn't the daylight offer protection? Evil was most at home in the dead of night—and evil was all around us.

My father came to a stop and he and his brothers and uncles all came together, gesturing wildly, yelling.

They were acting as afraid as I felt which only made it so much worse. There was a loud scream, followed closely by a second and a third and out of the darkness they came . . . there were so many of them and they all seemed to be carrying weapons and torches. We ran, trying to escape, but our way was stopped by more of them. Forced back. Each route blocked until we were funneled into the only shelter we could find, huddled together, hoping that our numbers would protect us, that the sanctuary of the building would be honored. And then the flames came—

I sat bolt upright, terrified. My heart and head were racing until I realized it was only in my dreams. That they couldn't get me, not here and not now. The flames, heat and blazing light of my sleep were replaced by the dark and cold of the night. I was bathed in sweat and started to shake—partly from the chill of the night air, and partly from what I'd seen in my head before I'd started awake.

I lay back down and pulled up the thin blanket, trying hard to get some protection, to generate some warmth. I took a deep breath and tried to calm my head. There was one thing I needed to do to make my mind slow down.

Quietly I got up off the ground and went to the cot where my mother and sister were sleeping. In the dark it was hard to make out their entwined forms,

my sister in my mother's arms—sleeping, safe and protected. At least she was as protected as she could ever
be. Would *I* ever feel safe again? Would *I* ever feel protected again? Even sleep wasn't an escape for me.

I heard a slight moan and moved closer. My
mother was sleeping but her teeth were chattering. It
was more than the cold—her fever was coming back
again. I reached around and took my blanket from the
ground, carefully draping it over both of them. The
one blanket they shared wasn't enough. Gently, so as to
not wake them, I tucked it in at the bottom and then
at the sides. It wasn't much, but there was nothing else
I could do. My father would have known what to do—
or his parents, or my uncles or aunts, or—but there was
nobody left to help. My whole body shuddered. The
chill in the air hadn't caused that.

There was no point in even trying to go back to sleep.

I groped around on the ground for my shoes,
slipped them on and then quietly lifted the flap of the
tent. I stepped out and let the flap fall back down to
seal them inside. That flimsy piece of canvas, with the
blanket, was a second layer to guard them.

It was still dark, still night, but not pitch black.
The sun wasn't up yet but there was a hint of light just
below the horizon. In the distance a rooster crowed.
Then a second rooster called out from the other direction, joined by a third and fourth.

As I stood there, my eyes started to adjust. Our little tent was one of hundreds and hundreds, side by side, as far as the eye could see. There was tent after tent, row after row—a field of white canvas stretching across what had once been an open dusty expanse. The dust was still there beneath and between the tents, and when it rained, it turned into a sea of mud churned by the thousands of people moving through it. Today it was just dust and tents, however—lots and lots of tents. If I'd spent all morning trying, I wouldn't have been able to count them all. And in each tent was a family—two, three, sometimes seven or eight people. That would have been much more crowded, but much better. They were the lucky ones. They *had* more family. We were only three now.

I wrapped myself in my own arms, the only protection from the chill air aside from my thin clothing. It would be better to do something than stand and do nothing. Moving would make warmth.

Carefully I pushed aside the tent flap and reached back inside, fumbling around until I found our water container. We needed water and this was a good time to get it, before the morning, before there was a line at the tap. I didn't know how many people were in the camp, but I did know how many taps there were—only three. Large black plastic tanks had been placed on high wooden platforms, and water trucks came daily to

fill them. They were the water for all of us. Sometimes
the lines would snake away from the tower, hundreds
of people and hundreds of containers sitting side by
side, marking the owners' place in line. With each container filled, the remaining people would slide forward
in the dust. They shuffled forward patiently, silently.
There was never any pushing or shoving or arguing—
or conversation or laughter. Just people quietly waiting
their turn.

There was usually enough water for everybody,
but the tanks sometimes ran dry toward the end of the
line and the end of the day. When that happened a thin
thread headed out through the gate and off into the
distance. A thirty-minute walk away there was a small
stream, almost dry now, where a trickle of water could
be scooped up and put in the containers. The water
wasn't clean but it could be used for washing and cooking, and boiling it made even bad water fit for drinking.
I'd gone to the stream a couple of times with my sister to
get water when there was none to be found in the camp.

I had no way of knowing if there was water in the
tanks now as I walked toward them. They could have
run dry last night, and then there wouldn't be any until
the water truck rumbled in. It didn't matter. I'd put my
container in line and be first when the water did arrive. It
wasn't like I could head out in the dark to the stream by
myself. It wasn't safe. There were wild animals out there.

And other dangers as well.

This was all so different from the life I'd always known. Our homestead had a well full of sweet and clean water, plentiful enough to irrigate our crops. I'd never known what it was like to worry about water. It had always been there for us when we needed it.

I walked softly and silently now, trying to be invisible as I moved between the tents. They called out to me—a gentle *flap, flap, flapping*, as the wind pushed against the canvas. There wasn't much wind, so there wasn't much noise. It was almost reassuring, as if each tent were offering a quiet greeting to me as I passed—a rhythm like music.

That was so different from the sounds made when the wind was strong or the rain was heavy. Then it was desperate. The tents flapped wildly, like the wings of big white birds — like storks—trying to take off and fly away as if they were crying out because they too wanted to be sheltered from the storm. The noise—rain on canvas and canvas flapping—was almost deafening.

On those stormy nights, we could hardly hear each other talk, and the noise was very troubling to my sister. She was so sensitive, so scared of loud noises now. During the last heavy rain, she'd sat on the cot, hands over her ears, blanket over all of her, rocking slightly. I could only wish we were back on our homestead. There, the rain had pinged off the metal roof, softly and safely.

Now our house wasn't safe. Now it maybe wasn't even there anymore. Maybe everything was gone.

Each week every family in the camp was given a ration of food—mostly beans, rice and maize flour. On weeks when extra refugees flooded in or the trucks didn't arrive on time, there was less food. Some families ran out by the fifth or sixth day and went hungry. My mother never let that happen.

Whatever we got each week, big or small, was divided into eight parts—enough for seven days and one extra in case the next relief supplies were late in coming. It had been late three times—once a full two days. There was always a lot of complaining and hunger on those days, especially when nobody knew if the truck would be a day or two or even a week late.

My mother said it was better to be a little bit hungry all the time than starving for a short time. She said we could adapt to having less, and we had. We weren't eating nearly as much as we had before, but we seemed to be able to get by. I didn't mind that much. I was more worried about her. Sick people needed food. It was medicine to fight the sickness. I tried every day to persuade her to eat just a little bit more, but she refused.

We now had a little supply, almost five days' worth, carefully hidden under the thin mattress on which my mother and sister slept, where nobody could see it. Most people respected their neighbors' things, so there wasn't much theft, and those who did steal were chased out of the camp under a hail of rocks and angry words and threats. But hungry people could be desperate people. I knew it wasn't much food that we'd stored, but it was something—a little cushion standing between us and nothing that could be a temptation to some. Still, it made my mother feel good. It made me feel good. It was nice to have something to feel good about.

In the still and quiet dark, sounds seemed to travel so much farther. The roosters still called out in the distance, but closer at hand was the constant sound of coughing and sneezing. Lots of people were sick. Pneumonia and malaria were everywhere, and rumors about the rise in tuberculosis and cholera were spreading throughout the camp. So far it was mostly rumors, but the big hospital tent was completely filled with people suffering from one condition or another. Outside of that tent, in the dirt, were those who were unwell but not sick enough to warrant a bed.

Up ahead I could make out the dark shapes of people standing beside the water tank, and then I saw the ember of one cigarette and then a second. The smell of tobacco drifted over and drew me forward. I stepped into the clearing and the men stopped talking. I nodded respectfully and looked down. I knew they were looking at me.

"Early to get water," one of the men said.

"Yes, sir."

"Too early. No water in the tank," the man said. He reached up and tapped it with his hand and it made a hollow sound.

"Hopefully by morning light," another said.

"You can put your container in line," said a third man, gesturing to the five water containers already waiting by the spigot.

I didn't like to leave our container unguarded, but there wasn't much choice. I put it down on the ground at the end of the line.

"Come, boy. Have a seat," said the third man. He was clearly the oldest of the group.

I didn't know any of them, but it would have been rude to say no because they were my elders.

"What is your name, boy?"

I hesitated for an instant. I knew what the reaction would be.

"Muchoki."

They all burst into laughter. Of course I knew why—my name meant "the one who returns."

"You have a most hopeful name," the second man said. "I hope we all can return to our homes."

"Those who have homes to return to," the first said, and the last of the laughter stopped short.

"After all that has happened, they should have

called you the one who keeps having to return," the eldest added.

I shrugged. "It is my father's father's name."

"That is the Kikuyu way. It is good to be named after our ancestors. That way we never die. Has your grandfather gone ahead? Has he died?"

I nodded my head. "He is gone." My father was gone too. It had only been a few weeks and I hadn't seen it with my own eyes, but if he had escaped, I would have known. It was so hard to believe that less than five weeks ago I'd lived in the town of Eldoret with my parents and sister. We had a house and livestock, a store, and so many relatives, and schoolmates. I was happy then, and now it was almost all gone. Along with my happiness. My sister and my mother were all that remained.

"You are Kikuyu?" the older man asked.

"Of course he's Kikuyu!" the second man exclaimed. "Do you think they are putting Luo and Kalenjin in the same camp as Kikuyu?"

"He could be other things. He could be Meru or Embu or Mbeere or Kamba."

They all looked at me. "Well, are you Kikuyu?" the eldest man asked again.

"Yes." I paused. "My father is Kikuyu and my mother is Kamba."

"Ah, we have with us a Kikukamba!" the first man exclaimed, and they all laughed again.

I cringed slightly. I *hated* being called that. It was bad enough when schoolmates said such things, but shouldn't adults know better—especially now?

"Do not take offense, young man," the older man said. "It is meant only as a jest. The Kamba and Kikuyu are brothers. We are all Bantu . . . the same."

"The two are similar enough that the Luo or a Kalenjin would see no difference," declared the second man. "For some, the only place for even a trace of Kikuyu blood is on the dirt at their feet."

We always knew who was a Kikuyu and who was a Luo or a Kalenjin. It was important, but it really didn't matter. Our homes were side by side; we sat together in school and went to each other's stores. Then all at once, tribe was all that did matter.

"Where are your people from?" the old man asked.

"Eldoret."

"Then you know about blood. What was the business of your family?"

"We have a parcel of land—our homestead—and a store in the main market."

"Why is it that every Kikuyu wants to be either a soldier or a shopkeeper?" the old man asked.

"Or the president," the first man said. "None of this would have happened if he had stopped being president and let the other take office after the election."

"And let a Luo become president?" the second man demanded.

"If he had, this would not have happened," the first replied.

"No, much worse would have happened. Our president stayed to protect us, to keep us safe!"

"Do you feel protected? Do you feel safe?" asked the first man.

"But how much worse would it have been if the Luo controlled the military? The slaughter would have been even worse and—"

"Silence!" the oldest man said as he got to his feet. "There is no point in arguing over what is the past and about things we do not know. We are not the only ones who have suffered. We are not the only ones who have tasted death."

I knew he was talking about the rioting and killing in Nairobi and other places. Across the country there had been killings—members of one tribe slaughtering members of another. Luo and Kalenjin and Maasai killing Kikuyu and Kamba. Kikuyu and Kamba killing Luo and Kalenjin and Maasai.

"There is a difference between them killing us and us killing them," the second man said. "That was done because the Luo had to be stopped. They had to be punished and—"

"Burning a home or killing a child is the same no

matter who wields the machete or tosses the match," the oldest man said.

That seemed to silence everybody, although I wanted to argue against what he had said. Our killing was done in self-defense or to avenge the deaths of our people.

"What is done is done. It is over," the old man said.

"Not all," said the first man. "It is not done until we return to our stores and our homes."

"There are no homes to return to. They have been burned to the ground."

Is that what happened to my home? I'd heard rumors that our store was torched, and I knew what had happened to the church. Still, I wanted to believe our house continued to stand.

"We can rebuild," insisted the first man. "They can burn a house to the ground, but they cannot take away the ground it stands on."

"I have been driven out before—four times," the older man said. "Why return to be driven out again?"

"I will return and plant my crops."

"If you go back, the only act you will perform with a shovel or hoe is to dig your own grave. Do you think it is safe to bring your family home now?"

The man shook his head, and I could see the sadness in his face in the growing light. "Not now. Later."

13

The man who had been arguing so fiercely with the first reached over and placed a comforting hand on his shoulder. "Someday we will return. I will go with you. But not now . . . not yet."

"In the meantime, we are here," the old man said. "And we will do the best we can with the little we've been given. At least we are safe."

"I wish I felt so sure," the second man said. "Those guards are few. Do you think they could stop a mob if it attacked us? Would they even try? Maybe they would just run away to save their own lives."

"We are not helpless," the first man said. "We will not be driven and slaughtered like sheep. If they come, they will meet men who are prepared to fight."

He pushed back the blanket over his shoulder to reveal a large machete dangling from his belt. The second man did the same, and another pulled out a club. I wished that I had a machete or a club. All we had was a small knife for cooking, and it was back in our tent.

"We are Kikuyu and we will fight if we need to fight."

There was a low rumbling sound—an engine—and then two headlights came into view and marked the path in front of the truck coming slowly toward us. It was the water truck. There soon would be water to replenish the tanks and fill my container.

Chapter Two

The camp was coming to life: tent flaps open, bedding lying on top of the canvas to dry and breathe and catch the fresh air; little fires going and pots of water bubbling away; children laughing and playing. It hadn't taken long for that to happen. The smaller the child, the sooner he or she acted as if nothing had happened. I wished I were young enough to forget. I felt so old. I couldn't even remember what thirteen felt like. Did I used to laugh? Did I used to play football with the other children at the school? I remembered, but I didn't believe it.

My mother squatted beside the fire, our little pot held in place over the flames by a wooden spit. She smiled at me as she stirred the porridge. I smiled back, but I knew neither of us was truly smiling. In her eyes was sadness, worry, a weariness that extended throughout her whole body. She seemed so much older, as if she had aged before my very eyes. I felt the same sadness and worry. I wondered if she could see those things in my eyes too.

Her clothing was as worn and dusty as her face. It was all she owned, the clothes she was wearing when we had to flee. I wished I'd known then what was going to happen. At least I would have put on warmer clothes or better shoes. I looked down now at the little hole in the toe of my shoe.

I set the water container next to my mother with a loud thud. "I went for water."

"I saw that the container was gone," she said. "You couldn't sleep?"

"I slept fine. I just wanted to get the water before there was a line. How are you feeling?"

"Much better every day."

I didn't know why I asked. She would never tell me the truth about how she was feeling. She wasn't shaking or sweating, I noticed, but her eyes were cloudy and yellow. That she couldn't hide. Anymore than she could hide the fact that she was thinner, her shoulders more hunched, the lines on her face more deeply etched. I knew it was more than just the malaria flaring up again.

"Where is Jata?" I asked.

"Still sleeping."

"I am not sleeping," she called out from inside the tent. "I was waiting for breakfast in bed." She giggled.

"You will be waiting for a long time," I suggested.

"Come, little one. It is ready," our mother said.

She giggled again and came out of the tent. Our mother took the wooden spoon and portioned out the porridge onto three plastic plates. One serving was big—that one she would give to me—and the other two were much smaller. She scraped the spoon against the pot until the last little bit of porridge was taken. She handed us both our plates and returned the spoon to the empty pot. I picked up my own spoon, took some food from my plate and transferred it to hers.

"You need the extra food!" she protested. She tried to take the spoon from me, but I held it away from her.

"You need more than a child's serving," I argued.

"I am not growing," my mother said.

"I *am* growing," Jata said.

"You are." With her fingers, my mother took the spoonful I'd put on her plate and plopped it onto my sister's.

Before my sister could react, I reached out, grabbed it and popped it into my mouth.

"Hey!" she protested.

"You may be growing, but you are not working," I said. "You will be sitting in a classroom and I will be doing chores."

"I could work too!"

"You need to go to school," I said.

17

"Why don't you need to go to school?" Jata demanded.

"They have only set up school for nursery and standard one and two," I said.

"That isn't fair!" Jata protested.

"It is not only fair but fortunate. You should thank your teachers for setting up the school at all," my mother said. "Now finish your meal and your brother will walk you to class."

"I can walk myself."

"No," I said. "I will walk you. I will be going out to search for firewood, and it is on my way." I gestured toward the dwindling pile of twigs just inside the flap of the tent. Like everything else of value, our fuel was stashed away inside the tent.

"I could go for firewood," my mother offered.

"No, I will. I have nothing else to do." I had no school or studies, no games or friends to play with, no chores to do on the homestead. "You can stay here and watch our tent."

What she could do was lie down and rest. I knew from the doctor that when the malaria flared up, rest and sleep were the best medicine. My mother didn't argue, which worried me even more. She had to be more tired and sick than I thought if she was letting me go off by myself without a fight.

—

The flaps were up on the big tent that had been made into the school. Crates that had once held supplies had been made into desks, and someone had found a few chalkboards. There wasn't much more—no books or writing paper, pencils or pens—but they did have teachers. Within this camp there were teachers, drivers, shoemakers, seamstresses . . . well, everybody except for the rich. They had been forced to flee as well—if you were Kikuyu in our area, you ran or were killed. But those with relatives or money or connections were able to go elsewhere. They didn't need to be in the camp. Here were the people who either had nothing to start with or had to flee with nothing, leaving behind their homes, possessions and money.

My family wasn't poor. Before coming here, I'd never known what it was like to go hungry. There were always crops growing—the land was good—and we had our store and home and cattle. We *had* all of those. Now we had a cooking pot, a knife, two blankets, a cot, the clothes on our backs and one extra week's worth of food stuffed under the mattress.

"Muchoki?" my sister called.

"Yes?"

"You were staring again."

"I was *thinking* again. You should try it. Now go to school. I will be back to get you at the end of the day. Do not leave without me, understand?"

"I can find my way back to our tent. I am not a baby."

"I know, but you are my little sister and you need to listen to me. You need to respect what your older brother tells you. Understand?"

"I understand."

"Now go."

She skipped off toward the school tent and was greeted by one of the teachers, then instantly swallowed up into a group of girls. They were all smiling and laughing and talking. I wished *I* were young enough not to worry. I wished *I* could go to school. Not here, of course, but *my* school. Last year I was third out of forty-seven students. This year I would have been studying for my high school admissions. I knew I could get the marks to qualify to get into a good school—at least a provincial school, although my parents hoped for national. That would have been much more money, of course, and I might have had to go farther away, but still, to go to a national school was a dream.

I missed my teachers, my lessons, sitting at my desk, running in the field chasing a football, playing with my friends. My friends—people I had known for years whose fathers and uncles and brothers had come after us in angry mobs, carrying machetes and clubs and torches . . . I turned and walked toward the gate. I didn't want to think about any of this. I just needed to get more fuel for the fire.

The entire camp was now up and moving. Almost all the tents had at least one flap up, letting in the sun and allowing the breeze to blow away the stale air. In front of each tent was a small fire pit for cooking. Each one was made of a few rocks to contain the fire and ashes. Many women used small whisk brooms made of leaves to sweep the front of the family tent. The sweeping couldn't clear away the dirt, but it left smooth patterns in the hard red clay. Fires were being tended, food cooked, and clothes were slung across the tops of the tents—some to dry after being washed, and others just to catch the breeze. Life went on.

Two soldiers, rifles slung across their shoulders, came strolling toward me. I moved to the side to let them pass and looked down at the ground. There were soldiers who patrolled the camp—usually in groups of two or three—and those who stood on guard at the perimeter fence and the gate. The fence itself was nothing more than strands of wire nailed onto rough poles. It was not much higher than a tall man and was topped by razor wire. It would perhaps have been possible in places to pull it up at the bottom and crawl under, but it would have been very difficult, and painful, to try to go over the top. I guess I should have been grateful for the fence and the guards, but strangely it somehow made me feel trapped, almost penned in like livestock. They were there to safeguard us. Still, they made me feel uneasy and I wondered if the man from the water tank was correct—would they fight to protect us, or flee if there was an attack? Where were the soldiers when we were being attacked? Had they had just turned and run away or hidden in their barracks the way the police hid in their stations? When we needed them the police were nowhere to be seen. Would these soldiers be any different? I wondered how many of the soldiers were Kikuyu, how many of them were *our* people.

I wished I had taken our little cooking knife with me. It wasn't much, but it was more than I now had.

I slowed down as I came up to the gate. During the night it was closed and nobody was supposed to go in or out, but now it was wide open and the guards didn't even seem to notice the people flocking through. I was happy not to be noticed.

There was a trickle of people leaving the camp. A few were men but most were women, and some were my age or a little younger or older. I knew I wasn't the only one going out for wood, although I also knew there were many reasons for people to leave. Some were heading out to the highway to catch a *matatu*—the buses that carried everybody and everything—and take it to the city. Those people might have relatives in Nairobi or were going to find work. I'd never been there, but I'd heard stories of big buildings, road crammed with cars and people on all the streets. The city was supposed to go on forever—houses, apartments, people, cars, carts and *matatus*. Sometimes my father had had to go there for business. He said he was always grateful to come home because Eldoret was paradise compared to Nairobi.

For me, Eldoret was all I'd ever known. It was where I was born and raised, and where my father said I would eventually marry, have children of my own, take over the homestead and store, and someday die. All that talk about marriage and taking over the homestead just seemed like so much talk, it made me laugh. Little did I know how soon the store and homestead would be gone, and how close to death I almost came to be. Eldoret had changed from paradise to hell.

Those in the camp who had been to Nairobi and were fortunate to find a job or a benefactor would come back with new cooking pots, thick blankets, warm clothing, a new mattress, or even a chicken or goat to be slaughtered. How long had it been since I'd tasted goat meat? We'd always had goats at our homestead, enough to milk and butcher for meat for holidays.

If I were a little bit older or my mother a little bit stronger, one of us would have gone looking for day labor outside the camp. Now, all she could do was rest and all I could do was search for wood and fetch water.

I felt a sense of relief as I stepped through the gate. I took a deep breath, hoping that the air would feel different. It didn't. I looked back through the wire to all the tents and all the activity. The crowds, the smell, the dust when it was dry and the mud when it was wet—it all drew me back. Part of me wanted to turn around and go back inside the wire. When I was inside I wanted out, and when I was out I wanted to be back inside.

What I really wanted was to be home.

Just outside the gate, sitting under the shade of a bush, were two girls and a boy. All three of them were about my age—maybe a year older or younger. They seemed to be waiting for something. It wasn't wise to go out alone, so if they were going out for wood, they might be waiting for more people to join them. Maybe four would be enough. I walked over.

"Hello, I am Muchoki," I said, speaking directly to the boy, because it would not be proper to address the girls.

The boy got to his feet. He was no bigger than me. "I am Jomo. These are my sisters, Kioni and Makena." All three were dressed in clean clothing with no holes, although only the boy wore shoes. "We are from Webuye. And you?"

"Eldoret."

They all took on the same look of concern that people did whenever my town was mentioned.

"It was bad there," Jomo said.

"It was bad everywhere, but I've been told it was among the worst there." I paused and offered a nervous

24

smile. Somehow it felt shameful to be from an area that had had so much violence. "I am going to find fuel for the fire and was looking for company," I said.

"As are we," Jomo said.

"Do you think the four of us would be enough?" I asked.

"The two of us would be enough," Jomo said. "We could send the two of them back to the camp to cook, but they both have strong backs."

"We could work together and split what we find in quarters, each getting our share," I suggested.

"You are fair. Do you have a knife or an axe?" Jomo asked.

I shook my head.

He pulled up his tattered sweater to reveal a machete hanging in a sheath around his neck. "We will use this, to cut the wood and to have—just in case it is needed to cut something else. Let us set off."

Jomo started off toward the highway and I fell in beside him. The two girls got up and trailed behind us. There were people—in ones and twos—extending over the hill ahead of us, marking the way. In the beginning we'd have had to only go a few hundred meters, but now, less than a month since we'd moved here, the walk could be close to an hour to find the deadfall.

"How long have you been in the camp?" Jomo asked.

"A little more than a month. We were one of the first, and the camp has grown around us. You?"

"Two weeks. Maybe we will be here only another two or three weeks."

"You're going back to Webuye?" I questioned.

He shook his head. "No, to Isiolo."

"I don't know where that is."

"It is past Mount Kenya. My family, we are Meru and we have relatives. It is very far."

"But how will you get there?" I asked. "Will you walk?"

"I *could* walk," Jomo said.

Behind him, his sisters started giggling.

"What are you chickens cackling about?" he asked.

"It is hundreds and hundreds of kilometers away! You could never walk that far," Kioni said.

"I could walk across all of Kenya if I needed to. Walking is simple: Every journey begins with one step. Step after step until you reach your goal. Maybe it would be harder for a couple of chickens."

"Our father has gone ahead," Kioni explained. "He is arranging for a place to stay and a vehicle to come and get us."

"And until he returns I am the man of the family."

"If we are chickens, then you are nothing more than a rooster," Makena said, and the two girls burst into laughter.

"And not even a *big* rooster," Kioni said.

"A rooster that sleeps in each morning and must be woken up," Makena added. "Not *much* of a rooster."

"Little sisters," Jomo said, shaking his head. "Do you have sisters?"

"Just one. She is much younger."

"You are so lucky to have only one. Would you like a second or third? As the man of the house, I could give them to you."

"Thank you for your generous offer, but I am happy with just the one," I said, laughing.

"I understand not two, but one certainly—" He stopped mid-sentence and dropped his voice. "Do you see them?"

He pointed and I looked. There in the scrub, not too far away, were three small gazelles.

"They are so close," Jomo whispered. "I just wish we had a gun."

"Or even a spear," I said.

"We have a spear," Makena said. "A *flaming* spear."

What was she talking about?

"She is making a bad joke," Jomo explained. "My name means 'flaming spear.'"

"If we all picked up our brother, we could throw him at the gazelle," Kioni suggested.

"Are you *sure* you do not want another sister or two?" he asked me.

"I would rather have a gazelle," I said. "It would taste good."

"Have you eaten gazelle before?"

"Never, but I imagine it would be good. Before coming here, I had never even *seen* a gazelle. There are only goats and cows and sheep around Eldoret."

"The same for Webuye. There are lots of animals around here, though—even elephants and giraffes and lions."

"You have seen them?" I exclaimed.

He shook his head. "I have heard about them. I have only seen gazelles and some zebras. I wonder what zebra meat would taste like?"

"If we see one, we can throw you at it instead of the gazelle," Makena said. "It is a bigger target."

Jomo turned to me. "If I give you a dowry, will you at least marry one of them so she will live somewhere else?"

One of the gazelles—the one with the biggest horns—turned and looked at us then. He ran off, and the others followed close behind. We started walking again.

"When will your family leave the camp?" Jomo asked.

"I do not know."

"Surely you have family somewhere and can go there."

"My mother's people are Kamba. They live in a place called Kikima. Have you heard of it?"

"No."

I shrugged. "Nobody has. I only know it is in Kambaland, up past Machakos."

"I have not heard of those places either," he said. "But all roads in Kenya lead to Nairobi. From there, you can go anywhere else. Have you ever been to Nairobi?"

"Never. You?"

"No. My mother said it is a big, black hole."

"No, it is a city, a very big city. It is not a hole."

"I think she meant it was *like* a hole." He laughed. "She said that once people go there, they never leave. They fall in and the hole is so deep that they cannot climb out again."

I could easily picture that—a hole so deep that you could never get out, so dark that you could hardly see the sky above. Sometimes it felt like we'd already fallen into one.

We followed the beaten path up a little rise. Up ahead, the people disappeared as they dropped over the dip. I looked back over my shoulder. A curve cut off from view anybody else following behind. We were alone. It seemed so strange after spending all this time at a camp so crammed with people. You were never more than a few steps from other people, and even when you closed your eyes you could still hear them, coughing or talking, laughing or sobbing, even breathing. There was even a smell of people.

I slowed down slightly, hoping to hold on to the moment before we made the rise and saw the people ahead again. I even thought about stopping and letting Jomo and his sisters go ahead without me so I could be completely alone. Some part of me wanted to be alone, but another part craved the company of others. I was already living a life that was so much closer to being alone than anything I could have imagined. I realized I was relieved when we reached the crest of the hill and could see the other people once more.

From the little rise we stood on, I could see the highway leading off in both directions until it curved and dipped out of sight. Even this early in the morning, the heat was building up and there were wavy lines rising up from the tarmac as the air wiggled and shimmied. There were people waiting by the road, their colorful clothing standing out against the red of the dust and dirt. Along the road there were a few vehicles moving. They were so far away—so small—that they looked like toys.

"If you travel to the left, you will reach Nakuru," Jomo said.

I nodded. "We traveled through there to get here."

"And if you go to the right, you will reach Nairobi.

My father will be coming back from that direction, and then we will all leave together."

I couldn't help thinking how lucky they were. I could only wish that my father was coming to get us.

Chapter Three

"Time for bed, Jata," my mother said.

"But I am not tired!" she protested. "Can't I just stay up with you a bit longer?"

"I am not staying up. It is time for me to go to bed too."

"Can you tell me a story?" Jata asked.

"I have told you every story I know dozens of times."

"Please," my sister begged.

"Only one, and only if it will help you get to sleep."

I was pleased. I was too old to ask for stories but still young enough to enjoy hearing them.

"Which one do you want to hear?"

"Can you tell us a new one?" I asked. "Something we haven't heard?"

"Are there any that I know that you do not know?" she asked.

"How about a story from when you were a girl?" I suggested.

"It was so long ago that they did not even have stories," she said and laughed.

"Your mother didn't tell you stories?" Jata questioned.

"She told me stories."

"Can we hear one of those? Can you tell us a Kamba story?" I asked.

She nodded her head. "You know what 'Kamba' means, right?"

"It means 'people of the string,'" I said.

"What does *that* mean?" asked Jata.

"That is what I will explain. That will be the story."

I moved closer to the fire pit. The fire was almost out, but beneath the ash there were embers that still gave off warmth. I poked the ashes with a stick, and it sent up a puff of smoke and a gust of red and warmth. Both were good. The smoke chased away the mosquitoes, and the embers chased away the cold. I still found the smell of fire disturbing, but the other benefits outweighed the distress.

"The Kamba people did not originally come from what we now call Kambaland," our mother began.

"Where did they come from?" asked Jata.

"Very far away."

"Did they ride in a car or a *matatu*?"

Mother laughed. "This was long ago, before there were any cars or *matatus*—or even trucks or motor-cycles. Not even bicycles. They walked."

I thought of what Jomo had said about each journey, no matter how long, starting with just one step.

"There was a boy and a girl," our mother explained, "and they loved each other, but their families told them that they could not marry."

"So what did they do?"

"They decided that they were going to marry anyway. They would run away in the middle of the night and be together. They knew they would have to run far away, but after they were married, their families could not object anymore and they would return."

"But if they went far, especially in the night, weren't they afraid they would get lost and not be able to find their way back?" Jata asked.

"Yes, they were. You are a very smart girl."

Jata beamed and sat up straighter.

"The girl had with her a big, big ball of string. She tied one end to the door of her home, and as they walked she let out the string."

"So they could follow the string back, even at night!" Jata exclaimed. "*She* was a very smart girl!"

"She was," Mother agreed. "They went off through the night, through the forest, down the side of the mountain, over a river and to a place where nobody lived. As they walked, they let that string out behind them, knowing that they could go as far as the string was long."

"That must have been a very big ball of string," Jata said.

"It was big, but it was also very, very thin, so it went far," she explained. "The boy and girl became one. They built a house and had a child and farmed the land—it was very good land. Then finally it was time to go home to show their parents their new grandson. They followed the string back. It guided them over the river and up the mountain and into the forest, and that is when it happened."

"When *what* happened?" my sister asked.

"The string had broken."

"That is terrible!" Jata cried out.

"It *was* terrible. They could not go back to find their families. All they could do was go back the way they had come, still following the string. And that is how the Kamba people—the people of the string— came to be. We are all the relatives, the descendants, of that first man and woman."

"Were that boy and girl your grandparents?" Jata asked.

Again my mother laughed. "I am not quite that old, although some days I feel like I could be! Those would be your great-great-great-great-grandparents. Did you like the story?"

"Yes, it was very good. It reminded me of you and father," Jata said.

"Why would you think that?" our mother asked.

"You were not supposed to marry, and you had to leave your home."

"Who told you that we were not supposed to marry?"

"Mundi."

"Our cousin has a big mouth," I said. "And little brains."

"But did he tell the truth?" Jata asked.

Once again my mother nodded her head. "My parents did not want me to marry a Kikuyu—especially one they had never met."

"So you had to leave?"

"I had to leave." She looked so sad.

"And you could not find the string to go back," Jata said.

Our mother shook her head. "I wish I had been able to find the string to bring you home. Your grandparents would have been so proud and happy to meet you."

"Why did we never go back?" I couldn't stop myself from asking.

"It is complicated. There was never enough time or money, and there were always other things happening. My sickness . . ." She let the sentence trail off. "Besides, you are both Kikuyu."

"We're Kikukambas!" Jata sang out. "We are Kamba too."

"No, *I* am Kamba. I married a Kikuyu, and when a female marries a Kikuyu, the children are Kikuyu. You are both named after your father's parents, as is the Kikuyu tradition. You speak Kikuyu and you know the Kikuyu traditions."

"You could tell us more stories," Jata said. "We could learn the Kamba traditions and—"

"No, it is too late," our mother said, cutting her off. "It is too late tonight. It is time for bed." She got to her feet and took Jata by the hand. She looked shaky. Just before they entered the tent, she turned to me. "Do not be long, and make sure the fire is out."

"Yes, I will make sure to do that." I wasn't ready for bed or sleep.

I knew the story my mother had told. Before my sister was born, my mother used to talk to me in Kikamba when we were alone late at night. There were so many words that were similar to Kikuyu, and although they were now foreign to my tongue, they were still familiar to my ear.

She also used to tell me about her home, growing up as the only girl with seven brothers and the grandfather and grandmother I never met. She talked about how someday I'd meet them all, about how we would go back to her home one day. But when her sickness came, she stopped talking about them and stopped talking to me in Kikamba. And we never went back.

I took the stick I had used to poke the ashes and snapped it into four pieces, throwing them on the fire. I knew it was a waste to use fuel just to sit by, but I wanted to. Besides, Jomo and I had gathered a great deal of wood that day, and my share, my quarter, would keep us supplied for days to come.

Jomo and his family would be leaving soon. They didn't need to follow a piece of string: their father was coming to get them. I didn't have a father. I didn't even have a piece of string.

Just then, I heard a voice coming from the tent. It was my mother, and she was singing. Her voice was soft and gentle. She was singing to Jata to help her fall asleep. I recognized the melody before I could pick out the words. It was a song she used to sing to me when I was little. It was a song about a little boy and his grandfather going on a trip together. She was singing in Kikamba.

Maybe I did have a piece of string.

Chapter Four

The sun was hardly up, but church had already begun. I could hear the singing drifting across the camp. It was a familiar hymn. I stopped to listen and it brought me back to our church on the outskirts of Eldoret. It was where my family—all of our family—went to worship. After my homestead it was the place I felt most familiar with, most happy being there. My father was an elder in the church and our pew was close to the front. I'd sit there, my father on one side, my sister and mother on the other. All around us would be relatives and friends. The music was always good, and even if the minister went on too long I knew there would be time afterwards to play with my cousins, and visit and share a meal.

Jata tugged at my arm, pulling me back to the present, and we started walking again. I was in no rush.

It wasn't as if church was going to end soon. The service would be at least three hours long, and every minute I spent walking *toward* church was another minute I didn't have to be *in* church.

The voices got louder and the tent came into view. There were hundreds and hundreds of people gathered together, but there was still a great deal of open space underneath the gigantic tarp that served as the church. Funny how we didn't always have enough food or water but this gigantic tent had suddenly appeared so there could be a church. The ministers would say that God's Kingdom was more important that this one, but we were living in this one right now, and more food and heavier blankets would have been good. Would Jesus have built a temple or fed the poor first?

It was also hard to get away from my memories. Church was supposed to be God's home, a sanctuary, a place of safety. Instead it had been nothing more than a trap for me. How many times had my mind gone back to the last time I was in a real church? We were gathered under God's roof, and what did he do? Did he protect us? Did he save us? Or did he let . . . I tried to force those thoughts out of my mind. I couldn't risk inviting any more of his wrath upon my family.

Standing at the side of the tent I saw many familiar faces—people I had gotten to know in the camp—but I was looking for one: Jomo. Over the past two weeks he had become my best friend. And his sisters, who could be truly annoying, were so kind and gentle with Jata. They had almost adopted her as their own. It meant that they would watch her for me and give me a little time free.

My mother seemed less able to do things as the sickness got stronger. Malaria was like that. Sometimes it was so powerful a person couldn't work, sometimes so strong a person couldn't even walk. I had seen it that bad with my mother before, and then it had passed. It would pass this time. I'd seen it worse. And yet that thought scared me more. Did that mean it was going to get worse before it got better? Jata needed to be cared for. I was there for her when mother couldn't be. She also needed me to tell her that everything would be alright, that mother would get better. I offered her reassurances I had no right to make.

I scanned the group but didn't have to look for long. Jomo was standing at the back and waved wildly when he saw me. Jata and I went over to him.

"Being late for church is not a good thing, you know," he said. "God is watching."

"Then I'm sure he saw me walking," I said. "Where are your sisters?"

"Under the tent in the shade."

I nodded and had started to walk away when he grabbed me by the arm and my sister kept walking down an aisle.

"Do you really believe that God is everywhere?" he asked urgently.

"Um, yes . . . I guess he is."

"Good. Then we do not need to go to church to be with God. Come with me."

He started to walk away, but this time *I* stopped *him*. "Where are we going?"

"Come and you shall see."

"I can't leave my sister alone."

"Alone? Just look—she is with my sisters."

I looked back. She was sitting on Kioni's lap with Makena on the bench beside them. She was laughing and happy, and I knew she wasn't going anywhere without them.

"Do you think they would let anything happen to her?" Jomo asked, seeming to read my mind. "Besides, we will be back long before church is over. So are you coming?"

Part of me didn't want to go, but the bigger part was curious to see what he had in mind. It *had* to be more exciting than church. I decided to risk making God angry. Anyway, he wasn't the only one who had reason to be angry.

I walked wordlessly beside Jomo. I knew there was no point in asking him questions when he was being mysterious. He had quickly become a good friend, somebody I trusted. Of course, I'd trusted my friends and neighbors in Eldoret, and that trust had proven to be nothing but empty hopes.

He stopped in front of his tent, reached inside and pulled out a spear!

"Where did you get that?" I asked.

"I made it. I found the stick and attached a knife to the end." He handed it to me. "What do you think?"

I moved the spear up and down, feeling the wood in my hand, the weight of the weapon. "It feels good, but does it work?"

"Who would be better to make a spear than a boy named after a spear?"

"I do not think it works that way. It could just be a toy."

"A *toy*? There is only one way to find out if it is a toy or a weapon." He took the spear from me and then reached back into his tent and removed the machete. He handed that to me. Once again he started walking.

"Where are we going now?"

"Were you not listening? We are going to try to find something worth throwing my spear at."

"Here in the camp?"

"Outside the camp," he replied. "Come, and stop asking so many stupid questions."

I trailed behind him. I did have questions, but going with him would answer them.

As we moved, we attracted a great deal of attention.

Two boys carrying a spear and a machete were worth watching. People gawked and pointed at us as we passed. I didn't think that was so good.

"Jomo, slow down! Let me at least hide the machete so people do not stare."

"They will be staring harder when we come back with an antelope or a gazelle—or even a zebra."

"Do you really think we can catch a zebra?"

"Not 'catch'—kill. And not 'we'—me. I am the one with the spear. You can help carry whatever I kill and then we will share it—your family and mine."

I liked his confidence, but I wasn't sure that a hastily made spear would be enough. He would need skills in tracking and hunting and using the weapon. I had never even held a spear before a few minutes ago, so I couldn't be counted on for anything.

We came to the gate. Two soldiers, one with a hand on the holster of his sidearm and the second with a rifle on his back, came toward us.

"Why do you have a spear?" the first solider demanded.

"It would be foolish to go hunting without one," Jomo declared.

"What did you say?"

"He said we are going hunting," I replied, answering before Jomo could trouble or annoy the soldier further. "We are going hunting."

"You two squirts are going hunting?"

"Yes, out there." I gestured beyond the fence. "We hope to kill a gazelle."

"With that little spear?" he asked, and the two soldiers laughed.

"If it is so little, why did you need to ask about it?" Jomo snapped.

Both men stopped laughing.

I leaned in close to the first soldier. "Please forgive him. He is my cousin, but he is not so right in the head," I said. "His mother dropped him when he was a baby."

"If he isn't careful, he may suffer another blow to the head."

"I will keep him careful. Come, Jomo. Come!" I grabbed him by the arm and dragged him out the gate and away from the soldiers.

"Those two were just acting like big men because they have guns," Jomo said.

"They *were* big men—bigger than you and me—and they *did* have guns. It is not wise to be impolite to soldiers."

"They were the rude ones," he complained. "But enough about them. We are here to kill an animal, and when we do, we will bring it back in through that gate and wave it under their big noses!"

"They will be seeing it, because there is no way into the camp except through the gate. But we will not be waving anything under anybody's nose—and especially not the noses of men with guns. Now what is your plan?"

"Plan?" Jomo asked.

"To kill an animal."

"I thought we would walk through the brush until we find one and then I would throw my spear at it." He shrugged. "Simple."

"It is simple. Very much like you."

Jomo gave me a playful shove. "Let us walk until we see some animals."

We walked off into the bush, away from the path that led toward the highway.

"When I leave the camp, I will miss you," Jomo said.

"And me too."

"I did not believe we would still be here this long. My father could be here today or tomorrow."

I didn't reply. He'd been saying the same thing for the past week. I think he was starting to worry.

"He must be taking longer because he wants our home to be perfect for us."

"I'm sure that is why." But I wasn't sure. I had heard rumors that there was continued violence, that people were still being hurt and killed. When there was no information, there were only rumors. I wondered if Jomo had heard the rumors too.

He suddenly ducked down, so I did the same. "Do you see them?"

I nodded. There were half a dozen gazelles ahead, almost on the top of a small rise.

"I want you to wait here, quietly," he said. "I will circle around and get behind them on the hill below. Wait until you think I am in position, then charge and drive them toward me."

"How long should I wait?"

"One minute. Count."

Jomo took off, heading in almost the opposite direction from where the gazelles were grazing peacefully. He disappeared into the scrub brush. I couldn't see him or hear him, and the gazelles didn't seem to have noticed either. Maybe this could work, I thought. Maybe I should give him a little more than a minute to get in position.

I tried to stay perfectly still. My grandfather had once told me that animals only see movement. As long as I didn't move, they wouldn't see me. I just had to stand there and wait. I focused on one gazelle. It had been so long since I'd had meat—so long since my mother had had meat—and I wanted it. She *needed* it. Meat would be good for her. Meat and the marrow from the bones helped malaria. There was hardly anything better for somebody who was sick.

The animals were starting to edge across the face of the rise. If they moved much farther, they wouldn't run toward the place where Jomo was—or at least where I hoped he was—when I started to chase them.

I inched to the right, trying to cut them off but not startle them. The closest gazelle, the one with the biggest horns, stopped grazing and looked up. I froze. Slowly he looked all around with his nose up in the air, smelling. His tail twitched nervously. He knew something was wrong, but he wasn't sure what. And then our eyes locked. He'd seen me. They were going to flee, but in which direction?

I screamed loudly and waved my arms wildly as I ran to the right, cutting them off from that direction. All the animals jumped and then followed the big male as he ran over the rise! I kept running and screaming, up the hill, right to the spot where I'd seen them disappear. Scrambling across the rough ground was taking all my air, and I staggered, almost falling over the loose earth and rough rocks as I made the top.

And then I saw it.

There was a gazelle lying on the ground, still twitching, with a spear sticking out of its side! He'd done it—he'd hit the gazelle! But where was he? Where was Jomo? He was nowhere to be seen . . . but how was that possible?

"Jomo! Where are you?" I yelled out.

"Here! I am here!"

He followed after his voice, running out from behind some brush, and he was still carrying his spear.

I looked over at the gazelle—which had now stopped moving—and at the spear sticking out of it. How was that possible?

Then I saw the Maasai warrior. He was standing stone-still beside some rocks, the red of his clothing the only thing that marked him. He glided forward, straight for the gazelle, and stopped right over top of it.

"Hey, that was our gazelle!" Jomo yelled as he ran toward him.

He skidded to a stop in front of the man. The Maasai was a full head taller than him, but Jomo continued to yell. I hoped the man didn't understand Kikuyu.

I ran over. "My friend does not know what he is saying," I explained, switching to Swahili in the hopes that he'd understand the common language.

"He is saying it very loud," the man answered. "I don't know the words, but I know he is angry with me."

I knew the Maasai from Eldoret. They often traded in our store. My father had told me that they prided themselves on being short-tempered, and that they always carried weapons. And, if what I had heard was true, those weapons had been turned on Kikuyu in parts of the country. He had a machete hanging from his belt.

"That is our gazelle!" Jomo yelled as he too started using Swahili.

"How did *my* spear get into *your* gazelle?" the Maasai asked. He took the handle of his spear, twisted it into the animal, placed his foot on its side and pulled the spear free. Blood and guts dripped from the end of the weapon. He held it up. "Does your spear have blood?"

"We were chasing it," Jomo said.

"A dog can chase a *matatu*, but that doesn't mean the *matatu* is his," he said. The warrior turned to me. "You were the one screaming like a girl?"

"I was driving the gazelle toward my friend."

"Instead you drove it to the tip of *my* spear."

"He was chasing it to my spear, but you got in the way," Jomo cried.

"*That* is not a spear. *This* is a spear." He held it even higher and I felt afraid.

"Come on, Jomo. We have to get going."

"We are not going anywhere without *our* gazelle!"

"You did nothing to deserve any part of this kill," the man said. "There is only one way this can be settled."

Lightning-quick he drew the machete from its sheath. I staggered backward as he pointed the tip of the blade directly at me.

"*You*," he said menacingly, looking at me. "*You* did something. You drove the gazelle to me. Part of the kill belongs to you." He plunged the blade into the side of the animal.

Chapter Five

All eyes were on us as we walked through the gate. Each of us supported one end of the spear, the remains of the gazelle concealing the middle section. The Maasai had given us the back legs and part of the torso. It would have been more impressive to have the head and horns balanced between us, but still it was obvious that we were returning with a kill. Besides, you could not eat the horns or head.

I felt like a proud hunter. Of course, neither of us had killed this animal, but the people watching didn't know that. The man, the Maasai, had said I could decide what to do with my portion of the kill and I could share it with my friend if I wished, "although he deserved none." Of course I was going to share it. Jomo had started to complain again when the man portioned out what looked like less than half the animal, but I told him that if he didn't shut up, I would not only give him nothing but also kill him myself. Luckily, he had closed his mouth.

"Do you see the kill?" Jomo asked now, goading one of the guards who had teased us on the way out. "Not bad for a toy."

He seemed incapable of not causing problems.

The soldier removed his hat and bowed his head slightly. "My apologies for doubting you." He paused. "I have never tasted gazelle before."

"And you still aren't going to!" Jomo yelled back.

The guard scowled.

"But if you come to my tent," I said, "you are welcome to share a bowl of soup made from the meat. I would be honored if you joined us."

"Will *he* be there?" the guard asked, pointing at Jomo.

"No, he will not."

The soldier smiled. "Then it would be my honor to join *you* at your table."

"My family tent is in the center, in the row that runs from the central water tank."

"I will follow the smell. Thank you."

I started walking again, towing the gazelle and Jomo behind me.

"He is not getting any of *my* share," Jomo declared.

"You must spend your entire day thinking of ways to get in trouble."

"You are so wrong! I hardly think at all!"

I laughed, and he laughed too.

"First you fight with a Maasai with a machete, and then you taunt a soldier with a rifle. Neither of those is very wise."

"Maybe not, but I just do not like being bullied. That soldier would not act that way if my father was here. Maybe he will arrive in time to share my part of the animal."

"Maybe. I look forward to meeting him."

We continued to walk, with every eye in the camp on us. I did feel proud, even if all I had done to deserve this was scream like a girl. Nobody had to know that part.

Our pot simmered over the fire. I stirred it so the food wouldn't burn. It was a mixture of beans and rice—nothing different there—but the gazelle was a welcome addition. The smell of the meat drifted across the whole camp. I'd taken one section of meat for our meal, while my mother had begun drying a bigger section in the tent to preserve it. Still one more section had been traded for a warmer blanket and a few other items. I was so grateful for that blanket—my mother needed more warmth to chase away the chills that seemed to be overcoming her each night as she slept.

Jata joined me at the fire. "It smells so good," she said.

"It will taste even better. It will soon be ready."

"Do not start without me!" our mother called from the tent. She pushed open the flap and came out. Her stride was uneasy, and although she was smiling, she didn't look well. Her eyes were yellow and somehow she looked like she was faded.

"Come and sit," I said, offering her my hand.

"You are a hunter, a cook *and* a gentleman."

I eased her down so that she was sitting on a rock. That was the closest thing we had to a chair.

"I also have a guest joining us," I said.

"Is it your friend Jomo?"

I shook my head. "He is eating with his family. It is a soldier from the gate."

She gave me a confused and concerned look.

"He is a nice man, and I offered him the chance to taste gazelle," I explained.

"You are such a kind boy . . . despite everything."

There was no need for her to say anything more. We knew what "everything" meant. Kindness was important for its own sake, but this was done with something else in mind. It was important to ensure that people with weapons were our friends.

I picked up a wooden spoon and ladled the soup into one of the three little plastic bowls.

"Did you borrow those bowls from somebody?" our mother asked.

"No, they were part of the trade, along with the blanket."

"You are a businessman, just like your father," she said.

I had so many memories of time spent with my father in his little shop. Our store was on the main street of Eldoret. It was far from the biggest store but it was very busy. It was co-owned by my father's brother—my uncle—and the two brothers worked together. My uncle's two sons and I would help out, but we were all still too young to be left on our own. The walls of the store were lined with clothing and racks of shoes. Behind the counter were the radios, flashlights, cellphones and other electronic items—safe from any potential thieves.

"Your love of business makes you a true Kikuyu," my mother said.

"And a true Kamba," I added. "I would like to meet my Kamba family someday."

"The meal tastes so good." She was ignoring my comment, which meant she wasn't comfortable with what I'd said. I shouldn't have said anything. I wasn't trying to make her feel worse than she already did.

She sipped quietly from the bowl—I wished I had traded for some spoons as well. Perhaps someone would swap for some of the soup. I had seen people in the camp with lots of spoons and little food.

"This is just so good!" my mother exclaimed.

"It *is* good," Jata said as she sipped from her own bowl.

"And you and Jomo caught it!"

"Mainly we just helped the Maasai warrior."

"They can be very dangerous," my mother warned. "Always be wary around the Maasai."

"I was wary, but he was kind and fair."

"Your father always said that they drove a difficult bargain but were men of their word," she said.

Jata used her fingers to scoop up the last of the food in the bowl. Then she licked the bowl and her fingers.

"Do you want more?" I asked her.

"Can I go and play with my friends?" She pointed down the passage, where two of her little friends were waiting, holding a skipping rope.

"It is getting late and—"

"Go and play with your friends," our mother said, cutting me off. "But stay where we can see you."

Jata put down the bowl and skipped off.

"She needs time to play, to be happy."

My mother was right. It was good to see her happy. It almost made me feel happy too.

Without asking, I scooped some more of the meal from the pot and put it in my mother's bowl. "Eat."

"I think you have come to believe that you are my mother rather than my son."

"You need to eat. Food is the best medicine when you are ill," I said.

"It is the only medicine we have, and we only have it thanks to you." She paused and looked at me thoughtfully. "Actually, I can see my mother in you."

"Your *mother*?"

"In the eyes. You have my mother's kind eyes. You would know that if you had ever met her."

"Why haven't I ever . . ." I let the sentence trail off. This was not what she needed.

My mother took another slurp from her bowl—a long slurp—and then looked right at me.

"I always thought I would go back. At first I did not because I was afraid."

"Afraid of what?"

"Of facing my family. My father—your grand-father—is a very, very proud man, and I know how much I hurt him." She took another long, slow sip of the soup. "Then with the coming of you, caring for a baby, the distance, and the money that we did not have, it seemed like it would have to wait. But the longer I waited the harder it was to stop waiting and go. And then, in the end, I did not go because of hope."

"I don't understand. Hope?"

"I knew that the longer I waited, the harder it would be for my father to accept me back to his home. By not going, I had hope that he would not turn me away. By going, that hope could have been crushed and I would have had nothing."

"We have nothing now," I said. "Not even hope."

"I know what you are saying. I just do not know if I could go back now with nothing, with everything gone. It would be hard to face him."

"It sounds like your father is not the only person with too much pride."

She laughed. "My father always said that of all his children, I was the one who was most like him."

"I would like to meet my grandfather and grand-mother."

"It would not just be them. You have aunts and uncles, and I would imagine there are dozens and dozens of cousins by now. But I do not even know if my parents are still alive. I wish I knew."

"There is only one way to find out."

She took a deep breath. "It is very far and I am not well."

"But when you get well?"

"Kikima is not close, Muchoki."

"Every journey, no matter how far, starts with one step," I said.

"That is very wise. Who told you that?"

"Jomo. He said that he could walk to Isiolo if he had to."

"Isiolo is very far, even farther than Kikima. But

hopefully we will not have to walk."

"But if we had to we could," I said. "It is not as if we have much to carry. As you said, you would return with nothing."

She smiled. "I would return with something very important. I would return with my children—my parents' grandchildren, the niece and nephew of my brothers, the cousins of their children."

I understood why, for all those years, returning to her home village had represented the possibility of the end of hope for my mother if she was to be turned away. For me, now, it was the start of hope. And maybe it had rekindled her hope too. But first all that hope had to be in my mother getting better again. Right now she couldn't even walk to the front gate.

"Good evening!"

The soldier was standing there, a rifle on his shoulder and a smile on his face.

"Good evening, sir," I said.

"I hope I am not too late for a sample of gazelle."

"No, sir. I made sure to save you a portion."

"I thank your son, and I thank you as well, ma'am, for this invitation to join your family."

"It is our honor," she said. "Please sit."

He pulled off the rifle and laid it carefully on the ground, taking a seat on a rock on the opposite side of the fire.

I filled a bowl and handed it to him, and also gave him the serving spoon. It was not right to have a guest use his hands.

He took a big mouthful. "So good," he raved, looking at my mother. "So very good! You are a cook who is a match for my wife!"

"You are most gracious to say so," my mother said, "but it was more my son than me."

"It is wonderful. I must admit, though, that as much as I appreciate the food, it is also good to be sitting around a fire with a family. It has been more than a month since I was with my family." He took another big mouthful. "Not that I should be complaining, of course, when I know how much worse it has been for the residents of the camp."

"It is better to be in a tent with your family than in a mansion alone," my mother said.

"And your family is all here with you?" he asked.

"All that remains." The last word was said so quietly that it almost couldn't be heard.

"You are not well," the guard said to my mother. "Malaria?"

"It has been there for a long time, but it has flared up again of late. Thank goodness my Muchoki is here to care for me."

"A son is a blessing. I have two sons and a daughter. Not that having a daughter is *not* a blessing," he added quickly. "Do you have medicine?"

She shook her head. "Rest, food, warmth are the best. So many here have malaria."

"So many have other things as well. The hospital tent and the medicine are for those who have diseases that can be spread. The fear is always of an outbreak of cholera or typhoid."

"And malaria can be suffered by many and spread by none. I understand."

"I am only a sergeant," he said, "but if there is help that I can give, please come forward and ask, and I will offer my humble services."

"You are most generous," she said. "We greatly appreciate your offer of help. But for now, you must finish your meal and then have more if you wish."

"I will finish this, but I will not take more."

"You do not like it?" my mother asked.

"I like it very much, but your family has greater needs than mine. I will not take advantage of the kindness you have offered—especially to me."

"I do not understand."

"I am Kalenjin."

"Kalenjin!" I gasped. "But you speak Kikuyu."

"I speak many languages. Kalenjin is my tribe."

I tasted bitterness in my mouth. If I had known he was Kalenjin, I would never have invited him to our tent, never offered an invitation to dine at our side.

Suddenly those fears of the soldiers guarding the camp came rushing back. How many of those who were guarding us were Kalenjin or Luo, and how many were Kikuyu?

"Most of the soldiers here are Kikuyu," he said, answering my unasked question. "But I am a soldier first and Kalenjin second. I am here to defend the people of my country. I am a Kenyan. I am here to defend *all* my people."

Those were brave words from a man whose people had attacked the defenseless.

"That is how it is supposed to be. We owe you even greater thanks and are even more honored that you sit with us to share a meal," my mother said. "Do have news of things . . . out there?"

"I hear things, but that does not make them true."

"And have you heard if things have settled?"

"There are still problems. Parts of Nairobi were still aflame this week."

I thought about Jomo's father—he had to pass through Nairobi to get to Isiolo. Was that why he had not returned? Because something had happened to him? Should I speak of this to Jomo?

"It was particularly bad in Kibera," the soldier said.

"Kibera?" my mother asked.

"It is a shantytown in Nairobi. There are so many

people there they cannot even count them. It is reputed to be the biggest slum in Africa."

"And there were problems in Kibera?"

"Homes were set ablaze, whole sections destroyed and hundreds killed. There, many Luo and Kalenjin were killed by Kikuyu."

"That is so awful."

"I heard it was in retaliation for what was done in the western regions, but really it is nothing more than an excuse for people of violent natures to act violently. Still, those people may have spread the fire, but they were not the ones who started it."

"What do you mean?" I asked.

"The politicians who should unite us as Kenyans divided us as tribes. The fault lies with them." He paused. "I understand that some people were simply reacting to what they saw as violence being done to their people. I don't excuse their actions, but they were responding to what they heard had happened in the Western Province. It was particularly bad in the area around Eldoret. Stores and homes were burned to the ground, and many people were killed. There were terrible rumors—even reports of a church being set on fire with people in it."

"No," my mother said. "Not rumor. We are from Eldoret. We saw it. We lived through it."

"Now that you have told me, I will never again

call it a rumor. I beg your forgiveness if my words have caused you offense."

"No offense was taken. I am sorry if I caused upset to our guest," my mother said.

"We are all upset, but you are not the cause."

"Rumors replace facts. It is wise to question. Can you tell us about things here in the camp?" my mother asked. "That is, if you are permitted to discuss such issues."

"I will discuss them with you and trust your discretion," he said. "What information do you request?"

"Is it true that there are over ten thousand of us here?" she asked.

"There are now over twelve thousand. The number has gone up as new people have come and down as others have left. At one point there were more than fourteen thousand, but others have left for resettlement."

"Have they gone back home?"

"There are no homes for some and no safety for any."

"I thought things had settled," she said.

"Settled but not finished. Violence continues to flare up as retaliation. An eye for an eye will leave everybody blind."

"If they cannot return to their homes, where are those people going?"

"Many are returning to their tribal areas. Luo are

fleeing Nairobi for the west, and Kikuyu are flooding back into the central areas, especially Nairobi. Do you have people in Nairobi?"

"I think everybody has people in Nairobi, but my family is from the hills of Mbooni district."

"You are Kamba?" the guard asked.

"I am Kamba. My children are half Kamba and half Kikuyu."

"It is a shame that every person in Kenya is not half Kikuyu and half Luo. Then none of this would have happened," he said.

"Within the camp," my mother asked, "are we safe?"

"All the displaced person camps are being held with integrity by the military."

"How many camps are there?"

"There are twenty-two larger camps containing almost three hundred thousand people. This camp is large but not the largest."

"And here things have gone well?" she asked.

"Everybody is hungry, but nobody has starved. Everybody is parched, but nobody is without water."

"And disease?"

"There have been outbreaks of dysentery and a small pocket of cholera. There have been deaths, but the doctors and nurses are caring for the sick and disposing of the bodies to prevent disease from spreading."

"We should be grateful," my mother said. "So many people, so close together, so weak and tired—I'm surprised there has not been more sickness, more death."

He shrugged. "In time it might get better, or it could get worse. It is wise to leave if you have a place to go." His expression darkened, and I knew what question was going to come next. "Do you have a place to go?"

I waited for her answer, holding my breath . . . hoping.

"Yes, there is a place, but it is far away."

"Close is better than far, but far is better than not," he said. And with that, he placed the bowl on the ground, stood and picked up his rifle. "I am so grateful for you sharing your meal and kindness and company. If there is some small way I can repay your kindness, I am at your service."

"No, no. We should be thanking you," my mother said. "You are a good soldier. You are a good Kenyan."

Chapter Six

I placed the wet rag on my mother's forehead. It was hot to the touch. She was burning up, so fiercely that I finally had to move my sister away. She slept on the ground, a blanket wrapped around her to protect her from the cold ground beneath and the cold air above.

The chill couldn't break my mother's fever, but at least she was now asleep. For the past few hours she'd been awake, but not really awake. She would cry out, say words and look wild-eyed. I tried to talk to her, to answer her words, but she didn't seem able to hear me. She was like a madwoman, a woman possessed. And she was—by the fever.

Some of what she yelled out made a twisted sense. Many of her words were so garbled as to not even be words, but still I knew what was haunting her mind.

The anguish in her voice and that look in her eyes—I just knew she was back in Eldoret, in the church. It seemed like the fever in her blood had brought back memories of the fire in the church. It was something she couldn't drive from her mind, and something that would never leave mine.

"Muchoki!"

I started out of my thoughts. My mother was looking up at me, her eyes wide open and staring into space.

"Yes, Mother, I am here."

"Your father—go and get your father."

She was so feverish she was out of her head.

"Go! I need him."

She did need something, but I didn't know what more I could do. Maybe a doctor or a nurse at the medical tent would know.

"I'll go and get help," I said. "You just stay here and I'll be—"

Her eyes were closed and she wasn't moving. Was she . . . ? Was she . . . ?

She took a deep breath and her whole body shuddered, then her eyes closed and she was asleep again. She was just asleep. For a brief second, I thought she had died. That was crazy but not so crazy. People did die of malaria—but not here and not now and not her. I wouldn't let her. She'd get better, just as she had done a dozen times before, and then we'd leave this camp. I didn't know how we'd get there, but I knew where we were going—Kikima. We were going back to the homestead where she was born, and once we got there, everything would be fine—as fine as it could ever be again.

I tucked the extra blanket around my mother to keep her snug in bed. Next I took the cloth from her forehead, dipped it in water and wrung it out, finally placing the cool, damp cloth back on her forehead. Slowly, so as not to jostle the cot, I went over to my sister. She was still sound asleep. In the little bit of light coming from the candle she looked peaceful, as if she didn't have a worry in the world. Maybe she didn't. I owned all of those. All the worries were mine to hold, mine to solve . . . but how?

"I'll be back," I said softly, whispering in my sister's ear. "It'll be all right. I'll always be here for you." Even though she couldn't hear me, I needed to say those things. Maybe I needed to say them for me to hear.

I slipped out of the tent. The sky was filled with a hundred million stars and a big, bright full moon. Between them was an eerie glow that seemed to reflect off the white tents. I'd never seen snow, but I'd read about it in books. Was that what snow would look like? I took a deep breath and in the silence could hear it release. There was no wind at all. It felt like the camp itself had fallen asleep. It must have been as exhausted as the people.

On silent feet I moved among the tents. There

were no sounds other than my muffled footfalls. I was struck suddenly by the terrible thought that all the tents were empty, that all the people had gone, leaving me and my sister and my mother alone. I knew that wasn't true—that the tents were filled with sleeping people, hundreds and thousands of sleeping people— but really we *were* all alone. Alone in a crowd. We had nobody. Well, except for Jomo.

I was near his tent. I had an urge to lift the flap and shake him awake so I would have somebody to talk to, to ask questions of. Of course I wouldn't do that, but tomorrow I would ask his mother for advice. She was a good woman, and she and his sisters had been very kind to Jata, to me, to our mother.

I hesitated for a half second by their tent. It was identical to all the other tents in the row, in the camp, but there was one difference: the people inside lived in hope. They still went to sleep every night and woke up every morning hoping that this would be the day their father would return and take them away. And with each passing day, the hope both grew and faded. It grew because it only made sense that each new day was one day closer to his return. And it faded because with each day he didn't return, some of their hope was replaced by the fear that he never would. How could something get bigger and smaller at the same time? I didn't know, but I knew it was true.

I had hope too—hope that my mother would get better and we would then leave and her family would welcome us. I had started to realize how powerful hope was. After water and food, shelter from the weather and a place to sleep, it was the most powerful thing that could sustain a person. That was why my mother had never gone back home. She needed that hope, and I worked to convince her, to allow the hope to grow and the fear to fade. It would soon be time for us to test our hope. As soon as she got better.

As I approached the hospital tent, the silence was replaced by a gentle hum. It was the sound of the generator. In a sea of darkness, the hospital tent was a little island of electricity—a few dribbles of light leaking out through the cracks in the canvas. I wasn't sure what I would say, or if anybody would even talk to me, but I had to try something.

I circled around the side where the entrance was located. There was a big truck parked right by the tent and two men came out, carrying something between them. As they heaved it into the air, I suddenly realized they were tossing a human body. It landed with a thud in the back of the truck! I skidded to a stop and then darted over to the side so I was sheltered in the darker shadows.

Two more men came out of the hospital tent, and they were also carrying a body. They were more delicate in placing it in the truck. It looked to be smaller. Could it be a child? All four men disappeared back inside. In the light, I could see that they were all wearing masks over their faces and gloves on their hands. The first two reappeared with another body. How many were there? I stood there, frozen in place and barely daring to breathe, and watched and counted—five and six . . . seven and eight. And then nothing. Was that all of them? I continued to wait, giving the men more time to return, until I realized I didn't want to see any more bodies. I turned and rushed off. There was nobody in there I wanted to talk to tonight.

Chapter Seven

I opened an eye and closed it immediately to the bright light. It was morning. I didn't even remember drifting off, but I must have at some point. I forced my eyes open and allowed them to adjust to the brightness. I looked over at the cot—my mother wasn't there! I jumped to my feet. My sister was gone as well. I pushed through the tent flap and there they were, sitting around the fire eating porridge.

"Good morning, Muchoki," my mother said.

"Good morning." I looked at her hard. "Are you fine?"

"Much better . . . Weak, but better."

"I'm sorry I fell asleep."

"You needed to sleep. Come, have some porridge."

I felt so relieved that my whole body seemed to melt to the ground right beside my sister. I watched my mother intensely as she served me some porridge. She said she was better, but I had to see it with my own eyes. Her hand had a slight tremor but her color was good—except for the yellow in her eyes. Had they ever been that yellow before?

"After breakfast, I will walk Jata to school and then go out and get more firewood," I said.

"Perhaps I can come out with you," my mother said.

"I can handle the wood by myself. You should stay here. Sweep up, or lie down if you need to." Resting was what I wanted her to do, what she *needed* to do.

"You are a very considerate son."

If I was considerate, I would have stayed up all night to watch over her.

"Muchoki!"

I turned around at the sound of my name being called. It was Jomo.

"Thank goodness you are here!"

"Where else would I be?" I asked.

"You could be fetching water or outside gathering wood, and then I would have missed you!" He was louder and more excited than usual.

"If you had missed me, you would have found me later."

"No, no. There is no later. I am leaving!"

"Leaving?! You mean . . . ?"

"Yes, my father has returned! We are leaving, we

are leaving!" He picked Jata up and twirled her in the air, then tossed her up high until she squealed with delight. He caught her and set her down.

"I am so happy for you," I said.

"We are all happy. I just wish you were going to be leaving too."

"We are talking about leaving," I said, glancing in my mother's direction.

She nodded her head ever so slightly in agreement.

"Wonderful. Could you come to meet my father? Could you come to say goodbye?" Jomo asked.

"Of course . . . if that is all right?" I asked my mother.

"Yes, yes, of course."

"I need to say goodbye too," Jata said.

"If you did not come, my sisters would be very disappointed."

I got up, but before starting away, I turned to my mother. "I will clean away the dishes when I return," I told her. "You need to go and rest."

I expected her to argue but she didn't. She nodded in agreement.

Jata took one of my hands and Jomo the other, and we started off for his tent.

"I am so happy that my father is here," Jomo said. "I did not wish to mention it, but I was starting to get worried."

"I knew he would come," I said.

"I *knew* but I did not *know*. I was worried about him and worried that we would have to stay here forever. It would be terrible to have no place to . . ."

He let his sentence trail off. We both knew what he was thinking.

"But I am sure you will leave soon . . . I am sure of it," Jomo said. "I just wish you could come with me. You are my best friend—no, you are more like a brother!"

"And you are my brother."

"I wish that you and your sister and mother could come with us."

"I understand it would not be possible."

He nodded his head. "It will be hard already. My father has told us. We are going to something but not too much—it is a single-room hut with a patched roof. We will be sharing beds, and the fields are rocky."

"You'll get more beds, and in time you will remove the rocks," I offered. "It will be better than living in a tent."

"I just want *you* to have more soon."

"My mother has said that once she is well, we will try to go to her people in Kikima."

"That is so good." He looked away. "How is your mother?"

"Better today than last night, but not as good as she will be tomorrow."

"Malaria can be strange," Jomo said. "It comes, it goes; it gets better, it gets worse. Sometimes it disappears for years, and other times it can be so bad that . . . it can disappear again."

Or it can kill. Once again, I knew what he wasn't saying. Sometimes friends agree not to mention things. I hadn't talked about the possibility of his father not coming back, and he didn't talk about my mother and what could happen to her.

There was an old car parked in the passageway between the tents. Jomo's mother and sisters, along with two men—one of whom I knew must be his father— were loading their possessions into and onto the car.

"Papa!" Jomo called out.

One of the men stopped and looked over just as Jata broke free of my grip and ran to be swept up by Jomo's sisters.

"This is my friend Muchoki."

Jomo's father handed the load he was carrying to the other man and came over to offer his hand. We shook.

"It is good to meet you," he said.

"And you, sir."

"I have been told that you are a good friend of my family's," he said. "Thank you for standing by them in my absence."

"Jomo also stood by my family."

"As it should be with friends. Jomo is distressed that we are leaving you behind."

I didn't know what to say.

"If there was more space, or we had more—"

"I understand, sir. I understand."

"I have written down the name of our village and my family name." He handed me a small scrap of paper. "Someday, perhaps, you will come and visit our homestead. You will be an honored guest."

"The honor will be mine. Thank you, sir."

"We are taking our few possessions with us."

"But not all," Jomo said. "This is for you." He reached down, picked up a blanket and gave it to me.

"I can't take your blanket." I held up my hands to stop him.

"It is for your mother," Jomo said.

That I couldn't refuse. "Thank you," I said, accepting the blanket.

"I wish we had more to leave for you, but we have so little where we are going."

"You have also left me with your friendship and an invitation to visit. That is worth much." But I had one more question I wanted to ask Jomo's father. "Sir, out there," I said, gesturing beyond the fence. "What is happening?"

He moved in closer. "There are still problems," he said very quietly—so quietly that only Jomo and I could hear. "Nairobi has remained a tinderbox."

"What does that mean?" Jomo said.

"There are still protests against the elections. There is still some violence spilling out from the slums. There are still clashes between different groups and with the police. There are still roads blocked with rocks or tires set on fire in parts of the city."

"But don't we have to travel through Nairobi?" Jomo asked.

"There is no other way. All roads lead *to* and *through* Nairobi."

"But how will we get through?" Jomo looked anxious.

"The protesters block the roads, and then the police clear them away. We will travel during the day, when it is most safe. The police and army will protect us."

"They didn't protect us in Webuye," Jomo said.

"There are more of them now, and they are more determined. Still, we will be most safe when we get to our village. Sometimes you must pass through danger to get to a better place," Jomo's father said. "We have to leave soon or darkness will delay our trip one more day."

"Thank you for speaking of this to me," I said. "I will leave you to finish. I need to get back to my mother."

His father and I shook hands again, and then Jomo came over and offered his.

"Goodbye, Jomo."

"No," he said, shaking his head. "Not goodbye. We will meet again, my brother."

"Until again," I said, smiling.

The girls were hugging Jata, and all three were in tears.

"You must promise us you will bring her to see us," Kioni said.

"I promise."

"Perhaps we could trade?" suggested Makena. "You keep Jomo and we get Jata!"

"No," I said. "Jomo is my brother, but Jata is my sister. She must always be at my side to be cared for."

"As it should be," Jomo's father said. "As it should be."

I stood sheltered from the sun by the tents, Jomo's blanket draped over my shoulder, trying to see but not be seen. I wanted to be there to watch them leave. I knew it was going to happen, but somehow I needed to see it with my own eyes.

I heard the little engine first and then saw the car—the one carrying Jomo and his family away. It had mattresses on the roof, and they were all crammed inside. I was close enough to see, but not close enough to see well. I could make them out inside the vehicle, but I couldn't see their faces clearly. I didn't have to, though, to know that they would all be smiling.

They were going to a new home, and they were going together.

The little vehicle rocked and bumped along the footpath until it came to a stop at the gate. One of the guards walked up to the driver's side of the vehicle while the second opened the gate wide enough to let them pass. The car started up again and eased through the narrow opening. Once outside it picked up speed, kicking up a cloud of dust that trailed behind. I just hoped they didn't look back at the camp as they left. I wanted them to only look forward. Forward was where they were going, toward their future. Behind was nothing worth seeing or remembering. I wished them the gifts of forgiveness and forgetfulness.

The car got smaller and smaller until it took the rise and disappeared over the other side. Soon even the plume of dust was gone. I felt sad and happy. Sad that they were leaving—that my friend was leaving—and happy because it meant it was possible to leave. Somebody I knew and cared for was going to a better place. I was happy for my friend, and I was happy because it meant that maybe someday I could go through that gate to a better place as well.

Chapter Eight

"Could you tell me about Kikima?" I asked my mother as we sat around our fire, and she stirred the food in the pot.

"It is a village like any other village." She shrugged and offered a sad little smile. "It has been a long time since I left."

"So long that you don't remember?"

"So long that it has changed, I am sure."

"Is it like Eldoret?" Jata asked.

Mother laughed. "Eldoret is a big city. Kikima is a small town, more like a market. Or at least it was then. Most days it is a sleepy little place, but Mondays and Thursdays are market days. People flow in from the whole Mbooni district to buy and sell. The square is filled with stalls and blankets laid out with produce and merchandise, and it is so filled with people that you can hardly move. It is very exciting."

"It would be fun to be there on a market day," Jata said.

"When I was a little girl, those were my favorite days."

"Was your school far away?" I asked.

"It was no more than a twenty-minute walk to Kyangoma—that is the name of the school I attended."

"You and your brothers?"

"My brothers and my cousins. And now I'm sure my nieces and nephews must go there as well."

"Do we have lots of cousins?" Jata asked.

"Dozens and dozens and dozens I am sure."

"It will be wonderful to meet our cousins," I said.

"If we go, you will meet them," she replied.

"It should not be *if*," I countered. "It needs to be *when*."

She looked hesitant, almost afraid.

"We can't stay here, Mother, and there is no place to go back to. Our home is not safe . . . if it is even there anymore."

"The government will help us go back to Eldoret," she insisted.

I shook my head. "Nobody is being allowed back. The government says it isn't safe."

"And how do you know this?"

"I listen. I ask questions. I speak to the sergeant every

day. He has told me. He knows." Our dinner guest had become my friend—almost against my will. Who would have thought that I could become friends with somebody of his tribe after all that had happened? We spoke often about the weather and other small pleasantries, but sometimes we also talked about things that were significant.

"You know that Kikima is not close," my mother said.

"Is it as far as Eldoret?" I knew how far that was from the trip to the camp.

"Not as far," she admitted. "But right now, it is far for me. I cannot even go as far as the front gate."

"We are not leaving today. We need to wait for you to recover."

"Yes, I must get better before anything can happen. Even then, it will still be far away."

"Do we travel through Nairobi?" I asked.

"Through Nairobi, and then toward Mombasa. Along the route to Mombasa, we head north toward Machakos Town. It is almost as big as Eldoret, except that all the people are Kamba."

"All of them?" I asked.

"The whole region. That area is called by some Kambaland."

"And from there where do we go?" I asked.

"From there, Kikima is not far. The people of Machakos all know of Kikima."

"The sergeant told me that the government is giving money to people to help them get back to their traditional homes," I explained.

Slowly my mother got to her feet. She stood there, looking a little unsteady, swaying a little bit, but still standing. She was silent, staring into the distance, not talking but thinking.

"I miss my brothers," she said finally. "I miss my parents. I do not even know if they are still alive."

"They are," I said.

"How would you know that?"

"I don't know. I just feel and hope."

"Hope is all we have when everything else has been taken away. But I am afraid that we would arrive and then . . . well, perhaps we would not be welcomed."

"Why would they not welcome us?" Jata asked.

"I have been gone a long time."

"If I was gone a long time, would you welcome me home?" I asked.

"Of course. I am your mother."

"And they are your parents."

A small smile came to her face. It was a sad smile. "They are still my parents. I can only hope that they still think of me as their daughter."

"There is only one way to find out," I said.

"Yes. Only one way. When I am able, we will leave.

We will travel to Kikima. It will be a long journey, but we will do it."

"We'll be like those Kamba in the story," I said. "We will follow the string to find our way home."

"Let us hope that this time the string has not broken," she said.

I couldn't allow myself to think that it had.

Chapter Nine

I walked along the fence, looking for the sergeant.
I'd already gone to the gate, but he wasn't there.
They said he was on patrol around the perimeter of the camp. I just hoped that we were walking around in different directions so that we would eventually meet.

As I walked, I noticed that there had been a shift in the fence. New poles had been set farther out and the fence restrung to allow more room for tents to be put up. The camp was still growing. There was a saying that misery loved company. We had more and more company. More people meant that more food and water had to be brought in, more latrines dug, more soldiers to guard us, more tents to house us, more of everything.

Some of the new arrivals moved into tents that had been vacated by people like Jomo and his family.

But this expansion was filled with tents that were obviously new. They were bright white, not weathered by the sun or coated and made dingy by the dust, or ripped and worn through use or abuse.

Our tent was still holding up well. We'd weighed it down with rocks so it was anchored to the ground. I'd dug a little trench to catch the rain and direct it around rather than through our tent. My mother had stitched up the two places where it had started to rip. It was secure. It kept us dry and out of the sun, held our possessions and sheltered us at night. But still it was just a tent and could never be a home. We needed to leave to find that home, even if it was far away in a place I'd never been. Kikima . . . when I went to sleep, I repeated the name in my head again and again to make it feel like a place I'd known before.

Just then, three soldiers came into view. I didn't know two of them but the sergeant was the third. I waved and he waved back.

"Good afternoon, my young friend," he said.

"Good afternoon, sir. I was wondering, if you have the time, could I ask you some questions?"

"Certainly." He turned to the other two soldiers. "You will continue your rounds and I will meet you on your next circuit."

They both saluted and then continued their patrol.

"How is your family?" he asked. "Is all well?"

"My sister is fine. My mother is still feeling the effects."

"Malaria is a difficult disease. She would be better in a hospital, or at least in a home with a bed and shelter from the elements."

"That is why I am here to talk to you," I said. "We are going to leave the camp."

"To the faraway place that your mother spoke of?" he asked.

"Kikima, my mother's village. It is in Mbooni district, by Machakos Town."

"Machakos I know of, but it is not close. Would somebody come to get your family?"

"There is nobody who even knows we are here. We have to travel to them."

"Then you would need funds to pay for a *matatu* ride."

"We have nothing," I said. "You told me before that the government will provide some assistance for those who are able to move out of the camp."

"It is not much, but some resources are there for families who receive a recommendation for assistance."

"Who makes the recommendation?" I asked.

"Any of the camp administrators, or a ranking soldier, such as myself."

"Would you make that recommendation for us?"

"Most certainly. You know that. You are good people. Is your mother able to travel?"

"I think she will be ready soon."

"Excellent. I will put forth the recommendation for a travel allowance so it will be ready when you are ready. I will miss my visits with you, but I wish you well as you rejoin members of your family." He paused and his expression became serious. "I have never asked— and you have no need to tell if you do not wish—but your father . . . was he a casualty of the uprising?"

It was one of the things we had never discussed. I nodded. "My father, and his father and mother, and my uncle and cousins."

"All of them?"

"All of them. It was just after dark when it began. We were already in bed. We were pulled out and told to run. My parents had been told the rioters were coming for us. It was my mother, my father, my sister and my grandparents, as well as my uncle, his wife and their three children."

"You must have been very afraid," the sergeant said.

"Even my father was afraid. I had never seen him afraid before. We fled with all the other Kikuyu we knew, trying to stay ahead of the mob. We were many, but they were so many more. They had clubs and machetes, knives, picks and shovels. And they were everywhere. We tried to get away along different routes, but they were blocked. Rocks and tires strewn across the road, fires set, men chanting and yelling. They were pulling people out of vehicles and killing them. Unable to run away, all of the routes blocked, we took refuge in the village church.

"There were so many of us. It was crowded and dark and confused. But I was there with the men who had always taken care of me—my father, my grandfather and my uncle—and I knew they would keep me safe.

"Then they came. First it was the voices. Then we could see torches bouncing up and down in the darkness, like they were living things moving toward us on their own. They came from three directions. Then as they closed in I could see the people who were holding the torches, burning bright and lighting their way. My father and the other men went outside. I went too.

"My father took me aside and commanded me to get my mother and sister and flee through the back. I begged him to flee with us, but he refused. He said he could not stop them, but he could slow them down enough to allow us to escape through the fields. I asked if I should take my cousins and my aunt, but he said that was for his brother to decide, not him, and then the mob arrived and I ran back into the church.

"I looked through the windows as others turned away, afraid to see. I was too afraid *not* to see. I saw more and more torches coming toward us, and more and more people gathering out there. In the light from the torches I could see some of their faces, and even though I knew some of the people, I could hardly recognize them. There was something so different about them."

"And there were no police to stop them?" the sergeant asked.

"There was nobody," I answered. "At first the mob stopped just outside the fence marking the church property. It was sacred land and they didn't want to enter. It was difficult then, telling my mother what my father's wishes were. She did not want to leave, did not want to leave him behind. I understood, but I insisted.

"As the crowd grew, they started tossing rocks. I remember people jumping and screaming as that first rock pierced the stained glass and sent shards into the air. Those shards of glass compelled my mother to listen to what I had said.

"Then it all happened. They swept through the front gate of the church grounds, screaming and yelling, and people inside and outside the church answered with their own anguished screams. I grabbed my sister in my arms and carried her through the crowd to the back of the building and out the rear doors. I yelled for my mother to run! I looked over my shoulder as we stumbled into a cornfield. Desperately I looked back for my father, but I knew he was gone."

"And through your actions, you and your mother and sister escaped."

"It was my father's actions that allowed us to escape. He stayed behind to give us time to leave," I said sadly. "My mother, unsteady on her feet, clung to my other arm for support. The corn was thick and high and we were hidden in the stalks."

"And then?"

"I left my sister and mother and went back to the edge of the field. The mob had by then surrounded the church on all sides, so there was no hope of escape. Again I looked for my father, but he was not to be seen. I knew. I knew. I could not do anything. I hid there, able to watch but not to be seen."

"If you cannot talk more about this, I understand. This must be difficult for you to speak of," the sergeant said.

Strangely, it wasn't. I'd relived it so many times in my thoughts and my nightmares that the words simply flowed out. I was more of a distant witness than anything else, as if I were telling him of something I'd read in the papers.

"I can talk." It felt like now that I had started I had no choice but to keep telling him the story, that I couldn't have stopped the words if I'd tried. "The mob barred the doors, barricaded them so none could escape. And then they set the church on fire."

"So awful. So terrible. I am so sorry for your loss."

"Thank you."

"If I had been there, I would have tried to stop them," the sergeant said. "If I had to, I would have opened fire upon the mob to drive them back."

"They were Kalenjin, your people. You would have fired on them?" I asked.

"I would have fired upon enemies of the country because that is what they were, whether they were Kalenjin killing Kikuyu or Kikuyu killing Kalenjin, as was done in other parts of the country." He stopped. "All those responsible for these atrocities are the same. They are nothing more than savages, animals looking for an excuse for violence, hyenas reacting to the smell of blood."

"It might have been different if the police and soldiers had come," I said.

"I have spoken to some of the men who were in those garrisons. They said there were more in the mobs than they had bullets in their guns. They were afraid. I understand the fear, but that is not an excuse. Those men were sworn to uphold the laws of our land. They did not keep their oath."

I should have felt angry at the soldiers who did nothing to protect us, but I didn't. I could still taste the fear I felt lying in the stalks at the edge of the field. I didn't have a gun, but even if I had, would I have done anything? Would I have been brave enough to help my father? I just lay there and watched as the church was set on fire.

"The flames started from the inside as windows were smashed and torches thrown in," I said, resuming my story. "Soon the thick black smoke poured out through the windows, and then the flames licked up the sides of the building and the roof caught fire. The light from the fire was so bright that I was afraid I would be seen and the mob would come after me. I needed to get my mother and sister and get away—as far away as possible.

"When I reached them, my mother wanted to wait for my father. I simply told her that he would not be coming and said no more. She knew, but we agreed not to speak further of him. I pulled her to her feet and took my sister into my arms. We staggered away, stumbling through the darkness, trying to be quiet while trying to listen. We bumped into other people—Kikuyu fleeing for their lives, and sometimes Luo, as confused and almost as frightened as us. We walked throughout the night, each step putting a little more distance between us and the mob, between us and the church. It wasn't until the morning that we stopped.

"My sister had fallen asleep in my arms, and I'd put her down in the safe spot we'd found to wait. We waited with two other Kikuyu families who were also fleeing. Then I took my mother aside and told her what had happened. How do you tell your mother that your father has died? How do you find the words? It was the hardest thing I had ever done. It was much harder even than watching the church burn. That had not seemed real. Telling her was all too real.

"It was so strange. I'd been somehow preparing for my mother's death for years. The malaria had weakened her and made so many illnesses appear. I didn't expect it to be my father. He was so big, so strong, so healthy. I thought he would live forever. I was wrong."

"I wish I could have been there that night," the sergeant said again. "Instead all I can do now is make arrangements for funds to be disbursed to your family. I wish to make sure that as soon as you are able to travel, you will be ready."

"You have shown friendship and kindness to my family," I said.

"It is important that Kalenjin show friendship to Kikuyu, and that Kikuyu do the same to Kalenjin," he said. "You must try to do this."

I understood what he was saying, but could I ever do that? Could I ever show kindness to the people who had killed my father? Wouldn't that be to disrespect his memory, to dishonor his passing?

"You cannot fight evil by becoming evil," he said, seeming to read my thoughts. "The only cure for darkness is light. Not that you should forget what happened."

"I cannot forget what happened!" I snapped, but then I felt badly. This man had done nothing but offer me friendship. He had shown us kindness . . . but that was different. *He* was different. He was Kalenjin, but he was different.

"But please also remember the kindnesses that have been offered. Do not let the bad—no matter how bad—erase the good. Those people have taken so much from you, please do not let them take everything."

I slowly nodded in agreement.

He placed a hand on my shoulder. "You are a good boy. A boy a father would be proud of. Now you go and tell your mother, and I will go and make the arrangements. I will try to make things happen quickly, but it could be two or three weeks."

"Thank you."

I *would* remember this small act of kindness by a Kalenjin, but that act would never make up for the evil that was done by other Kalenjins. I would never forget what those people had done. Helping to get us a few shillings for a *matatu* would never undo those deeds.

I would not forget any of it. Ever.

Chapter Ten

There was a loud cry from somewhere outside the tent—sad and loud and desperate—and then I heard my sister react. She started crying. I jumped up from the ground and went to her side.

"Jata, it is all right. I'm here," I whispered. I tried to keep my voice calm, although I felt my heart racing too.

The sobbing continued. I scooped her up and she wrapped her arms tightly around my neck. For somebody so little and thin, she had such power.

"It's all right. It's just a noise in the distance."

At that instant, the person cried out again. I felt Jata tighten her grip, felt her body begin to shake as she cried louder. I had to comfort her, but I also had to make sure she didn't wake our mother. I stood up with her in my arms and walked over to the tent flap, pushing it open and stepping outside.

"See, there's nothing out here to be afraid of," I said.

She loosened her grip slightly and peered around. I looked around too. She wasn't the only person who needed reassurance.

"Everybody is asleep. That was probably somebody having a bad dream," I said. I knew about bad dreams.

I felt her relax a little bit more. I needed to offer her more reassurance.

"We are safe here in the camp. Nobody can get in."

My fears here weren't from the outside. They were about diseases being spread, the water being tainted and of course fire. And there had been fires. It was inevitable when there were so many people, so many tents and so many cooking fires. Although most only burned a few tents, others spread rapidly and destroyed dozens and dozens of tents before they were put out. Those affected were without shelter except that offered by their neighbors until a new tent could be brought. It seemed so cruel for those who had so little to lose the little they had.

The fires scared me just as much as the loud sounds bothered Jata. She had *heard* the mobs, but I had *seen* the flames. The nightmare had entered not just through my eyes but through my nose. The smell of fire caused me great distress. How sad that something that warmed our bones and cooked our meals could also be used for something so evil. Fire wasn't our friend or our enemy, it just was.

"I'm scared," Jata said.

"Scared of what? You have your brother here, so nothing can ever harm you. You know that." I needed to distract her, calm her. "Look at all those stars in the sky. Aren't they beautiful?"

She nodded. They weren't just beautiful but bright. Between them and the moon—which was almost full— there was a gentle blanket of light that filled the night. The tents seemed almost to glow, and I could see clearly into the distance, tent after tent, row after row, until they disappeared.

"Do you see it?" I asked.

"See what?"

"It is very hard to see, so I'm not surprised you can't."

"See what?" she demanded.

"The string."

"The string?"

"Yes. I see it going down the passageway between the tents." I pointed with my finger to trace the path of the invisible string. "It goes out through the front gate and then down the road to Nairobi. And do you know where it goes then?"

She shook her head.

"It goes all the way to Kikima, to the home of our grandparents."

"You can't see that."

"Of course I can't see it all the way! I can only see it as far as the gate. I'm just surprised that you can't see it at all."

She strained to look, trying to make out the string in the moonlight.

"It glistens, reflects the light. Look harder. Can you see it?"

"I think I can see it . . . I think."

"It's okay if you can't. I can see it. It will lead us to our grandparents' home, to our *new* home. But don't worry if you can't see it, because I can."

She gave a big yawn.

"Are you ready to go back to bed?"

"I'm ready."

I opened up the flap and carried her back inside. I pulled back the blanket with one hand and set her down on the bed to snuggle back down. It was good that none of this had woken up our mother. She was quietly sleeping. In fact, she hadn't moved at all. I held my breath, listening for hers. I could hear her . . . or was it Jata?

I bent down and placed my ear by my mother's mouth, straining, praying, hoping for a sound. There was nothing. I touched her face with my hand. It was cold.

My mother was gone.

—

"I am sorry for your loss," the man said.

"What?"

"I am sorry for your mother's death."

"Thank you, sir." I took a deep breath and worked hard to keep the tears inside. It would not be right to cry in front of a stranger—especially a stranger who was this important. It was time for me to be strong. That was what my father would expect, what my mother would want and what my sister needed. She was in the hospital tent being watched by a nurse. I needed to get to her soon, but right now, I needed to be here.

The stranger was a large man and he sat behind a desk piled high with papers. I had never met him before, but I had been told that he was the chairman of the camp—the man in charge—so he was *very* important. Before coming here—being forced to come here, like all of us—he had been a very successful business-man and a respected elder in his community.

"How old are you, son?"

"Thirteen . . . fourteen in a few months."

"And your sister is how old?"

"She is seven, sir."

"Do you have any other family in the camp?"

"No, sir. We were alone." If Jomo hadn't moved, I could have claimed that his family was our family— they would have helped us. "We were going to be leaving soon, sir."

"So you have some family elsewhere? Excellent, most excellent." He smiled—a big smile. "Can they come and get you?"

I shook my head. "They do not know we are here . . . I do not know how to contact them."

"But you were going to go there?" he asked.

"When my mother recovered." Now she would never recover. "We were going to return to her village."

The smile disappeared and the man let out a big sigh.

"Sir, may I be excused? I need to be with my sister, to care for her."

"The matron at the hospital will provide care." He sighed again. "It is most unfortunate that you are not turning sixteen in a few months. Then I could ignore the things that need to be done, lose the paperwork for a while . . . I could perhaps do something by doing nothing."

"I do not understand, sir."

"You are not of age to care for your sister, or for yourself. I must take action to provide supervision."

I nodded in agreement, although I still had no idea what he meant.

"I have to sign the papers," he said.

Did he mean the papers for the funds to help us get to our grandparents?

"When can we leave, sir?"

"It will be soon. Probably your sister will leave first."

"I do not understand," I said again. "She is too young to be going on her own."

He looked as confused as I felt. "She will not be going alone. A matron will escort her."

I felt a sense of relief—we were not going to have to go alone—somebody was going to take us to our grandparents. But still . . . "Why am I not going with her at the same time?"

"Because you are not going to the same place," he said.

"But we are both going to our grandparents."

He shook his head. "You are going to where you can be cared for as orphans."

"Our grandparents will care for us."

"You tell me that their village is far away, and that they cannot come and get you. That they do not even know you are here. How would you get there?"

"There is money given to help some families leave," I said. "I was told that."

"There is some money for families, but not for two children. Do you expect us just to give you money and allow you to walk out of here alone? Do you think that would be responsible?"

I didn't know what to say.

"And how do we even know these people will take you when you arrive—if you arrive?"

I hadn't considered the possibility that they wouldn't, so again I had no answer.

"You will both be well cared for. You will be provided for at the children's homes."

"We cannot be separated. We need to go to the same home."

"That is not possible. One is for girls and the other is for boys."

"But . . . but . . . she is my sister. She needs my care."

"She will remain your sister and she will be cared for—far better than you would be able to."

"My mother has been ill for a long time, sir. I have always been there to care for both my mother and my sister. I *can* care for her."

"Not legally. You are too young. Do you know the trouble I would get into if I allowed you to care for her and something happened?"

I didn't care about trouble for him, and anyway nothing was going to happen.

"Besides, it is not like you will never see her. I have been told that visits are possible."

"Visits?"

"Yes. During school breaks, you will have an opportunity to see her—perhaps for an entire afternoon, if the two homes are not too far apart."

"You don't even know where they are?"

"I have enough to do inside this fence. Once people leave, they are not my concern."

If we were outside the wire, would we be his concern?

"Would you like to tell your sister of the plans, or would you prefer I tell her?" he asked.

"No, you cannot do that . . . I will tell her." But how? Telling her of our mother's death was the hardest thing I'd ever done, and now she was going to lose me as well. "When will this take place? When will she leave?"

"Do you think you can provide care for the night?" he asked.

"Yes, sir. I can care for her."

"It could even be two nights. You must watch and feed her, put her to sleep. Can you do that?"

"Yes, sir."

"Does your sister go to our school?"

I nodded.

"Tomorrow you go there and tell them that she will be leaving and there is no point in her taking up a seat." He stopped and considered me carefully. "I know this is not what you want, but what choice do I have?"

He could have somebody take us to Kikima, I thought, or at least give us the money to go there ourselves.

"You have to have faith that what is being done is what is best for you. And who knows? Maybe once you're in the orphanage, somebody there will be able to connect you with your family."

"They could?"

He shrugged. "Anything is possible, although I would imagine it would not happen soon. There are so many orphans and only so many resources. Nothing will happen quickly. Are you of faith?"

"What do you mean?"

"Are your family churchgoers? Are you a believer?"

"Of course. We go to church each week. Sometimes twice a week."

I thought about my last brief glimpse of our church, the flames engulfing it, the smoke rising into the sky and—

"Then you must know that sometimes things happen for reasons we do not understand. It was God's will that brought you here, and it is God's will that you go to a children's home."

"No, sir."

"No? What do you mean?" he asked.

"It is not God's will. It is *your* will. You are sending us to these places. You are sending my sister away from me. God would not do that."

His mouth dropped open. He looked shocked. And then he started to look angry.

"You are only a boy, and you must understand that adults—your elders—are wiser. Do you think you are wiser than me?" he demanded.

"No, sir, but I—"

"You have taken enough of my time. I am a busy man." He got to his feet. "Go and take your sister. Be prepared to leave by tomorrow. There is no point in discussing this further. Go."

I got to my feet and stumbled out of his office. He was right. There was no point in discussing it further, and we did need to go . . . just not the way he intended.

Chapter Eleven

Jata lay sleeping on the bed. It had taken a while for her to fall asleep. I'd rubbed her back until the tears had finally stopped and she'd drifted off. Then I was able to let my own tears flow. It was important that she not see me break down. Now more than ever, she needed me to be strong, to be in control. The only way she could believe was if I believed . . . or at least pretended to believe. Did I really think we could do this? I wasn't sure. I felt all scared inside, so much so that I felt sick to my stomach. But I couldn't show the fear. I had to act. What choice did we have? When there is no hope, even a little glimmer is better. Besides, the longest journey starts with one step. That was how it was done.

I sorted through our meager possessions. We didn't have much, but I still didn't know if we could take it all. Everything had weight that I would have to carry, and at some point I might have to carry Jata as well.

Definitely we should take a blanket . . . or should we carry two? That would leave one—a small present for the people who would take up this tent when we were gone. The cooking pot definitely would be needed. The water container, the knife and most certainly all the food. Two bowls and two plates and a spoon. Would a second spoon weigh that much more? I had proudly traded some of the gazelle meat for those three spoons.

Thank goodness my mother had always planned ahead. There was extra food for three of us for five days. That meant there was enough for seven or even eight days for the two of us, although we were going to need to eat more than usual. We weren't going to be sitting around doing nothing.

There was a gentle rapping on the flap of the tent and a rush of panic overcame me. Had they come early to get Jata? Was I foolish to have waited for morning?

"Muchoki, are you there?"

I recognized the voice. It was the sergeant. Had they sent *him* to get Jata?

I stayed perfectly still. If I didn't respond, maybe he would go away. But the flap of the tent opened and he poked in his head.

"I needed to come to express my condolences," he said.

"Thank, you, sir."

"Your mother was a good woman. I am sad for your loss. I just wish she had survived long enough for you to go to the homestead of her parents." He paused. "I inquired about your circumstances. I was told they are sending you both away."

"They want us to be separated in two places."

"I was told of the plan, but it is not right to separate family," he said.

"Do you . . . ? Do you think that perhaps you could . . . ?"

"Ask that they reconsider their plan?"

I nodded.

"I could ask, but my words would fall on deaf ears. I am merely a sergeant. Besides, the chairman looks at me and sees not a soldier but a Kalenjin, and he is Kikuyu. He will not change because of my words."

"Then there is no choice."

He looked at me hard, as if he were trying to look inside my mind.

"I hear your words agreeing to this, but I am not sure I believe them. The boy I know—the one who has cared for his mother and sister all this time—would not so easily agree. You have something else in mind, I think."

111

I wanted to lie, but even more I needed to trust somebody and he was all I had.

"In the morning I will leave the camp with my sister. We will go to the village of my mother, to the village of her family. *Our* family."

He shook his head. "You cannot do that."

"I have no choice. I cannot allow my sister to be taken away."

"No, you should not allow her to be taken, but you cannot wait until morning. By then it will be too late. I have been told that the matron from the children's residence will be here at first light to take your sister."

"But . . . but . . ." I buried my head in my hands. "I do not know what to do."

He bent down until I could sense that his face was right beside mine—I could feel his breath. "You will not wait for morning. You will leave now."

"But the gate is closed. No one is allowed to leave. Are you going to let us leave?"

"I cannot let you out in front of other soldiers or I will be punished."

"I don't want you to be punished."

"And I do not want you or your sister to be punished either. You will not leave through the gate. You will leave through the back. There is a spot where you can squeeze under the fence."

112

"*Under?* But how can I find that spot?"

"You will find it because I will be there to show you." He got up. "You must gather your things and then go to the back of the camp. I will be waiting outside the fence at the correct spot. Do you know where you are going?"

"To the back fence," I said, puzzled.

"I meant after you leave the camp. Do you know the way to travel?"

"To Nairobi, then to Machakos and finally to Kikima."

"That is far, but it can be done," he said. "You must be strong and you must be brave."

I didn't feel either strong or brave, but what choice did I have?

"You need to move quietly in the camp. You cannot be discovered as you leave or they will stop you."

I suddenly felt a rush of emotions swelling up inside of me—fear, uncertainty and, strangest of all, hope. I wasn't going to let anybody stop me. I would do whatever needed to be done. Maybe I was stronger and braver than I thought.

Chapter Twelve

My sister had a blanket draped around her shoulders. Not only did it provide her with warmth against the cold air, but it was dark red and so it would also help her blend into the night. I had a second blanket tied off in a knot and inside was everything we would take—the pot, our supply of food, three bowls and three spoons. I knew we didn't need the third bowl and spoon, but they had belonged to my mother and I couldn't bear to leave them behind. They were all we had left of her.

Everything was in that little bundle—everything except the water container, which was too big and heavy, and the little knife. I'd wrapped the knife in a piece of cloth and then tucked it into the belt of my trousers. I wanted to have it close if I needed it, but I couldn't think of much that could be solved by my little knife. I just wished Jomo had left me his machete. That would have been something.

"Are you ready?" I asked.

"I want to sleep more."

"There's no time for sleep. We have to leave now."

"Why?"

What was I supposed to say to her? She didn't know the reason we had to leave.

"Um, I can see it best at night—the string."

"Really?"

"The string seems to reflect the soft glow of the moonlight even better than it does the bright rays of the sun."

"Does that mean we have to travel only at night?" she asked.

I hadn't thought of her asking that. What was I going to answer? "Um, right now we are very far away from where we are going, so the string is very thin. As we get closer, I'll be able to see it by sunlight."

I threw the bundled blanket over my shoulder and picked up the water container. It was full, which made it heavy, but there was no telling where or when we would find clean water.

"It is time to go."

I offered my sister my hand and helped her to her feet. She stood up, leaving the cot empty. It seemed strange to think that my mother wasn't there, lying hidden in the shadows. We were leaving her behind just as we had left our father behind in Eldoret. Just as we'd left behind our grandparents and aunt and uncle and cousins. They were all gone. It was just me and my sister moving forward.

The air outside the tent was cool and quiet. Everybody was asleep, and all was still. Even the wind seemed to have stopped, as if it were waiting for what we were going to do. Carefully I did up the buckles to seal the tent closed. I was hoping that when they came in the morning, they would think we were still asleep and perhaps not enter as soon, and that would give us a little more time to escape.

"Do not be afraid," I said.

"I am not," she replied. "I am with you."

That made me smile. She trusted me. I just hoped that trust was justified. And I hoped even more that she couldn't sense the fear inside me.

"We want to move as quietly as possible," I said. "We don't want to wake anybody up. That would not be *polite*."

"I will be as quiet as a mouse."

We started off, and then I stopped and turned around. Even a few steps away, our tent seemed different now. It was the same as all the other tents in the camp, and it would soon be occupied by another family. It would no longer belong to us—it no longer belonged to us now. All it held was a bed—just a simple cot and a mattress. Would the bed even remember that we were once there? Silly. It was just wood and stuffing and cloth sheltered underneath a piece of canvas. None of those could remember or forget.

But *we* could remember. Jata and I could remember our time here, our mother, our father, what had happened to us and where we had come from. We could not forget our lives in Eldoret, but now we were setting out to do something more—we would return to where our mother had come from. Even though we'd never been there we were going to be walking home.

"Why are we waiting?" Jata asked.

I couldn't tell her what I was thinking. "I was just waiting for a cloud to pass overhead," I said, gesturing to the sky, "so that the light from the moon will show me the way. Do you see the string now?"

She seemed to be straining her eyes, tilting her head slightly, looking for the string that would guide us. "I think I see it."

"I can definitely see it," I said. "Strange, though—it is leading us away from the front gate."

"It is? Before you said it went through the front gate."

"Before it did, but now it doesn't. Just keep holding my hand and I'll keep my eye on it."

She tightened her grip on my hand and I squeezed hers a little tighter too. I was never going to let go of her, not ever. She was all I had left and I was all she had left, and nobody was going to separate us.

Carefully I chose our route. I wanted to stay away from the administrative tent in case I ran into somebody who knew us. I was sure the chairperson was asleep—did he even sleep in the camp?—but we were known by other people. I didn't want to be asked any questions that I couldn't answer. As well, I wanted to stay away from the hospital. My fear wasn't just that some of the nurses might recognize us, but that we might see something we shouldn't. How would Jata react if she saw them moving our mother's body? It was in the middle of the night when I'd seen them throw those other bodies into the back of the lorry. I couldn't think about them doing that with her. I couldn't.

The nurse at the hospital had told me that our mother would be "laid to rest" at a cemetery they'd created outside the camp. She'd also told me that family members weren't allowed at the burials. All goodbyes had to be said there at the hospital. So that's what we'd done, leaving her in that bed.

"Is everybody asleep?" Jata asked now.

"Almost the *whole* world is asleep."

"Is Mommy sort of asleep?"

I felt my heart rise up into my throat. "It's like being asleep but never waking up again."

"*Never?*"

I shook my head. "She's with our father. She's at peace now and has been reunited with him. We are doing what she wanted us to do. We're following the string."

"And you can see it?"

"It's faint but I can see it. It's leading us to the fence at the back of the camp."

"Are we going to climb the fence, Muchoki?"

"It's too high to climb, and anyway the razor wire at the top would stop us," I said.

"Then what will we do?"

"There will be a way. The string will lead us. Just have faith, okay?"

She nodded. It was important that she have faith so she didn't have fear. I didn't want to lie to her, but the truth wasn't as secure or as certain. The truth was far from either of those. I wished I had somebody who would lie to me so I didn't feel the fear and the uncertainty.

"There's the fence," Jata said.

We were coming up to the edge of the camp. The wire of the fence glistened, catching the rays of the moon the way I'd described the string reflecting the light. Now, I saw the fence differently than I had before. Rather than a ring of protection, keeping us safe from the outside world, it was a barrier standing in our way. What would we do if the sergeant wasn't there? Would I be able to find the one place where we could squeeze under the fence? Surely we couldn't climb it, and I had nothing to cut it with. In fact, the only tools I had were those three spoons and my knife. A shovel would have been better, but if I really needed to, I'd just take that little knife and one of the spoons and dig my way underneath. I wasn't going to be stopped before we had even started. Not by the chairman and not by a fence.

We came to the base of the fence, but I didn't see the sergeant—I didn't see anybody.

"What are we waiting for?" Jata asked.

"I'm just trying to decide whether we should go left or right."

"Shouldn't we just follow the string? You do see it, don't you?" She sounded hesitant.

"Of course I do. I can see it right outside the fence. I just can't see where it goes through the fence. Let's go a little bit to the right and then—" I heard a sound . . . feet against the dirt. It was either the sergeant or somebody else. Either good or bad. We'd know soon.

"Somebody is—"

"Ssshhh. Stay quiet," I whispered. I slowly dropped to one knee and pulled Jata down beside me, using my body to shield her.

The footfalls got louder, and then I saw a darkened figure walking just outside the fence. Was it him?

"Muchoki? Muchoki? Can you hear me? Are you there?"

It *was* him!

"Come," I said. I pulled Jata to her feet and we rushed over to meet the sergeant at the fence. He had his rifle over his shoulder.

"It is good to see you and Jata."

"It is even better to see you."

He bent down and grabbed the bottom strand of wire. It was a few centimeters above the dirt. He pulled it up until there was a gap wide enough for us to slip through.

"You first, Jata," I said.

I dropped the bundled blanket to the ground and grabbed the wire as well, pulling it up to make it easier for her. Jata easily slipped underneath. I pushed the bundle and the water container under, then slipped under as well.

"You came to almost exactly the right spot in the fence. Did you know about it being right here?" the sergeant asked.

"He followed the string," Jata said.

"What?"

"I just came to the back and it was by chance," I said. I turned to Jata and quietly said, "It is a secret."

The sergeant motioned for us to follow him as he walked away from the fence. Finally, well away from the fence, he stopped. "Stay this distance from the fence so that you cannot be seen by the guards but are still close enough that it can guide you. When you can see the main gate, you will be able to find the path leading out to the highway. I wish I could lead you that far, but I must continue my rounds or someone will become suspicious."

"I can find the path."

"Be careful of your steps. This is the time when snakes are out . . . as well as other things."

"What other things?" Jata asked anxiously.

"There are lions."

"You have seen lions?" I asked.

"Not me, but others have. Have you seen zebras?" he asked.

I nodded.

"The Maasai have a saying: 'If you see zebras, think of lions.' It means that lions always follow zebras."

Instinctively I put my hand against my small knife.

"They have not been seen close to the fence or along the path to the highway. I think they smell and know to not come close," he said. "Do not get too close, but do not stray too far. Understand?"

"I understand."

"The people who will be coming to get you, the government people, will be distressed when they find you are not here and will look for you—in camp first and then perhaps on the road. But they will not look too hard or too far. There are more than enough orphans to keep them occupied. Regardless, you must get far from here before they arrive."

"We will walk as quickly as we can."

"You will do better than that. Here, this is for you." He pressed some shillings into my hand. "I only wish it were more, but it is the end of the month. I have almost nothing left. The rest has been sent to my family."

"Thank you. What more could any person do than give everything?" I asked.

"When you get to the highway, you must flag down a *matatu* that is going to Nairobi."

"Is this enough to get us to Nairobi?" I asked.

"Not nearly, but it will get you down the road far enough that nobody will suspect you have come from this camp. It will take you twenty or thirty kilometers, maybe more."

"Thank you so much."

"When you get to the highway, remember you are going toward Nairobi. It is to your left."

"To the left," I repeated. I knew that already, but it was good to hear it again. Nothing could be worse for us than traveling in the wrong direction and having to retrace our steps.

"I just pray to God that I am doing the right thing," he said.

"What do you mean?" I asked.

"I am helping you to leave. It is giving you a chance to be together, but it is also giving you a chance to die together."

"There is always that chance," I said. "Even when you are in a church with your family."

"You are right. Besides, I think it would be better to die together than survive apart."

His words hit me so strongly. I had thought about that so much—how it might have been better if we had all perished as a family. But I couldn't let those thoughts overwhelm me, especially now.

"We will live together," I said. "And I will remember that is was because of you, a Kalenjin."

"First I am a Kenyan. Second I am a Kalenjin. Now, go. I will walk along the fence in that direction. You go the same way so you can see me even if I can't see you. Follow along."

I offered my hand and we shook.

"God be with you," I said.

"And with you, my son." He released my hand. "Now hurry! Another guard will be here shortly."

I took my sister's hand and then picked up the water container. It was heavy, but that was good. It had all the water we'd need for the next few days.

The sergeant walked back to the fence, and Jata and I started along through the scrub. I tried to move quickly and silently and carefully. I pulled my sister up a little incline and then down the other side. Suddenly, the sergeant and the camp were gone from view. It was almost too late to turn back. No, it *was* too late.

"Come, Jata," I said soothingly. "Stay silent and we will be fine."

We walked along the base of the small rise. As it ended, I was reassured to see the fence once again and even more reassured to see the silhouette of the sergeant. He coughed loudly, which I suspected had more to do with letting me hear him than actually having to cough. We hurried our steps to keep pace with him. His circle was smaller than ours, so we needed to move faster to stay with him. It was dark but not completely dark. The sky was sending down enough light to guide our feet and keep the fence in sight.

"Do you think we will die?" Jata asked.

"Of course not. I will not let us die. Why would you even think that?"

"I heard the words of the sergeant. It would be all right if we did," she said. "It would be God's will, and then we would be with our parents and our aunts and uncles and our cousins."

"We will be with other cousins and other aunts and uncles, and also with our grandparents," I said. "There will be time later for us to join our parents. Right now, there is a different plan that we must follow, and right now, you must be silent."

The way was rough and it was hard to keep one eye on the fence and the second on the ground beneath our feet—harder still to keep one ear on the sounds of the sergeant and a second on any hints of noise from the brush. Maybe God's plan was for us to be eaten by a lion, but it was not *my* plan and I would try to stop it.

We continued to circle around until the gate and the guardhouses came into sight. The path would not be much farther ahead of us. The sergeant walked right to the gate and stopped. There were two other guards there. He raised a hand and gave a wave in our direction, and I waved back even though I knew he couldn't see us.

I turned away and headed forward, away from the fence, not wanting to chance entering onto the path where I could be visible to the guards. Jata and I went over another small rise and then I turned us back toward the path. Almost instantly we came upon it, worn and wide from the thousands of feet that traveled it daily from the camp to the highway. It was reassuring to have it to guide us, just as it was reassuring to have had the fence and the sergeant guiding us. I only wished there *was* a trail of string leading us to Kikima. But in a way, there was: it was a black ribbon of tarmac that led from here to Nairobi. I wasn't sure of the steps after that, but I was sure of the first. In fact, we'd already taken them.

We followed the path up another rise until we stood at a place where I could make out the outline of the camp if I looked back, and I could see the dark line of the highway if I looked forward. The camp was completely dark, but I could see two pinpoints of light coming along the highway—the headlights of a vehicle. It was coming in our direction and then would pass us as it continued to Nairobi. As it got closer I could hear the engine straining and see the lights stretched out before it, showing the surface of the road.

"There, I can see the string!" Jata yelled.

I almost told her to be quiet, but I didn't. She needed to see the string, and so did I. The truck passed by the spot where the path met the highway, and as it did, the white headlights became dull reddish taillights, visible but not giving off any light, just a glow.

We started down the hill, and I stopped myself from looking back. There was nothing behind us. I just hoped there was something in front of us. The weight of the water container pulled me forward, and I pulled Jata with me. The path was smooth and straight, and there was nothing and nobody to stop us from reaching the highway. We were moving faster and faster. I had to fight the urge to run. At the end we could run, but now we needed to walk. I slowed our pace and then came to a complete stop at the highway.

We stepped onto the tarmac. It was empty and dark and solid and there was a little bit of warmth rising from it. I released Jata's hand and put down the water container. I felt lighter, hopeful.

"This road leads to Nairobi," I said. "All we have to do is follow it."

"Is it far?"

"Very far, but not too far."

"How long will it take?"

"If we stand still, it will take forever." I picked up the container and Jata took my hand and we started.

"We're closer now," she said.

"Yes, we are."

"And closer now."

"Yes, another three steps."

"And even closer—"

"Less talking and more walking."

"Sorry, sorry," she said.

We walked in silence for a few moments. I felt badly for snapping at her.

"Jata?"

"Yes, Muchoki?"

"We *are* closer now."

She laughed, and her laughter made the darkness seem to lift.

Chapter Thirteen

All through the night we walked. We slowed but never stopped. Jata kept pace with me, even though she had to take four steps for each three of mine, which meant her journey would be longer. She never complained. That was Jata. That was my *mother*—always looking for things to make her smile, always making other people smile. She was exactly what my father had always said: a small copy of our mother.

As we traveled, most of our time was spent in open country. In the darkness I couldn't see far, but I could make out the darkened shapes of trees and hedges, and the imagined images of lions lurking behind them. I tried to stay in the very center of the road, feeling somehow that the tarmac would protect us—as if lions couldn't scale the side of the roadway. But maybe it *was* safer. If they didn't like the smell of the camp, they certainly wouldn't like the lingering smell of the tar and the fumes of the vehicles.

Frequently the country gave way to homesteads or small settlements, a few or a few dozen buildings huddled together. It was as if even the buildings did not like being alone. Their shadows were almost always dark, with only a very few showing any signs of life, light leaking out from beneath doors or around drawn curtains. Light was too precious to allow it to escape, but it wanted to find its way out to freedom.

With the night starting to give way to morning, there were more signs of the world awakening. Roosters started to crow, an invitation to all to wake up. While vehicles were still rare, they were more frequent. They were also coming in waves—not one or two but sometimes ten lorries, all moving together. Maybe they didn't want to be alone right now either.

Now we walked beside the tarmac. For the first few kilometers we had moved off at the sight of traffic and then back on again. Now the stream was so steady that there was no point. Those first few trucks that had come along were a welcome sign that we weren't alone. I could hear the engines and then see the lights and feel warmed by their passing. Now they were just noisy and smelly. I kept my eyes open for a *matatu*, but so far there had only been lorries.

"Are you tired?" I asked Jata.

"I can walk farther. How far is it?"

"We will walk for days," I said.

"How many days?"

"It depends on how fast we walk." I would have given her a better answer if I'd had it. I had no idea how many days it would be.

"I can walk faster." She tried to pick up our pace, but I held her back.

"Do you not remember about the tortoise and the hare?" I asked.

"I remember that story, but I do not necessarily believe it. It would be better to move faster to get there sooner. If we moved very fast, how long would it take?"

I still had no answer. I didn't know the distances, and I didn't know how far we could move each day. "We will get there when we get there."

"That is not a good answer," she said reproachfully.

"It is the best I can give." Just then, I heard an approaching vehicle and looked behind us. It was a *matatu*! "Do you want to move faster?"

"Yes, much faster!"

"Good, because we will move very fast now." I put down the water container and raised my hand high for the driver to see. He blew by us, leaving nothing but a hail of stones and dust and . . . he pulled off to the side! I grabbed the container and we ran after him. It was a big yellow *matatu* and its roof was piled high with boxes and barrels. By the time we arrived, the door was open and the conductor was hanging out.

"Nairobi?" he yelled at us.

"Yes." I pulled the money out of my pocket and handed it to him.

He unfurled the bills, then said, "We are going to Nairobi, but you are not."

"What do you mean?"

"This is not enough to get you there—not even one of you."

"Can you carry us as far as the money will allow?"

"That I can do, but it will not be far. Climb aboard, quickly now!"

Jata jumped into the open door and I climbed up after her, burdened with the bundle and the water container. My feet had hardly hit the step when the conductor thumped against the side and the vehicle leaped forward, practically knocking me into the arms of an old woman in the first row of seats.

"Sorry, sorry!" she yelled as she offered me support.

The *matatu* bumped back up onto the tarmac, but this time I was ready and steadied myself with the side of a seat. Jata and I stumbled down the aisle. There were people sitting on the floor toward the back, which signaled that all the seats were taken. I wanted to move as close to the back as possible, some-how hoping that the conductor would forget about us a little longer and allow us a few extra kilometers. Slow and steady won the race, at least between the tortoise and the hare—but I didn't think either could outrace a *matatu*.

As I passed each row of seats I looked at the people. Most were still asleep and couldn't look back. There were men and women, some with their children, sleeping together in tangled groups. At their feet and poking into the aisle were bundles and bags—their possessions. I couldn't help wondering how many of them were fleeing from the same storm we had left behind.

Jata slumped down onto the floor at the back. I put down the water container next to her. It was lighter from a night of drinking but still heavy. I heard the water sloshing around inside. Next I removed my bundled blanket and set it down as well. Finally I sat down on her other side and she settled into me, resting her head on my shoulder.

"Go to sleep, little one, and I will watch over you."

Instantly her eyes closed and her breathing changed. She was asleep. I decided I'd just close my eyes for a few minutes too.

"Hey, wake up, boy!"

My eyes popped open and I was blinded by a bright light and confused as to where I was. It was the *matatu* conductor standing over top of me.

"You have ridden more than your fare! It is time to get off the bus!"

"Yes, we will get off." Jata's eyes were only half-open. "Come, sister, we need to get off."

I stood up and pulled her to her feet. The conductor retreated down the aisle toward the front of the still-moving *matatu*. We may have traveled too far, but with each second we were traveling farther. Deliberately, I grabbed her blanket and then the bundle with one hand and the water container with the other. I went slowly down the aisle, pushing past others who had boarded since we did. Now not only every seat but also most of the aisle was taken by passengers. I looked out the windows at the passing country. It didn't look much different from where we had started, and I wondered how far we had come.

When we finally arrived at the front, the conductor signaled to the driver and we pulled off the tarmac onto the dirt shoulder, a big cloud of dust rising up behind us.

"Where are we, sir?" I asked.

"We are as far as your fare could take you and then more."

"And Nairobi?"

"It is sixty-five kilometers ahead on this road."

"How far did we ride?"

"It should have been only twenty kilometers, but

it is now closer to forty. You should be paying more."

"We have no more to pay, sir. Thank you for allowing us to ride longer," I said.

"I did not allow. I simply forgot."

He opened the door and I jumped down, helped Jata off with my free hand. Her feet had hardly touched the ground when the engine roared and the bus started off. The conductor leaned out the door. "And do not forget: it is this way. You cannot miss it!" he yelled.

The *matatu* bumped up onto the tarmac, driving off. Soon, the dust it had created dropped down and the sound of the engine faded to near silence before it was replaced by the noise of an oncoming truck.

I looked around. No homesteads, stores or people. We were alone in the middle of nothing. Behind us—well behind us—was the camp. We were far enough away— they would never bother chasing us this far. Stretching out ahead was the road leading us onward. I knew that the road would lead to another and then another until it finally reached our destination. I just prayed that we were on it when it got there. I felt that sense of fear rising in my chest again. We were alone, so alone.

The sun continued to rise until it was directly above our heads. We had passed through dozens of little towns and markets—some no more than two stores together, and so broken down that they seemed to be leaning against each other as a way to stay upright. There were always people in the markets—little roadside stands put there to sell food or services to the passing trucks. Mostly we just passed through, ignored. I was grateful. We were not the only people moving between these places. We would come across others—by themselves, in pairs, sometimes whole families—who were either passing us or moving in our direction. Some would overtake us, and others we would overtake. Some moved slowly because they were burdened heavily with their possessions. We were not the only ones who had no better way to move than on our feet.

As we passed these people I would be respectful in how I observed them, but I still observed. Some seemed friendly, and almost all gave us a greeting. Others, though, had that look I'd seen in the eyes of people in the camp—a look I'd seen in the eyes of my mother. They were beaten down, afraid; they had witnessed things, and things had been done to them. It was in their eyes, visible in that instant when we passed, in a nodding of the head. I wondered if they could see those same things in me?

I was vigilant and wary of all but still welcomed their presence. In the great stretches of road that we were walking, even the company of strangers made me feel less alone. We were sharing a journey, even if we were headed in different directions.

Jata and I were walking to leave farther and farther behind everything that we had ever known, every place we had ever been, to go to people we had never met in a place we'd never been. But I couldn't allow myself to think about that. I was already carrying enough weight.

As the sun climbed throughout the day we slowed. It was hot and we were tired and hungry. A rest was needed, as was food.

"Are you hungry? Do you want to stop?" I asked.

Jata slumped down to the ground.

I offered her my hand. "I did not mean right here and now. We need to find the right spot."

She took my hand and got up. "I do not see any right spots," she said. "I only see this." She motioned around.

In front and behind were open sections of road. There were no homesteads or shops, and even the trucks had seemed to abandon this stretch. Off to both sides, as far as I could see, was only scrub brush, cactus and the occasional tree. The only thing that broke the scene—the thing that gave me hope—was in the far, far distance: the rising rim of the Rift Valley. I knew we'd be climbing it eventually. I wasn't looking forward to it but I knew it was the high point that stood between us and Nairobi, so it would have to be scaled.

"I want to find a spot off the road," I said. I was still thinking that sometime today those people who had been sent for us would be traveling this road. They might not recognize us and would view us as nothing more than two of the hundreds of people walking along the highway. Still I would rather not chance being seen by them at all. We were far from the camp now. Between the forty-kilometer ride in the *matatu* and the distance covered by foot, we had traveled perhaps fifty-five kilometers. That meant that Nairobi was only another fifty kilometers away. We couldn't get there today, but we could be there in two days. But after that I had no idea. How far was Machakos from Nairobi, and how far was Kikima from there? Was it two hundred kilometers or three hundred or more? I wanted to know, but perhaps knowing would have been bad. It was easier to walk these steps at least having hope that it was close.

Twice it had looked as if it would rain, but then it hadn't. The rainy season was upon us, but the rain wasn't. Rain was a blessing from heaven, and there appeared to be no blessings this day. At least when the clouds came, they shaded us from the sun. There were times when the tarmac was so hot that it was spongy under foot. It was better to travel along the side of the road, not simply to avoid the traffic but to be free of the heat rising from the tarmac.

Up ahead I could make out the outline of a few little buildings. Smaller still were the figures moving slowly about in the midday heat. They were moving because there was some cause to move. I knew that if I had no reason, I would surely be sitting in a spot shaded from the sun instead of walking along the side of the highway.

Between us and the buildings, there was a vehicle off to the side of the road. It was a vehicle, but it was not a vehicle. At least not anymore. It was a wreck of some sort, I was certain. Getting closer, I could make out the skeleton of a small *matatu*. Gone were the tires and the glass of the windows, and even the white of the frame was scarred and blackened by fire. It had been in an accident; a fire had consumed it.

"What happened to it?" Jata asked.

"An accident. You know how *matatu* drivers are. I'm surprised the roadway isn't littered with more of their remains."

It sat there, at the side of the road, facing forward, sitting right side up, and the body, other than the black-ened frame, was not dented or damaged. The roadway, though, had been swept clean of any pieces from the collision, and there were none of the glistening pebbles of glass that usually lingered on the road for months or even years after an accident. This must have happened long ago, because nobody would ever clean up after an accident, especially out here where there was nothing but scrub bush to witness it.

"Do you think we could ride on this *matatu*?" Jata joked.

"It's about the only one we can afford, although it would not go very far."

It did look as if it was simply waiting for passengers the way it was sitting. I could almost picture the conductor hanging out the open door.

As we came right up to it, I could see that it would be a most uncomfortable ride. The seats had been completely consumed by the fire, so there was no place for the passengers to sit, and there was a blackened mass in one of the seats. In an instant of trying to make sense out of nonsense, then denying it and then realizing it was real, I knew. It was the burned remains of a man, still covered in shreds of clothing, the white of his skull the only contrast to the blackened, burned body.

I pushed Jata away, still holding her hand, trying to get some distance and to use my body as a screen between her and the dead man. I wanted to protect her, to stop her from seeing, or suffering from the sight.

"Up ahead in the next village we will stop for water," I said.

"I am thirsty."

"So am I. Very thirsty. How about if you sing me a song to pass the time?"

"But you told me not to sing because it takes away my breath and makes me more thirsty."

"You are only going to sing until those next buildings, and then you will have something to drink."

She began to sing. "*Charity, charity, charity, charity . . .*"

We left the *matatu* behind. Her little sweet voice had blocked the sight from her eyes. She hadn't seen. I just wished I hadn't either.

I started humming along with her.

I could tell there was something happening on the highway, but I couldn't be certain of what. The trucks and cars were slowing down and then stopping. Was it rioters? I couldn't see any smoke, and nothing was on fire. It would be easy enough for us to leave the tarmac and go into the bush, where we could detour around without being noticed. I didn't want to do that, but if necessary I'd try to take as short a detour as possible. I needed to get closer to see exactly what was happening and how I would need to act. There were people coming slowly toward us on foot. Not only had they not been harmed, but they could tell us what was happening ahead.

I put down the water container and grabbed Jata by the hand, the better to move her fast if I needed to. With my free hand I sought the comfort of feeling the knife tucked into the band of my trousers. It was there. That was reassuring in a small way.

"Excuse me, sir," I called out to an old man moving slowly toward us.

"Yes, young boy? What can I do for you?"

"I was wondering, sir, what is happening on the road ahead?"

"Security. The police and army are checking vehicles."

"So there is nothing for me to fear?"

"Not unless you are a thug or a rioter." He gave a raspy laugh.

"Thank you, sir."

I picked up the water container and started back along the road, towing Jata along behind. Up ahead, the line of vehicles was growing. I took us on a route farther off the road so that I could see around the cars.

There were dozens of vehicles and more than double that number of police and soldiers. Across the road were metal barriers that completely blocked one lane of the highway, forcing vehicles in each direction to alternate in passing through the opening when the soldiers allowed. The gap was blocked by two soldiers, each holding a machine gun. Soldiers moved down the line in pairs and stopped at each vehicle. They were on the road to provide security. I should have felt safe, but instead I felt frightened. They were soldiers, but they were still men with guns.

I tried not to look at them as we passed, but it

was hard not to. They were in green uniforms with red berets. They wore big black boots and each held either a rifle or a machine gun. They were giving loud orders—yelled out in Swahili—to the drivers. Nobody seemed to be saying much in response. The drivers listened, allowed the soldiers to look inside their vehicles and then drove off when they were allowed.

"Do you think any of them are friends with the sergeant?" Jata asked.

"I'm sure he knows them all," I replied. I wanted her to feel reassured.

We passed by the checkpoint and continued to walk in silence, unnoticed and untroubled. The soldiers by the waiting vehicles didn't even glance in our direction. It was as if we were invisible.

Chapter Fourteen

"There's one over there," I said to Jata, pointing out a piece of wood off to the side of the road. She ran over and picked it up, adding it to the bundle she was carrying. We were gathering fuel as we walked so that we could have a fire to cook our meal over.

"Do you think this is enough? It is getting heavy."

"Here, give me the pile to carry," I said.

"It is not *that* heavy."

"Well, you will not need to carry it much farther. I think I see the spot."

Up ahead was a small bridge in the near distance. As we got closer, I could see a deep gorge. At the bottom were a few pools of dirty, brown water and a thin thread of water linking them together. This was the spot. We wouldn't use the water, of course, but the depression would shield us from other eyes, from the wind, and from the sun until it set. It was—I believed—close to evening, and time was passing into the distance. Within two hours the light would be gone completely, but until then I wanted to escape its glare and the eyes that could be upon us. This might be the place to stay for the night.

Carefully Jata and I worked our way down from the road and into the gorge. It was hard going, with one hand on the water container and the other steadying my sister. The banks were damp. During the last rainfall—which had been recent—there must have been a raging torrent of water filling up the entire gorge. Now it had all run off, leaving nothing but the damp reminder of a trickle in the sand.

Reaching the bottom, I edged over into the shade provided by the steep carved wall of the gorge. The sand was giving off a coolness that was a welcome change from the heat of the tarmac. There were droppings from goats and cows. The little water that was there was being used to quench the thirst of the local herds. Jata dropped the bundle of wood and then slumped down to the sand. I wanted to do the same, but there was work to do before we could eat and nobody else to do it.

I started gathering stones and placing them in a circle as a fire pit, with one stone in the very center for the cooking pot to rest upon. For good measure, I also hauled back two larger rocks that we could sit on. After that, I took the branches Jata had gathered and broke them into small pieces, arranging them in the circle. Next I pulled up some fine dry grass that made the perfect starter for the fire. I tossed the grass onto the kindling but also threaded it into the twigs and branches. Satisfied, I took out a small box of matches. There were eighteen left—enough for the rest of our journey, and probably more than enough for the amount of food we carried, but still not even one to waste.

I squatted low and struck the match, shielding the flame with my hand, and then lit one part of the grass and then a second and a third. All three caught, and soon the fire spread to the twigs and the branches. I put more branches on top so that there would be more fuel.

Finally, I undid my bundle and pulled out the pot, a big serving of beans and maize, two cups, two bowls and two spoons. I just wished that we'd needed three of each—that my mother had been sharing the third. I took the water container and carefully poured water in both cups and then into the pot. The container had grown lighter throughout the day as we drank, and now it was lighter still. That was good for carrying but bad for our ongoing needs. There was no telling when I could get us more clean water. Still, there was plenty for tonight, tomorrow and a little into the third day.

I put the pot onto the stone in the middle of the fire, poured in the beans and maize, and gave it all a stir.

"Jata, it won't be long until—" I stopped myself when I saw she was sound asleep. I'd wake her when the food was ready.

I took one of the blankets and draped it over her. If I hadn't been afraid to wake her, I would have placed the second beneath her to offer some protection against the ground. The thin mattress on the cot in our tent would have been most welcome now.

Perhaps it would have been wise to travel farther, but it was better to stay out of the sun and heat than to keep going now. I knew that to beat the hare, the tortoise had to keep moving, but that tortoise did not have as far to go as we did. We needed to rest, and this was a good time. Any thoughts of moving for the night were now gone. This was where we'd sleep. Not that I could rest yet. We'd need much more fuel for the fire first—both for the warmth it offered and for the protection it provided. It wasn't just cows and sheep that needed water. But I knew that animals were afraid of the fire, and that it would keep them away. Strange, that. You'd think it would only show them where you were so they could come and make a meal of you.

Jata finished the serving I had put in her bowl. The walking had made us both hungry. Very hungry. I would have to rethink how many days of food we had. Our supply would not last as long as I had hoped. Still, there was some left in the pot. The portion had been too large. In my head I knew it was only for two, but in my heart and in my habit I had put in enough for three.

"My feet are sore," Jata said.

"So are mine." I looked down at my shoes. The big toe on my right foot was peeking through a hole that had become larger throughout the day. Would my shoes last through this journey? If I had to, I'd walk barefoot. The lack of shoes wasn't going to stop me.

"Do you hear it?" Jata asked.

"Mostly I can just hear you talking and singing."

The rest and the meal had raised her spirits and she was my Jata again, talking to herself, softly singing and—

"There it is again," she said.

I had heard it that time too. There were voices . . . and maybe a bell tingling. I got to my feet just as two goats spilled down the side of the gorge! They were fol-lowed by two more, and then more still, until a whole herd was sliding and surging down the slope. Cattle followed. The first few hesitated at the top, but they were propelled down by those coming from behind. It was a big herd—dozens and dozens of goats and many, many cattle. They all rushed forward, ignoring us as they found the water they were seeking. The cows, which were far larger and had bigger horns, plowed aside any goats that weren't wise enough to scamper away on their own.

I looked back to the top of the slope to see if there were any more animals still to come. Standing there, with the setting sun behind him, was a Maasai warrior! In his hands was a long spear and strapped to his side was a machete, the fading sun glistening against the blade. He stood there like he was frozen, as if he were a statue made of stone. Then he started skidding down the slope himself, coming toward us.

He stopped a few meters away and looked at us. He towered over me. I moved a few steps forward, not to threaten but to put myself between him and Jata. He remained silent and still, staring, as if he was studying us.

Suddenly, Jata moved past me. In her hands was her almost empty bowl.

"Greetings," she said. "Would you join us for dinner?"

The Maasai didn't react.

"We have enough to share," she added. "We have more than this."

His expression didn't soften or change in any way.

I stepped forward again to shield her. "Perhaps he doesn't understand," I suggested. "Or—"

"I know some Kikuyu," he answered in Swahili.

149

Of course he now knew that we were Kikuyu—just as I knew that as a Maasai he was of the Nilotic people, like the Kalenjin who had killed our father.

"Would you join us?" Jata asked, this time in Swahili.

"You two are alone out here?" the man asked. His head swiveled from side to side, looking around.

Before I could even think to deceive him, Jata answered, "We are alone."

"Are you sure you have enough food?" he asked.

"We do not have much," I said. "But we have enough to share." It was wise to offer because he could have taken it if he'd wanted.

He nodded his head and offered a small smile. "That is kind. Thank you."

Jata extended her bowl, but I stopped her. "I will get you a fresh bowl. We also have water. I wish I had tea to offer."

"Water, milk and blood are what I drink, so water would be fine. Thank you, friend."

We sat on our rocks around the fire, which was now the only heat and light left in the land. I missed the heat of the midday sun, although I never would have thought that possible as I passed along that scorching tarmac. An occasional vehicle would roar up and then past us on the road, leaving behind the smell of fumes and a silence that seemed deeper. All around us, moving in and out of the light thrown by the campfire, were parts of the Maasai's herd. They were corralled by the sides of the gorge, and one of his sons stood watch up on top. He had come after we finished dinner—his name was the same as his father's, Wilson—and after he was introduced, he had silently taken up his position caring for the herd . . . and for us.

"You have traveled far," Wilson the father said.

"We have much farther to travel still."

"The Maasai can travel from sunrise until sunset."

"We started before the sun came up and traveled nearly until it set," Jata said proudly.

"Perhaps you are not Kikuyu but Maasai." He laughed.

He laughed a lot. He was very happy and friendly. The few Maasai I'd known—or had *seen*, not really *known*—always looked so fierce and intimidating and they always carried weapons. Wilson had a spear, a machete and a club tucked into his belt. I remembered what I'd been told about how the Maasai were short-tempered and quick to anger, but Wilson only seemed quick to laugh. Still, I was careful of what I said, trying not to give him reason to be angered.

"I am saddened for you for the loss of your parents," he said.

We had told him everything.

"How old are you, boy?"

"Fourteen in a few weeks." I knew I should probably lie and say sixteen, but I didn't. If I had told that chairman I was sixteen, would he have left Jata in my care?

"Then perhaps I should not call you 'boy' any longer. You are a man, in age and in responsibility. You are now the father."

"And mother," Jata said.

"It is unusual how people are related and what they are called. Kalenjin think of us Maasai as cousins," Wilson said. "But we are not. We are Maasai. Do you know that if a Maasai takes the life of a person who is not a Maasai—even one who is a Kalenjin—then it is not murder?"

"It is not?"

He shook his head. "It is only murder if a Maasai kills another Maasai."

"That is not right," Jata said.

"It *is* right. I know our customs and laws and legends." Wilson's expression had hardened.

"She was not meaning to question you," I said, trying to ease her words in case they had offended. "She knows you are wise."

"Your sister is also wise," Wilson said. "To take the life of any other is to murder. We Maasai have tried to stay separate always—to follow our own ways—but some things are simply wrong. Many of us have stayed separate from the problems that are out there. We are content to mind our herds."

"That is wise."

"We have neither killed nor been killed. Although as warriors we are armed and trained to take a life if necessary."

"Most people know and understand that," I said. "We show respect."

"As it should be. We ask for respect and we show respect in return." He paused for a moment. Deep in thought, he stared into the distance before turning back to face me. "I have no interest in politics or politicians or political events."

"None?"

"We ask only that politicians leave us to live our lives in the traditional way."

Everybody knew that the Maasai were the tribespeople who most followed their past. Some admired them, but others called them "dirty primitives," although never to their faces—short-tempered, proud and well armed was a bad combination to offend.

"Of course we have different ideas about livestock. Do you know that all cattle in the world belong to the Maasai people?"

"They do?" Jata asked.

He laughed. "It is one of our creation legends. In the beginning, God gave all the cattle to the Maasai.

That means that other people with cattle have either stolen them themselves or inherited them from ancestors who stole them."

"Really?" Jata asked.

"We believe that when we take cattle from other people, we are merely taking back what is rightfully ours. Of course, neither the politicians nor the other tribespeople believe that."

"And what do *you* believe?" I asked.

"If I raised a boy from the time he was a baby—if I fed him, cared for him, defended him, gave him my name—then he would be my child. It is the same with cattle. I will not allow the convenience of an old legend to justify what is clearly wrong."

"You are most wise," I said.

"I am old. Someday you will be wise . . . if you are blessed to live that long."

A tingle went up my spine. Was that an innocent statement or a warning of what was to come? As if in answer to my thoughts, Wilson pulled back his robe to reveal the machete. It glistened in the light from the fire.

"Of course I would never allow *my* cattle to be taken. I would be prepared to kill or die in their defense." He let the blanket fall closed again to hide the weapon. "I care not who is the president. I care only that my family, my tribe and my herd are left in peace."

"That is most important," I said.

"Your sister has gone to sleep," he said.

Jata was lying on the ground, half on and half under her blanket, close enough to the fire to be warmed. This time it was no nap. You could see that she was in the deepest of sleeps.

"It is time for me as well." He stood up. I'd forgotten how tall he was. "I will sleep close to my herd, and you can sleep close to yours." He nodded at Jata. "You can sleep secure. I know that this is a time of worry, but at least tonight you will have no concerns. You are under my protection. No one would dare to bring you harm."

"Thank you, sir."

He walked away into the darkness and was gone—but not far. I threw the remaining pieces of wood into the fire. There weren't enough to keep it alive until morning, but I was not going to go out in the darkness and gather more. I was going to sleep. I had no fear. I trusted Wilson. Besides, if he was going to take my life, he had no need to wait for me to close my eyes.

I took the second blanket—the one holding our remaining food—unloaded it and draped it over Jata, covering her legs and feet with a second layer. Then I lay down behind her, offering her whatever protection I could from the darkness and what it might contain.

Up above there were stars twinkling in the sky. The ground beneath me was cold and hard. All around was openness that disappeared into darkness. I thought back to my bed in my room in my house. To being safe and warm and protected. It was all gone, no matter how much I wished it wasn't so. Even the tent was gone. I closed my eyes and hoped for a sleep that would bring me escape, if only in a dream.

Chapter Fifteen

The smell of fire caused me to jolt awake. It was nothing—just the small fire I had made, still glowing and flickering and crackling. But the sky was also starting to show the first rays of morning light. How could both be possible? The fire should have died out hours before the arrival of dawn. Then I saw Wilson—the son—come forward with branches in his arms. He stopped by the fire and fed the branches into the flames, one by one.

"Good morning," I said.

"And to you. That is for you and your sister." He pointed to our pot. It was filled to the brim with porridge.

"It is special," he said. "Made with cereal, and milk from our cattle." He picked up the pot and handed it to me. "Eat, but leave some for your sister."

"I will leave enough for everybody," I said.

"There is no everybody. My father has eaten. I have eaten. It is for you and your sister."

"We could never eat that much."

"Never?" he asked. "Perhaps not this morning, but it will be there for later today and perhaps even tomorrow. It will not last till 'never.'"

"Thank you for your kindness."

"You offered your food and we offer ours. It is our way. You should awaken your sister. We will be leaving soon."

"How soon?" I asked. It had felt calming to be under their protection, and now again there would be no protection except for my little knife.

"We will leave soon."

Jata and I would not be ready that quickly, but this was a safe spot to be left.

Wilson the father walked over and offered his morning greetings.

"We will soon move our herd to graze. I have chosen to move them that way." He pointed down the road in the direction we were going. "I ask if you would travel with us."

"Yes, that would be most wonderful!" I exclaimed. "We will quickly ready ourselves for the journey."

"But our journey together will not be for the full day. We will travel until the sun is overhead. Then we will rest, feed and come back this way for evening water."

"Your company would be most welcome for as long as you offer it."

"The road along this section is not safe, but you will be walking with us," he said.

"I know, then, that we will be safe. Again, my thanks."

We traveled well off to the side of the tarmac. We were close enough to the road to see it in the distance but far enough away that we could only hear the largest and loudest vehicles passing.

Wilson's goats and cows moved slowly forward, nibbling from the brush and bushes. The goats would eat almost anything, but the cows were much more selective. Our pace was slow—certainly slower than yesterday—but at least we were moving forward. The tortoise would have been proud of us. And we were safe. I felt as secure as a goat or a cow knowing that both Wilsons—father and son—were our shepherds.

I looked around for Jata. She was being carried by Wilson the father. She looked tiny in his arms. She was smiling and laughing. He was smiling and laughing. She was my little star, twinkly and shining even during the day.

"This is where we will stop," Wilson the father said.

"Thank you for your protection, but we must continue forward."

"But there is danger for strangers. The road is not safe."

"We could travel off to the side, away from the road," I suggested.

"Then there will be other dangers. You will not travel alone."

"I do not understand."

"My son will accompany you farther in your journey. He will lead you." He squatted down and picked up a stick. "This is the route of the road." Wilson made a line in the dirt. "It must cut far to the west to allow the trucks to travel up the steep valley wall. But you can go more directly." He drew a second line cutting through the curve of the road in an almost straight line. "This way is shorter and safer—as long as you are in the company of a Maasai."

"Thank you again, sir. I'm . . . I'm . . . so grateful for your kindness." I didn't have the words to let him know how truly appreciative I felt. To continue to travel in safety under the protection of Wilson the son was more than I could have hoped for.

"Offering to help is our way. The route you will walk is rough and very steep, but it is the path our people travel."

"Today, with your permission, sir, we will walk as if we are Maasai."

—

Wilson the son led. Free of the herd, he started the trip quickly, eating up ground with his big, bouncy strides. At times Jata was forced to run to keep pace. Finally he noticed her plight and slowed.

"Wilson, are there lions here?" she asked.

She sounded concerned, so I had to ease her fears. "Of course there are no—"

"Not many," he said, interrupting me.

"So there are some?" I asked.

"Not many," he repeated.

"What will we do if we see one?" I asked.

"It depends on what the lion does. If it allows us free passage, then I will allow it free passage."

"And if it doesn't?"

"I have my spear," he said, holding it up.

"You will kill it?" Jata asked.

"I have been a part of slaying a lion before."

"When you say 'a part,' does that mean you were not alone?" I asked.

"There were many of my age mates in the hunt."

"But here it is just you."

"Even better!" he exclaimed. "That way, both the tail and the mane will be mine. I will have all the honor of the kill."

"Or you will *be* killed," I said.

"Perhaps, but then I will die in a way that will be sung about."

"Aren't you afraid of lions?" Jata asked.

"I am Maasai. Lions are afraid of me." He paused. "But an elephant is different. One needs to be afraid of them."

"Are there elephants around here?" Jata asked.

"You will not see one today."

That was reassuring to hear.

"They are even more rare here than lions. But there are some, nonetheless."

I looked all around to see which bush could hide an elephant. But I realized that any elephant that could hide in that brush would be so small it could probably be handled.

"If we see an elephant, you must stay close by my side. We will go downwind so that it cannot smell us. But if it sees us and comes in our direction, you must run very fast away from him in a straight line, and I will wait this long"—he held up four fingers—"because I am faster than you. We will hope that it chases me, but it will probably chase you, because even elephants are afraid of Maasai."

"Do not worry, Jata," I said. She had no need to worry because I was worrying enough for both of us.

"Do not worry, but run. If it does chase you, then stop running straight and start running zaggy-zaggy."

"Zaggy-zaggy?" I asked.

He waved his hand back and forth like a snake. "Elephants do not turn very well and he might fall over." He started laughing.

"Isn't there something else we could do?" I asked.

He shook his head. "It is an elephant. Unless you have a gun, it cannot be stopped."

It was a sign of progress to leave the flatland behind and start up the face of the cliff. The path was challenging—steep and curving—but it had to be free of elephants and lions. Wilson led the way and we struggled to keep up with him. As we climbed, the valley opened up behind and beneath us. It stretched out so far into the distance that it didn't look real. On the horizon darker clouds had formed, and they seemed to be chasing after us. A storm was coming.

Wilson stopped and turned around. "This is where I leave you."

"Is the road just up ahead?"

"Ahead, but not just. Continue up, and when the path divides, take the fork to the right."

"Couldn't you come with us until we reach the tarmac?" Jata asked.

He shook his head. "I must leave to return to my father. I will not find his camp until after dark."

"I understand. Thank you, Wilson the son, and thank Wilson the father," I said.

163

"I will. You will be safer now. If you come upon other members of my tribe, you tell them you are still under the care of Wilson."

"Thank you so much."

"Goodbye, my friends."

We stood there watching until he disappeared down a small rise and into some trees. He was gone and we needed to continue moving forward—and up. The road awaited. I just didn't know how far it was.

I thought about the distance we had already traveled. On this section we hadn't followed any imaginary piece of string. Instead, we had been guarded and guided by two Maasai warriors. Someday it would make a wonderful story. I just wished my parents had lived to hear it. I leaned into the slope and started to climb again.

A few more steps forward.

Wilson had not lied—the road was not close. We struggled on up the hill, which never seemed to end. The forks in the path were few, and I followed Wilson's advice and always chose to go to the right. It had been a long day. Jata and I had traveled for nearly six hours with both Wilsons—father and son—and then another four with Wilson the son. Now, it had been well over an hour since the son had left us to walk alone.

Behind us, the storm was gaining ground. The wind was offering a push forward and the sun had been chased behind the storm clouds. It hadn't started raining yet, but the sound of thunder and the sight of lightning were common. This was threatening to be a big storm.

I turned my head to the side to listen. I could hear something more than the wind in the trees. It was the roar of an engine. That could mean only one thing—the road was close. If not the highway, at least some road was ahead. It would be good to be free of the trees and the constant climb.

"Come, Jata, we must hurry."

I reached back and took her by the hand to pull her forward, something I hadn't been doing very often. The slope of the hill was more than I could handle with my heavy load and her in tow. We came through the trees. In front of us was a small homestead—a small but neat home and rows of knee-high maize—and beyond that was the highway. Two big trucks crossed in opposite directions. The road was lined with small stores and stalls, and I could see a few people moving quickly along the paths that lined the highway. A few drops of rain started to fall.

"Do we have to go much farther?" Jata asked.

"Not much. Our day is almost over and we have covered more than thirty kilometers. If we had some place to get out of the rain, then we could stop."

"There is a house."

"We do not know the people who live in that house—or which tribe they belong to. Just come and we will look for the right spot."

We reached the road just as a big truck roared by in the direction we wished to travel. Behind it were a third and fourth and fifth—all traveling together. If any of those drivers had allowed us inside for a ride, we would have been in Nairobi in hours and not days. We carried on along the road, the sky darkening by the minute, more drops starting to fall. We didn't have much time to get away from the rain.

Ahead was a small building. As we approached, I realized it was deserted and partly destroyed. On front, in big letters, was written THE STAGE SHOP. The name remained but the windows were gone, as were the door and part of one wall. But the tin roof still survived. I pulled Jata inside. Almost instantly the rain began pounding noisily, demanding to come through, but the roof would not allow it. Wind blew in through the openings, but there was a corner—two full walls— away from the windows and doors that seemed to be safe and hopefully would remain dry.

"Tonight we will sleep here."

"It is already cold."

"But it will stay dry, and I can chase away the cold if I can find fuel for a fire."

I couldn't go outside without getting soaked, and

all the wood would soon be wet. I looked around. There, in the far corner, were the remains of a chair. I walked over. There were wooden slats, two of the legs, part of the back, and some ripped cloth and foam from the seat. That would be enough kindling for the fire. This chair would never be sat on again, but it could still be counted on. Raindrops were coming in, but the pieces of the chair were still dry enough to burn—at least I hoped.

I brought them back over to the corner where Jata was sitting. She had her back in the corner and her blanket draped over her. I smashed the wood into small pieces and then stacked a few in a way that I hoped would quickly catch fire. Next I ripped the seat pieces, shredding the foam and sprinkling it about, then topping it with some ripped pieces of the cloth covering. Finally, I removed the matches from my bundle. The first was blown out by the wind before I could coax the cloth into lighting. That left only sixteen. I turned my body to act as a shield from the elements and then lit a second match, nursing it in my hands.

"Come on, come on," I begged the flame.

It listened to my desperate plea. The cloth caught first and the foam quickly followed. Soon the flames licked against the wood. I just hoped the pieces I'd placed weren't too big to be ignited by the kindling. I looked around the little floor. It was the only place where dry existed in my world. There, against the wall, were a few plastic bags and a scrap of paper. I gathered them up. They were damp but not wet. They would smoke, but they would also burn. I went back and tossed them on the fire. The flame got brighter and bigger, and the wood started to bubble as it got hotter. The flames licked around the wood until it charred and then began to be consumed. The fire had caught, and now it would last until the fuel was all used.

"Do you want your supper hot or cold?" I asked Jata.

"I am not hungry." Her arms were wrapped around her legs and her face was buried. That was not a good sign.

"Since you are not hungry, it is my choice and I say it will be warm." I hoped that the warmth of the food in her stomach would spread through her body and chase away her tiredness and despair.

I opened up our bundle and removed the pot. Throughout the day we had been nibbling its contents, but it was still half full. I was tired of porridge but more tired of being hungry. Besides, I couldn't cook anything else in the pot until the porridge was finished, and worse than that, it would spoil before long. It needed to be finished.

I placed the pot beside the fire, where it could start to heat without burning. I'd just have to stir it about and maybe add a little water to make it moist. At least water wasn't going to be a problem. I poured a cup from the container into the pot and then went to the doorway. There was a stream of water coming off the roof and onto the ground. I reached out and cupped a handful of rain and drank down what didn't escape through my fingers. It was cold and clean. Whatever sand and dirt had collected on the roof had already been washed away. I placed the water container outside and positioned it so the stream of rain danced around the opening. Soon—within minutes—it would be full.

Jata was stirring the porridge when I turned back. "I didn't want it to burn. It started to smell good."

"That's because it will taste good! You are so lucky to spend the entire day walking across the savannah with a Maasai and eating his food. Wait until you tell your friends. They will hardly believe you!"

"I do not know where my friends are," she said. "I do not have any friends anymore."

What had I said?

"You will make new friends when we arrive, and they will become your best friends, you mark my words. But for now, would you do me a favor?"

She nodded. There was sadness in her eyes.

"Could you tell me all about today? So many things happened that I don't even believe it! I need to hear it from you to believe it was real!"

Her smile lit the small building even more than the fire.

Chapter Sixteen

We were awakened early by the cold and the sound of trucks rushing past on the road. We got up, said our thanks to the little building that had sheltered us and joined the trucks on the journey to Nairobi. The air was cool and the road was downhill. I was grateful for both, for I knew the sun would soon be blazing hot and the road could turn up at any time.

We walked on the right side of the road, facing the vehicles as they came toward us. Sometimes the path shifted away from the road, and sometimes it was so narrow that rather than hold Jata's hand, I had her walk behind me. Deliberately I walked closer to the traffic to try to shield her—as if a vehicle hitting me would stop and go no farther. And there was one other constant for the trip this morning: the mud.

The heavy rain had gone, but it had left much behind. Dirt had turned into mud and large puddles blocked the way; water ran from the hills and into the ditches beside the road, turning them into small streams. In places that were lower, those streams and puddles came together to create ponds, and goats and cows were wading through them, eating. They seemed not to even notice their early morning bath as they continued to graze. Life had to go on for them as well.

"Wait!" Jata called out.

I turned. She was much farther behind than I would have liked. I had got so caught up in my head that I hadn't been exercising enough care. As she tried to catch up, she slipped and slid toward me. Her shoes wore a thick sole of mud that made walking difficult.

"Here, do this." I rubbed the bottom of my shoe against the edge of the tarmac until a layer of mud peeled away. I did the same with the second shoe as she copied me.

"I do not like the lorries," she said. "Those trucks are so big and loud and scary."

"Their numbers will increase as the day fully dawns."

"Do you think it will rain more?" she asked.

I shook my head. "There is not enough water left in the skies because it all fell last night. Besides, if somehow it does start again then we will walk between the drops."

"At least we know how far we have to go," she said.

"We do?"

She pointed beyond me. There was a large green sign in the distance, close enough that it could be read: NAIROBI 45 KM.

"We are almost there," she said.

"If we walk strong today and tomorrow we will be on the other side of the city by the second night." My hope was not to have to sleep within the city itself. I remembered what the sergeant had said—that I should treat the city as a dangerous animal, best approached in the light of day, when it could be watched.

"Are you ready to continue?" I asked.

"I am not ready, but we will continue."

"First you need to take a drink. It is better that you carry some of this water in your stomach than I continue to dangle all of it from my arm."

"There is so much water all around. Do you need to carry so much?"

"I'd rather carry water that we don't need than not have water that we do need. I will carry it."

I couldn't help admiring the land we were passing. The crops were thick and lush and green. It looked as if the rain was a blessing to them on an ongoing basis. I thought about how my father would have envied these fields. If his family had possessed such land here, they would never have moved to Eldoret and then none of—I stopped myself. No point in thinking that through. As constant as the movement of our feet was the need for me to put those thoughts away. They would weigh me down even more than the load on my back and the thick mud under my feet.

More and more traffic—both driving on the road and walking beside it—was flowing by. We exchanged greetings with people. At first I used Swahili, but the greetings repeatedly came back to me in Kikuyu. The people were Kikuyu. That made me feel much safer. The homes here were many, and none seemed to have suffered damage. There were so many Kikuyu here that no one had been forced from their dwellings.

I slowed and came to a stop. Ahead of us the road was pressed against the cliff on one side and a drop on the other. There was barely space for a person to pass, and certainly not enough to pass with confidence of not being hit. Yet a steady stream of people had come toward us. They had to be coming from somewhere. I waited for somebody else to come into view.

Jata came up behind me. "Why are we stopping?"

"I'm not sure of the way."

"Can't you see the string?"

"Of course I can. It leads along the road. It is just that the way is only wide enough to allow two trucks and one strand of string. We have to find a way around this section of the road."

"And walk without the string?" She sounded worried.

"Yesterday, with Wilson, we walked without the string. When we went back to the road, it was waiting for us."

"Ah, yes, yes. So if we leave for a little bit, we can find it again," she said.

"Most certainly. I'm waiting for a guide to appear."

A woman was coming up behind us. She was about the age of our mother, and she was bent under the weight she carried on her back.

"Excuse me," I said. "We are looking for a way to Nairobi."

She stopped and straightened to look at us. "A *matatu* will come by soon." I was relieved to hear her speak in Kikuyu.

"We do not have the fare for a *matatu*. We are walking."

"All the way to Nairobi?" She sounded surprised.

"Yes, but we think better of following this road. Is there another way?"

"There is always another way." She hefted her bundle again. "I will lead you. This is a shorter way by foot. Come."

We waited for a big truck to pass and then crossed the road.

"Why are you going to Nairobi?" the woman asked.

"We are going farther—to Kikima," my sister said.

"That place is not known to me. Are you sure you are saying it correctly?"

I hadn't even thought of that. I was positive that was how to pronounce it. I thought back to the way my mother said it and realized I had to strain to hear her voice. It saddened me to think it could fade that quickly, but I could still hear it saying the name.

"It is very small and very far," I said in explanation.

"And you are going by yourselves? Have you no one with you?"

"There is no one to be with us. We are going to find our family."

"And how did you lose them to begin with?"

"In the violence," I said.

"Where are you from?"

"Eldoret. We lost our home and we lost our parents."

"Poor babies. Such evil . . . such evil has been done to you." She stopped. "This is my home. I go no farther. You need to continue on this road until you come to a large crossroads, not small. You will cross over many that are small, as you will go many kilometers."

"And at the big crossroads?" I asked.

"You will turn right."

"And that will lead us back to the tarmac?"

"Oh no! There are many, many twists and turns over many, many roads and paths."

"But how will we find our way back?" I gasped.

"At each step, there will be people close by. Ask them and they will direct you. You are Kikuyu and you will be helped by your people. There is no need to fear. It is even safer here since the political problems."

"How can that be?" I asked. "How can it be safer than before?"

"People are pulling together, for one thing, and those who were the cause of trouble—the small-scale thugs—have all left."

"Left to go where?"

"To wherever they could be involved in the most trouble. Like moths to a flame, they are attracted to violence. Some of them will get burned. Now, travel safely."

She turned up a path to a house, leaving us alone, but not too alone. We would meet others along the route, and those people would be our guides, one after the other. If we were helped, I had to expect it would be by other Kikuyu.

At each crossroads, I stopped and asked questions about our route. Sometimes we were ignored, but most gave us answers. If I was not confident in the answer or the person who gave it, I waited and asked another passerby to confirm. We were walking too far to travel even a step in the wrong direction.

Two little black sheep nuzzled against their mother at the side of the road. She was trying to graze and they

were trying to nurse. They were frolicking and jumping and bumping into each other. It made me smile.

"Look at those babies," Jata said.

"Those two little ones are like me and you," I
joked.

"No, they are not. They have their mother."

Her words entered my heart like daggers. I felt
sadness, but much more for her than for me.

"You are right. There is a difference—in fact, more
than one. Neither of those little babies has a big brother
who is there to provide for them. You have that."

She took my hand. That was her answer.

"Do you know what we would be doing today if
mother were here?" she asked.

"It is Sunday morning, so we would be in church."

We had passed by a dozen churches already this
morning. At times we could hear the singing flowing
out the window to meet us on the road.

"I like church," Jata said. "It is good to be close
to God."

"God is everywhere," I said.

Almost as if in answer to that, God spoke—or at
least sang to us. The sounds of singing came drifting
through the air. Somewhere up ahead was a church, and
with each step we took, the sound got louder. I knew
the song. It was the one that Jata had been singing—
"Charity, Charity." She started to quietly sing along.

We quickly came up to a wire and wood fence that surrounded the church compound. We stopped and peered through. There were a few people outdoors, but most were inside, singing and worshipping. I could see them across the courtyard, through the open doors and windows.

"Muchoki, do you think we could go in?"

"It is not our church."

"But wouldn't we be welcome to worship?"

"Well . . . yes."

"It would make our mother happy if we went to church."

It would. And we could use a rest. "Come."

Jata squealed as I took her by the hand and led her up to a path.

The church was a big building, solid brick, with a cross on the side of the tower. Some of the windows were wide open, while others were filled with colorful stained glass. It was a church of substance. Would we— two strangers, two orphans dressed in mud-stained clothing—be welcomed? I put my water container beside a bush and then tucked it in so it was hidden by the leaves.

The music of the church got louder with each step.

"Good morning, children. May God be with you!" a woman called out in greeting. She was dressed in her church clothing.

"And with you," we answered in unison.

"You have missed more than you will hear."

"We were just passing by," I said.

"And God called you in?"

"God and the singing."

"Joyous singing. I do not know you. Where do you usually worship?"

"Far away."

"Welcome. Go in, go in!"

We entered the church. The pews were mostly filled, and the people at the back turned as we passed by, looking for an open seat. At the front, five men sat on a raised platform. Off to the side I saw an electric organ and two men playing guitars. In front of the platform two dozen young girls were singing and dancing. The song was in Kikuyu. It made me feel both at home and uneasy. I'd been to church a number of times in the tent at the camp, but this was the first time I'd been inside a real church since . . . well, since it all happened. Anxiously I looked around to find the doors, the ways out. What I didn't find was anything that suggested danger. The fear subsided and faded away until only a sense of being safe and at home remained.

We sat down as the singers came to an end and the parishioners gave them a cheer. One of the men at the front got to his feet, clapping, and then went to the microphone in the center of the platform.

"Some items have been brought as an offering," he said. "We will auction them to raise money for the church." He held up a plastic bag and pulled out a pea pod. "This is filled with sweet peas. Will somebody give me a bid?"

"Fifty shillings!" a man called out.

"Does anybody wish to bid more?"

"Eighty shillings!" a woman offered.

"Any other offers?" the man asked. "Any?"

There was silence. He came over, and he and the woman exchanged the bag for the shillings.

Three more items—a pumpkin, some pears and some beans—were also auctioned off. This happened in our church as well, although I'd never been so interested in items of food.

The middle man on the platform got to his feet. He wore a suit and tie, and there was a large red Bible in his hand. I assumed he was the pastor.

"Good morning, and may God be with you!" he called out.

"And with you!" the congregation called back.

"If a lion were to kill your goats, would you be justified in killing that lion?" he asked.

"Of course!" a man called out. Others agreed with raised voices.

"Yes, you would," he said. "We all know what is going on out there." He gestured beyond the wall. "Kikuyu have been killed by Luo. Kikuyu have been killed by Kalenjin. So are we not justified in killing them?"

The parishioners roared out their approval and agreement. I understood what he was saying, but that didn't stop me from feeling sick to my stomach. Did these people know what any of that meant beyond just words?

The minister raised his hands to silence the members of the congregation. It took a while for some to notice and others to react, but finally the room was quiet.

"No," he said softly. "No, no, no, no!" Each word got louder until the final one was like thunder. "Jesus said, 'Love thy neighbor.' He did not say, 'Love *some* of thy neighbors.' He did not say, 'Love only your *Kikuyu* neighbors.' Each of us is God's child. Each of us was made in his image, and we have no right to strike down that image."

His words caught me by surprise. This wasn't what I had expected. I could feel the tension in the air. I could read in some faces expressions of confusion or even anger.

"Some of you may not agree with me," the minister bellowed, "but you would be wrong. *I* know the Word. When Moses went to the mountain to receive the Commandments, God did not simply speak to him. Words can be misremembered and misspoken. God did not simply write the Commandments on parchment, because parchment can be ripped. He did not simply write the Commandments on wood, because wood can be burned. He wrote the Commandments on stone, because stone is eternal—as eternal as our lives if we accept those Commandments."

There was a rumble of approval from the congregation.

"And while each of the Ten Commandments is sacred, and it is not for me—a mere man—to place one above the others, I will speak of only one: Thou shalt not kill."

He said each word with emphasis, making each one louder than the last.

"I know that the commandment does not say, 'Thou shalt not kill a Kikuyu.' It simply states, 'Thou shalt not kill.' If each of us is made in God's image—if each of us is precious to God—then who am I, who are *any* of us, to take that life and kill God's image?"

I leaned forward in my seat not only to hear his words but to be drawn closer.

"In time, each of our lives shall pass. Ashes to ashes, dust to dust. When you stand at the gates of heaven, before your maker, before the Almighty, you will be held to account. None of us is perfect, all of us have sinned, but some sins will not be forgiven. Some sins will block the path through the gates."

He took a long pause and not a sound could be heard.

"Thou shalt not kill." He thumped his hand against the pulpit and I jumped, as did Jata and half of the rest of the congregation.

"A Swahili proverb states, 'The hurt of one finger is a hurt of the whole body.' Our body—our country—has whole arms and legs that are hurt. You do not heal one arm by harming another. You do not heal the loss of one eye by blinding the other. We will stand strong as a community of God.

"Now, I am not saying that we will not act in our own defense. We will not allow ourselves to be killed, but we will not kill. We will defend, but we will not attack. We must go forth as Christians, as Kenyans, as Kikuyu and spread the message we have been taught. These are not just my words—this is *The* Word." He held his Bible high. "Let us pray for peace."

As one, the heads of the congregants dropped. I closed my eyes as the minister started to pray. I listened to his words, but the images inside my head were stronger. I thought back to all that had happened. It was easy to say those words, sitting here inside this church where there was so much, where it seemed as if nobody had lost anything. Would he still be saying the same things if his father had been murdered? Would I kill the men who killed my father if I had the chance? Yes. It would be my duty. Would I kill those who were innocent, even if they were Kalenjin or Luo? I knew what I would have answered in the weeks that had passed before we were befriended by the sergeant, before we were helped by the two Wilsons, before I'd heard his words. I felt my whole body become lighter, as if the heaviness of anger was seeping into the ground at my feet. Thou shalt not kill. I would not take the life of one who meant me no harm. I would not do to another what had been done to me.

He finished the prayer. "Now go forth, and may God be with you."

"Come, it is time to leave," I said to Jata, as everybody started to get to their feet. I took her by the hand and led her down the crowded aisle. We had been close to the back and were among the first to leave. The courtyard filled up as the entire congregation spilled out. I kept moving away, stopping at the bushes to retrieve my water container. I felt lighter, but it still felt heavy.

"Wait!"

I turned. It was the woman who had spoken to us as we entered the church. She had two other women with her—one of them was the woman who'd bought the peas, and she still had the bag in her hand. They came over to us.

"Are you not staying?" the first woman asked.

"We have far to go before we can sleep."

"You said you were passing by. Where are you passing to?"

"Today we will travel to Nairobi."

"By foot? And by yourselves?" She frowned and looked concerned.

"We have no other way to travel, and nobody to travel with us."

"And you know the way?" the first woman asked.

"We have needed assistance through this section to get us back to the highway. People have been kind," I said.

"People can show such great kindness."

"And such cruelty," the third woman added.

"Today we will only offer kindness," the first woman said. "I have no vehicle to offer, but we will have somebody help you move to the next stage of your journey and get you back to the highway."

"That would be most thoughtful."

"And I would like you to take these," the second woman said, offering me the bag of peas. "They are sweet and you can eat them as you walk."

I hesitated but then took the bag. "Thank you so much."

"It is not much that I have offered," she said.

"It is an act of kindness and nothing could be greater," I replied. "Thank you for that act even more than what the bag contains."

"We have heard the Word," she said. "You may spread that Word as you travel."

Chapter Seventeen

I took one more look back. The man was still standing at the place where the path met the tarmac. He waved and we waved back.

He had been with us for over an hour, guiding us through the twists and turns of roads and paths that led us back to the highway. I didn't know if we could have done it without his help. Now he was going back home and we were walking forward again. I wasn't sure how short the shortcut had been and wouldn't know until we saw another sign announcing the distance still to travel, but at least we were back on our route.

With a quick glance I saw the man disappear around a bend in the road. I felt afraid and alone once more. For these last few kilometers we had been in his care, moving under his direction. Now there was nobody but me, leading us along a road I had never traveled to a place I'd never been to be met by things I could not predict. At least my fear had reason.

"Can you see the string?" Jata asked.

I started from my thoughts and for an instant didn't understand. Then I recovered myself. "I'm so surprised that *you* cannot see it," I said. "Take my hand and we will begin again."

The day had become increasingly hot and the sun brighter. Between the two, the water had been drawn back up and the mud had dried, making the puddles smaller and the walking easier. The way continued to be downhill, and that helped pull us forward.

The peas the church woman had given us had all been eaten. They were as sweet as candy. Along the shared journey the man—his name was Njoroge—had asked people if we could pluck plump pears overhanging the road and they had given permission. We had eaten our fill. I had felt warmed by the sun and by the people who had helped us get this far. I had felt hopeful. Now, walking alone again and passing by people who did not speak to us, I felt that hope drip away with each step. Once again we walked and walked until many hours and many kilometres had passed since we had left our friend behind. Would I have any hope left when we reached Nairobi?

The road was now wider, with two lanes in each direction. On both sides of the tarmac were wide walking paths, and set back from them was an almost uninterrupted line of shops and stores, homes and homesteads. With the extra buildings came extra people. It now seemed as if it was impossible for us to be alone. There was a constant flow of people that made the time pass quickly.

There were also reminders of what had been going on. We passed more burned-out and overturned vehicles, their contents gone. There was the usual assortment of closed buildings, but some had obviously been put to the torch. A storm had passed through that had come not from the sky but from the people beneath it. But had it passed in the direction we had come from or the direction we were going? And even more important, was the storm going to sweep over us again?

We continually passed by roadside markets. There were dozens of stalls and hundreds of people flocking around, buying and selling everything in sight. Although I was still full and satisfied, the food stalls were the ones that most caught my attention. We had not gone hungry and still had many days of food with us, but it remained my greatest worry. Thank goodness for the kindness of the people we had met.

"There is a sign!" Jata called out.

Farther down the highway was indeed a large

green sign. I could read the word "Nairobi," but I couldn't make out the distance. We'd need to be closer to read it. I felt a sense of anticipation. What would it say? Fifteen kilometers? Twenty? No, it couldn't be that far anymore. It might even be ten, but better not to get my hopes too high.

I stopped in front of the sign. It only said NAIROBI. What good was that if it didn't tell us how far away it was? Unless . . .

"Sir," I said to a passing man. "Is this the line where Nairobi starts?"

"Where the government says it starts," he replied. "The real starting point?" He shrugged. "That is for Nairobi to decide."

"We're here!" Jata yelled out. "We're here!"

"Yes, in a few more steps. But we need to find a place to stay. I saw a place just back there where we might spend the night."

"We should go forward and enter the city," Jata said.

There was not enough sun remaining in the sky to allow that to happen. "No. We do not know what is ahead, but I know what is behind. Come, we will rest. Tomorrow we will travel *through* Nairobi."

I turned and led her back the way we came. I knew it made no sense, but I didn't want to go forward just yet. Nairobi was dangerous and would be most dangerous at night. Today we would sleep beside the beast but not within it.

I opened my eyes and was surprised to be greeted by light. I must have drifted off again. Throughout the night I had tried to fight sleep—my back pressed against the building, Jata nestled with her head on my lap. She still slept.

The air was misty and the sky overcast. That didn't necessarily mean a storm but it didn't mean that it wasn't going to rain. We had been blessed by a dry night. The overhang of the small broken building I'd found wouldn't have provided much protection against rain, and there were neither doors nor a roof to offer more shelter inside. It wasn't the best, but it was the best I could find. The building's chief asset was that it was far enough away from the road and from people to allow us to sleep alone. Here the people were so plentiful that there was no fear of animals but it had been replaced by the fear of the people who chased away the animals.

Jata stirred from her sleep.

"Are you hungry?" I asked.

"I am tired . . . and hungry."

"We can fill your stomach, but you need to be awake."

"My feet are tired. Do we have to walk far today?" she asked.

"Maybe not *as* far, but still far."

That was a reassuring lie. I was planning on walking until we reached the far side of Nairobi, even if it meant going all day and into the dark. I would not have us stay there even one night.

"Let us gather wood for a fire to cook our breakfast. How about beans and maize?"

"Yes, that would be a good breakfast to have instead of porridge," she replied.

Jata rose to her feet. Before I could stand too, she draped her blanket over top of me.

"You stay and rest. I will gather the wood. Even big brothers need to close their eyes sometimes. I will watch you."

The road was like a never-ending river of cars and lorries, *matatus*, pushcarts and donkey carts. So many of the trucks spewed out clouds of black exhaust as they roared along the road. At the sides and tentatively venturing out between the lanes of traffic were scores of people on foot. I gripped Jata's hand tightly as we walked, hour after hour. I hadn't known what to expect from this city, but it was more. More of everything. It never seemed to end. Not only had I never *seen* this many stores and people and vehicles, but I had never even dreamed there could *be* so many. I was beginning to worry that I had miscalculated and it would not be possible to cross the city in one day. If that were the case, would this city swallow us up? Would we be able to come out the other side at all? I hurried my pace.

Jata seemed overwhelmed by the movement, the roar, the foul smell. I was overwhelmed too, but my fear could not be shown. As disturbing as the bustle of the city was, it was also reassuring. Despite the crowds, nobody here was fighting or seemed to be afraid. The world was going on. Had I finally come to a place where there was peace, if not quiet?

The road started to rise up, and the traffic slowed and bunched together. Horns sounded as those trying to go around the carts changed lanes. Some boys who had been standing at the side of the road jumped out into traffic, put their shoulders against the carts and began pushing, helping them up the hill. That was so kind that they were helping . . . but no, there had to be more to it than that. They must be getting something for their trouble.

"Hey, boy!" a man called out in Swahili.

I looked at him. He was not an old man. He was leading a donkey and trying to pull a big cart laden with oranges up the hill. It looked as if the hill was winning.

"You, boy. I am talking to you," he yelled directly at me. "If you help, I will give you two oranges."

I looked down at Jata. "We could use oranges, come."

I looked for a break in the traffic, then ran out and started to push.

"I only want you, boy," he said.

"She is my sister. She must be with me."

"She can try to push, but it will still be only two oranges."

He led the donkey and we started to push. The cart was heavy and seemed to push back. I fought against it and it finally gave way, moving up the hill.

"Good, good! Put your shoulder into it!" the man called out. "We shall do this!"

The hill became steeper, but our speed still picked up. Cars zoomed up behind us, narrowly missing before they swerved and changed lanes to pass us by. Maybe, I thought, it would be better if Jata did go back to the roadside . . . no, if I was hit and killed, it would be better for her to suffer the same fate than to be left alone without me.

Finally the hill flattened out. We had done it! Now I just had to get the oranges.

"Come here!" the man called out.

I took Jata's hand again and ran to the side of the cart.

"There are two more hills to come. If you come along with me, I will give two more oranges."

If he was offering me two oranges for one hill, I thought, shouldn't he give me six oranges for three hills? But I couldn't afford to argue. Four oranges were better than two, and it looked like we were going in the same direction regardless.

"Yes, we will do it."

"Good, good." He jumped onto the seat of the cart. "Come ride with me. There is space for both of you." He offered a hand.

I hesitated for a second but quickly realized that riding would be better than walking. Especially for Jata. I picked her up and swung her up beside him. Then I tossed up our bundle and water container and jumped up myself. The cart sank with my weight and the donkey slowed slightly.

"Thank you, sir," I said.

"No need to call me 'sir.' I am not a teacher or a minister. I am simply a man with a donkey and a cart."

"It is a fine donkey and a good cart and a full crop."

"We have come far. That is why my donkey needs a push." He leaned far forward and gave the donkey a little slap on the rump. "I have heard that there are problems in Nairobi. Is that true?"

"I do not know. We have just arrived."

"Arrived? Where are you from?" he asked.

"Eldoret," my sister blurted out before I could say anything.

"Eldoret! There was so much violence. Is that why your family came to stay in Nairobi?" he asked.

"We are not staying. We are passing through on our way to a town called Kikima," I said.

"I have never heard of such a place. Is it far?"

"Not as far as we have already traveled." I didn't know that, but it was what I wanted to believe and what I wanted Jata to hear.

"And where are your parents now?" the man asked.

"They are gone. My brother is my mother and my father," Jata said.

"Your parents are dead?"

"Our mother died of malaria last week," I told him.

"And your father?"

"He was killed in Eldoret. In the violence." Saying that suddenly made it seem real again. My father had been killed. My mother was dead. Our home was gone. In a few short weeks, all of life had changed.

"And what are your people?" he asked.

I was afraid to answer. What if he was from one of the other tribes? I'd noticed a club and a machete strapped to the seat by his side. But he couldn't strike out at me right here on this crowded street. The worst that could happen was that he would kick us off the cart, maybe deny us the oranges. But I would fight back and take two oranges from the cart as we left. That wouldn't be stealing. They were ours—we had earned them!

"Well?" he asked.

"My mother was Kamba and my father Kikuyu."

"Then I must offer an apology. My people are Luo, and they killed many Kikuyu in the uprising."

"My father and his family were killed by Kalenjin."

"Are you certain?"

"I heard them chanting in their language . . . I was there. I saw them when they set the church on fire."

He shook his head. "I have heard of that church in Eldoret. Those people who did that were animals, but there were animals on all sides."

"I have heard that. I know there were Kikuyu who did evil against Luo. They set a house on fire. They were just as evil. I owe you an apology too."

"Some of my family reported problems, but none were killed. I just wish for it to be safe here in Nairobi. I have heard rumors that there are problems in many areas of the city."

I glanced around hesitantly, looking for unseen danger. I had heard the same things from Jomo's father.

"Why did you come into Nairobi if it is safe where you were and dangerous here?" I asked.

"Safe or dangerous, a man must eat. If I do not get our crop to market, we will not have money for food. Here there is a chance of problems, but not coming here there is a certainty of problems. Where I am going, I will avoid the worst places."

"And where is the worst?" I asked. I needed to avoid those places too. I just hoped the Mombasa highway was not one of them.

"Kibera has been the worst. Do you know of Kibera?"

"A little. I was told that it was not a good place, and that it was filled with people," I replied. I remembered the sergeant telling me of the dangers of that shantytown.

"Some say it holds six hundred thousand people."

"It is a city?"

"It is a city within the city of Nairobi. Tens and tens of thousands of little tin houses pushed so close together that residents can hardly move. People from different tribes flow into Nairobi—Kikuyu, Luo, Kalenjin, Kamba—and when they have no place else to live they end up there, side by side by side."

"But if they are side by side . . ."

"That's right. Neighbors are fighting neighbors. I heard on the radio that Kibera has been on fire and the flames have spread to the streets and neighborhoods that surround it. It is time to push again."

"Oh, yes." I hadn't noticed that we were starting up another slope. "Come, Jata."

"No, no, she can sit here. I will pull and you will push and we will succeed together—one Luo, one half Kamba/half Kikuyu, and mostly one donkey!"

I went to the back as he climbed down and went to the front. I knew that the cart would be heavier with Jata aboard, but somehow it felt lighter. I was so happy that she was able to move forward without having to use her feet, if even for just a short time.

The cart bumped up a curb and onto a smaller street. Soon there was rutted dirt under my feet, which made the work harder. We had left the main road behind—left people behind. Was the man being friendly to my face but luring us to a place where he could use that machete? If he drew that weapon, I would grab the club. No . . . he was friendly. He could not be that good an actor to hide his true intentions from me. Still, I would keep alert.

The hill flattened out once more and we surged forward. I ran around the side of the cart just as the man was climbing back to his seat.

"I should have asked earlier. What are your names?" he asked.

"I am Muchoki and this is my sister, Jata."

"And I am Omolo. Tell me, this place—this Kikima—where is it located?"

"We are to go up the Mombasa highway until we reach a place called Machakos. From there it is not far."

"And do you know where to find the Mombasa highway?"

"It is in Nairobi."

"Nairobi is made of thousands and thousands of streets," he said. "But do not worry. I will guide you to it."

"Thank you so much. Once we find the highway, we can—"

I stopped speaking. Ahead of us were five men. I counted. In their hands were clubs, and they were coming toward us.

Omolo drew the machete from its holder. "You and your sister must leave. Get her off the cart—go now. There will be trouble, I am certain."

"You must come with us. We can all leave," I said. "We can get away."

"I cannot leave," he said. "I must stay to defend my property."

"My father stayed to defend us and he did not survive."

"If they take my donkey and my cart and my oranges, I am dead anyway. I will not give them up without a fight."

The men were coming closer, moving faster, and there was something about them I recognized, a wildness and ruthlessness in their eyes.

"You must go quickly or there will be no time," Omolo said.

"No," I said. "I will stay. Two is better than one."

"And five is better than two! Just leave. I cannot have your blood on my hands."

I reached across him and grabbed the club. "I will not run and I will not leave you."

"Are you sure?"

"I am sure."

I moved to jump down, but he grabbed my arm.

"You stay on the seat and defend your sister."

He jumped down from the still moving cart and yelled something to the men. They didn't answer. Instead they fanned out so they could come at him—at *us*—from all sides. What had I done? Why hadn't I taken my sister and fled when I had the chance? Now it was too late.

"Do not worry," I said to Jata, hoping my words would calm us both. I gripped the club tightly in my hand, swinging it slightly to test the weight. It was strong and would deliver a blow if needed.

The men blocked the road completely and I brought the donkey and cart to a stop.

"Who are you and where are you going?" one of the men yelled in Swahili.

"I am going to market," replied Omolo.

"You are going nowhere. Give us your cart and go while we still allow you."

"Let us pass." Omolo said as he held out his machete.

One of the men started to circle around to my side, away from Omolo. He had to be stopped. I jumped down, but as I landed he rushed at me. I swung the club wildly and it came down hard, striking his shoulder and dropping him to the ground! I grabbed his fallen club and now held two. Omolo looked at me in shock, as did the other four men. The fifth remained on the ground, whimpering and writhing in pain.

"You are nothing but thugs!" Omolo yelled. "My brother has dealt with one. Move aside or we will harm the rest of you."

They didn't move—not back or forward—but I saw a change in their eyes. There was uncertainty, even fear.

"Move now or you will taste my machete!" Omolo threatened.

All at once, they scampered off to the side. They looked less like a gang of thugs and more like a group of beaten dogs. Omolo grabbed his donkey by the lead and pulled the cart forward. He held the machete high and waved it threateningly as we passed them by. I stayed close to the side of the cart and then moved to the back as we passed, guarding our escape. What did I have to protect me other than my club? I held on to the cart with one hand, looking anxiously over my shoulder, certain that the men would give chase at any second. Instead they gathered around their fallen member, who was still struggling on the ground.

"Muchoki, come onto the cart!" Omolo cried out.

I leaped up as he took a small twig and smacked the donkey on the rear. It roared out in response and jumped forward, moving us faster than I thought it could. I steadied myself with one hand, then stood up and looked back. The men had grown smaller in the distance. We had made our escape.

"It is all right, little one. We are safe," Omolo said to Jata.

I looked down at my sister. There were tears in her eyes and she was shaking. I had been looking so hard behind that I hadn't looked beside me. I put my arm around her.

"They are gone," Omolo said. "We are all safe now."

"What tribe were they?" I asked.

"They were a tribe of hoodlums. They were just thieves, punks, criminals."

"That wasn't about the election?"

"There are always criminals—and Nairobi has more than its share—but now there are many who are using this election as an excuse for more crime and more violence. What does stealing and looting have to do with a political decision?"

"I do not know," I said.

"Nothing. Yesterday I saw a man running down the street carrying a television on his back. At first I thought he was running from his home with his most valuable possession. Then I saw others coming out of a store. They had smashed the window and were looting it. People who are bad will look for a reason to do bad. Now, here is the last hill coming up."

I stood up, ready to get off again, but he reached over to stop me.

"You do not need to get off yet," he said, "and you won't need those." He gestured to the clubs in my hand. I'd forgotten I was carrying them. I handed one to him, to return to its spot, and gave the other to Jata to hold.

"If those thugs had attacked us here at the hill it might have been a different ending, but here and now, there is nobody. Now I pull and you push and you little Jata will drive." He handed her the reins and jumped down. I followed.

At the back of the cart, I looked around. There were a few people nearby, but they were all very young or very old. Nobody looked to be a danger. I put my shoulder against the cart and pushed with all my might. It was hard, but I felt strong. The blood was rushing through my body. The road was rutted and pocked, but it didn't seem to be slowing us down. I wondered if Omolo and the donkey felt as strong as I did.

Finally the way flattened, and after one more backward glance, I ran forward and jumped back into the cart.

"That was the last of the hills," Omolo said. "You have done your work. Would you like to continue riding along? I am still heading in the direction you wish to travel, and your company would be welcome."

"Thank you for your offer," I said. "It is good to ride."

"Especially for your sister. She has walked a long way for one with such little legs."

"We have not always walked. Once we took a *matatu*."

"And Muchoki sometimes carries me," Jata said.

"I have no doubt. There was a part of this trip when your brother carried a whole cart full of oranges, a donkey and its driver on his back."

"I did not see that!" Jata laughed.

"Oh, there is no question that he did. And I am most grateful," Omolo said. "Where will you two sleep tonight?"

"I do not know. We will find a place."

"Up ahead is where I am going. I will bring my cart inside the gates, and people will buy my oranges tomorrow. Tonight I will sleep there, safe behind the gates. You are welcome to take sanctuary there as well."

That was a kind offer . . . wasn't it? I had to think before I answered. Perhaps we should just take our oranges and go elsewhere.

"It is not fancy. You can make a bed with the empty

burlap sacks used for the oranges. They can be both mattress and covers if you wish. I would like to offer more, but that is what I myself will use. You have probably slept in worse on your journey."

"Much worse."

"And there are guards who watch the compound. You can sleep knowing that you will be safe for the night." He looked at me. "I imagine that most nights you have been sleeping with one eye open."

"Sometimes two," I admitted.

"Then this will be good. Please, it is my way of offering a small gesture in return for what you did for me. I would not feel right sleeping tonight unless I knew you were safe." He seemed to sense my hesitation and turned directly to look at me. "You will be safe, Muchoki. You have my word."

"Thank you," I said. "It will be our honor."

Omolo guided the cart to a building with a high cement wall looped with razor wire and topped by broken glass. He stopped in front of a closed metal gate and then yelled out something that I didn't understand. He was speaking in Dholuo, the language of the Luo people—which meant that the people inside the building were also Luo.

A small metal door opened in the gate and a guard appeared. He had in his hands both a club and a machete. A second guard stepped out after him. He said something in Luo and Omolo answered, but in Swahili this time. I think he did that to reassure me and it worked.

"Yes, many troubles. The last just down the road," Omolo explained. "That is why we are glad to be here, where we can sleep safely."

The first guard replied in Dholuo. I didn't understand the words, but his expression was hard and his gestures large.

"What tribe are they?" Omolo asked. He was repeating what had been asked of him. "You know me for many years, and you know that I am Luo."

The guard spoke again.

"They are my friends and that is what matters," Omolo said.

"We can go if it is too much—" I began.

He motioned for me to be silent.

"You let them in or we all sit out here," he told the guard. "What would your boss—my *cousin*—think of that?"

The first guard mumbled something but the second started to open the gate. It creaked and groaned in protest until it created enough space for us to pass. I wasn't so sure I wanted to go inside. Would these Luo guards protect me and my sister? But then I realized that it didn't matter. Even if they didn't, Omolo would offer us his protection. I knew that.

The donkey started forward once more and the cart bumped over the threshold. I heard the gate squealing behind us, then there was a loud clang and it sealed shut.

Shutting us inside.

We were either safer than we had been in days or in more danger than ever before.

Chapter Eighteen

Slowly my eyes opened, adjusting to the light. Light? What time was it, and where was Jata? I sat up like I was on a spring. There she was, practically buried in the burlap sacks, eyes closed, still asleep. There was motion off to the side. I looked over to see five men, including Omolo and one of the guards from last night, sitting around a small fire in the open section of the compound. All around them were bins filled with oranges and piles of empty sacks. There were pushcarts and donkey carts off to one side, but I didn't see any donkeys. They were probably sheltered in stalls elsewhere in the compound. The air was sweet with the scent of oranges and something cooking.

"Good morning," Omolo called out. "Come and join us for breakfast."

"Good morning," I replied softly, not wanting to wake my sister.

I peeled back the sacks that covered my legs and got up, carefully making my way over to them.

"Here," the guard said in Swahili as he offered me a bowl. "It is porridge."

"Thank you, sir. I will wake my sister so she can share."

"Let the girl sleep," he said. "There will be a full bowl for her as well."

I dipped my finger and popped some warm porridge in my mouth. It was sweet—sugar had been added. It was wonderful. Maybe it was the best thing I had ever tasted! Or at least the best thing I had tasted since my mother last cooked for us in our home.

"Did you sleep well?" Omolo asked.

"Better than I have in many, many days."

"You should have slept well knowing that you had guards to watch over you."

"Very good guards," the guard said. "And perhaps it is time that we went back to guarding." He stood up, as did a man I now recognized as the second guard from the night before.

"And we should also get to work . . . before the boss arrives," one of the remaining men said, and he and the final man rose and walked off, leaving me with Omolo.

"I told them what you did when those men threat-ened me and my cart," Omolo said. "They took note, as did I." He pulled something out of his pocket. It was money—paper and coins. "This is all that I have: two hundred and twenty-three shillings. I will keep seven-ty-three and offer you the rest."

"I cannot take all that. It leaves you with so little."

"You must take it. I will get more for my oranges. You must take the money—if not for you, then for your sister."

I took the three wrinkled notes from him. "Thank you so much."

"I know you will use it wisely, perhaps for food or for a ride along the way. I wish I had more to give, but the money I receive for the oranges I will need for my family."

"I understand. I thank you for what you have given." I stuffed the three bills in my pocket—the one I knew had no holes.

"I will leave before noon, so that is when you should leave too," Omolo said.

"We will leave earlier. Morning is the best time to travel."

"It is not as hot," he said, nodding.

"Or as dangerous."

"Aye, bad people seem to be afraid of the morning sun," he agreed. "You could stay with me, but I now travel in the direction you have come."

I would have liked to continue traveling with him, riding on the seat of the cart. Even more, I would have liked that for Jata.

"I thought that perhaps you could come and be sheltered in my family compound, but I realize that would not be wise," he said.

I knew what he meant. No Kikuyu should be going to a neighborhood of Luo.

"I have spoken to the guards about your route and the dangers that are ahead. They did not know of this place Kikima, but they knew of Machakos. They said you can reach it by two means—by train, which travels from Nairobi through Machakos, or along the Mombasa highway, as you are already aware. I know you do not have enough for rail travel, so I will show you the way to the highway, first traveling along and then offering directions. But you must be aware that there have been problems along the route. Many problems."

"Problems?"

"Road blocks, burning vehicles, people being attacked and killed by both protesters and the police."

"The *police* are killing people?"

"They are trying to wrest control from the rioters, but a fired bullet does not know you or your sister from a rioter. Of all areas, you must avoid Kibera particularly. But everywhere you go, beware and keep safe."

"I will keep my eyes and ears open."

"Once you are east of Nairobi, you are free of the worst. The guards told me that, from what they have heard, rioting has been absent in the Machakos region."

"There has been none?"

"That region is all Kamba people, so there has been no tension, no rioting, no looting and no need for people to flee to their traditional lands. But you must get safely through Nairobi before you come to Machakos."

I stood up. "First I must leave here."

"No. First you and your sister must eat. I will walk with you for the first part, to make sure your route is reliable."

We walked together to the top of a hill. Stretching out before us was an endless city. Houses and stores blurred together until I could no longer see where one stopped and another started. Vehicles bumped along already busy roads. In the distance, I could make out gigantic buildings reaching into the sky. I had heard of these buildings—these skyscrapers—but never before had I seen them. What would it be like to stand beneath them looking up? What would it be like to stand at the top and look out? From there, you must be able to see forever. Maybe even Kikima could be seen.

It was still early, but not as early as I had hoped to leave. Jata had continued to sleep and I didn't want to wake her. Dreams were a place of refuge. When she had finally stirred and eaten, she'd seemed reluctant to leave. I knew that reluctance. It felt good to be behind strong walls, with guards to protect us, a friend beside us and warm food to fill our stomachs.

At least some of Nairobi was still slumbering. That didn't mean it was quiet or empty, but not every space had been filled with a car or a person yet. Not like yesterday.

"Follow this road until you find yourself beside a large sports stadium. The sign will say NYAYO STA-DIUM. At that point, you will find the highway. It will be marked and you turn toward Mombasa."

"Is it far to the highway?" Jata asked.

"You see those buildings that stick up in the distance?"

There were buildings everywhere, but I knew he was referring to those that stood tallest against the distant horizon.

"Yes, I see them."

"Those buildings are as tall as the cliffs of the Rift Valley, but they are so far away that they appear to be small. You will reach the heart of the city, although right now some would argue that this place has no heart, or soul, just anger and danger. From that turn you will be halfway to the highway."

I thought back to what the sergeant had said about Nairobi grabbing us and not letting us escape.

"If you walk with speed, you will be at the stadium by midday. Once there, your destination is to the right, but be certain to look for the cutoff to Machakos. It will be no more than fifty or sixty kilometers along the highway."

That was two or three days' walk, depending upon Jata's pace.

"You will go to the left when you find that junction to Machakos Town. I am sure there will be signs to show you the way."

"We don't need signs," Jata said, "because we have the string."

Omolo gave a questioning look.

"It is a Kamba tale," I explained. "We simply need to follow a trail of string to return to our home."

"In that case, I wish you not a string to follow but a thick rope. May God go with you."

"And you."

We shook hands.

"Goodbye, little sister."

Jata wrapped her arms around him in a big hug.

"Jata, can you do me one more favor?" Omolo dug into his pocket and pulled out some change. "At some point on your journey, when you are tired and hungry, I want you to purchase two *mandazi*, one for you and one for your brother." He offered her the money.

Jata's eyes brightened at the thought of one of her

favorite treats—a sweet, sugary, doughy snack. It made my mouth water to think about it.

"We cannot take any more of your money," I said.

"I am not offering it to *you*. I am offering it to your sister. And it is not wise to refuse a gift from a Luo. It is an insult, you know." He smiled broadly.

"Thank you so much, my friend," I said.

"You have fresh water, correct?" he asked.

"I filled the container."

"And you have oranges?"

"You stuffed my bundle so full I can hardly carry them."

"Eat them and trade them. Oranges are as good as shillings. Now, go and remember me, as I will remember you."

Omolo turned and started walking away. I expected him to turn back again, but he didn't. His back was straight and his stride strong. He was practically marching.

"Goodbye, Omolo!" Jata yelled out.

He hesitated, then turned and waved. We waved back, and then all three of us, at the same instant, started walking toward our different destinations.

Chapter Nineteen

With each step, I became more hesitant. The city was growing more active, the streets getting more crowded with people, and all along our path there were signs of struggles. Burned-out cars and trucks were spaced along our route. We saw storefronts and homes that had been set afire, their charred timbers standing upright, their twisted iron gratings not able to withstand the looters.

Piles of rocks that were used as blockades had been pushed to the side of the road to allow the traffic to move again. Fires that had once burned on the highway were now crushed down by passing cars and carts. The remains of burned tires littered the road and their foul odor filled the air.

The smell of the city was everywhere. It was what I imagined hell would smell of—not just fire but brimstone. It came not only from the vehicles and the small fires people set to burn garbage at the side of the road, but from everywhere and nowhere all at once. The smell of fire brought back what I didn't want to remember. It brought me back to Eldoret, to the church, to the fire, to my father. Would I ever be able to smell fire again without my father being in my memory? Maybe it was right that he should never be gone from my thoughts.

But there was something more in the air than the smell of the fires. I think it was the smell of fear and anger and desperation. It filled my nostrils and it filled my heart.

"There are so many people here, I cannot believe it," Jata said.

"They are everywhere."

Surely that should have meant it was safer, but it just made me more nervous. The more people we saw, the more I had to be watchful of. But how could I watch all these people at once?

"How many are there?" Jata asked.

"Many more than you could ever count."

"I am the best in my class in mathematics. I can count to thousands."

"But you cannot count to a million, and they say that there are six million people in the city of Nairobi," I explained.

"I cannot believe there are that many people in the world!"

"You are so young. My teacher told me that there are billions of people in the world, and that is so much more than a million."

"Why did God make so many people?"

"Because he loves us."

"If he loves us, why did he let all those people die at the church? Why didn't he stop those men from killing everybody?"

I shook my head. "I do not know."

"Maybe it is because he made so many people that he didn't need *those* people anymore. Maybe he didn't need our mother and father."

"They are in a better place, Jata. They are in heaven, looking down on us."

"I want them here with us, not looking down on us from above."

"So do I, but it is God's will."

"God wanted them to die?"

"Well . . . I . . . there are many things we cannot understand."

"Did God make those men kill our father?" she asked.

"Of course not! What they did was the work of the devil!"

"But isn't God stronger than the devil? Couldn't he have stopped those men?"

"God is great and most powerful."

"Then why didn't he stop them?" She started to cry.

"God cannot be everywhere all the time."

"The minister told us that God is everywhere, so where was he when those men came?" she asked.

"I don't know," I said. "I am not a minister. I do not know what God is thinking."

"But I just—"

"I do not wish to talk about this. I do not have any answers, so you have to stop asking me questions. Understand?"

"I just—"

"No more. Stop right now!" I yelled.

We walked along in silence. I think we were both stunned by my words and my reaction. But I was so distressed by her questions. She was asking things that I didn't want to speak about. Why had it happened? Why was God not there in his own home, the church, to protect those people? Was the devil stronger? Would thinking such things invite the devil to take me over the way he had taken over those men?

I reached out and took Jata's hand. She gripped my hand tightly. I could feel her quivering. She was fighting to hold back tears. I stopped and bent down so that I was looking her directly in the eyes.

"I am here to make sure that you will be cared for, that you will always be protected," I said.

"Wasn't our mother supposed to care for me? Wasn't our father supposed to protect me?"

"They did. Our father died protecting both of us. He gave his life so we could get away. And our mother cared for you until she had no life left to live." With the back of my hand I gently brushed away her tears. "And now I am not just your brother, but also your mother and father. I am *your* family and you are *my* family. I am sorry that I spoke harshly to you just now. I do not have the answers to your questions and I was sad, so it came out as anger. I do not know why those men did what they did, but evil overtook them—just as it overtook those Kikuyu who killed other people simply because they were of another tribe. Evil was waiting for the moment to come forth."

"And that was the moment?"

"That was an excuse for evil to come out. Maybe there is evil in all of us."

"Is it in me?" she asked.

I smiled. "Not in you."

"And you?"

I thought about what I would do if I could find the men who had killed our father. Would I kill them if I could? Would I do to them what they had done to him? Wouldn't it be right to avenge his death? But then I thought about what the sergeant had said—evil was evil. Light was needed to take away darkness. I had once felt that it was my duty to avenge my father. But now, when I thought of the sergeant and the minister and Omolo—when I thought of all the people who had helped us along the way—I knew that I had already chosen a different path.

"The devil speaks to us in moments of desperation, but we decide if we are going to be his instrument, the weapon of his evil. I will not listen to the whispers of the devil. I will do no evil to any of God's children. Not even if they have done evil to me."

She laughed. I hadn't expected that.

"You think these words are funny?"

"No, it is just that what you are saying makes me think that you would be a good minister."

I did listen in church. I knew the Bible—our mother always had us study the words and what they meant—but still . . . a minister?

"Do you really believe that our parents are looking down at us from heaven?" she asked.

I shook my head. "I do not *believe* it—I *know* it. It is certain, and they will guide us the way the string is guiding us now. Do you see it?"

"I don't need to see it," she said. "All I need is to keep holding your hand, because you see it. You are a good brother . . . and a good father and mother."

"Then let us walk forward together."

Suddenly the smell of the air changed. It was more

pungent, and people who were in front of us started running back in our direction.

"What is happening?" Jata called out to a woman rushing toward us.

"Tear gas!" the woman yelled. "There is a demonstration ahead, and the soldiers are coming! Run, little ones! Run!"

We turned and rushed along with the group. Some people passed us and we passed those who were older or struggling with heavy loads. The mass of people flooded onto the road. Vehicles jockeyed about, some almost hitting people and other vehicles as they tried to turn and drive away.

There was a loud crack, followed by another and another. I knew without asking that it was gunfire!

"We must move faster!" I said, pulling Jata along. I had the urge to drop the water container, but I knew our life depended on it.

We came to a set of railroad tracks that we had passed a few minutes before which cut across the road. People were streaming off the road and onto the tracks in both directions. Railway tracks! That was the other way to Mombasa, along the tracks.

I grabbed an old woman by the arm. "These tracks—do they lead to Mombasa?"

"Yes, yes," she yelled. "They run between Mombasa and Kampala, Uganda."

"Which way is Mombasa?"

"That way, that way," she said, pointing to our left. "Now leave me alone! Let me go!"

I released my grip and she fled down the road. I was going to ask another person, just to be sure, but I didn't need to. The way the sun was shining, reflecting off the rails, I was positive that I could see the string.

"Come, Jata."

We walked right down the middle of the tracks. We were not alone. There were many people in front of us and even more joining from behind, flooding off the road and onto the rails. There were more gunshots coming from behind, and that awful smell was stronger. My eyes felt itchy and my lungs began to burn. Whatever was chasing the people this way was still chasing us. We had to move fast not to be overtaken.

I overheard two men talking ahead of me. "The police are as bad as the rioters," one said.

"But what would happen if there weren't any police?" the other asked.

It was then I noticed that the side of the first man's head was gashed, with blood flowing down his neck and staining his shirt.

"Sir, did the police do that?" I asked, venturing a question.

"No, a protester threw a rock that caught me. But the police have done far worse to many, believe me. I have seen it."

"We have all seen it," the second man said. "It is like there is no safe place to go."

"Certainly not here," the first replied.

"Will they come here?" I asked. "Will they follow?"

Jata gripped my hand tighter.

"Maybe they will. Maybe they are in front of you already. Sometimes you fear the police, and sometimes you fear that there are no police."

"I do not understand."

"The only thing worse than the violence committed by the police is the violence committed because there are no police. You will soon see that."

What did that mean? I wanted to ask, but I was afraid of the answer.

All at once I skidded to a stop, getting bumped and jostled from behind before I could move us off the tracks. I was just so shocked at what I had seen. Ahead there *were* no tracks. They had been uprooted—the rails and ties torn from the ground and thrown about as if an angry giant had been at work. All that remained was the gravel of the railbed, as if the small pieces of rock were too insignificant for him to bother moving. Of course, it had been the work not of an angry giant but of angry men—many angry men.

I turned to a woman who was moving slowly nearby. "What happened here?"

She shrugged. "Even God does not know what happens in Kibera."

"*This* is Kibera?" I gasped.

"It is not the Garden of Eden." The woman walked on.

"We cannot be here," I said to Jata, trying to steady my voice. "We cannot go on." I could see that she was feeling the same fear I was feeling.

I grabbed her and turned around, then realized we couldn't go back either. The crowd behind us was large and moving fast, and those who passed had panic in their eyes. Was there another way? I looked to one side and then the other. Both ways were blocked by small tin buildings—sheds, stores and homes—that stretched out into the distance. If there was a path, I didn't see it. There was only one way: we had to follow the string. With Jata in one hand and the water container in the other, I plunged into the fleeing crowd.

As we walked I looked cautiously from side to side. The little buildings pressed in around us, but then suddenly a gap opened up. The buildings that had surely been there had been reduced to tangled piles of twisted metal, burned timber and wooden beams. A whole swath of homes on both sides of the railroad had been destroyed. The scar created a large opening over ground littered with the remains of what had once stood there.

While the buildings had been pushed away from the tracks, we were pressed in by the smells. The odor of burning was everywhere, and I could see that there were still small fires smoldering. But it was more than that. There was a stench—the foul air of human waste, so much more pungent than that of animals. It seemed to be oozing out of the thick black muck that was everywhere, extending out in all directions. Sometimes in their haste to pass, people would slide down the gravel of the railbed, sinking ankle-deep in the very muck they wanted to escape. Other times people would leave the tracks deliberately, disappearing along one of the small side paths into the endless shanties that stretched out into the distance. Kibera seemed like it was all one big tin roof. I couldn't see where one shack stopped and another started.

Even with people leaving the path, we were constantly pushed from behind. But the pace seemed to have lessened—as if people were still running, but possibly not being chased.

Suddenly the rails were in place again, held together by metal ties. A few paces back they were gone, and now here they were. Had the giant grown tired of destruction? At almost the same instant, the shops at the side of the tracks started to press in upon us once more. The thick black mud was still there, but there were people moving through it. Some were in fresh pressed shirts, and others in suits and ties. Women were sitting at the thresholds of the little shops, some using whisk brooms to sweep away the garbage. In one shop there were green bananas and even greener cabbage for sale. With the reds of the tomatoes piled on the counter, it almost looked pretty.

The rusty tin buildings were still cluttered and crowded together, but there was an order to things. Did this mean we were past the worst?

"Sir, is this still Kibera?" I asked a man just behind us.

"It is until we reach the road."

"But this part seems so different," I said.

"Different from back there, but the same as it was before. People are born, raised, schooled, shop, work and die in Kibera. It is just that too many died too soon these past days."

"But there are shops open and people doing business," I said.

"People can be killed, but life goes on. It is going on." He left the tracks and disappeared down one of the narrow corridors leading past the shops and into the shanties.

"Are we safe?" Jata asked.

"We are safer than we were but not as safe as we will be. Keep with me."

We continued to trip along the tracks. The line of people behind us grew thin, and nobody passed us as we walked. The shops thinned out and then stopped as we crossed a small bridge over an even smaller stream. Ahead was a road. My whole body felt light, free, almost as if I could fly.

A big *matatu* rumbled toward us along the tarmac. In the window sat a big sign: MOMBASA.

The string was still showing us the way.

Chapter Twenty

Being finished with Kibera did not mean being through with Nairobi. It stretched out along the highway—people and shops and homes and vehicles in an endless line, as if we weren't really moving forward but simply passing the same spot again and again. But I had made sure we were moving in the right direction. Three times I'd asked people to confirm our route, and three times they had pointed us toward Mombasa. And then, finally, we had seen the sign: MOMBASA 495 KM. We didn't have to travel the whole way, but what if it was half the distance? Omolo had said he thought Machakos was no more than sixty kilometers. That would take us at least two days. But then how far was Kikima from there? We could get more water, but we might not have enough food unless we only ate smaller portions. If nothing else, being put into the camp had shown me that I could eat less and less often. I had gone two days without food when we first arrived. But then we had only been sitting, shifting around, trying to stay out of the blazing sun. Here we were walking endlessly, and there was no escape from the sun unless a cloud drifted over top. We would need more to eat and more to drink.

Little by little, the city became less and less. There were fewer people on the side of the road, and fewer homes and stores as well. The only thing that remained constant was the traffic on the road. Lorries and *matatus* formed the bulk, but there were also cars, some holding only one or two people. There in the back, free and empty, were seats that could have carried us on our way. What would take us days would take the drivers only hours. I wondered who could be rich enough to have an expensive car all to himself.

Almost all the vehicles left behind a trail of dust and a stench of fumes. You could see the thick black smoke coming from some of the trucks, but you could smell the results from all—so strong I could taste it in my mouth.

"Look," Jata yelled out. "That *matatu* is going to Machakos!"

There, written in big letters above the windshield, was its destination: MACHAKOS. Without even thinking, I waved at the driver and he pulled off the road, bumping onto the dirt and pushing up a thick cloud in his wake. He was not going to be pleased when I simply asked questions and didn't climb on board, but he had knowledge I needed. A few days ago, I would never have flagged him down or dared to ask him questions. Days ago felt more like another life ago.

I struggled through the dirt cloud, running as fast as I could with Jata in tow.

"Sir, are you going to Machakos?" I asked the conductor.

"We are. Climb aboard, quickly."

"How far is it?" I asked.

"Not that far."

"But how far?" I persisted.

"Are you stopping to ask questions or to ride?"

"What is the fare?"

"Three hundred and fifty for you and another three hundred for the girl."

I knew the little money in my pocket would not be enough. "Sorry, we do not have that much. But thank you for your time."

"How much do you have?"

"Not nearly enough. Sorry, sir. Could you tell me the distance?"

He gave me a scowl and then slammed his palm against the side of the vehicle, signaling not just his anger but his impatience for the driver to leave. The *matatu* squealed away, leaving us in another cloud of dust, but also in a state of hope. I didn't know the exact distance, but that fare wasn't too much. Machakos wasn't ten days away, but maybe two or three, confirming what Omolo had told me. We had enough food to last at least until then. We could make it.

"Giraffes!" Jata yelled.

There they were, not more than a hundred paces away—three giraffes pulling leaves from a tall tree.

"They are so beautiful! I have never seen one before."

"I have," I said. "I was with my classmates when my school took a trip to see them in a pen. They have the most wonderful eyes, so big and moist."

"I would like to be close enough to see their eyes," Jata said.

"That was in a pen. Here they would run or kick if we got too close. Did you know that even a lion fears a giraffe?"

"No, I did not."

That got me thinking. I hadn't seen any lions or zebras, but this looked like the landscape for them.

"I wish I could have a giraffe as a pet," Jata said.

"I thought you wanted a dog."

"I did, but you cannot ride on a dog."

"And you think you can on a giraffe?" I asked.

232

"You could on *my* giraffe. It would be very gentle and have a special seat so I could ride everywhere."

"Would you let me ride your giraffe sometimes too?"

"Of course, but not alone. You would ride behind me."

"That would certainly be better than walking. Can you imagine the scene we would make when we entered Kikima? I would lean down and ask directions to our grandparents' home. Perhaps from up there we could even see their home!" I exclaimed.

One of the giraffes turned in our direction. I got the strange feeling he had heard me and understood that I was making fun of him. I didn't want him to kick me, but fortunately he turned away, far more interested in the leaves than us.

"Muchoki, I was wondering about the string story."

"It is a good story."

"Yes, but in the story the string was broken and they couldn't find their way home."

"It will not break for us," I said. "It will lead us all the way home."

"And if it does break?"

"Then we'll do without it. We do not need a string when we have brains and roads and signs. Even if we cannot follow the string, we can still follow the tarmac."

"But you can see the string, right?"

For a split second I thought about telling her the truth, but I quickly realized that a kind lie was better than a cruel truth.

"I can see it as clear as I can see you. Let's keep looking for more giraffes."

There were more giraffes scattered along the route. And some antelopes, a few little gazelles and some zebras. I wished we hadn't seen the zebras. I knew it made no sense because lions ate all of the others except the giraffes, but it was that saying—see zebras, think lions. That thought kept us from venturing out into the scrub bush that extended into the distance on both sides of the road.

Behind us the sun was starting to set. We were walking east and it was setting in the west. I didn't need a watch tell to me that our shadows were becoming longer and the day was growing shorter. It was good to have the sun on our backs instead of in our eyes, but soon it would be good just to have it. It would be missed. We needed to find a place for the night. There were very few homesteads around, and those few were set well away from the road and surrounded by walls and barbed-wire fences. We hadn't seen a store for over an hour, and I could see none in front of us either. There was nothing more. And dusk was approaching quickly, falling from the sky faster than we could move forward. We needed shelter and there was none. There was nothing except for shrubs, cacti and scattered trees. Trees . . . lions did not climb trees. I remembered reading that. Now I just needed to find the right one.

We traveled on until we came to what I was looking for—a large tree that we could climb with a crook where we could sleep. I stopped below the perfect tree. I could push Jata up and then climb up after her.

"We'll have our evening meal here," I said.

"And sleep in the little ravine?"

I'd been looking up for trees so hard that I hadn't looked down for water. We needed that as well.

"No, not in the ravine, but close. You sit and put your back against the tree while I gather wood."

She didn't argue. She was tired but had never complained, not even once. She was as brave as I was pretending to be.

I didn't have to go far to get wood. There was deadfall everywhere, and it was as dry as old chicken bones. This whole area was dry. There had been no rain here for a long time. I didn't miss the mud, but I missed the water. We had no more than a few mouthfuls left in the container, and I'd have to find water early tomorrow. We could go without food, but we couldn't go far without water.

I dropped the wood at Jata's feet and picked up the water container. I poured some into the pot—just the amount we'd need to cook the beans and maize.

"There isn't much water left now, so I want you to drink it."

"I am not thirsty."

"Of course you are."

"You should drink it," she said.

"Do not worry. We'll get more water, and I'll drink it then."

"Is there water in the ravine?" Jata asked.

"I have not looked. But even if it is dry, there will be water if I dig into the sand."

"Clean water?" she asked.

"I hope, but I cannot know. That is why you need to drink this water from the container. I know it is clean. I do not want you to get sick."

"I do not want *you* to get sick," she said.

"It is more important that you are well."

"No," she said, shaking her head violently. "It is more important that you are well. If I am sick, you can carry me. If you are sick, I cannot carry you."

I didn't know what to say. What she was saying was true.

"We could share the water in the container," I finally suggested, "and then get more from the ravine."

Jata shook her head. "That would be worse. If we

both drink from the ravine and it is bad water, then we
both will get sick."

Again she made nothing but sense. When had she
got so wise?

"Just take a sip from the container and I will finish
the rest," I suggested.

She put her hands over her mouth. "I will only
drink once you have emptied the container," she said,
her words muffled.

"You are a very stubborn girl."

She nodded her head. I couldn't very well force her
to drink, and there wasn't that much time. We had to
make a fire, cook, eat and possibly dig for water before the
sun set, and then we had to find a way to sleep in a tree.

"Fine."

I opened the container, tipped it back and drank.
The water tasted so good. I needed it so much. Back
and back I tipped the container, until the last drop fell
into my mouth.

"You get the wood ready for a fire and I will get
the water."

I grabbed a cup from my bundle and the water
container and set off. The lip of the ravine was steep
and undercut, but at the very bottom was a thin trickle of water that stained the sand. It wasn't much, but
it was good that I didn't have to dig. I slid down the
side and walked across the sand to the water. It slowly

snaked through the ravine, gathering in small puddles scattered along its route. I didn't want the sitting water, but that which was moving.

I dropped to my knees, straddling the stream, and dipped the edge of my cup into the thin flow, tipping it ever so slightly so that water could gather at the bottom. I brought the cup up to my face and eyed the contents. It was full of sand but looked clean. I took a little sip— Jata didn't need to know. It was cool and tasted fine, just a little gritty. If I'd had a basin and enough time, I would have filled it and allowed the sand to settle. But I had neither. I decided to try to pour only the clean sliver at the top of the cup into the water container. Less than a mouthful went from cup to container.

I dug down into the sand in the middle of the stream and then sank the cup up to the rim. It quickly filled with water. I had an idea. I removed my shirt and stretched it over the top of the cup. As I poured, the material caught most of the sand and the water fell into the container. That still didn't mean it was fit to drink, but it was better. I repeated this process time and time again, until the container was two-thirds full. That was much more than enough for tonight. Tomorrow I'd fill it to the top.

Lugging the container back up the slope, I was surprised to see that Jata had not only prepared the fire but also started cooking our dinner on it.

"It took three matches," she said. "I am sorry."

"We still have matches left. Thank you."

Jata smiled up at me as she stirred the pot. I knew that I was leading, that I was the one caring for her, but she kept giving me reasons to move forward. Even in the darkness, she always gave me hope.

"We will eat and then seek shelter," I said.

"Where will we sleep tonight?"

I pointed up.

"In the sky?"

"In the tree."

"We cannot sleep in a tree!" she protested.

"You think we can sleep in the sky but question if we can sleep in a tree? I know that you have never flown like a bird, but I have seen you climb a tree. But first, we eat."

I tied the end of the blanket in a knot so that it held both Jata and the branch that supported her. She was wrapped up snug in a crook of the tree.

"There you are, as safe as a baby being carried by her mother."

Almost before the words came out I felt badly for saying them.

"Was I carried like that when I was a baby?" she asked.

"Of course you were. I remember."

"I wish I could remember more."

And I wished I could remember less.

"Do you miss our parents?" she asked.

I was going to say "every day," but I didn't because that was a lie.

"Every minute. I miss them every minute." I smiled at her. "Now go to sleep."

"Will you sleep?"

"I will try, but I will also watch," I said.

"Watch what?"

"Hopefully my sister sleeping! But if you fall, I will be there to catch you. I will sleep when we rest tomorrow. Then you can watch me and make sure I don't fall."

I lowered myself to a branch below Jata. I'd already tied up the blanket with our remaining food to keep it safe from marauding animals. For good measure, I'd also hauled up our water container and crammed it into another crook. I wasn't sure why I'd bothered, because I couldn't imagine any animal clever enough to undo the lid and take a drink. But it seemed better to have all of what we owned up in the tree with us.

Below us, the fire continued to burn brightly. I'd taken every last bit of fuel and thrown it in. It provided not just the light to guide our climb but also ongoing protection. Animals feared fire, and this was a good fire. It continued to bathe us in light even high in the branches. I only wished I could feel the heat. The sky was cloudless, which meant the night was going to get cold.

I settled in my own crook and wrapped my arms around the branch, locking them together on the other side. There wouldn't be much sleep for me. There *couldn't* be much sleep for me. I closed my eyes and tried to remember and to forget.

My eyes popped open and my whole body jerked as I gripped the branch even tighter. I'd done that same thing dozens of times since drifting off. I had no idea how long I'd been asleep this last time. It could have been two seconds or two minutes or longer. The fading fire gave the only hint of the passage of time. It was nothing more now than a few embers throwing out more shadows than light.

Most of the light was coming from above. With no clouds, the millions of stars in the sky all gave their small token of light. Those and the half moon gave shading to the ground. The moon changed each night. It was more and more and more until it became full, and then it was less and less and less until it vanished completely, only to repeat again. The stars were different—they stayed the same. They could be covered by clouds, but they still remained in place. They were that way when I was young, and they would be that way when I was old—and even when my grandchildren were old. In this tree, at the camp, at our homestead near Eldoret—they were always the same. And I was sure they would be the same in Kikima. I just wished that I could find out soon.

I looked up at Jata. I couldn't tell if she was asleep, but I could tell that she was motionless, at rest. My little star in the sky above my head.

Just then, there was a sound below, so soft that it could have come from inside my ear. The fire crackled, one of the embers calling out in pain. Before the fire at the church, I would never have thought about a fire that way—that wood tossed into the flames would cry out in pain. Now I did.

A large shadow shifted on the ground and my heart seemed to stop beating. There was the unmistakable outline of a lion! It edged forward silently, more shadow than substance, caught in the glowing light of the smoldering fire. It moved hesitantly, alternating between sniffing the ground and looking ahead. It had appeared from the ravine where I'd gathered our water, and I was sure that it was following my path. It was following its nose, tracking, hunting—for me.

As it approached, it grew in size. It was male with a tremendous mane framing its head. He moved warily forward, then stopped before reaching the fire. He was cautious, perhaps even afraid of the glowing embers. I was sure a full fire would have sent him running. That thought was calming—lions *were* afraid of fire. That gave me more certainty that my other piece of knowledge—that lions couldn't climb trees—was also correct. Jata and I were safe up here. I just wish I *felt* safe up here.

The lion was leading with his nose, searching, being pulled forward by the scent that I had left behind. He circled around the embers until he came to the spot where we had sat to eat. He started snuffling, drawing in scent so strong that he appeared to be not just smelling the air but tasting it.

He continued in a wide track around the fire, following the invisible trail until he came to the base of the tree. His ears and nostrils twitched, and then ever so slowly he raised his head until he was looking up at me and I was looking down at him. The light caught his eyes—glowing green eyes unlike any color I'd ever seen before—and those eyes were looking right at me.

His tail swished back and forth, almost like another living animal. Did a swishing tail mean the same as it did with the cats in our village? Was the lion angry? And if he was, was the anger directed at me or at the tree that blocked his path to me?

Slowly I reached for the club I'd taken from the man who'd attacked us when we were with Omolo. It wasn't much, but it was the only thing I had. I held it in front of me. The tree trunk, height and this small piece of wood were the only things that stood between me and the lion. And then there was a little more height and one more obstacle between it and Jata. That was me. If he ate me, would that be enough? Would he leave her alone?

Suddenly the lion placed both front paws on the side of the tree and started up the trunk! I was so afraid I couldn't scream, and it happened so fast I couldn't react. Higher and higher, paw above paw, he stretched his full length toward me . . . and then stopped! He was standing on his back legs and stretching toward the sky, but he wasn't able to climb. Then he reached up and took a swat at me with his gigantic paw, missing my feet by a few centimeters!

I struggled farther up my branch and knocked over the water container in the process. It tumbled over and flew past me, hitting the lion right on the tip of his nose! The massive cat roared out in pain, dropped down and ran away, vanishing into the darkness!

"Muchoki!" Jata called out.

I tried to respond but no words came.

"Muchoki!" she screamed again.

I swallowed hard to try to make words come forth.

"I'm here. Everything is fine."

"I thought I heard the roar of a lion," she cried out.

I didn't want her to know what had just happened. "How would you even know what a lion sounds like?

You have never seen one or heard one roar. You must have been dreaming."

"But it sounded so real."

"Dreams can be like that." I had to say more. "I am just surprised you were not dreaming of giraffes. Those you have seen. Maybe one will come up to the tree and give you a goodnight kiss!"

She giggled and I felt relieved.

"If a giraffe comes, I will wake you. Now go back to sleep."

"Goodnight, Muchoki."

I looked around for signs of the lion, but I could not see any. The water container was lying on the ground below. The lid was off and water was leaking out. It looked as if it had been hurt in the battle with the lion and blood was flowing from a wound suffered in our defense. What a brave water container. Certainly braver than I had been.

I pushed myself up higher, getting closer to Jata and farther from the ground. I wasn't going to sleep now, but I wanted to not sleep higher up in the branches.

Chapter Twenty-one

"**B**ut why can't we go down yet?" Jata asked.

I hadn't told her anything about the lion, and I wasn't going to. It was best that he remained part of a dream she hadn't had.

"I'm waiting for the giraffe to come to kiss you good morning, since it did not kiss you goodnight. If you get down, it will not work. Giraffes do not bend down to the ground very well."

It was no longer dark but it was not yet light. There were too many places still left for a lion to hide.

"But my legs are sore. I need to stretch," she said.

"There is plenty of space in the tree to stretch. It is a big tree. Do you ever hear monkeys complain about being cramped?"

"I am not a monkey," she protested.

"That is only *your* opinion."

"I am hungry. Can we have food?"

"I can hand you some raw maize if you want. But we are going to walk before we eat."

"So can we walk, then?" Jata asked.

"We will rest before we walk, and walk before we eat. Rest your legs and your mouth."

I continued to peer out, trying to pierce the gloom with my glare. The sun was coming up quickly, and I was starting to be able to see farther, clearer, truer. Still I saw no sign of the lion. That didn't mean he was gone, of course—only that I couldn't see him.

"I have to go," Jata said.

"We will go, but not now."

"I mean I have to relieve myself."

That she couldn't do in the tree. I took one more long look around.

"Wait," I called out to her.

I climbed down and then jumped to the ground, trying to land as softly as possible. Still, it would not have been soft enough if there was a lion close by. I turned the water container and picked it up. It was less than a quarter full. I took the lid from the ground and wiped it on my shirt before putting it back in place.

"Can I come down now?" Jata yelled.

"Yes, but be quiet."

In the dust were the tracks of the lion. They were enormous! With my foot I smudged them, brushing them away. I didn't want Jata to see the tracks—dreams didn't leave footprints. Head up, eyes still looking, I used both feet to destroy the evidence. The tracks led back to the ravine. Any thought I'd had of going for more water was gone. We'd take what we had and leave.

"Here," Jata said. She was holding my bundle and lowered it to me as I reached up. I slung it over my shoulder and then helped her down the last part of the trunk.

"We have to go right now," I said, picking up the water container.

"But I told you I need to stretch."

"And I need to walk."

I grabbed her hand and practically dragged her toward the road. Glancing from side to side, I moved as quickly as possible, imagining the lion hiding everywhere. My club was right there, sticking out of the waistband of my trousers. If the lion came, I would meet him. I wouldn't be able to win a battle, but I could win enough time for Jata to escape—as my father had done for us at the church.

Just then, a big lorry thundered past, barreling down the highway. It was gone in an instant, but for that brief second we were not alone. Surely the sound and sight and smell of the big truck were enough to drive away a lion. Surely. I dragged Jata right up onto the road with me. There was another lorry in the distance and we'd have to step aside before it came, but right now we needed to be there. Those few centimeters of roadway separated us from the lion. There was now nothing to fear. And if he did reappear, I still had my water container to protect us.

Jata sat on my shoulders, hanging on tightly. I supported her with one hand while I held the empty water container in the other. We'd traveled far and fast. The rush of the lion had driven me forward, and that rush had lasted throughout the morning. We hadn't stopped for breakfast or lunch. We ate oranges as we walked—three each. We peeled each section and popped it into our mouths, slowly chewing, sucking out every little drop of juice before swallowing what remained. No oranges had ever tasted more succulent.

In my mind I thanked Omolo and wondered and worried about him. Had he been able to get home safely? I felt bad that I wasn't able to help him the way I know he would have helped us—the way he *did* help us.

As we walked, we left behind a trail of orange peels. Peels behind and a string in front. I could picture a lion following the peels just as we were following the string toward Kikima. Neither was real, of course, but that didn't stop me from imagining lions behind every shrub we passed. But I had no need to fear. Between the traffic on the road and the people walking beside it, no lion would come near.

Up ahead was a market. There were stores with small stalls in front. Many lorries and *matatus* had pulled off to the side of the road. Others slowed almost to a stop as they came up to the big speed bumps on the tarmac. The lorries groaned in protest as they thumped over the bumps, and then roared and belched out black smoke as they struggled to pick up speed again.

Off to the side was a man sitting on a bicycle that he'd converted to a sharpener. There was a grindstone where the front wheel would have been, and he used that stone to sharpen knives and axes. He sat there, pedaling away, his efforts turning the grinding wheel. He had on pink plastic sunglasses—the kind that would be worn by a child—to protect his eyes from the sparks that flew into the air. In his hands was a machete. I felt uneasy but watched transfixed as he moved it back and forth, back and forth across the stone, sparks flying as the blade became razor sharp. I both feared it and wished I possessed it. A machete could do so much more to protect us than my little knife. I tightened my grip on Jata's hand and pulled her into the crowd.

"I am thirsty," she said.

Our water had run out more than an hour ago. This marketplace needed to have water to survive.

"There will be a place to draw water here, I hope."

We crossed a small bridge over a river . . . well, at least a riverbed passed beneath.

"Stay," I said to Jata.

I looked down over the side of the bridge. The river was dry and men were working with shovels, putting sand into piles. They weren't digging for water but gathering sand to be used with cement. If there was any water beneath the sand, it was so far below the surface that I could never dig deep enough to get it.

I started back—but where was Jata? In a panic I looked around, then spotted her next to a man roasting maize. I rushed to her side.

"Do not wander away from where I have placed you, little sister."

"I am sorry."

"No need to fight," the man said in Kikamba. "Buy some maize and be friends."

"No, thank you, sir," I answered back in hesitant Kikamba.

"I offer the best prices and the most tender maize in the market."

"I am sure, but we do not have money." That was a lie. We had money, but not for maize.

"Where are you from?" he asked, this time in Swahili. "Your Kikamba is . . . well, not so good."

"Our mother is Kamba," I said, still using my Kikamba. "We were forced from our home by the problems with the election."

"Terrible, terrible." He had switched back to Kikamba.

"I was wondering, sir, is there a place where we might get water?"

"The ravine."

"But it is dry."

"Up farther the water still runs at the surface. Not much, but it is there and it is fresh. I need to go myself. I am almost out of water." He pointed down at the container by his feet.

"I could fill it for you," I said.

"I have no money to give you."

"I am not asking. The distance is the same to walk whether I carry one container or two, and I have two hands."

"Your Kikamba is bad, but your manners are good." He picked up his water container and handed it to me. "Go down the ravine and up the dried-out bed. You will find the water."

"Come, Jata." We went back along the road to the bridge. It always felt bad to retrace our steps and move in the wrong direction, but at least there was purpose this time.

Carefully we crossed the highway. It was much

easier here, with the traffic slowed to a crawl by the speed bumps. When we came to the ravine, we skidded down the steep sides until we stopped at the sandy bottom. I looked back and could see the high-water marks along the bridge. It appeared that during the rainy season, the river almost flooded the road. We would have had water more than three times my height above our heads.

It was easy to see that we were headed in the right direction. Some children were coming toward us, struggling under the weight of full containers of water, and others were going in our direction, carrying containers that were empty. One group was moving with much more speed.

Eventually the sand of the creek bottom gave way to rocks and a small but steady stream. The water danced among the rocks and then vanished beneath the sand. I joined the others filling their containers. Dropping to my knees, I took the man's container, turned it on its side and allowed the water to enter to the level of the flowing water. Next I removed a cup from my bundle and cup by cup poured in the water until it was full. I did the same with my container and put the lid back in place. His container lacked a lid.

Standing up, I grabbed both containers and lifted them. I was caught off guard. The two seemed to weigh much more than twice the one. Perhaps my offer had been too generous. Both containers were too heavy for Jata to carry. Laden down with the water, I shuffled slowly along the dry creek bed. When I reached the road, I put one down and scaled the slope, leaving the other at the top, and then repeated it and returned with the second.

"Come now," I said to Jata. "The way is clear."

We crossed the road, dodging between the slow-moving trucks, and then made our way back to the stand.

"Here is your water container," I said to the man.

"And here is your maize." He offered me a cob of roasted maize.

"But I still have no money."

"You have done a favor for me. I will return a favor to you. Now take the maize or I will be offended."

I took it from his hand and turned to Jata. "For you."

"For *us*," she insisted.

"You start and I will finish."

She took the maize from me and started eating.

"There is one more favor that I would ask," I said, turning back to the man. "Could you tell me how far Machakos is?"

"Sixteen kilometers."

"It is only sixteen kilometers!" I exclaimed. "Are you certain?"

"That is what the sign says."

He pointed up the road. Sure enough, there was a large green sign confirming what he'd told us.

"So you are going to Machakos?" he asked.

"We are going to a little place beyond it."

"And it is called?"

"Kikima."

"Ah yes, I know Kikima."

"You do?"

"It is not that much farther. Maybe another forty kilometers. You could be there by nightfall."

"It will be longer. Maybe three days—two if we walk long hours each day."

"Walk? You are going to *walk*?"

"Yes, sir. We have already walked for many days, so two or three more is possible." In my head I thought it was not just possible but a certainty.

He shook his head. "You stand here and watch my maize. I will be back."

He walked away and I felt anxious. What was he doing? Maybe we would be best to leave. There was more than enough light for us to get at least part of the way to Machakos if we left right away.

"Hey, boy! Come, and bring your sister!" the maize man yelled. He was standing beside a big lorry filled with sand.

I picked up the water container, grabbed Jata with my other hand and hurried over.

"This is my friend Henry," the maize man said.

"Hello, sir. I am Muchoki and this is Jata."

Henry nodded his head in response.

"He is the driver of this lorry. It is going to Machakos, and you are going with him."

I could hardly believe my ears!

"Climb up in the back," the driver said. "Quickly, I have to get this and another load in before dark."

"Come, there is a ladder on the side," the maize man said.

I helped Jata start the climb up, then followed close behind, struggling with the water container in one hand. Finally, I got to the top.

"Thank you!" I called down to the maize man.

"Good luck and offer my greetings to your family!"

I shooed Jata to the center of the truck, and we both positioned ourselves on top of the load of sand. Almost instantly the truck started moving, bumping along the dirt side of the road and then up onto the tarmac.

"Do not be afraid," I said to Jata.

"I am not afraid. I am happy. We are moving without me having to use my feet. Wake me when we get there." She lay back in the sand. That seemed like a good thing to do. Still holding the water container with the one hand and taking her hand in my other, I lay back as well. The sand was slightly damp and cool, and it felt so good as both soaked through my shirt and into my body.

Chapter Twenty-two

The lorry slowed and I sat up. I had fallen asleep. We were circling a roundabout. It was a big place with stores, a bank and a church. The roads were filled with cars and motorcycles, and people passed along narrow walkways that separated store from road. This looked to be a fine city. It reminded me very much of Eldoret—at least how it was before.

When we had left Eldoret in the back of the lorry, I saw what it had become. There were looted stores and burned cars on the streets. Rocks littered the road, and everywhere there was a smell of the fear and terror and anger that had gripped the city. It was there and still growing as we left. Even the rain that had fallen that day hadn't been able to cleanse the air. But here, there was none of that smell.

The truck exited on the far side of the roundabout

and then went a short block and made a turn, the brakes complaining as the driver slowed through the turn. Up ahead sat a yard full of lorries just like this one—some full and some empty. Behind them was a gigantic pile of sand and a large building. The brakes squealed again and the engine roared as the driver downshifted and turned into the yard. He moved into a space beside the sand pile and then brought the lorry to a stop. Was this the end? Was this Machakos?

"Okay, you must get down now!" Henry called up.

Jata and I went down the ladder to where the driver was waiting.

"You are now in Machakos," he said.

"It looks like a good town. Sir, could you tell me, was there any violence here? Has it been quiet?"

"Most quiet. There was no violence in the heart of Kambaland."

"None?"

"Well, there were two men who came. They wished to instigate violence. We told them that we did not believe in violence . . . so we killed them."

"You killed them!"

"It was not me—it was others. They beat the men with sticks until they were dead, and then they set their bodies on fire. The men had to know that there would be no violence in Machakos."

His answer was disturbing and reassuring all at once. The citizens had stamped out violence and I was safe, but I shuddered at the thought of how that safety was accomplished.

"Thank you, sir. We now have only one more step to travel. We have to get to Kikima."

"That is a fine town."

"You know Kikima?"

"Everybody around here knows Kikima."

"Is it far?"

"The roads are rough, but by vehicle it is no more than an hour."

"And by foot?" I asked.

"It depends on the speed of the foot. It is twenty-five kilometers."

"It is one day's walk."

"One day," he said. "Not one night. The roads are not safe."

"But you said there was no violence here."

"There are always thugs. The roads are much safer during the day." He glanced over his shoulder toward the building behind him. "Now go before my boss sees that I brought cargo with me that was not sand."

"Thank you, sir. Thank you so much."

I led Jata away through the gates and onto the busy street outside. Traffic buzzed around us and people brushed by. We had no time to gawk.

"We need to find a place to sleep for the night," I said.

"We aren't sleeping in a tree again, are we?"

"No trees." Here it was not animals I feared but the people.

Machakos Town was big and we were close to the center. We needed to get out of the heart and into a part that was deserted. How far would that be? I thought back to the places we had slept the last five nights— under the protection of a Maasai, in an abandoned building, under the overhang of a building, in a warehouse filled with oranges and in a tree with a lion at our feet. Last night had been the worst. Tonight would have to be better than that.

As we walked, I made an inventory of the things we possessed. The water container was solid and almost full of clean drinking water. We had enough beans and maize for at least five more meals—far more than we would need before we arrived. We had our pot, the cups and bowls and spoons, and of course my little knife and the club. The two blankets were still in good shape. And we had one more thing.

I put my hand into my pocket and felt the shillings folded in the bottom. It wasn't much money, but tomorrow we would use it. Tomorrow we would get on a *matatu* and ride toward Kikima. We might not have money to pay the fare the entire way, but each kilometer that we didn't have to walk was good. Jata was starting to struggle. And I was beginning to struggle as well. I could continue to move forward, but I might not be able to carry her on my back . . . no, I would carry her as long as I had the strength if that was what she needed.

I knew I should have felt excited—our goal was in reach—but instead I just felt afraid. What if my mother's fears had been correct and we wouldn't be received? With her we had their daughter and a claim to kinship. Now we were only strangers claiming to be family. Then what would we do? Where would we go? How would we move forward? The only other person I knew was Jomo, and while I had a slip of paper that gave the name of his new village I had no idea where or how far it was or how we could ever possibly get there. I felt such a sense of panic and dread that I stopped walking, suddenly weighed down by so much more than what was on my back and in my hands.

"What is wrong?" Jata asked.

"Nothing, nothing."

I reached out and took her hand and started walking again. Standing still meant we were finished. None of the steps that preceded this one meant anything.

The streets became much quieter as we left the center of town behind. The setting sun was a signal for us to seek shelter. We passed by a government office and the local hospital. Ahead were some bushes. I wondered if we could find shelter in their midst, safely away from the prying eyes of passersby.

"You stand right here," I said to Jata. "Do not move from this fence, and watch our water container." I set it down at her feet.

I walked across the street to the bushes. Almost instantly, I was disappointed. They weren't thick or deep enough to hide us from passersby or the people in the small dwellings behind. We would have to go farther from the town, and we would have to go quickly.

Jata was still where I'd left her but she was on her knees, facing the fence. It looked like she was peering through the wire and into a little compound. As I came closer, I could hear voices—she was talking to somebody. There was a little girl about her age, and she was pressing her face through a small opening in a building where a board was missing. The girl was speaking Kikamba, and Jata was replying in Swahili.

"Come, we have to go," I said.

"But I am talking to my friend."

"Tell your friend goodbye."

"My friend's name is Mueni."

"Tell Mueni goodbye. We need to find a place to sleep."

"I asked her for a place and she was telling me where we could go."

"She was?" I turned to the girl. "Do you know of a place where we could sleep?"

She didn't answer.

"It is polite to call her by her name," Jata instructed.

"Mueni, do you know where we could sleep?"

Again, no answer.

"She has probably been told not to talk to strangers," Jata said.

"But she talked to you, and you are a stranger."

"I *was* a stranger. Now we are friends. I will introduce you. Mueni, this is my brother, Muchoki."

"Hello, Muchoki."

"Hello, Mueni. It is a pleasure to meet you. Do you know a place where we could sleep?"

"Yes, there is a shed at the back of our compound."

"And what is this compound?" I asked.

"It is Suvia."

That was the Kamba word for "taking care."

"Is it a school?"

"It is a children's home. We are all total orphans who live here."

I had a rush of fear. We had walked hundreds of kilometers to escape being placed in orphanages and now we were pressed against the fence of one!

"What is a total orphan?" Jata asked.

"Those who live here have no mother and no father."

"We are total orphans," Jata said before I could stop her.

"We need to leave," I said. "We cannot stay here." I took my sister by the hand and started away.

"But why not?" Jata resisted, digging in her heels and refusing to move.

"We do not know these people, and we do not have permission to stay." There was so much to fear that Jata didn't know about—things I had not told her and could not tell her about the authorities wanting to put us in separate orphanages.

"It would be a secret," Mueni said. "You would be where no one goes—at least not until later tomorrow, after you have gone. Inside the fence is safe."

All of what she said played in my mind. To have a roof over our head and a fence around us would be good—like the night we spent with Omolo. But what if we were discovered? Would the people running the orphanage try to keep us? Would they separate us?

"Go around to the side," Mueni said. She pointed to the left. "I will meet you."

With that, she disappeared into the darkness of the opening.

"It will be safe," Jata said.

She was not afraid because she was unaware. But having a look would not cost us anything except time.

"Come," Jata said. She took me by the hand and started to lead. I did not resist.

We circled to the side of the fence, and it gave way to a wall made of blocks. It was high and was topped by pieces of jagged glass. The ground sloped away, making the wall even higher. I certainly saw no place where we could get through such a formidable obstacle.

Just then, Mueni appeared. Jata broke free and ran over, and the two girls hugged like long-lost friends. There was a hole in the wall—or *under* the wall—where rain had washed away the ground, creating a gully. The hole was protected by strands of barbed wire that had been pushed aside. Mueni started to lead Jata through.

"No, I will go before my sister."

She nodded and released Jata's hand, taking mine. Mueni ducked down and edged through the wire. I was pulled along, but since I was larger, the hole became smaller. I had to ease through, careful not to snag myself or the bundle slung over my shoulder. Jata pressed in behind me. She was not waiting to be invited in.

Once on the other side, I poked my head up, released Mueni's hand and looked around. There were some bushes and a small shed—was that the place she meant? Farther along were patches of cultivated land, and behind that two large buildings blocked the view of what was beyond. The wall provided protection to keep the outside from entering—and the inside from leaving. I could hear children's voices but saw no children.

"Who lives here?" I asked. "How many?"

"There are twenty-six. Seven are boys and nineteen are girls."

"And adults?"

"There are eight staff members, but all have left except the matron and the patron. Soon the night watchman will arrive."

"There is a watchman?"

"He sits in a shed by the main gate. He is very old and does not walk back here. Soon after he arrives, he is asleep. I will show you where you can stay."

Mueni led us toward the little building and opened the door. I noticed that it did not have a lock. That was good. I feared being locked in. Inside was dark, but there was still enough light to see. There were tools along one wall. The floor was empty except for a pile of burlap bags. I now knew that they could make good beds and blankets, but I still needed more before I could allow myself to stay here.

"Where are all the other children?" I asked.

"They are studying in the dining hall."

"And why are you not there too?"

"I am so smart that I do not need to study as much."

"You are?"

"I must be, because I was smart enough to sneak away without being noticed!"

I couldn't help smiling at that. "Why are you doing this for us?"

"You are my friends and we have been taught to help our friends, especially those who are in need."

We were in need—there was no arguing with that.

"Thank you for helping," Jata said.

"But in the morning, you must leave or we will all get in trouble."

"We will leave at first light." If not long before, I thought.

The two girls hugged again, and then Mueni was gone. Part of me wanted to follow—not back to the dining hall but out the door and under the fence. The other part just wanted to make a bed from the burlap bags, lie down and go to sleep. That part won.

Sometimes you just had to trust. Even new friends.

Chapter Twenty-three

 Sweet voices filled my head. It was a lovely sound.
Where was it coming from? I snapped awake and
sat bolt upright. It was dark and it took a moment
to remember that I was in a shed in the compound
of the orphanage. We had to leave. It was still dark,
but why were there voices? Why was there singing? I
reached over and felt for Jata beside me. She was there,
still sleeping, a soft whistle coming as she breathed in
and out.

The door creaked open and a beam of light entered, and before I could even react, Mueni poked in
her head.

"Are you still here?" she whispered.

"Yes."

"You need to go soon, before you are discovered."

"Yes, of course. Jata, you must get up."

She yawned and stretched, and I threw off the burlap sack I'd been using as a blanket and got to my feet.

"This is for you," Mueni said. She handed a banana to me. "I wish there were two, but I only get one for breakfast."

"I cannot take your breakfast," I said.

"There will be porridge. I will have some of that. You take this."

Reluctantly I did as she asked. Jata needed to eat.

Mueni opened the door wider. "It is time."

I slung the bundle over my shoulder, handed the banana to Jata and picked up our water container. We followed Mueni out into the yard, hidden by the walls of the shed. The voices were much louder now. Mueni peeked around the edge of the building.

"Go now," she urged. "All is clear."

"Thank you so much. We will not forget your kindness. Someday we will come back for a visit," I said.

"I will look for you both."

Staying low, trying to keep the shed as cover, we reached the gully.

"You first," I said to my sister.

Jata waved to Mueni, who waved back. They exchanged a last smile, and then Jata ducked down and was gone. I waved as well and then followed after my sister. Quickly we circled back the way we'd come, along the wall until we reached the road.

"Where do we go now?" Jata asked.

"To Kikima, of course."

"But how do we get there?"

"Today, we ride." I pulled the shillings out of my pocket. "We will take a *matatu*."

"All the way that remains?"

"As far as our shillings will take us."

The *matatu* station was a crazy mass of people and vehicles. Hundreds and hundreds of people were pushing and shoving, trying to get on the *matatu* that would take them to their destination. If there was sense, I couldn't find it. *Matatus* both small and large rumbled in and out, almost bumping together as they passed. Their conductors were busy, screaming destinations and collecting fares. There were vendors selling everything from newspapers to roasted maize to sunglasses and maps of the world. Who would buy a map of the world at a *matatu* station?

I felt overwhelmed, pushed in on all sides by the sounds and smells and movement. The few other times I had been in such a place—and I had never been in a station so large—I was watched by my mother and father. Here I was the one doing the watching. I tightened my grip on Jata's hand as we wove through the crowd.

"Excuse me, sir," I said to one of the conductors. "Can you tell me where I can get a ride to Kikima?"

"Over there," he said, waving to the far side of the station.

"Thank you, sir."

He had already turned away before I finished speaking.

"Come, Jata."

We walked along, trying to avoid the hordes of people rushing on and off the vehicles.

"I want a *mandazi*," Jata said.

"We do not have the money . . ." I began. But then I remembered that she *did* have the money. "I do not need one, but you can get a *mandazi* with the money Omolo gave you."

"He said I need to buy two—one for me and one for you." She pulled the money out of her pocket, balancing the few loose coins on the palm of her hand.

I wanted to say that we would be wiser to pool our money so we could ride closer to Kikima, but I didn't. This was what Omolo had wanted—and I really did want a *mandazi*.

"Come." I led her to a little stall that had a shelf filled with *mandazi*. "You make the purchase."

I allowed her to step forward and talk to the woman who was selling. That was what my mother always did with us. She said that we needed to know about money. I watched but allowed Jata to make the purchase on her own.

She turned around holding two *mandazi*, with a smile so bright that it was worth the price even without the treat—although I did want the treat too. Jata had eaten most of the banana this morning, and I'd had only a bite. I knew we had at least three more oranges in my bundle, but we would save those for the ride.

She handed me one *mandazi*. "Thank you," I said, and took a big bite. The pastry was fresh and warm and sweet, and it practically melted in my mouth. It was the best thing I'd ever tasted in my life! I took another bite and another. I hardly needed to chew as the soft dough slid down my throat and filled my stomach.

When I finished, Jata tore off a piece of hers and offered it to me.

"I had more of the banana," she said. "You give me more of everything."

I took the piece from her and ripped it in two again, handing back half. Together we popped the last two pieces in our mouths.

"It is time to go to Kikima," I said.

I led Jata back through the crowd, searching for the right *matatu*. The drivers all yelled out encouragement to the potential passengers, trying to convince them that their bus was the best. I tried to ignore the voices and looked instead for the names posted in the windshields. There were so many places I'd never heard of—Kalawani, Tawa, Tuvilani, Nzaini and Emali—but there was no Kikima. Still, there were so many *matatus* that I wasn't worried . . . yet.

I reached into my pocket and pulled out our remaining shillings. They were a crumpled ball, dark and worn from where my fingers had held them, wedging them in and making sure that they were safely buried deep in my pocket. Slowly, deliberately, I straightened them out. Three notes—three fifty-shilling notes—for a total of one hundred and fifty shillings. Would that be enough? There was only one way to know.

"There is our *matatu*!" Jata exclaimed.

She was pointing at a bright orange bus. On the windshield was its name and motto: MUM—YOU ARE GREAT. But I couldn't see where it said Kikima.

"That is a fine *matatu*," I agreed, "but we need to locate the one going to Kikima."

"It is that one, I am sure," Jata said. "Come and look."

Before I could stop her, she ran toward it. She was so much smaller that she was able to move through the people quickly. She stopped by the *matatu* and I ran to her side. There, in the side window, was a smaller sign: KIKIMA. Jata burst into laughter and started jumping up and down. I felt like doing the same. This was the *matatu*—and she had known it all along.

"I knew our mother would lead us home," Jata said.

She *was* leading us home. We would travel the last part of our journey with our mother. We were returning to her home with her.

If we had enough money.

A conductor was standing at the door, taking fares. The bus was already filled with people, and the roof was piled high with items.

"Good morning, sir. We wish to travel to Kikima," I said.

"You are most fortunate, since that is where we are going. The fare is two hundred shillings for each of you."

I let out a big sigh. My heart and my hopes sank.

"Do you not have enough money to pay the fare?" he asked.

He must have read my reaction. I shook my head.

"This is not a charity. You must pay to ride."

"Yes, sir."

"How much money do you have?" he asked.

"One hundred and fifty shillings."

"That is not even enough for one, but I could take you partway."

"That would be good."

"And that partway could be longer if you ride on the roof instead of inside."

I had often seen people doing that but had never done it myself. Our parents would never have allowed that, and when we were with them we would never have needed to do it.

The conductor saw my hesitation. "Or you can ride inside—just not as far."

"We will take the roof," I said, handing him the money.

"Climb up, and make sure you help the little one. And stay low so nobody sees that I'm letting children ride on the top."

Jata started up the ladder on the side of the bus. I climbed up after, shielding her from a fall. The conductor handed me my water container and I placed it on the roof, then followed up myself.

The roof was full of all manner of items. Barrels, boxes and bags, even a bed, a chesterfield and a cabinet were all tied in place on the rack. There was a spare tire tied down at the front. That would be our seat.

"Sit," I said to Jata, directing her into the center of the tire so she was surrounded by its rubber walls. That would be the safest place. I sat on the rack itself, leaning against the tire, easily able to reach out for Jata if needed.

The engine roared to life and the low rumbling became a full shaking. I leaned over the side and watched as the *matatu* started to move. Slowly it edged its way through the other buses and the people dodging between them. It slipped through impossibly small spaces, practically pushing vehicles and people out of its path.

When we came to the gate, the conductor and the gatekeeper yelled back and forth. If it not for the smiles and laughing, I would have thought they were fighting. Instead they were sharing a joke until the man opened the gate to allow us to pass. The conductor continued to talk to the gatekeeper as we rolled by and started off. Finally he ran after the *matatu* and jumped aboard as it began to pick up speed. We were off! We were either on the last leg of our long journey or else the first leg of one that I didn't think I had the strength to finish.

The streets around the station were hardly less congested than the station itself. There were so many people and vehicles. Despite the crowds, the *matatu* began to pick up speed. Occasionally I could feel the driver apply the brakes, but mostly he used his size and his horn to open a way through.

We quickly left Machakos behind. The stores and stalls, people and homes spaced out. The driver passed several slower-moving lorries, swerving onto the other side of the road and back again before hitting any oncoming traffic. From up top I could see how close he sometimes came to running headfirst into those vehicles. But I wasn't afraid. It wasn't that I trusted this stranger, but I had lived through so much already that I had no fears of a crash. Somehow we had been protected, and I knew we would remain protected all the way to our destination. It had been our destiny to reach Kikima.

We raced forward, the ground at the side of the road a reddish blur. If we could find a way to stay aboard for the entire trip, I knew we would be there within an hour. One hour and we would be in Kikima. And then what? We would try to find our grandparents. I would ask questions of people until they were able to direct us to them . . . if they were still alive. Many years had passed since my mother had had contact with them and they had to be very old.

"Do you still see the string?" Jata asked over the rush of the wind.

"Not now, but the driver can see it. Have no worries."

"I am not worried. Our mother is taking us home."

For an instant, I forgot that she was referring to the name of the *matatu*.

"It is like you said—our father and mother will guide us," she said.

It did feel like they had been watching from overhead. There was no other explanation. We had got here through more than my efforts.

"I cannot wait to be welcomed by our family," Jata said.

"Yes, that will be most special. But first we must find them."

Finding them was a task I could control. Being welcomed was still in question. Would we be accepted and embraced, the children of the daughter who had defied her parents, the children of a Kikuyu father they did not approve of, the grandchildren they did not even know existed?

Walking had moved my legs and left my mind quiet. Whenever those questions had arisen, I had pushed them aside. Now my legs were still and my mind was active, and there was no escaping them. I opened my bundle, pulled out two oranges—leaving one remaining—and handed them to Jata. "You peel them for our remaining breakfast."

She started to peel, tossing the pieces over the side. No worries about a lion following our path now. Perhaps those little orange peels would help us find our way back to Machakos if there was no place for us in Kikima.

I sat there and for the first time allowed that thought to sink in—what if we were not wanted in Kikima? What would we do and where would we go? There was no place for us at the camp anymore. I would not travel across the country twice just to end up back where we'd started. We hadn't gone through all this to go back to the beginning. If we stayed in Kikima, at least there was peace. We would be free of the violence. And we would be in the home village of our mother, so at least a small piece of her would still be with us. We had followed the string.

Wherever we were, Jata would remain at my side.

The *matatu* slowed and I had a rush of fear that it was to let us off. But I looked down the road and saw three people waving it down. When we came to a stop, the trail of dust we had been leaving behind caught up and surrounded the vehicle. Up top we were clear of the hovering red cloud.

After a minute, we started moving again and the conductor appeared, clambering up the side and tossing a bag onto the roof.

"Enjoying the ride?" he asked.

"Yes, sir. This is a good place to ride."

"It is my favorite," he said as he tucked the bundle under a rope and made sure it was secure. "This is where I always ride when I am not the conductor. It is mostly above the dust, and you have air in your face and lots of space. I think we should charge a higher fare up here than we do down there."

"Can we still ride farther?" I asked.

"Still farther. But why did your parents not give you more money for this ride?" he asked.

"We have no parents," I said.

"Orphans—there are many. You have never been on my vehicle before."

"Never."

"Why are you going to Kikima?"

"Our grandparents live there."

"And you live with them?"

"Yes." I hoped so badly that I wasn't lying.

"Tell them to give you more money next time. Now I'd better be a conductor."

More people on the road ahead were waving for us to stop. The conductor climbed down the ladder and was gone.

Repeatedly the *matatu* stopped to let passengers and parcels on or off. The conductor appeared and disappeared, putting things on or taking them off from the roof. Most stops were quick, but others—such as when he had to untie and lower the chesterfield—were longer. Each time we stopped, I wondered if this was where he would tell us that our fare would take us no farther. But each time, we traveled on.

Despite the bumps and the stops, Jata had fallen asleep, held safely in place by the rubber of the tire. I wished I could fall asleep too and wake up in Kikima.

The road had gradually become rougher. We passed over dried riverbeds, between huge boulders, down rutted roads and through mountains. Along the way, the homesteads grew smaller and were set farther back from the road. Crops, where they grew, seemed to be suffering. There was as much brown as there was green. Had the rains failed, or did they simply not come here very often?

Once again the *matatu* slowed. There were no people waiting by the roadside, so I had to hope that passengers inside were wanting to get off. The conductor appeared at the side—perhaps to get a parcel for that passenger?

"We are stopping for you," he said. "Your fare has passed."

I roused Jata and gathered my bundle. "Are we far from Kikima?" I asked him.

"Closer than your shillings should have allowed."

When the *matatu* came to a full stop, the conductor offered Jata a hand to get her started down. Then he took the water container from me, handing it down to Jata on the ground. No sooner had I landed beside her than the *matatu* started moving again. The conductor ran alongside and then jumped into the open door, hanging out and looking back at us.

"Follow us!" he yelled. "It is just up the hill. Not far. Follow the dust!"

The *matatu* raced away, disappearing into the dust cloud it created.

I picked up the water container one more time. How many times had I set it down and picked it up? More important, would this be the last time in this journey?

"Muchoki, are we going?"

"Of course. I was just waiting for the dust to settle."
And waiting to settle my fears as well.

We started walking.

"Do you think it will be big or little?" Jata asked.

"What will be big or little?"

"Our grandparents' home."

"Does it matter?" I asked.

"Not really."

I was more interested in the door of the house—
would it be open or closed?

We were not alone on the road. Women with heavy
loads on their backs were slowly walking up the hill,
and they were joined by pushcarts filled with produce
and bicycles piled high with merchandise. We were not
the only people heading in this direction.

"Look!" Jata exclaimed, pointing at a store. The
window said, in big letters, KIKIMA WEST SHOPPING
CENTER. "We are here!"

"I think this is just the outskirts, but we are close.
There is more ahead."

Jata's steps became lighter. She was almost skipping
she seemed so happy. My feet, on the other hand, felt
heavy, burdened with worries she knew nothing about.

We moved to the side of the road as another *matatu*
came up from behind. I turned and shaded my eyes from
the dust. Many people were going to Kikima, it seemed.

Up ahead were more stores, more vehicles and many, many more people. We had come upon the center of the town, and we were here on a market day. The square was filled with stalls, the ground covered with burlap and plastic to display merchandise. There were tomatoes and potatoes, onions and oranges, mangos and passion fruit piled high.

The square was crowded with people, young and old alike. Were any of these my grandfather and grandmother? Were my uncles and aunts and cousins standing around me? How would I know other than to ask? I looked around for the right person—somebody who was older, who would know the people of the community. At one stall I saw a woman old enough to be a grandparent, carefully stacking potatoes into little piles.

"Good morning," I greeted her. "I am asking of you, do you know the Kyatha family?"

She shook her head. "I only know potatoes."

We started walking again. The market space was crowded with only small aisles of dirt left open between the blankets and stalls. People bumped through and loud voices—those of the vendors and those of the customers—seemed to make it seem even more chaotic and crowded. I was reassured that every voice seemed to be speaking in Kikamba but that made it even more difficult as it was harder for me to understand and it strained my mind even further.

All along throughout the whole journey I'd only thought of reaching Kikima but not the difficulty of finding my mother's family when we did arrive. It was so much bigger, more confusing than I had imagined. My head felt like it was spinning, my legs were shaky. All I wanted was to find an empty spot and quietly think, but there was no empty and no quiet.

I led Jata through the market, being bumped from behind, people and produce crowded in all around us, never allowing her hand to slip from mine. Finally in what seemed like the very center I stopped and put my water container down. It felt like we were in a small island of calm within the middle of a sea of chaos. I looked all around, trying to see an answer that wasn't visible in my eye or clear in my mind.

"Do you see our grandparents?" Jata asked.

I answered with only a shrug. What else could I say?

"I do not know where they live," I said to her. "I only know they are the Kyathas."

"Did you say Kyatha?" a man passing by asked.

"Yes, do you know them?"

"I *am* Kyatha," he said.

"You are?" I gasped, unable to believe my ears or my luck.

"Yes. Why do you ask for the Kyatha family?" he questioned.

"We are looking for *our* family. Our mother was a Kyatha."

"*Was?* Has she passed?"

"Last week. Her name was Mutanu."

The man's eyes got wide in shock. "You need to wait right here. Do you understand?"

"Yes, we will wait."

"Right here—do not move . . . understand?"

"Yes, sir. But who are you?" I asked.

He didn't answer. Instead he stared directly at us, as if questioning whether we would wait. Finally he said, "Your mother was my sister."

"Your sister!" I exclaimed. "Then that makes you—"

"Your uncle. Now wait. Do not move."

He rushed off. I had to fight the urge to run away, as well as the urge to run after him, not to allow him to leave my sight in case he vanished. That option was quickly removed, though, as he was almost instantly swallowed up by the crowd and disappeared. Where was he going and why did I let him leave?

"Is he really our uncle?" Jata asked.

"I do not know why he would lie to us."

I tried to calm myself. I felt afraid, but I couldn't allow Jata to sense my fear.

She took my hand and I looked down. "It will be fine." She smiled. She didn't need my comfort—she was comforting me.

Within minutes the man reappeared, and he was not alone. There were others moving with him, pushing through the crowd. I tightened my grip on Jata's hand to check my rising fears. Six men and three women stopped in front of us, and behind them were some children and finally an old man and old woman, walking slowly. The crowd parted to allow the old couple to come to the front.

"I am Kyatha, the father of Mutanu," the old man said. "And this is her mother. Who are you?"

"We are her children," I said. "I am Muchoki and this is Jata."

"And where is my daughter?"

I took a deep breath. "Our mother—your daughter—she is dead."

He staggered slightly, and the man who had spoken to us first offered a hand to steady him.

"How? When?" the old man asked.

"Only a week ago. It was malaria that took her," I said.

The old woman—our mother's mother—began to cry.

"And what of your father?" he asked.

"He was killed. In Eldoret, in the violence. We have no parents."

"And how did you get here?"

"Mostly we walked."

"From Eldoret?" the old man asked in disbelief.

I shook my head. "From the camp. From the place they put us in the Rift Valley, near Maai Mahiu."

"That is over two hundred kilometers! You walked from there?"

"Yes . . . almost all the way."

"Do you expect me to believe that?"

"Yes, sir. We walked because there was no other way."

"You have come so far to bring me such terrible news. I always dreamed that one day she would return, and now you have told me she never will. You have taken away the last thing of her I held—the hope that she would come back."

Without thinking, I smiled.

"You think this is funny?" the old man demanded.

"No. It is just that our mother always said that. She did not wish to return because she feared she would be turned away, and she said she wanted to live with the hope."

"We would never have turned her away. *Never*." The man reached out and took his wife's hand. "You say that you are my grandchildren and that my beloved daughter is dead, but I do not know either of you. How do I know that what you are saying is true?"

"Can you not see?" his wife asked. "Look in their eyes."

He looked at my sister, hard, like he was studying her, and then turned and stared at me too.

"I do not see my daughter when I look at you," he said to me. "But there is something in the girl."

"My father always said she was like my mother, and that was why he loved her so much."

Tears were starting to form in the old man's eyes.

"And you say you walked that far, not knowing where you were going, and still you found us here, in Kikima. How is that possible? Did you have a map?"

"No map."

"Then how?"

"Our mother told us the way to travel. Before she died, she had decided to return."

"If only she could have. There is so much I wanted to say." He choked back a sob. "It is hard to believe you could come all that way on your own and find us."

"We just followed the string," Jata said.

He turned to her. "What did you say?"

"The string. We followed the string to find our way home."

"It is nothing," I explained. "She is telling you a story."

"I *know* the story," he said. "It was told to me by my father, as it was told to him by his." He paused. "As I told it to *all* of my children."

"And our mother told it to us," I said. "It is just a story."

"But it is a *true* story!" Jata protested. "Muchoki

saw the string and we followed it here. Sometimes it was so thin that I had to squint to see it, and mostly I could not see it at all. But my brother could *always* see it."

In my mind, I realized, I *had* always been able to see it.

The old man looked at me. "Do you see the string now?"

I shook my head. This was the end. It led me no farther. We'd always been moved forward by the vision in my head and the hope in my heart. Now there seemed to be neither.

"Do you have any money?" he asked me.

"We have none."

"And the water container?"

"It is half empty and half full."

"And food? Do you have any food?"

"Some beans and maize for a few days."

"And nothing else?"

"One orange."

He shook his head and smiled. "You *had* an orange."

I turned to follow his gaze. Jata was sitting on the ground in a little circle with some other girls. She had peeled the orange and was giving out the pieces!

"You have come with empty pockets, empty stomachs and only enough water to last a day. Both of you wait here!" he ordered. With that, he turned and walked away, leaving us with the others.

ERIC WALTERS

"My sister," the first man—our uncle—said, "was always so kind and gentle." He pointed down to Jata in the dirt, talking and laughing with the other little girls. "My sister would have done that. Two of those little girls she has given that orange to are my daughters—your cousins."

Suddenly the old man returned. He opened his hands and revealed a ball of string. He unraveled it until it dangled to the ground. Then he turned and started walking away, the string dragging behind him in the dirt. After a few steps, he stopped and turned back around. "Do you see the string?" he asked.

"Of course," I said.

"Then why are you not following?"

"Are we going . . . going to your home?" I asked.

He shook his head. "No, we are not going to *my* home." A smile came to his face. "We are going to *our* home. Together, we are walking home."

290

Author's Note

In the summer of 2011—accompanied by four children from the Creation of Hope Orphanage, four young Canadians, and my good friend Henry Kyatha—we walked the route traveled by my characters Muchoki and Jata. From an internal displacement camp on the Mara, up the Rift Valley, down to Nairobi, through Kibera, along the Mombasa highway, to the mountains of Kikima, we walked home. As you'll know if you've visited www.ericwalterswalkinghome.com, along the way we talked, filmed, interviewed, experienced, made notes and wrote as I tried to put myself in the shoes of my protagonists. They say if you wish to know a man, walk a mile in his shoes. Over six days we walked more than 150 kilometres so I could know Muchoki and Jata. I hope you got to know them as well as you followed along on our journey.